Charlotte

A Marked Heart Novel

M. Sembera

I0685974

"A real man would know that every mark on your body

is beautiful because it's a part of you."~Auggie

To my sister Heather, your courage and faith is something every woman should aspire to.

❧ Table of Contents ❧

The true measure of a person's worth lies not within what they can offer you but what you have to offer them. No matter how desirable, are they worth your time, patience, forgiveness, loyalty, friendship, love, respect, understanding, compassion, trust? If not, they are worth more than you have to offer. They deserve for you to let them go.

❧1❧

Home

An uneasy feeling filled Charlotte as Trace drove through her small southern hometown. The trip from the airport felt like they were moving in slow motion. Nothing seemed to have changed. Hoping only the appearance of the town was the same, the last thing she wanted was to spend the next three months feeling like she did before she left for Spain.

Five and a half years ago, Charlotte's adoptive parents, Emerson and Amila Roberts, agreed to let her move to Spain with Emerson's mother. A clean slate to start over, far away, where no one knew her. Erin Roberts opened her home and many opportunities to Charlotte. Her life became better than anything she could have imagined. The decision to go back, although only temporarily, came at an unexpectedly convenient time. With Trace, who Erin liked to refer to as Charlotte's suitor, just days away from months of investment meetings with his father, the timing was perfect.

The decision was made that Trace accompany Charlotte on her trip home. He would then be introduced to her adoptive father before flying out to meet his father in Europe. It was a show of respect as Erin had explained. Trace never mentioned proposing to Charlotte. However, Erin swore she knew he would. When Trace's meetings were over, he would fly back to the small southern town that she was staying in, ask Emerson for permission and then propose.

Formalities aside, Charlotte was going back for a different reason. It wasn't that she didn't believe what Erin shared with her and she intended to say yes. There was something Charlotte left without five years ago that she needed in order for her life to be complete. It was promised to her the moment she returned.

Two days ago, Charlotte received a phone call that let her know, the one thing keeping her from truly enjoying the life she now led, would be gone forever if she wasn't there to receive it within a week. Forgiveness.

৯৯৹৯

"Your father will love me," Trace assured.

Pulling her eyes from the scenery, Charlotte laughed, "Of course he will, everyone does."

His messy brown curls bounced around his head as he nodded.

"Isn't that what you're worried about?"

Shrugging a shoulder, Charlotte focused on the large two story house in front of them, saying, "I don't worry."

"You have been acting strange since we arrived."

As they pulled up to the front of the house, she shared, "I'm not ready to go in yet."

Leaning over and flashing an 'I'm too perfect' toothy grin, he suggested, "The sooner we go in and do a meet and greet the sooner you and I can go out and then to my hotel."

"There's no going out here and it's an inn, not a hotel," she assured recalling how absolutely boring this town was.

His brown eyes reflected a hint of indecency as he responded, "I will be more than happy to drive us straight to the inn then."

Tilting her head to the side, Charlotte closed her eyes for a moment as Trace ran his lips across her jaw line.

Easily sliding out of the driver's seat, Trace walked over to the passenger side opening the door for her. Looking him over as she stepped out, his slacks still held a perfect crease down the center even after their twelve hour flight. He always dressed as if they were going out. Trace was incredibly fashion forward. Suit jacket, dress shirt, no tie and dress shoes, his theory was if you are always dressed for any occasion then you never have to decline an invitation. He was all about appearances.

As they made their way up to the front door, she stopped as Trace gave the bottom of her skirt a slight tug.

Glancing down at his hand, Charlotte griped, "There is nothing wrong with my skirt."

"The line is off," he stated, continuing to tug at the hem.

Brushing his hand away, she assured, "Amila isn't going to care."

"Isn't she Society?"

Nodding, she fussed, "I said she won't care and neither do I. Now let go and walk to the door."

Trace scowled at her in disappointment as he complained, "If you do not care about your appearance, how can I trust that you will be suitable for more."

"The same way I trust more includes our being exclusive, I imagine."

Giving her skirt a final tug, he questioned, "Why are you being this way?"

Silently counting back from ten in her head, she wasn't entirely sure.

"Perhaps it is not necessary for me to be here," he stated.

Wanting to blurt 'bye' to him but knowing he was her future, she fluttered her eyelashes, "Is that really what you want to do?"

Placing his hand on the small of her back, he replied, "That depends, will you be acting like this the entire time I am here or will you be the girl I know in Spain."

Moving her shoulder's back, she faced forward and headed to the door.

Trace was all about formalities and courtesy, on Charlotte's end that is. He could be sweet and charming when he wasn't preening her like she was a misfit of some sort. Normally she had no problem with the guidelines he held her to. They actually helped her learn to control herself. But now that Charlotte was back in her home town, she was having trouble. Wondering if maybe it was in the air here, after tonight, Trace would come to dinner with her family and then be away for three months. The least she could do was hold it together long enough for him before he left.

The moment Trace rang the doorbell, the front door flew open and Amila threw her arms around Charlotte.

"I can't believe you're finally home," she cheered squeezing her tight.

While hugging each other, Charlotte replied, "It's good to be here," appreciating how much Amila cared about her even from the beginning.

Placing her hands on the sides of Charlotte's face, Amila said, "You look so grown up."

"Where is everybody?"

Releasing her hands from Charlotte's face, she reminded, "The Rec Center, its Wednesday."

Shifting her focus, Amila stated, "And this must be Trace."

"Yes, it is a pleasure to meet you Mrs. Roberts," Trace replied.

Giving him a sweet smile, Amila offered, "Come in, come in."

Trace gave a polite smile before declining, "We have a previous engagement. I apologize for our haste and look forward to dinner tomorrow evening."

Her smile faded as she asked, "You're not staying?"

"I'll be back in a few hours," Charlotte assured before giving her a tight squeeze."
Amila's pleasant demeanor was noticeably forced as she told them to be careful and that she would see Charlotte later."

৯৵৶

Stopping at a local diner, they stood in the parking lot. Charlotte cringed as she glanced across the street at The Dog House, a local bar owned by Jackson Thomas. It wasn't the thought of Jackson that upset her or his wife Ren. She cared a great deal for Ren. It was the knowledge that Augustus Caffrey was tending bar there. He hated her and the feeling was completely mutual.

Trace appeared hesitant about going into the restaurant.

"What do they serve?" he questioned.

"Burgers and fries are the best here but they have steak-finger baskets too."

Taking a look around with a disgusted expression, Trace offered, "Let's go there."

"That's a bar, not a restaurant," she spit out hoping he didn't notice the apprehension in her voice.
Without paying her any attention, Trace took her arm and led her in the direction of The Dog House.

"Wait, I can't."

Continuing to pull her in the direction of the bar, he said, "No need to be uppity, think of it as trying something new."

"I'm not, I can't go in there."
The doors to The Dog House were propped open, allowing passer's by to hear the band playing inside.

Trace insistently tugged at her, saying, "There is live music."

Struggling to break away from his hold, without making a scene, Charlotte looked up and noticed they were already across the street and right outside the open doors. With one final effort, she jerked away from him.

∾⧫∾

It was a slow night at The Dog House, Wednesdays were always that way. The band was there but only to rehearse for the weekend crowd. With around fifteen patrons in the bar, most of which were regulars, Auggie stepped from behind the bar. He raised his hand in the air to catch his brother Braden's attention. The second the music stopped something outside the doors caught Auggie's attention. Stepping to the side, he saw a pair of long legs attached to a woman with blonde hair being manhandled by some overdressed jerk.

Hot footing it to the doors, he shouted, "Hey!"

The second Mr. Fancy let go of her, she turned around. Instantly, filled with anger, Auggie glared at her. Visibly stunned at the sight of him, her blue eyes were wide before she narrowed them at him in an equally hateful glare.

Auggie was about to tell her where she could go when Braden stepped up to them with a surprised, "Charlotte!"

Assuming the misunderstanding could be quickly resolved, Trace held his hand out saying, "This is not what it looks like. I was trying to convince her to come into your establishment. Trace Delgado, and you are?"

Auggie pulled his eyes away from Charlotte long enough to glance down at Trace's hand and state, "Augustus Caffrey," while refusing to shake it.

"Braden," his brother introduced himself, shaking Trace's out stretched hand.

With no interest in pleasantries where she was concerned, Auggie griped, "What are you doing here?"

"Anything I damn well please," Charlotte snapped back at him as she refused to let him rattle her.

"She's a bit jetlagged and doesn't realize how rude..." Trace tried apologizing for her when Auggie took a step toward him.

"Was I talkin' to you?"

Knowing how this was going to play out, Braden tried to diffuse the situation by offering, "Trace, how about you and I step inside and grab a beer. On the house."

Confused by what was going on, Trace questioned, "I do not understand the problem here."

More than happy to answer his question, Auggie stepped closer.

Gritting his teeth as he got directly in Trace's face, Auggie growled, "For starter's you brought that..."

Before things got too far out of hand, Jackson quickly made his way behind Auggie and pulled him back by his shirt.

They all turned in the direction of a woman's voice, warning, "Knock it off."

Slowly walking up to them was Ren Thomas, shaking her head with a smirk across her face.

Auggie instantly barked, "She's not stepping foot inside."

Ren glanced at Charlotte before fussing, "That's enough. It doesn't look like she wants to spend any extra time with you either."

Jerking away from Jackson, Auggie gave Ren a dirty look before heading into the bar.

"Make sure he doesn't pick a fight in there," Jackson cautioned Braden.

Nodding, he shared, "Sophia and Ailin are inside."

Ren gave a smile, saying, "We'll be in in a minute."

As Braden headed back into the bar, Ren turned to Charlotte and raised an eyebrow at her.

"Of all the places in town, you decided to come here?" Ren fussed before saying, "So do I get a hug or what?"

Charlotte laughed and hugged Ren before turning to introduce her, "Trace, this is Ren."

His expression bordered on wonder as he stared at her. Barely five foot tall with long brown hair and light gray eyes, she was beautiful. He couldn't quite understand how a rough bartender like Augustus would instantly obey her. Just moments before she showed up, his face was redder than his beard and he was ready to fight. Quickly realizing he was standing there gawking at her, Trace composed himself and spoke.

"It is an honor. I have heard so much about you."

"It's nice to meet you too," Ren said before hooking her arm into Jackson's introducing, "This is my husband Jackson."

Reaching out, Jackson shook his hand as he gave Trace a courteous nod.

"I interned for your ex-husband last year," Trace shared.

Unimpressed, Ren asked, "Is that how you two met?"

Without answering Ren's question, Charlotte blurted, "Gah, Ren what were you thinking. He's such an ass."

Before Ren had a chance to respond, Trace turned to Charlotte scolding, "That is incredibly disrespectful. Mr. Herterand is one of the foremost successful businessmen in the world. Not to mention being a major investor in my father's company."

"You know what," Ren started as Jackson quickly wrapped an arm around her waist to prevent her from taking a step forward as she continued, "It's even more disrespectful to talk down to someone especially when you don't know the people you're doing it in front of or the character of the person you're defending."

Trace stood there staring at Ren as Jackson suppressed a laugh and kissed the side of her head.

"Have you been home yet?" Ren asked directing her focus to Charlotte.

"We stopped by and saw Amila, no one else was home."

Nodding at her, Ren informed, "Emerson should be back with everybody by now. Jacks had just enough time to shower before we came here."

"Trace needs to check into his room and then I'll head that way," Charlotte shared.

"You're staying at Emerson and Amila's though, right?"

"Yes, Ren," Charlotte replied with a smile.

Jackson and Ren turned to walk into the bar when Ren turned back and said, "Call me tonight after you get settled in."

Charlotte nodded, thinking, 'guess not everyone loves Trace after all'.

ॐ

After spending around fifteen minutes complaining that he had to carry his own suitcase, Trace scowled at his less than ideal accommodations. Thankfully he would only spend one night in the ratty little Inn. He would be even more thankful when he left town. It was no wonder Charlotte was behaving so badly there. Trace hoped Mr. Roberts would be more upstanding than everyone else he had met so far. Regardless, in three months he would return for Charlotte and propose. As far as he was concerned that would be the last time he would have to withstand this town or the people in it.

Doing her best to concentrate on Ren defending her, instead of the look in Auggie's eyes, Charlotte stared at herself in the bathroom mirror. It wasn't like she cared if Auggie hated her or not, she couldn't stand him. She didn't like to be reminded of why. If his reaction to her standing outside the bar was any indication, visiting his brother William, in the hospital, might give him a stroke. Thinking that might not be so bad, the memory of William's face the last time she saw him caused instant remorse. Charlotte didn't come back to town to cause trouble, she needed something from William and after receiving it she would steer clear of all things Caffrey for the next three months.

Stepping out of the bathroom, Charlotte was pulled onto the bed. Trace ran his hand from her ankle up to her thigh while roughly kissing the side of her neck. Normally she enjoyed their sessions of heavy petting. It thrilled her to invoke certain things from him without actual sex. It had been almost a year and a half for Charlotte. Trace had an interesting thought process when it came to sex. He, of course, did not go without. He was not exclusive with anyone until it progressed into more. His more, referred to an engagement and more could not be achieved if there was sex before a proposal. He was clear about it from the beginning, and it never bothered Charlotte before tonight. However, tonight it felt wrong.

Panting against her neck, Trace moved his hand under her skirt. Shifting to the side, Charlotte refused his offer of assistance. Focusing his attention back to himself, it wasn't long before he let go of her and swiftly made his way to the bathroom. Charlotte stood up and waited for him to come out. Not being able to shake the vision of William's face from her mind, she was ready to head to Emerson and Amila's.

Stepping out of the bathroom, Trace made his way to Charlotte. Resting his hand on the side of her face, he kissed her right below her ear, offering, "Are you sure? Three months is a long time."

"For you or for me?" she replied on an impulse.

"I understand you are under a certain amount of stress. After being here for only a few hours, I want to leave and never return. I will give you this allowance because of the effect this place seems to have on you. However, when I return, I expect you to remember what it is to be with me and act accordingly."

Charlotte counted back from ten in her head as she nodded. Nothing about him had bothered her before she came back. Trace was the exact same person in Spain as he was here and everything was wonderful there. Now everything he said and did made her want to run him over with the rental car, back up and do it again.

৯৯৯

Parked in the back driveway, under a carport, Charlotte had to admit she liked it better when there was someone there to get her bags for her. Stepping out of the rental car, she walked to the back and opened the trunk. As she pulled her suitcases out, Emerson walked out of the back door.

"Max and Luke can help you with those."

Looking up, she replied, "Thank you."

Making an effort with her, he said, "I have to admit, I was surprised when Amila said you were coming for a visit."

Keeping her tone short, Charlotte replied, "You couldn't have been that surprised. I know Erin called you."

With a quick nod, he shared, "It meant a lot that you stopped here first. Amila misses you very much."

"I'm sure she does. I miss her too."

"Charlotte, I would like your visit to be a pleasant one," Emerson assured.

With a knowing smirk, she replied, "Is that why y'all are leaving next week?"

"Amila said she told you we could reschedule and you swore to her it did not bother you."

"It doesn't," she spat at him before walking past Emerson and into the house.

Amila was in the living room with Lola when Charlotte walked in. The moment Lola caught sight of Charlotte she squealed and ran towards her. All together Charlotte had six siblings, all adopted like her.

Taking a step back, Charlotte placed her hands on her hips and asked, "Now who are you?"

Making a silly face at her, she said, "It's me Lola."

Narrowing her eyes, Charlotte teased, "No way, Lola is just a baby and you're a big girl."

Blushing, Lola gave a huge dimpled smile as she giggled.

"And I'm still jealous of your curls," Charlotte complimented her light blonde ringlets as she pulled her in for a hug.

As Amila hollered upstairs for the other kids to come down, Charlotte realized how much had changed in the five years she was gone.

Lola was five when Charlotte left for Spain. Aside from herself, the oldest was thirteen when she left. Now everyone else were teenagers, making Charlotte feel incredibly old at twenty-four. Emerson walked in just as Max and Luke were coming down the stairs. He told them to put Charlotte's luggage in her old room. Both of them gave her a 'What's up' before doing what they were told.

Smiling at Jenna, who sat quietly on the couch next to Amila, Charlotte asked," Where are Trent and Silvia?"

"Trent signed up for the outreach program right after graduation. He won't be back until the end of the summer and Silvia is at Cheer Camp, she will be back next week."

Nodding Charlotte asked Jenna, "What are you reading?" when she noticed a book in her hand.

Jenna's green eyes lit up as she tucked a strand of her long red hair behind her ear and softly replied, "Little Women."

"That's a good one. You like to read?" As Jenna nodded, Charlotte said, "Maybe you can loan me a few books so I have something to do when y'all go on vacation."

Enthusiastically nodding this time, Jenna smiled wide revealing a mouth full of braces.

৵৽

Settled in her old room, Charlotte grabbed her toiletry bag out of one of her suitcases before heading into the bathroom. Removing her lipstick first, it was always such a relief to take it off. She still appreciated Erin going to such great lengths to have it made for her but, unfortunately, it had a plastic feel to it. It was the only lipstick that covered the scar Charlotte had on her mouth. Taking her finger she followed the line of her scar from the top of her upper lip all the way to the bottom of her lower one. The left side of her lips was slightly firmer from the right, but it felt more natural to her than the lipstick.

When she finished washing the rest of her face, Charlotte stepped out of the bathroom. Grabbing her purse on the way to the bed, she grabbed her Clinique chubby stick and softly coated her bare lips with the wonderfully smooth balm. After tossing it back in her purse, she pulled her wallet out and opened it. Taking the bottle cap William gave her out of the zipper section she held it in her hand. Lying back on the bed, she closed her eyes.

She recalled meeting William at Ren and Jackson's wedding, sneaking off to meet with him in the park and the way he slowly ran his index finger down her pinky before asking if he could hold her hand. Suddenly, it occurred to her, she forgot to call Ren. Deciding a simple text message would do, she rolled over and grabbed her cellphone.

C: Home. Tired. Call you tomorrow.

Her phone dinged almost immediately.

R: If you want to see William, no one will be at the hospital from 10-11 TOMORROW.

C: K Thanks.

Tossing her phone on the bed before closing her eyes, she tried to fall asleep.

❧2❧

William

Standing outside William's hospital room, Charlotte stared at the door. It was already twenty after ten and she knew she only had until eleven. After being questioned by nearly everyone in the house on where she was going, she wasn't used to sharing her exact whereabouts with anyone. Erin basically let her come and go as she pleased because she was rarely home herself. In Spain, there was always something to do, unlike here.

It was crazy for her to be apprehensive about her mission at this point. Still, she wondered if he knew she was coming. Would he hold up his end of the bargain? Admitting to herself, if it were her, she wouldn't, Charlotte decided there was only one way to find out. Slowly peeking through the rectangle window on the door, she saw William lying in a hospital bed. Seeing him hooked up to IV's and with an oxygen mask covering his nose and mouth, she was grateful she had thought to look before walking into the room. He was far thinner than she remembered and he looked, sickly.

Closing her eyes, she counted back from ten, gave a slight huff and walked into his room. Aside from the machines, the room was quiet. Closing the door behind herself, she forced a smile at him.

Pulling the oxygen from his face, William gave a weak smile as he whispered, "Charlotte."

Focusing on his eyes and not his sickly appearance, even his auburn hair appeared dull.

Charlotte stepped to the side of his bed, saying, "I'm sorry."

His voice was weak and raspy as he replied, "You were never good...at...taking things slow."

As he placed the oxygen over his mouth to take a strained breath, she had to look away. Noticing a picture at his bedside, she scanned the unfamiliar face before taking note of how the girl's arms were wrapped around William in the picture.

"Who is that?" she asked.

Lowering the mask, he replied, "Mallory."

"She's kind of cute, I guess. If you like red heads."

As William started to laugh, a machine above his bed beeped.

Gasping at the same time, he choked out, "Don't...make me...laugh."

Charlotte's face fell and tears instantly welled in her eyes.

A nurse quickly burst into the room and rushed up to William. After checking his vitals, she gave Charlotte a dirty look.

"Who let you in here?"

Sitting up tall, Charlotte replied, "I let myself in," before questioning, "Is there a problem?"

Appearing agitated, the nurse suggested, "Would you step outside for a moment."

"No."

In disbelief, she snapped, "Excuse me?"

Motioning towards the door, Charlotte stated, "You're excused."

The nurse started to say something then glanced at William before turning and leaving his hospital room.

After standing up and walking to the door, Charlotte closed it and returned to William's bedside.

William drew a few ragged breaths into his oxygen mask, pulled it away from his face and whispered, "Hand me my board," as he pointed to the dry erase board behind the picture of him and Mallory.

Reaching around the picture frame, Charlotte lifted the board with a dry erase marker attached by a chain and handed it over to William.

Taking the board from her, he lifted the marker and wrote, 'She's gonna call Auggie.'

"So, I'm not worried about him," Charlotte insisted.

His eyes reflected sadness as he wrote, 'I am.'

With a slight huff, Charlotte shook off the flash of hatred in Auggie's eyes the previous night and apologized, "Look, you know I never meant to hurt you. The whole thing got blown way out of proportion because of your brother."

William scowled before writing, 'Why are you here?'

"Whether I meant to or not, I did hurt you and I'm sorry," she admitted before asking, "Do you forgive me?"

As Charlotte waited for his reply, she recalled her reason for visiting him.

Lying in William's bed, she could sense his hesitation. He was completely naked while she was left with only her camisole on. Propped up by his hands, William hovered over her.

"I might not be very good," he offered.

In an effort to nudge the moment along, she slid her hands down him assuring, "That's okay, I am."

Still holding back, he leaned down to kiss her. Turning her head to the side, to avoid their lips touching, she sighed as his kiss trailed across her jaw to right below her ear.

"Let me kiss you," he whispered before pushing himself back up.

Slowly shaking her head, she looked up at him, "It bothers me."

William nodded and gave a nervous smile before asking, "Are you ready?"

Charlotte started to guide him when they both heard a loud bang at the front door.

Freezing in place, he quietly stated, "Wait a minute."

"Do you think it's your brother?"

Shaking his head, William replied, "Even if he forgot his key, we keep a spare one under the rock on the porch."

Pausing a moment, Charlotte said, "I think they went away," right before they heard a crashing sound.

William quickly jumped up and wrapped the sheet around his waist before running out to see what had happened.

The next thing Charlotte heard was Emerson's voice shouting, "What the hell are you doing with my daughter?"

Sitting up, she pulled the comforter up to her waist when she heard Ren's voice next.

Smirking at Ren when she pushed William's bedroom door open and griped, "Get dressed and get out here," she waited for her to walk away before getting up and putting her clothes back on.

So close to combining sex with genuine emotion, something she never realized she had the desire for until she met William, she wanted to cry.

Not wanting either intruder to think they had effected her in any way, Charlotte stood up tall and walked to the living room just in time to hear William say, "I really care about her, I don't understand."

Ren answered him, blurting, "William, she's seventeen."

The only thing Charlotte could think to do to save face in front of all of them was to smirk at him, saying, "Oops," as if she didn't care at all.

The look on William's face and the hurt in his eyes made it impossible for her to look back at him as she walked out with Emerson.

The longer Charlotte sat waiting for William to answer her, the more guilt she felt over the situation. It wasn't like she lied to him, he never asked. If it had been up to her, she would have seen him so much sooner and apologized. But that night, Ren got involved, Emerson and Amila put her on serious lock-down and once his brother found out, she was lucky the apology letter she wrote made it to him.

Finally, the squeaking sound of the marker against the dry erase board let her know his answer.

'I forgive you.'

Charlotte started to feel the weight of guilt being lifted from her conscience until he pulled his mask down.

Raspy and weak, William waved her closer so she could hear him say, "If...you...do something for...me."

ॐ∽ॐ

Exhausted and downright furious, Auggie stormed up to the hospital doors. He almost didn't answer his phone but when he saw it was Sheryl from the hospital, he was instantly awake and feared the worst. When she shared that a blonde girl was in William's room upsetting him, he was just plain pissed. She had some nerve, not only showing up outside his bar but now she was in there with Will taking things one step too far.

Barely acknowledging anyone, he made his way through the hospital and up to the third floor, as they commented on his visit being earlier than usual. Today, Auggie didn't have time for polite conversation. In the last six months, he had spent four hours every day with William. Which made him sort of a regular there and he got to know most of the staff fairly well.

As soon as Auggie reached William's floor, Sheryl was standing at the nurses' station waiting on him.

"She is still in there," she spouted.

Stopping a moment, Auggie stated, "I'll take care of it."

Before he could take another step, she said, "I know who she is. Mallory's gonna be..." before he cut her off griping, "Nothing. You can keep this to yourself."

Giving him a 'whatever' look, Sheryl turned and resumed her duties at the nurses' station.

Taking the opportunity to see what he was walking into before barging into William's hospital room, as much as he couldn't stand Charlotte, his brother meant the world to him and he didn't want to upset him. Looking through the small rectangle pane, he placed his hand on the door handle. Slowly letting go, he suddenly couldn't bring himself to go into the room. Stepping to the side so he could still see without being seen, he watched the two of them. The situation was far different than what he'd expected.

William's oxygen mask was pulled down to his chin and his head was turned toward Charlotte. She was leaning close slowly shaking her head at him. Both of her hands were wrapped around one of William's hands and his other one rested on her shoulder. As Auggie continued to watch, he wished he knew what they were saying. When Charlotte hung her head and nodded, Auggie turned and walked away.

Auggie was still irritated by her presence, but it didn't look like Charlotte was upsetting Will. In fact, it appeared to be the opposite.

"You're not going in there?" Sheryl fussed from behind the nurses' station.

Shaking his head as he passed her by, he replied, "You have my number, text me when she leaves."

Quickly around the desk and at his side, she asked, "You're leaving?"

"I'm gonna get some air."

Sliding in front of Auggie before he could reach the door to the stairwell, Sheryl asked, "I do have your number, can I text you for other things?"

Glancing down at her, he shared, "I don't have time for anything right now."

Continuing to block his exit, she pressed her shoulders back against the door, saying, "Come on Auggie, surely you have time for a little somethin'."

Before he could turn her down, the head nurse called for her letting him off of the hook. He watched Sheryl roll her eyes and step away before he headed into the stairwell. She wasn't bad looking. Sheryl was a curvy brunette with big brown eyes and pouty lips, but she was also two faced and gossipy and that was a huge turn off for him.

୭∞ଈ

Charlotte took the opportunity to give Sheryl a sarcastic smile as she stepped out of William's hospital room. Sheryl started to make a face at her when another nurse called for her attention. If Sheryl would have said or done something to provoke her, it would have taken her mind off of what William asked her to do. It was going to be impossible, but she owed him. He said he wasn't punishing her for hurting him that she could consider it a penance for forgiveness. She cared so much about him, she couldn't deny him his last request especially after breaking his heart.

Wishing she was as cold and careless as she pretended to be, Charlotte started to feel overwhelmed with regret. Deciding to take the stairs, she needed some alone time to collect herself before anyone saw the tears building in her eyes as she left the hospital. Opening the door to the stairwell, she turned the corner. Slamming into a green flannel shirt, it took her a few seconds to take a step back as the smell of stale beer from the man she just ran into surrounded her.

"What the hell are you doing?" Auggie growled at her.

Taking another step back, Charlotte snapped, "Get out of my way."

Moving to the side, he stated, "Don't come here again."

Standing up tall, she took a step towards him assuring, "Trust me, I don't want to be anywhere near you or your little friend in there." Auggie narrowed his eyes at her as she added, "Oh, don't think I've forgotten."

"Stay away from my brother."

Charlotte gave him a disgusted look before turning and headed down the stairs.

∂∞∾

Auggie stood there watching Charlotte make her way down. Taking a minute, he hadn't forgotten either. After Charlotte and William got caught in bed together a few years back, it didn't take long for word to spread around town. Sheryl's younger sister went to school with Charlotte and took the opportunity to mess with her. Auggie wouldn't have cared except for the fact that, thanks to Sophia, Sheryl assumed since it was his house they were at, he was the one with Charlotte. He caught hell for a good month because of the ridiculous rumor.

It wouldn't have mattered to him that Charlotte was only seventeen and William was twenty-three but she lied to his brother, hid the fact that she was a minor and Emerson Robert's daughter. Her father was a big deal in town and Will could have gotten in serious trouble. She didn't even try to make things right, she just sent a fake ass apology letter to him that Ren probably made her write.

As he resisted the urge to cuss Sheryl out when he walked back in, Auggie walked straight to William's room.

Closing the door behind himself, Auggie said, "I heard you had a visitor."

William nodded as Auggie walked to his bedside. He hadn't intended on mentioning her at all, but William's room smelled of the same sweetness as when she ran into him in the stairwell. Thinking to himself 'someone like her shouldn't smell good, it's deceiving, she should smell like vinegar or liver and onions', he sat in the chair next to William's bed.

Catching sight of the 'I forgive you' written on Will's board before he wiped it and wrote, 'Don't be mad,' Auggie changed the subject, saying, "How ya feelin' today?"

Pulling his mask down, William wheezed, "Tired."

Nodding, Auggie cleared his throat before offering, "Let's both get some shut eye then."

William placed the mask back to his mouth before shaking his head as he pulled it away, whispering, "I need...you...to do...something...for me."

3

Dinner

Lola stood next to Charlotte in her bathroom watching her carefully applying a thick coat of lipstick to her lips.

"I think you are prettier without it," Lola assured.

Glancing down at Lola, Charlotte winked, saying, "That's why you're my favorite."

With a slight giggle, Lola asked, "Are you going to still be here when we get back?"

"I'll be here for three whole months," she replied. Charlotte made her way out of the bathroom with Lola close behind her.

Sitting on her bed, Charlotte reached down and slid her high heels on as Lola sat down next to her.

"Are you getting married?"

Charlotte smiled, answering, "That's the rumor but don't say anything. I don't think I'm supposed to know Trace is gonna ask."

"What's he like?"

Taking a breath, Charlotte turned towards Lola, replying, "He's very handsome."

"What does he do?"

Laughing, Charlotte asked, "Alright, what's with all the questions?"

Shrugging, Lola shared, "Silvia won't talk to me about her boyfriend. She says I'm too little and he's none of my business."

"That's because Silvia's a..." Stopping to filter herself, Charlotte continued, "A little on the uppity side."

Lola giggled, "You were gonna say a cuss word."

With a sigh, Charlotte nodded before imparting, "Don't be like that when you grow up. Just because Emerson and Amila have money, that doesn't make you better than anyone. Okay."

"Does Trace have a lot of money?"

Standing up to check herself in the mirror, Charlotte replied, "Yes but its mostly his father's."

"How did you meet him?"

Turning to Lola, still sitting on the bed, she answered, "At a party."

"Do y'all go on dates?"

Leaning down to hug Lola, Charlotte said, "I tell you what, if you let me go get him, you can ask him all the questions you want," and gave her a squeeze.

☜☞

Trace was waiting outside of the Inn when Charlotte pulled up. She rolled her window down and smiled as he walked to the driver's side.

"Hop in," she suggested.

Looking down at her, he gave her an absurd expression as he said, "I'll drive."

"I want to drive," Charlotte pouted, batting her eyelashes at him.

Trace gave a disapproving glance as he said, "What will it look like if you are driving me."

"It will look like I'm driving."

Taking a step back he, fussed, "You know I do not like being driven."

Charlotte pursed her lips, saying, "You get driven all the time."

"Not by you."

Mentally counting back from ten, Charlotte opened the door and stepped out of the car. This was the last time she would see him until he returned to collect her. She should behave for him.

Inspecting her from head to toe, Trace smiled. She was perfection. Her hair pulled into a perfect knot at the nape of her neck, the lines of her clingy blouse matched up perfectly to her fitted skirt that ended mid-thigh on her flawless legs that were elongated by the heels she wore.

Leaning close to her, he ran his hand down her side before kissing her right below her ear as he whispered, "No one will compare to you while I am away."

His compliment made her feel like he was reminding her, they were not exclusive and he intended on seeing other women while he was away.

"How can you say that, when you have never kissed me?"

Pulling away, Trace questioned, "This is a conversation you would like to have now, before I meet your father?"

It was a conversation, she never thought of before now. Charlotte had not been kissed on her lips since she was fourteen. Seeing William today and remembering how badly he wanted to kiss her properly, suddenly made it an issue. The scar on her mouth took a very long time to heal and when it did, it bothered her so much just the thought of someone kissing her upset her. But shouldn't Trace want to kiss her?

"Do you kiss other women you are with?" she asked.

Serious in expression, he replied, "I have no desire to deny the fact that I see other women. That was made clear to you from the beginning. If you insist on my disclosing every detail, I do many things with other women that I have yet to experience with you."

"I only asked if you kissed them because I was curious if you wanted to kiss me."

Looking down at her as if she was a child, he replied, "You know how I feel about imperfection."

"I'm full of imperfections."

Trace smiled at her, assuring, "And as far as I am concerned, if I cannot see them, they do not exist."

That was something she liked about him. Although she never told him exactly how she got her scars, he didn't care about where she came from, what had happened to her or what she was like before. There was no past with him. All he cared about was enjoying the now and preparing for the future.

☜❧

The formal introductions when they arrived went well except for Lola, who took one look at Trace and practically hid behind Emerson the rest of the time. Charlotte's brothers and sister had been fed already because this was more of a grown up dinner than a family one. Charlotte stood in the kitchen with Amila and Ren while Jackson, Emerson and Trace remained in the living room.

"So, what do y'all think?" Charlotte questioned.

Ren quickly replied, "About what?" before Amila gave a soft smile, answering, "Well, he's very handsome."

"Isn't he," Charlotte agreed.

"He seems very formal, is he like that all of the time?" Amila asked.

"Yea but so is Emerson," Charlotte replied.

With a hint of hidden meaning, Amila shared, "Not all the time."

Ren laughed out loud as Charlotte made a face at her.

"Sorry honey," Amila laughed before saying, "But these are things you should think about if you're getting serious. I mean, do you want a husband that politely asks or one that throws you over his shoulder and..."

Charlotte blurted, "Amila!" as Ren continued to laugh knowing Charlotte was horrified at the thought of Emerson and Amila in that type of situation.

When dinner was ready, the men joined them in the kitchen before heading into the dining room. Everyone settled, in pairs at the dining room table.

Amila started the conversation by asking, "So Trace, you don't have an accent, did you grow up in Spain?"

"I was born in Àlava. I attended American boarding school in Bethesda, Maryland."

With a compassionate expression, Amila said, "That must have been terribly lonely."

Appearing confused he asked, "Why?"

"It just seems like it would be," she replied.

Changing the subject, Emerson shared, "Dinner is delicious."

"Roasted pork loin is Charlotte's favorite," Amila replied before smiling at Charlotte.

Trace quickly chimed in, "It is exceptional. Who is your cook?"

Ren and Charlotte glanced at each other, trying not to laugh, as Amila gave him an offended expression saying, "You're looking at her."

"I did not mean to offend you," he quickly replied.

Jackson brought the next subject change, asking, "So Trace, do you follow basketball? I hear Spain is giving the European league a run for their money this season."

"I am not a fan of sports in general. The idea of running or sweating doesn't appeal to me."
Trace cleared his throat and adjusted in his seat as dining room went silent.

As Jackson tried to shake off the shock of what he just heard, his cellphone started to ring.

Reaching into his jacket pocket, he pulled it out, saying, "It's Penny."

Everyone at the table focused on Jackson as he answered the call.

"I can hardly understand you...She's right here," he said before handing the phone to Ren saying, "She said she's been calling your phone."

Ren quickly put the phone to her ear, saying, "I'm sorry sweetie. Is everything okay?"

Trace leaned to Charlotte, asking, "Penny?"
Before another word was said, Ren stood up and exited the dining room.

Jackson turned in his chair watching for Ren to return as Charlotte explained, "Ren's daughter is married to Ailin, Penny's brother. Ailin and Penny are Jackson's cousins on his mother's side."

Amila cut in saying, "I hope Sophia is okay." When Charlotte glanced at Amila, she shared, "Oh, I forgot to tell you. Sophia's pregnant."

Remembering their names being mentioned at the bar the previous night, Trace started to question, "Are they also..." when Ren stepped back into the room.

With a somber expression on her face and tears in her eyes, Ren stood there quietly for a moment holding Jackson's phone in her hand.

Jackson stood up as Ren informed, "William."
Charlotte sat there frozen as she stared at Ren.

"I'm sorry we need to go," Ren shared before Emerson and Amila stood offering their condolences.
Moments of time spent with William flashed through Charlotte's mind as she watched Ren and Jackson walkout.

Amila and Emerson made their way back to their seats after seeing Ren and Jackson out.

As Charlotte continued to stare at the doorway, Amila asked, "Honey, are you alright?"
She couldn't bring herself to answer.

"Did you know him?" Trace asked, taking note of Charlotte's reaction to the news.

Emerson answered for her, saying, "You know how it is. It's a small town. Everyone knows everyone."

Nodding, Trace replied, "Of course."

Charlotte looked at Emerson, who gave her a slight smile.

戴戴

Sitting in his truck in the hospital parking lot, Auggie stared out of the windshield at the building in front of him. He knew it was getting close but it was still a shock for William to finally be gone. Since Will was five, he had been in and out of the hospital. There was always a concern and he always feared the worst but William always got better. Not this time though.

Forcing himself out of his truck, he headed towards the hospital doors. His last conversation with William was about Charlotte. As much as he hated to admit it, if it wasn't for her showing up there, Auggie wouldn't have been able to talk to his brother before he passed. He had fallen asleep about an hour before Auggie normally would have shown up to visit, and now he knew he never woke up. He had no choice now other than to carry out his brother's dying wish. It was a last request and he gave William his word.

When Auggie reached the third floor of the hospital, it was filled with his family. His brother Ailin was holding Sophia close as she cried into his shoulder. It was clear he had been crying too. His other brother Braden was sitting in a chair against the wall with his arms stretched over his face. His sister Penny was with Ren and Jacks as Ren held her and Jackson patted her back. When he made it into William's hospital room, Jackson's parents, Carenza and JP, were standing with his mom.

JP and Carenza excused themselves from the room as his mom looked at him and said, "He's really gone."

Wrapping his arms around her, he assured, "It's okay, Ma."

She held onto him, mourning the loss of her son.

4

Uncomfortable

Standing in the cemetery, Charlotte stared at William's headstone. Reading the words *Beloved Son and Brother* over and over again. She could tell the funeral was the previous day, all the flowers that surrounded it were fresh. Her family left that morning to go on vacation for two weeks and it seemed like the perfect time to say everything she needed to, to tell William goodbye.

Crouching down by his grave, Charlotte squeezed the bottle cap he gave her in her hand.

"I know I already said I was sorry and you forgave me but there are some things I should have said when I had the chance. You were the sweetest guy I've ever..." Tears streamed down her face as she continued, "I wish I had loved you and I'm sorry I couldn't."

Opening her hand, Charlotte looked at the bottle cap before placing it on the ground next to his headstone.

Wiping her eyes before lowering her sunglasses, she admitted, "I should have let you kiss me."

Placing her fingers against her lips, Charlotte pressed hard against them before lifting her hand touching it to his name.

❧❧

Walking up to his brother's grave site, Auggie stopped when he saw Charlotte standing at William's headstone. Her blonde hair was swaying against her back with the breeze and she had a light blue sweater on and shorts. Incredibly short, dark blue shorts that showed the entire length of her legs. Looking down at the bottle he brought, he waited a few minutes before continuing on his way.

☞☜

Charlotte turned around just as Auggie walked up. Without the beanie he had on that night at the bar and at the hospital, Auggie's hair and beard had a copper tint to it in the sunlight. He had on the same work boots and Dickie's slacks as that day at the hospital. His shirt was red and blue plaid today and he didn't smell like beer this time either. It was a combination of men's deodorant and soap, but the pleasantness of it caught her off guard as she stared at him.

Pulling his sunglasses down slightly, he griped, "Not a word for five years and now I can't get you to leave him alone."

Giving him a dirty look from behind her sunglasses, she snapped, "Real classy drinking at a cemetery."

"It's for Will," he said twisting off the cap and setting it by the headstone.

Wondering if William truly expected her to keep her promise, she shook her head and stated, "I'm sorry."

"What?"

Holding her head high, and straightening the bottom of her sweater, she repeated, "I said...I'm sorry."

"What the hell are you apologizing to me for?"

"Because, I am a grown up and I felt it was necessary."

Scoffing at her, he replied, "A grown up? What are you like nineteen?"

Making a face at him, she sarcastically replied, "Nice math skills. I'm almost twenty-five, which must seem pretty young to someone as old as you."

Glaring at her, he took a step forward, stating, "I'm thirty-four little girl. That makes me a man, not old."

Auggie caught clear sight of the scar on her mouth as she slowly smiled, saying, "Good thing because it's certainly not your behavior."

"From what I saw the other night in front of my bar, you have no idea how a real man acts."

Charlotte was suddenly speechless recalling the incident in front of The Dog House.

Auggie had no idea why he brought that up or why he needed to defend himself to her. It was irritating that she could incite that type of reaction from him. She reminded him a little of Ren but when they argued it was all in good fun. He didn't like her, he was going to do what William asked but he wasn't going to like it, or her.

"When are you leaving?" he griped.

"Right now," she answered as she turned to walk away.

Hoping that was the case, he would be off the hook.

Making sure, he asked, "And you're not coming back."

"What are you talking about?" Charlotte snapped at him.

"You're leaving town right?"

Crossing her arms in front of her chest, she stated, "Eventually."

"When is that?"

Deciding she would have to figure out a way to keep her promise to William while having as little contact with him as possible, Charlotte replied, "Since neither of us wants to keep running into each other, why don't you just tell me where I can and can't go for the next three months."

Shaking his head, Auggie mentally told William, 'I can't do three months of her'.

When he didn't answer her, Charlotte walked off in a huff. He was impossible. She needed to go somewhere and do something but there was nowhere to go and nothing to do. Reaching her rental car, she stopped and pulled her phone out of her back pocket. There was a text from Trace.

T: Hello lovely.

Recalling the less than enthusiastic send-off she gave him, after finding out William had passed, she quickly typed back.

C: Hey there. Miss me?

T: Always my beauty.

C: Me too.

T: Are you lonely?

C: ♥ YES ♥

T: I told you 3months would be a long time.

C: So make a quick trip down here ;)

T: Tempted. Call when I can.

C: K bye ♥

Sliding her phone back into her pocket, Charlotte looked up to see Auggie standing there staring at her.

He had been watching her for a few minutes, without meaning to.

"So now you're following me?" she snapped.

"My truck is right there," he griped, pointing at his black pickup.

"Well, did you want something or you just wanted to take one last look at me?"

Scowling at her, he blurted, "Yea, you wish honey," before offering, "You wanna follow me to the bar?"

"Not particularly."

That was all Auggie could stand of her for the time being. Why did she have to be that way? Couldn't she see that he was using everything that he had to keep his composure and not tell her exactly what he thought of her? Shaking his head, he walked to his truck.

స్తూ

Sitting at the desk in the back room of The Dog House, Auggie leaned over, sorting through the week's receipts and eyeing the dreaded ledger book. When Will was first admitted to the hospital, he was offended that Jackson asked if he needed him to step in with his brother out. He could manage the bar. However, it was harder than he thought and although no one else knew, every Sunday he brought the ledger and receipts to the hospital with him. Will would walk him through it each time but now, no matter how many times his brother showed him, it never stuck and he was lost doing it by himself.

It had been a little over a week since his brother passed and that meant the cross he had his cousin Kieran tattoo on his back, the night William died, was starting to get uncomfortable. With every move he made, his shirt rubbed against his back. It was just like Charlotte, rubbing him the wrong way. Auggie'd had it with being irritated and not being able to do anything about it. Unbuttoning his shirt, he pulled it off and tossed it behind him. As Auggie opened the ledger and stared at it, his mind wandered to getting his life back to where it was before Will got sick. Six months was a long time for him. He didn't do dates or relationships, but he enjoyed taking home the random girl from time to time. Quickly realizing his mind had wandered in a less than productive direction, he stood up and left the manager's office.

☜•☞

Even though she tried to talk herself out of it, Charlotte's curiosity over why Auggie wanted her to come to the bar overruled her dislike for being around him. When she pulled up at the back of the bar next to his truck and walked in, she had no idea what to expect.

Stepping into the main area of the bar, Charlotte had to take a breath. Auggie was standing, shirtless, with his back to her, stretching his arms above his head. The muscles in his back flexed as he lowered them, rolled his shoulders and leaned his head from side to side. Fixated on the Celtic cross that covered his back, she had an overwhelming urge to make her way closer. As she tried to imagine him in those horrible plaid shirts he wore, instead of the images of him that were popping up in her mind, he turned around.

Eyeing the Augustus Carrick Caffrey IV tattoo across his chest right below his collar bone and the Celtic knots on his shoulders, Charlotte quickly spit out, "You wanted me?"

"What?"

Fluttering her eyelashes as she rolled her eyes at him, Charlotte reminded, "You asked me to follow you here."

Auggie scowled at her for a long moment before saying, "Will left something in the back for you."

Raising her eyebrows at him as he continued to stand there, she griped, "Well can I have it or are you just going to stand there staring at me?"

Auggie made a growling sound under his breath before he walked passed her, assuring, "You were starin' first sweetheart."

Following him to the back of the bar, she snapped, "My name is Charlotte."

Swiftly turning to face her, he didn't realize how close behind him she was as he shared, "Be happy I'm not callin' you..."

Standing a few inches from his bare chest, she interrupted, "Charlotte is my name, Augustus."

Another low growl resonated from his throat as he turned and continued to the office in the back.

Picking his shirt up off of the floor behind his chair, Auggie pulled it on and quickly buttoned it before sitting down behind the desk. He opened the bottom drawer of the desk and grabbed the box William left for her. Glancing up at Charlotte, who was standing in the doorway, he set the box on the edge of the desk before flipping open the ledger book.

"What is it?"

Shrugging off her question, Auggie grabbed his pencil and started adding numbers from the receipts into the ledger book.

Refusing to look up, he could tell she had made her way closer. The room suddenly smelled better. The subtle sweetness that accompanied her grew stronger causing him to lose focus.

"What are you doing?" Charlotte asked.

Erasing an entire line of numbers from the ledger, Auggie replied, "Trying to get this done."

Just as he started over, she questioned, "Why don't you use a computer?"

"Jackson likes it done this way first," he explained, rewriting the receipt balances.

"You look like you're having a hard time."

Erasing the row for the second time, Auggie griped, "I'm already a week behind."

Before he realized it, she was right beside him, leaning over the desk saying, "I can show you an easier way to do that."

As Charlotte placed her finger on the ledger book and started to explain, Auggie was overwhelmed by the smell of her. Without hearing a word she said, he closed his eyes and drew in a slow deep breath. He couldn't place the scent. Trying to think of what it could be, he felt her hair brush against his arm as she leaned closer.

Yanking the ledger book away from her, he slapped it closed and fussed, "I don't need help."

Standing up straight, Charlotte griped, "Keep doing it wrong then."

"I know what I'm doing."

Shaking her head at him with a disgusted expression, she stated, "Sure you do. That's why your totals won't balance out."

Auggie glared at her, knowing she was right but refusing to admit he needed help, especially from her.

৵৽

When Charlotte made it home to an empty house, she went straight to her room. Setting the box William left her on her nightstand, she threw herself onto her bed. She felt she was making an honest effort where Auggie was concerned. If he had let her help him, she could have been one step closer to fulfilling her promise to William. Reaching over, she grabbed her box and set it on the bed next to her. Propping herself up on her elbow, Charlotte opened it. Inside the box was a plastic bag filled with bottle caps.

With a loud exhale, she rolled onto her back and closed her eyes. No matter how hard she tried, Auggie standing in that stupid bar, shirtless, was the only thing she could think of. He wasn't even handsome. He wore ugly plaid shirts and his beard was scruffy, unkempt and far too long. Charlotte's mind wandered to how she felt standing close to him with his shirt off. She didn't like him, couldn't stand his attitude or the way he looked at her, but there was something about him that made her wonder what it would be like if they had known each other under different circumstances.

Slowly opening her eyes, Charlotte sat up. Closing the box William left her, she placed it back on her nightstand and stood up. Smiling with pride, she decided on just the right approach to take with Auggie. If she handled him as if he were any other man, she could do what William asked.

5

Deal

After a long night of tossing and turning, Charlotte stood in her bathroom brushing her teeth. The empty house was eerily quiet and she didn't like staying there by herself. In Spain, Erin was gone quite a bit but she kept a full staff at all times, even when it felt like it, Charlotte was never alone. In a way, she felt homesick for Spain. She missed having breakfast waiting on the table for her each morning, accompanied by Erin's 'Good Morning Dear'. Five years was a long time to spend there and it had become home for her. There, she fit in. No one knew anything about her there. It was a separate life from her small southern town, one that was everything she wanted her life to be.

Making her way to the closet, Charlotte stopped in front of her bedroom window when she heard a diesel engine idling right outside. Moving the curtain back, she peered through the mini-blind and saw a black Chevy Silverado 2500HD with custom chrome and mud tires. Making an irritated sound, Charlotte narrowed her eyes at the truck, knowing who was inside. To her surprise, the truck backed up and pulled away. Smiling to herself, she thought, 'chicken' before hearing the truck pull up again.

Wanting to watch and see if he got out of the truck this time, she opted to get dressed instead, just in case he did. Charlotte pulled on a pair of ultra-short knit baby blue shorts before pulling off her tank top and sliding on a fitted camisole and loose fitting white t-shirt. Grabbing her hair brush out of the bathroom, she ran it through her hair a few times before tossing it on her bed. Pulling her hair into a messy ponytail as she headed into the hallway. She stood at the top of the stairs for a while waiting to hear a knock. Wondering if he was trying to make up his mind, she heard his truck door close a few times before the doorbell rang. Taking a deep breath, Charlotte smirked to herself thinking, 'Game on'.

Charlotte took her time walking down the stairs through the living room and up to the front door. When the doorbell rang a second time, she counted to thirty, unlocked the door and slowly opened it.

Leaning onto the doorframe through the open door, Charlotte crossed one foot in front of the other and greeted, "Well this is a surprise."

Clearing his throat as he looked her over, Auggie questioned, "Do you really know how to do this?" holding a green ledger book up to her.

Drawing out a "Yep," she looked him up and down. Auggie was consistent if nothing else. The only thing that varied was his choice of shirt and even then it was still plaid. And what was with the beanie? Clearly he wasn't going bald, she had seen him at the cemetery without it and although it was fashionable to wear them, he didn't strike her as keeping up with trends.

Just about the time she started to think about what was hidden by his ugly shirt, Auggie said, "Sundays are my only day off."

"And?" she questioned, wanting him to come right out and ask her for help.

"That's the day I work on this stuff."

Rolling her eyes as she turned to walk back into the living room, Charlotte replied, "Thanks for sharin'."

Auggie followed her into the house, already frustrated by the way she was acting.

Closing the door behind himself, he griped, "You said you knew an easy way to keep books. Are you gonna show me or what?"

Continuing to the couch, she sat down, crossing one leg over the other, saying, "That depends."

"On what?"

Fluttering her eyelashes at him, Charlotte proposed, "Ask me nicely."

Narrowing his eyes at her, he snapped, "Kiss my ass."

Slowly shaking her head, Charlotte leaned back rebutting, "I do believe it's my ass you should be kissing, Augustus."

"You must be high out of your mind if you think I'm kissin' anything of yours."

Feeling a bit insulted, she sat up straight and offered, "Look, you don't like me and I don't like you so let's lay our cards on the table and help each other out."

Suspicious, he scowled, "Alright."

Charlotte patted the spot on the couch next to her, saying, "Have a seat."

"Yea, no thanks."

Fluttering her lashes as she rolled her eyes at him, she stood up with a loud huff.

∽•∾

Auggie watched as Charlotte made her way to a chair facing the couch. With a sarcastic expression, she motioned for him to sit on the couch by himself.

Taking the offer, he sat before asking, "You wanna get dressed first."

Crossing one of her long legs over the other, she replied, "I am dressed."

The spot where he sat on the couch still smelled like her, making him wish she would go put more clothes on.

"Let's hear it."

Placing her hands on the arms of the chair, Charlotte stated, "I made your brother a promise before he died and I need you to keep it."

Running his last conversation with Will over in his mind, Auggie asked, "Oh yea, how's that?"

She was silent for a moment before sharing, "He wanted me to make an effort with you. Since he loved us and we cared about him, he wanted me to be here for you."

Instantly furious, Auggie stood up correcting, "I didn't just care about him, he's my brother. I don't need anything from anybody and honey, if I did, you're the last person on earth..." until she cut him off, arguing, "Really? Then why are you here?"

Asking himself that same question, Auggie remembered Will making him promise he would look out for Charlotte while she was here.

Glaring at her, Auggie sat back down. He didn't want to spend time with her. He didn't want to have anything to do with her at all. Will had really screwed him over with this one.

"What did you have in mind?"

Sitting up a little straighter in her chair, Charlotte replied, "Sundays work fine for me, not that there is anything to do any other day. Pick a time and we can meet. I'll help you with your book there, be able to keep my promise to William then once you get the hang of it, we never have to see each other again. It's as simple as that."

Nodding, he replied, "I can do that."

Raising her eyebrows at him, she fussed, "I need a time and place."

"I don't want you at my bar. You can come by the house. Saturday nights are usually late ones so you can come around four in the afternoon."

He could tolerate her for a few hours once a week to keep his word with Will.

Waiting for her to argue, Auggie was caught off guard when she stood up, stepped to him and held out her hand.

Looking up at her like she was crazy, he griped, "What?"

"Shake on it," she demanded.

Clenching his back teeth, Auggie stood up and held out his hand. Staring at it, he watched as Charlotte slowly slid her hand into his. Her thumb brushed against the top of his hand as she softly held onto it. Tightening his hand around hers, he gave it a firm shake before letting go and making a beeline for the door. He refused to look back at her before leaving the Roberts' house.

❧❦

Pulling up at his mom's house, Auggie turned his truck off and sat there for a minute. The whole way all he could think about was how good Charlotte smelled and how soft her hand was. When his mind wandered to what the rest of her felt like, he turned the radio up as high as he could stand, trying to drown all thoughts of her out of his mind.

This wasn't going to work. How was he supposed to spend any time with her if she was going to have this kind of effect on him. It didn't make sense to Auggie. One minute she would appear disgusted with him and in the next, it seemed like she was flirting. In all honesty, he liked neither. Both of those expressions towards him were offensive coming from her. He knew women had their little games that they played with men and he could spot a come-on almost before it happened. Women were all the same and after a certain amount of time, there was nothing unique about any of them. Sure they varied in size, shape and appearance but when it came down to it, they all felt the same. She was just another girl, no different than any other but she had a way about her that kept catching him off guard. Not to mention, she smelled so good and those legs... If he couldn't get a handle on her at least he could get a handle on himself. Almost seven months was just too long to go without. That had to be it. Shaking his head at himself as he stepped out of his truck, Auggie knew what he needed before seeing Charlotte again.

Almost at the door, Auggie's cellphone vibrated in his back pocket. Pulling it out, he made a face at the text message.

S: Hi ♥ it's Sheryl LOL.

A: I know...?...

S: LOL do you have time for anything now?

It took him a minute to decide that might not be a bad idea.

A: What did you have in mind?

S: I'll be at The Dog House LOL tonight!

A: So will I.

S: Hahahaha! Was hoping we could hook up after.

Even over text message she was annoying.

A: Maybe.

S: LOL MAYBE???

A: Later.

Sliding his phone back into his pocket, Auggie ended the conversation before one more 'lol' caused him to throw his phone across the yard.

After giving the door a tap, Auggie walked in. He could smell meat and potatoes cooking and headed straight for the kitchen.

"Hey Ma," he said finding her standing at the stove.

His sister Penny rounded the corner and rolled her eyes, saying, "Oh, it's just you."

Sitting down at the table, he looked over at Penny, saying, "Aren't you ever gonna move out?"

Sticking her tongue out at him, when their mom Sarah, said, "Would you two stop."

"She needs to do something with her life," Auggie griped before Penny laughed, "Ha! You need to get a life."

Sarah turned around, fussing, "I swear, less than a minute and y'all are already at it. Enough," at the both of them.

Penny smiled wide, tossing her long auburn hair over her shoulder as she slid onto a chair at the table, saying, "Wanna know what I heard."

Auggie instantly stated, "Nope."

"Sheryl said Charlotte came to see Will at the hospital and..."

Holding his hands out, Auggie glanced at his mom before shaking his head at Penny.

"Oh please, mom was here when she told me."

Irritated, Auggie snapped, "See, all you do is gossip. No wonder you can't keep a man."

"Sophia is the biggest gossip in town and she has a man," Penny argued making an ugly face at her brother.

With a slight laugh, Auggie corrected, "She doesn't have a man, she's got Ailin."

As Penny snickered, Sarah fussed, "Auggie!"

"Just stating facts, Ma," Auggie shared as they heard the front door open.

Penny hopped up saying, "Sophia's here."

Sarah set a plate of Shepard's pie in front of Auggie as Sophia walked into the kitchen.

Sophia walked straight to Sarah and hugged her before stepping back and giving Auggie a slight smile. It was no secret that Auggie and Sophia didn't get along. He never understood what his brother saw in her. Sure she was cute with her big brown eyes and wavy brown hair but Ailin acted like she was the end all be all of women everywhere and he had since they were teenagers. Sophia was Ren's only child and he knew Ren had devoted everything to her. And boy did it show. Sophia was a princess in her own mind and expected everyone to treat her as such. Most everyone did too, except for Auggie who liked her alright for being his brother's wife, but that was as far as his attachment towards her went.

Sarah reached down and laid her hand on Sophia's belly.

"Well?" she asked with a smile.

With a heavy sigh, Sophia pouted, "We still don't know. We are going to try again next week."

Sophia was always pouty when she wasn't getting her way.

"Know what?" Auggie questioned.

"What we're having," Sophia sneered at him.

"Shouldn't it be a baby?" he teased.

Penny jumped in, saying, "Whether it's a boy or a girl, stupid."

Shaking his head at Penny, Auggie shared, "It's a girl."

Sarah rolled her eyes and walked to the sink as Sophia questioned, "How would you know?"

"Easy, its Ailin's kid so it's a girl."

Appearing put out with him Sophia said, "You're lucky he's your brother because otherwise I wouldn't invite you to our baby shower."

"Why would I want to go to that?"

Penny scowled at him as Sarah notified, "All the men are invited. It's going to be at the bar."

"What?"

Quickly making her way to Sophia, Penny said, "Come on let's go," urging her out before Auggie had anything else to say about it.

Watching them leave, Auggie noticed how slow Sophia moved as he thought to himself, she wasn't even that big and she already acted like she was carrying a twenty-pounder.

Sarah stood at the kitchen counter packing up leftovers for Auggie to take home.

"A baby shower at the bar?" Auggie questioned.

Sarah turned to him, saying, "I know, but that's what she wants."

Shaking his head, he griped, "I can't believe Ailin's letting her do that," then paused a moment before saying, "Yep, they're havin' a girl."

Taking a seat next to him at the table, Sarah fussed, "Stop talking about your brother like that."

Auggie laughed a little before asking in a compassionate tone, "You doin' okay, Ma?"

Nodding, she replied, "How about you? Did you think about what I said?"

"I'll get to it."

With a caring sigh, she said, "Auggie, he's not coming back. I know it hasn't been very long, but you need to accept that he's gone."

Trying not to get mad, he replied, "I said I'd get around to cleaning out his room and I'll do it. I've been busy."
Truthfully, Auggie had left William's bedroom door shut since the day he died and had no intentions on going in there for any reason.

"I can do it if it's too hard for..." Sarah started before he cut her off, blurting, "Ma."
Sarah dropped the subject.

Auggie finished his lunch and stood up, walking to the counter to grab his meals for the week. Scooping the containers up, he walked back to the table.

Leaning down to kiss her cheek, he suddenly took a step back when she asked, "So, Charlotte came back to tell him goodbye?"

Shrugging, he replied, "I don't know."

"Sheryl said you were there too."

"So."

"What really happened?"

Not caring what Sheryl's big mouth spread around, he answered, "Nothing. I got there, saw she was in his room and left until she was gone."

"That doesn't sound like you."

Shaking his head at her, Auggie said, "She didn't look like she was upsetting him and I didn't want to either."

"That's all?"

"Yep," he replied, not wanting to tell her about bumping into her in the stairwell or any other time he's seen her since.

"Is she back for good?"

Feeling like he was being interrogated, he spouted, "Why are you questioning me about her?"

"Because the second Penny mentioned her name, you looked guilty as hell and I'm trying to figure out why."

"I'm not guilty of anything. I let Will have his moment with her. I didn't even give him a hard time about it."

Sarah watched his expression carefully as she asked, "Did they make their peace with each other?"

Reminding himself he was talking to his mom, Auggie said, "How am I supposed to know?"

Sitting back in her chair, Sarah stared at him, assuring, "Son, you really think I don't know when you're lyin' to me?"

Staring back, he didn't say a word.

Shaking her head while pursing her lips at him, Sarah shared, "I know she was at the bar yesterday. Blabbermouth Sheryl came by all in a tizzy about it."

Exhaling as he lowered his head, he replied, "Will left something at the bar for her and she came by to pick it. That's all."

"You sure?"

"Yes, Ma," he stressed, pushing his plate to the center of the table before saying, "I've got to go, love you."

Sarah waited for him to peck her on the cheek before saying, "Love you too."

Gritting his teeth as he walked out of his mom's house, he thought if Sheryl was a man he'd kick her ass. He still needed to get Charlotte off his mind but it wasn't going to be with her.

6

Rumor

Charlotte was still fussing about her confrontation with Sheryl when she and Ren walked into the house. Practically throwing her bags and purse down on Ren's couch, she wasn't even excited about the new clothes she bought anymore.

Ren gave a loving smile to Charlotte as she complimented, "I am really proud of the way you handled the situation."

Flopping down on the couch next to her bags, Charlotte replied, "I should have broken her nose like I did her sister's in high school."

Sitting down next to her, Ren replied, "I think you got your point across just fine."

Shaking her head, Charlotte griped, "It hasn't even been a month and it's already back like it was before I left."

"Don't overreact. Not everyone here is like her."

"Oh no? Name one other person aside from you, Amila and Lola that's actually happy I'm back."

With a heavy sigh, Ren reminded, "Well, you didn't exactly leave on a high note."

Making a face, she blurted, "I never even did anything to him."

Appearing confused, Ren asked, "Who are you talking about?"

Giving Ren a stupid look, Charlotte replied, "You think its a coincidence that twice Sheryl said I was with him."

"Okay Charlotte, I see where you're coming from but I'm sure Auggie has nothing to do with this. In fact, he caught just as much flack as you did when Sheryl decide it was you two instead of William back then."

"He's such a jerk."

Tilting her head to the side, Ren gave her a soft knowing smile as she shared, "I know Auggie is pretty rough around the edges. Lord knows every conversation I've ever had with him has turned into an argument, but he's very loyal and he has a good heart. It's just a tad on the hard side."

"Sure," she spouted before Ren swore, "Trust me, Auggie's a lot of things but he doesn't talk about people. If he has something to say about you, he'll say it to your face." Charlotte sat there for a moment before leaning over, hugging Ren and standing up.

She was going to find out if what Ren said was true. If he thought he was going to spread rumors about her and she was going to sit there and take it, he had another thing coming.

As Charlotte grabbed her bags off of the couch, Ren snapped, "Where are you going?"

Whipping around, she replied, "I'm going over there so he can say it to my face."

"Charlotte!"

Defending herself, she said, "I'm not going to let anyone get over on me."

Shaking her head, Ren offered, "Call if you need bail money."

Charlotte gave a laugh saying, "Will do," as she walked out of the door.

❧

Pounding on Auggie's front door, the longer it took for him to answer, the harder she knocked. Finally, after fifteen minutes of banging, the door flew open.

Charlotte instantly blurted, "Let me in."

Appearing angry, Auggie griped, "Guess I should be happy you didn't kick it in."

Not even close to amused she stated, "You have something you want to say to me?"

"Yea, it's Tuesday, what are you doing here?"

"Sorry you don't have more time to come up with more little rumors."

Giving her a dirty look he stood there not saying anything.

"Let's get a few things straight, Augustus. I agreed to help you with your math skills. I don't want you. So, there is no need to run around telling everybody that I do. And the next time your tacky ass nurse comes up to me sayin' to stay away from *her* man, not only will she be a patient in the hospital, she'll be in serious need of plastic surgery."

Shaking his head at her, Auggie stepped to his couch and sat down.

Leaning his head back, he rubbed the sides of his face with his hands. It suddenly occurred to Charlotte she woke him up. His hair was messy, his shirt was buttoned crooked and his feet were bare.

Caught up in his appearance, it took her by surprise when he looked at her and said, "My turn."

Glaring at him, she waited for him to defend his actions.

With a matter of fact expression, he stated, "If you come over in the middle of the day, wakin' me up, it better be for somethin' more than tryin' to put me in my place." Shocked at what she felt he was insinuating, Charlotte started to say something when he continued, "You can shut that mouth right now, 'cause I'm not done."

Charlotte made a disgusted face and noise to match at him before closing her mouth.

"Now you listen here, being with you wouldn't be a step up for me, so rest assured if I was ever that drunk and desperate, I sure as hell wouldn't go around braggin' about it. I'm not with Sheryl, I can't stand her. The only reason, she's not already beat up is because I don't put my hands on females. So the next time you think you know what you're talkin' about, take it somewhere else. 'Cause sweetheart, I don't want you."

&~&

Staring at Charlotte in his living room wearing a khaki colored skirt that wasn't any longer than the shorts he'd seen her in, he waited for an excuse for her behavior.

Straitening the bottom of her white blouse, Charlotte stated, "Well, okay then," and turned to walk away.

In disbelief, Auggie stood up griping, "Now hold on. You come all the way over here, bang on the door like you're the law, wake me up to chew me out and all you have to say is okay then?"

With an unapologetic expression she turned back to face him, saying, "I suppose, I misjudged the situation."

"Oh, you suppose?"

"That's what I said."

Fighting the fact that he was impressed with her, Auggie questioned, "That's all you have to say?"

Shrugging her shoulders, she offered, "Situation resolved?"

Shaking his head at her, Auggie waited until he turned around before smiling to himself thinking 'Unbelievable'.

Walking into his kitchen, Auggie opened his refrigerator and pulled out a container of left-overs from his mom. Placing them in the microwave, he waited, thinking about the previous night at the bar. He had decided Sheryl was definitely off the table and aside from griping at her for not keeping Charlotte at the hospital to herself, he ignored her the rest of the night. There had been two other prospects but as the night went on, one had a seriously irritating cackle of a laugh and the other smelled like a mixture of perfume and hairspray. He'd just have to wait for the weekend when there would be a bigger pool to choose from.

Pulling his lunch out of the microwave, he turned to see Charlotte had seated herself at his kitchen table.

Grabbing a fork out of a kitchen drawer before joining her at the table, he grumbled, "Have a seat."

With a sarcastic smile, Charlotte suggested, "You should be careful, you know. Not all girls deal well with being one-night-ers."

Almost dropping his fork, he narrowed his eyes at her, saying, "A...Thanks."

"Isn't that why?"

Confused for a moment, he scowled before saying, "She saw you coming out of The Dog House Sunday."

"I see. She thought I was heels-up on the bar," as he stared at her she cocked her head to the side, "Or bent over it. I'm not entirely sure what the new rumor is."

A mental picture flashed in Auggie's mind, causing him to adjust himself in his seat.

∽∾

Fighting the urge to smile when she noticed Auggie's reaction to her comment, it was subtle but unmistakable. Eying him as he ate, Charlotte wondered why he was so adamant about not wanting her when it was fairly obvious he found her attractive, at least momentarily. Never in her life had she dealt with a man like him. One minute he was looking at her like he was an alcoholic and she was the last bottle on earth and the next moment like she was a pariah. It wasn't like he had anything to lose by being nice. She wasn't trying to broadcast spending time with him around town. No wonder William was worried about him.

Taking a slow breath, Charlotte suggested, "Since I'm here, you want to just go ahead and do it."

Stopping mid-bite, Auggie froze, glaring at her.

Bursting into laughter, she clarified, "The books...but now I know what's on your mind."

Resuming his bite of Shepard's pie, Auggie swallowed before intentionally changing the subject by offering, "You want some?" as he leaned the container towards her.

A tad disappointed he was refusing to play back and forth with her, Charlotte wrinkled her nose at his meal, asking, "What is it?"

"Shepard's pie."

"What's in it?"

"Meat, Potato..." he started before she blurted, "Gross!"

In disbelief, he questioned, "How can you not like potatoes?"

"Because they're disgusting."

"How can you say that?"

"Because I have tasted them," Charlotte insisted, recalling her mother force-feeding them to her until she threw up."

꒰◦ᵕ◦꒱

Baffled by her dislike for a staple he grew up with, Auggie had a hard time letting the subject go.

Remembering she was adopted, he asked, "Is that all you had to eat growin' up or somethin'?"

Appearing offended she snapped, "No."

"What are you?"

"What?"

Setting his fork down into the container, he asked, "I know you weren't always a Roberts, so what are you?"

"I don't know."

"What was your last name?"

Obviously growing uncomfortable, Charlotte replied, "Smith."

Narrowing his eyes at her, he asked, "What's your middle name?"

"Persephone."

Shaking his head, Auggie lifted the container to scrape the rest of his lunch to one side with his fork, laughing, "No way."

Sitting up tall, Charlotte insisted, "Persephone's a name."

"Oh, I know."

With a frustrated expression she griped, "Then why are you laughing?"

"I just can't believe your initials were CPS."

Before another word was spoken, Charlotte reached over and slapped the container of food out of Auggie's hand.

He jumped up, shouting, "What the hell?!"

Staring directly at him, she stated, "Interesting what people find amusing."

Furious with her, he griped, "That's not funny," walking to retrieve his container.

Without expression she stood up, "No?"

Auggie's aggravation with her quickly turned to confusion.

If he made her mad, why didn't she just say so? He was just teasing her. Auggie picked up his container and tossed it in the sink before turning towards her. She didn't look mad, she appeared indifferent. He honestly didn't mean to hurt her feelings but to be fair it didn't appear that he had.

Noticing her tug at the bottom of her blouse as she stood there, he fussed, "That was uncalled for."

"Yea well, you're very rude and you smell," she replied with a familiar expression of disgust.

Scowling at her, he worked at not smiling as he questioned, "I smell? That's the best you got?" as he tried to get her to fess up, "You knocked my lunch across the room because I smell?"

"Yes you do. Like stale beer and sweat. I believe I also mentioned your rudeness."

"What am I supposed to say to that?"

Softening her expression, Charlotte answered, "Feel free to tell me how rude I am, I guess."

It only took a second for Auggie to realize what she was doing.

Assuming he crossed a line with her, after all he had no idea what her history before the Roberts' was. He was fairly certain she was steering the conversation to something she was able to handle. There was an instant change in her disposition once she regained control of the conversation.

Shaking his head with a slight smile, he asked, "Should I tell you you stink too?"

With a curious expression Charlotte replied, "Do I?"
Caught off guard by her question, he snapped, "How should I know? I don't go around smelling you."

Charlotte instantly stepped to him, leaned her head back slightly and questioned, "Well?"

"Well what?" he asked in a low voice, not knowing whether to take a step back or lean closer.

"Do I smell bad?"
Breathing her in, he wondered, 'Can a smell be beautiful?'.

"Sorta'," he lied.

Charlotte fluttered her eyelashes as she rolled her eyes and turned her back to him, "See you Sunday...liar."
Auggie watched her walk out of his house admitting to himself, she got the better of him today and swore not to let it happen again.

7

Boredom

After a three and a half hour long conversation with Ren, Charlotte really needed to get out of the house. Ren wasn't fussing at her, even though it felt that way. She was checking up on her to make sure Charlotte didn't start acting out. She understood, after all when she first met Ren, Charlotte was out of control. Although she kept the notebook Ren put together for her, it was more out of reminiscence than instruction at this point.

Scrolling through her phone, there wasn't a single person to do anything with here. Frowning at her phone, she rolled over. Two a.m. on a Saturday night and she wasn't crawling into bed. She had been there since seven thirty. How incredibly depressing.

Charlotte's phone pinged with a text.
   T: Are you home yet, my lovely?
Rolling her eyes, she texted back.
   C: Been home.
   T: It is Saturday night there.
Charlotte thought, rub it in why don't you.
   C: Yes.
   T: ?
   C: Did you want me to have a date?

T: I do not throw stones.

C: Are you saying it's okay with you if I see someone?

T: I am not a hypocrite.

C: Maybe I will go out then.

T: Are you angry with me?

C: Do you want me to be?

T: I want you to be ready when I come get you.

Staring at her phone, Charlotte wondered what that meant.

C: This non-exclusive thing goes both ways?

T: Don't ask, don't tell works well for me.

C: K

T: I saw the perfect dress for you today. It will arrive next week.

C: Here?

T: To wear when I get there.

C: Thank you ♥

T: 10 weeks left.

C: :) K bye.

Well, that was a strange conversation, Charlotte thought as she got out of bed.

Pacing back and forth, Charlotte couldn't shake the nervous energy that had been building inside her since her return. She didn't intend to go on dates or even mess around. All she really wanted was to hang out with someone. It was now a little after two in the morning and there was only one person she knew that would be up at this hour or even be willing to see her for that matter.

Parked four houses down from Augustus Caffrey's house, Charlotte waited for his truck to pull up. It was now ten to three and she was getting sleepy. She could feel herself starting to doze off when the sound of his truck coming down the street gave her a second wind. She was actually excited. Reaching over she grabbed her purse, ready to wait for him to go inside before she got out of her car.

A sudden wave of nausea hit Charlotte when she saw a woman standing by the bed of his truck. Convincing herself it was disappointment, she leaned forward to get a better look. It was dark but from the streetlight she could tell it wasn't Sheryl. Then, to her relief, the man that threw his arms around the woman and started kissing her wasn't Auggie. It was his brother Braden. Curious, she watched as the two of them dashed into the street before stopping in the middle of the road. Braden spun the woman around before they started making out. Smiling to herself, Charlotte thought that was sort of romantic. She couldn't help staring as Braden turned his back allowing her to hop on. He piggy-backed her a bit farther down the street before they reached what Charlotte assumed was the woman's house.

Still shaking his head at Braden and Lily's inappropriate display of affection in the back seat of his truck, Auggie hoped his brother knew what he was doing fooling around with a married woman. Yea, she was separated because her muscle-head husband had beaten her up and gone to jail, but that didn't change the fact that she is married or that she left his brother to be with that steroid junkie in the first place. As he made his way to the kitchen and pulled a beer out of the fridge, there was a knock at his front door. Already thinking it was Braden, he was ready to say 'I told you so'.

Opening the door, Auggie was confused. Not only by the sight of Charlotte, in tiny turquoise shorts and a black tank top, but by the instant enthusiasm he felt seeing her standing there.

Appearing impatient, she blurted, "Can I come in?"

"Who said what this time?" he griped, moving to the side allowing her to walk in.

She stopped and looked at him before giving a slight laugh as she replied, "I'm sure lots of people are saying lots of things."

Scowling at her as she set her purse on the floor and walked to his kitchen, he questioned, "Why are you here, Charlotte."

Grabbing the six pack of Guinness with the bottle Auggie was holding missing from it, she headed back into the living room, answering, "I don't have a lot of options here and I'm tired of sitting around the house by myself with nothing to do."

Somewhat appalled by the way she made herself at home in his house, he snapped, "What's that got to do with me?"

"We're sorta stuck with each other while I'm here so why not make the most of it?" she replied, setting the beer on his coffee table.

As he thought 'unbelievable' he honestly didn't know what to say.

All he could do for the moment was watch her as she picked up a beer and walked back to her purse. When she bent over to rummage through it, Auggie just about lost his mind.

Snapping him back to reality, Charlotte stood upright, announcing, "Got it," as she waved a bottle opener at him.

Gritting his back teeth, Auggie fussed, "You got a lot of nerve walkin' in here makin' yourself at home."

Giving him a look as if he was being silly, she said, "Oh please, I'm not wanting us to be best friends. I'm tired of having nothing to do. You don't even have to talk to me. Just do whatever you normally do and it's not going to hurt you one bit for me to be here."

If she only knew how increasingly painful it was for him, having her there.

Pulling a bottle opener out of his back pocket, Auggie opened his beer. Before he could make his way over,

Charlotte sat in his chair. With a loud frustrated exhale, he sat on his couch.

"I know you don't like sitting next to me," she said, crossing one long leg over the other.

"Yea," he mumbled, knowing his comfy oversized chair would smell like her when she left.

They sat in silence for a few minutes before something occurred to Auggie.

"Isn't your boyfriend going to wonder where you are?"

"Nope," she said before tipping her bottle back and finishing her beer.

"You might wanna slow down."

With a lash fluttering eye roll, she shared, "I was planning on staying over."

"What?"

Charlotte leaned to the coffee table and replaced the bottle she pulled out of the six pack with her empty one, saying, "A responsible bartender wouldn't let me drive after drinking."

"You can't expect me to let you stay here!"

"You make it sound like I hired a moving van. I just tossed a toothbrush in my purse."

Shaking his head at her, he fussed, "Look I don't need some a-hole douche bag coming over here mad 'cause I let his drunk girlfriend stay the night."

"A-hole?" Charlotte laughed before saying, "I seriously doubt he would fly all the way from Europe to confront you, even if he did care."

"What kinda man doesn't care about that?"

࿐

Realizing Auggie may have been right about drinking that first beer too fast, Charlotte slowly sipped on her second beer, thinking, 'Yea why doesn't he care?'.

Leaning her elbow on the arm of the chair, she rested the side of her head against her hand, explaining, "We aren't exclusive until he proposes."

"Y'all are getting engaged," he questioned, as she nodded he fussed, "What kinda man wants to be with someone enough to get married but still see other women?"

Charlotte snapped, "You're being awfully judgmental."

Offended that she was taking offence, he assured, "Everyone judges other people."

Sliding up to grab her third beer, she stated, "Not me."

"Sure," he said in disbelief before sharing, "People can't help it. Deep down inside everybody thinks their better than everyone else. It comes from self-pride."

Changing her mind about that third beer, Charlotte leaned her head on the cushiony arm of the chair, saying, "I don't have that."

"You don't have any pride in who you are?"

Feeling herself drift off, she gave a lazy smile, swearing, "I know exactly who I am...and trust me, it's nothing to be proud of."

৯৯৩

Auggie sat on the couch looking at her. He wasn't sure if she had passed out or simply fallen asleep. It was already after four in the morning. Glancing down at the beer in his hand, he gave a slight laugh realizing he only had two sips to her two beers. Guessing he would be nice and get her a blanket, he stood up and walked to his room.

Returning to Charlotte, asleep in his chair, Auggie started to toss the blanket from his bed over her when he stopped. Twisted in an odd feet still on the floor and head leaned against the arm of the chair position, her tank top revealed a small section of her back. Leaning closer, he saw a wide scar about four inches long and two smaller ones right beside it. Without being able to help it, he carefully lifted more of her top to find the pattern repeated itself several more times across her back.

Out of nowhere, Auggie became angry to the point where he almost shook her awake to demand knowing who did that to her. Charlotte sighed and he jumped back a little knowing she would think he was trying to check her out in her sleep like some sort of pervert. When it was clear she was still asleep, Auggie covered her with the blanket and walked to his room.

Scars

Reaching to grab his cellphone, off of the table next to his bed, it sounded unusually loud vibrating against the wood.

"What?" Auggie griped into the phone.

Braden's voice was pleading as he replied, "Lily's mother in law is on her way."

"Thanks for wakin' me up to share," Auggie snapped before hanging up on his brother.

Slowly getting up, he'd slept in his pants so he grabbed his shirt off of the floor and put it on. Stumbling to the bathroom, he knew Braden would be over whether he invited him or not. It only took a few minutes for him to wake up enough to remember Charlotte was asleep in his chair. He was going to have to do something with her. No way he'd hear the end of it if Braden found her there. Hurrying into the living room, he stopped halfway to her.

The blanket he had laid over her was on the floor and her whole body had shifted in a different position than when she fell asleep. She was on her back with her legs folded on top of herself. Her head was turned towards him with one arm tucked under her legs and the other hugging her knees against her chest. For the first time the way she smelled matched her appearance, sweet and beautiful. He couldn't take his eyes off of her until there was a loud knock on his front door.

≈∾≪

Startled awake, Charlotte's eyelids popped open. Someone was knocking on the door. Rolling out of the chair she fell asleep in, she stood up and shook her head at Auggie, who was standing right in front of her.

"It's Braden," he informed.

"I don't want anyone knowing I'm here."

Slightly offended but in complete agreement, Auggie reached down and grabbed her purse and shoes before shoving them at her as he urged, "Down the hall, my room's on the left, I'll make sure he doesn't stay long."
She didn't appreciate his bossiness but did what he said.

Hardly considering it a hallway it was a square with three doors. Looking away from what used to be William's door, she opened the one to her left and stepped inside the room. Closing the door, she stood inside Auggie's room listening through the door.

"Took you long enough," Braden blurted.

"Call Brooks and have him come get you." Auggie griped.

"Nice hospitality brother. Thanks by the way. Lily said Keven's crazy jealous and keeps sending his mom to the house to check up on her while he's locked up."

"Wonder why."

"Don't get all judgy on me, she was mine first and besides they're getting a divorce."
There was a short break in the conversation giving Charlotte a chance to glance around the room. 'Figures his comforter would be plaid', she thought before hearing Braden's voice again.

"Dang man, your chair smells good!"

"Stop molesting my chair and call Brooks," Auggie griped before Braden asked, "Alright. I'm texting him. You're actin' really frickin' weird, you got a girl here?"

"No, I don't."

"Speakin' of girls...wanna know what I heard?"

"Nope."

"Bet ya do," Braden insisted before informing, "And it's not gossip."

There was no response.

"'Member that guy at the bar with Charlotte? He's some kinda businessman from Spain and he's loaded. Looks like she..."

Before Braden could finish, Auggie griped, "I shoulda shut his mouth for him."

"You're still mad about that?"

"I was letting her have it and she was giving it right back. She was handling herself. She didn't need him to jump in and correct her. He apologized for her."

"Never thought I would hear you defending Charlotte. Thought you hated her."

There was a long pause before Auggie replied, "I don't give a damn about her. I hope I never see her again. It's the principle."

Nodding at the door, Charlotte assumed that's what she deserved for eavesdropping. She thought for a moment that he was defending her too. With hurt feelings and not wanting to hear anymore, Charlotte stepped away from the door and sat down on the edge of Auggie's bed.

☜•☞

Irritated with his brother, Auggie didn't even mean what he was saying, except for maybe the principle part of it. He didn't feel that way about her. He used to, but he was getting to where he didn't mind her that much.

"Alright, alright, you know you really should learn to let things go. So did you hear, Sophia's havin' her shower at the bar?"

Grateful for the subject change, Auggie replied, "And we're supposed to go."

Shrugging, Braden shared, "It's some fancy somethin' or other, you gotta wear a suit." As Auggie scowled, Braden said, "Brooks is here." when they heard a horn honk.

"Be careful," Auggie advised.

Branden laughed, "Always man," as he walked out of the door.

The second Braden was gone, it occurred to Auggie, he'd sent Charlotte to his room. Quickly locking his front door, he wondered why he didn't just tell her to hide in the bathroom. He didn't want her in his bedroom.

When Auggie walked into his room, Charlotte was sitting on the foot of his bed with her shoes on holding her purse in her lap. Recalling the way she came in and made herself at home the night before, he was surprised she wasn't rummaging through his belongings.

"He's gone," Auggie shared.

Without a word, Charlotte stood up and walked right past him. She looked mad.

Thinking she was tired from just a few hours of sleep, he offered, "You wanna stretch out on the couch and get some more sleep?"

"No."

"Want somethin' to eat?"

Whipping around to face him, she snapped, "I'm leaving."

"You don't have to."

Holding her head high, Charlotte declared, "I don't want to be anywhere near you and I hope I never see you again."

Refusing to admit he didn't mean it or take back what he said to Braden, Auggie fussed, "I knew you were just lookin' for a way out."

"A way out?"

"I knew you wouldn't keep your promise or our agreement."

With a loud huff, Charlotte turned towards the door. Swiftly walking out of his house, she held her hand above her head and with a flick of her wrist she gave him the finger before slamming the door closed behind her.

Thinking to himself this is why relationships were a bad idea, Auggie sat down in his chair. He wasn't even in any kind of relationship with her but because of their agreement, she had tried to befriend him or something. Still unsure why she showed up at his house the previous night, that had to be it. She wouldn't understand of course, but he didn't have or need friends. Auggie had his family. Sinking back in his chair, Charlotte's scent, although muted because his brother sat there, still lingered. Closing his eyes, he thought about how she looked curled up in his chair as he fell asleep.

☙❧

Sliding into the car, Charlotte had parked in front of a for sale sign a few houses down from Auggie's. She had just taken the morning after walk of shame without the benefit of having done anything shameful. It was good to know where she stood with him and how he felt about her. Convincing herself, it was simply the disappointment in thinking he was something that he wasn't, she started the car and drove home. He should have just said it to her face instead of behind her back.

☙❧

Shivering as he stepped out of the shower, Auggie hadn't taken an ice cold one since he was a teenager. Falling asleep thinking about Charlotte had definitely, among other things, messed with his mind. Drying his hair with a towel, he threw his clothes on. Stepping into his boots, he pulled his beanie over his head and walked out to his truck.

Since he didn't feel like going anywhere, Auggie was glad everything was already in his truck. Assuming Charlotte would be a no show after this morning, at least he could work on the week's tallies from home. After grabbing the envelope of receipts and ledger out of the passenger seat, he closed the door. Turning back toward his house, he was surprised to see her standing there.

Instantly aware of the effect seeing her wearing a grey v-neck dress had on him, it might as well have been a t-shirt that barely covered the tops of her thighs.

Auggie griped, "Don't you ever wear real clothes?"

Giving him a dirty look, she followed him to his door, saying, "It may surprise you because you don't like looking at me, most men enjoy what I wear."

"I didn't say that."

Curling the un-scared side of her mouth into a curious smile, she asked, "So, you like looking at me?"

"I didn't say that either."

"What are you saying then?"

Auggie scowled as he changed the subject, "I didn't think you were coming."

Fluttering her eyelashes as she rolled her eyes at his avoiding her question, she replied, "We shook on it."

Nodding, he opened the door for her, saying, "Let's get started then."

🖘🖙

With receipts spread out on Auggie's kitchen table, Charlotte was growing just as frustrated as Auggie. She had showed him an easier way and even watched him carefully and still nothing balanced out. When she worked it out on a separate paper all the totals were perfect. 'What was he doing wrong', she thought before glancing between her paper and the ledger.

Looking over at him, Charlotte asked, "Are you dyslexic?"

"No," he blurted, looking at her like she was the rudest person on earth.

"Are you sure?" she asked before placing her paper right next to the ledger, saying, "You see this?"

"Why are your numbers different?" he questioned.

Hesitant, she replied, "Because you turned every six into a nine and vice versa." Taking note of his confused expression, she added, "No wonder you couldn't get the hang of it, I think you might be dyslexic."

"There's nothing wrong with me."

Frustrated for a different reason now, Charlotte snapped, "Whatever, let's just take a break then."

Grabbing two beers out of the fridge, Auggie set one in front of her at the table before walking to the living room and sitting down in his chair.

"Drink this one slow," he teased, provoking her to get up and join him in the adjoining room.

Making her way to the couch, Charlotte made a face at him, saying, "I'm not a light weight, it was late and I was tired."

"Sure you were."

With a slight huff, she sat down on the end of the couch closest to Auggie in his chair.

৵৽৹

Auggie could see all the way up the back of one of her thighs when Charlotte crossed her legs. As he tried to think about anything other than her sitting there, something came to him but it wasn't what he'd expected to think of.

Mentally swearing he intended to use more tact as he blurted, "So what's with your face?" when Charlotte gave him a crazy look, snapping, "What's with yours?" he took a moment before asking, "What happened to your mouth?"

Charlotte pulled her lips into her mouth, pressing them together before asking, "Why do you always wear that stupid beanie?"

Thinking that was an odd thing to counter his question with, she was usually pretty snappy with her comebacks. Recalling the scars he saw on her back, Auggie decided her lame distraction was just like when she told him he smelled. He was getting to know her and little by little he was figuring her out.

"No big deal, I was just curious," he replied, deciding it was a touchy subject.

"I'm sure you heard the rumors."

Standing up to throw his empty bottle away, he shared, "I prefer first-hand accounts," remembering all the trouble Sheryl and her younger sister caused Charlotte by saying it was a sex thing. That she liked it rough right before a group of her sister's friends, pulled her shirt over her head and shoved her into a room with nothing but boys. Now that he'd seen some of what was under her shirt he understood how the rumor caught on.

By the time Auggie made it to the kitchen and threw his bottle way, Charlotte was standing by the sink.

Leaning against the counter, she shared, "It's not a very exciting story. My mom told me to shut my mouth and I didn't so she shut it for me."

All he could say was, "Damn."

With a slight laugh and a shoulder shrug, Charlotte assured, "It doesn't bother me anymore, it's still a bit stiff on that side but other than not kissing anyone since I was fourteen..."

"Wait, what?"

Realizing she had crossed over into TMI territory, she'd already said it so she explained, "It was really painful and it felt like forever for it to heal. Just the thought use to make me a little sick to my stomach and now, it's just as well. Trace has a thing about perfection so there is no way..."

"He doesn't kiss you?"

Laughing, she shook her head, "Not on the lips. I even have this special lipstick that hides it. He would probably have an anxiety attack if he saw me without it."

Thinking back to the first night he saw her at the bar, Auggie remembered full red lips that had a lacquer-like shine as he asked, "But you don't wear it?"

"It serves a purpose with Trace, but it doesn't feel natural, I prefer my chubby stick."

Raising and eyebrow at her, he blurted, "Your what?"

As Charlotte replied with a light smile, "That's just what it's called, it's like lip balm but it has a hint of color to it," Auggie couldn't take his eyes off of her mouth.

How could any man in his right mind not want to kiss her? They looked so soft and so what if there was a scar, it was barely noticeable. If given the opportunity, he wouldn't think twice about it. Clearing his throat, Auggie realized he was out of his mind for thinking like that.

ॐ∾ॐ

Surprised at how effortless it was to talk to Auggie, Charlotte wasn't really a sharer. There were things that she didn't find worth talking about and her scars were right at the top of that list. Deciding it had to be the bartender in him, when he wasn't being a judgmental ass, he was unbelievably easy to talk to.

The moment was getting a tad on the awkward side, when Charlotte remembered she had asked him a question.

"Hey," she seemed to blurt out of nowhere, before saying, "Now, what about that beanie of yours."

With a blank expression like she had startled him out of deep thought, he walked back to the table, saying, "A couple of years ago, I got into a fight outside The Dog House."

Joining him at the table, Charlotte turned her chair to face him, interested in his story.

"This guy was runnin' his mouth about my sister. So we took it out to back. I was whoopin' his ass until he put my head through the passenger side window of Ailin's car."

Charlotte gasped, "Oh my gosh!" when Auggie pulled his beanie off, saying, "Twenty-two stitches," and held his hair back with his hand revealing a long thick scar that hooked around to the back of his head.

Without realizing what she was doing, Charlotte reached over and ran her middle finger across his scar.

"Sorry, go ahead," she quickly spit out when he jerked away and looked at her like she had electrocuted him.

It took him a few minutes before he continued, "It looked pretty nasty, so Jacks got me a couple of beanies to cover it while I was tending bar. I kinda got used to wearin' 'em and ya know it feels weird not to now."

Nodding, she turned back to face the table. Charlotte actually felt pretty bad about touching his scar. Knowing she would have freaked out if he had touched her mouth while she was talking to him, she had an understanding of how sensitive something like that was.

In an effort to get back to the task at hand, Charlotte stared at the ledger and receipts.

"I have an idea."

She could feel Auggie looking at her but kept her eyes focused on the table.

"Let's try this," picking up a receipt, saying, "I'll read them off to you and see if that helps."

"Okay."

Aside from reading the totals, not much more was said. Charlotte's idea momentarily solved a problem, but he still didn't quite have the hang of it.

9

Intruder

Another long and boring week had finally made its way to Thursday as Charlotte searched Auggie's front porch for his spare key. Grateful the street was empty at midnight, not only did she not want to be discovered at his house, she was sure she looked fairly suspicious out there. Finding his spare key, she unlocked the front door and let herself in.

Setting the information she found on dyscalculia, a form of dyslexia having to do with numbers, on his coffee table, she waited for him to arrive. He would definitely fuss at her for breaking and entering. In addition to helping him get to where he could handle the books on his own, she needed to catch him off guard. She needed a favor and let's face it, Auggie wasn't a do a friend a favor type of guy.

Finally, she heard the door knob turn before the front door opened. Leaning back in his chair, she watched as Auggie closed the door behind him with the back of his boot before walking right past her. Her initial amusement at him not realizing she was there was quickly replaced with a dull ache when he undid the first two buttons on his shirt before pulling it off over his head. Dropping his shirt on the floor, he kicked his work boots off on the way to the kitchen. Charlotte carefully memorizing the way the Celtic cross on his back started just below the nape of his neck, spread across his shoulder blades and ended just above his waistband.

The ledger, the information she brought, even the favor she was planning to ask all slipped away as he stretched his arms out to the side with a loud yawn. It was a downright sin for him to cover something so glorious with those hideous plaid shirts. As he continued to the fridge, Charlotte wished she could simply sit and watch what she assumed was his after work routine. Grabbing a beer out of the fridge, Auggie slid the top against the edge of the counter before catching the cap as it popped up off of his beer, in his other hand. After taking a long swig from the bottle, he placed his beer and the cap on the counter.

Turning back toward the living room, Auggie made his way out of the kitchen before glancing at Charlotte then jumping about two feet back.

"What the..." Auggie blurted before shouting, "You broke into my house?"

"No, I used your spare key on the porch," she replied, watching his chest move up and down as his shock wore off.

"You almost gave me a damn heart attack!"

Making an absurd face at him, she calmly stated, "I think you're overreacting a bit."

"You scared the hell out of me!"

"Sure, any guy would be terrified to come home and find a beautiful woman waiting for him," Charlotte teased, rolling her eyes.

Reaching down to pick up his shirt, Auggie demanded, "Why are you here?" before pulling it back on.

"Glad you asked."

❧❦

Still too stunned to be as angry with Charlotte as he should have been, Auggie watched her hop out of his chair, grab something off of his coffee table and walk up to him.

"First," she said with a hint of hidden motives, "You were right. You're not dyslexic. I think you have dyscalculia."

"That sounds horrible," he griped.

"I brought you some information if you'd like to read up on it."

"And?" he questioned, seeing the spark of something else in her eyes.

"I found a club twenty minutes from here."

"Good for you."

"And...I want you to take me Saturday night."

Thinking she was out of her mind, he stated, "Nope." Waiting for her to pout or start whining, Auggie was surprised when she whipped herself around and walked to the couch.

Charlotte narrowed her eyes at him and then smiled.

"Clearly, you have no idea how serious this is," she assured before adding, "I could literally die of boredom here."

"Now who's overreacting?"

Raising her eyebrows, she stated, "I have resorted to breaking into houses to keep myself entertained."

Trying not to smile, he said, "Really."

Nodding vigorously, she looked around saying, "If you don't say yes, I'll...I'll..." stopping to throw herself onto the couch, "I won't survive."

He couldn't help finding her amusing. Seeing Charlotte play dead on his couch, made it difficult to keep a straight face when she opened one eye to see his response. Pursing her lips at him when he held strong to his unwavering demeanor, it appeared as though she wasn't ready to throw in the towel.

Charlotte sat up, crossed her legs and sighed.

"Okay," she replied in a defeated tone.

Scowling at her, he didn't believe her for a second.

"Just know if I go alone, I could end up kidnaped, chained up in somebodies basement."

"No one here has basements."

Shrugging her shoulders, Charlotte stated, "In a freezer then."

"A freezer?"

Sitting up tall with a serious expression on her face she shared, "I could be enjoying myself at the club, a little tipsy, and up walks a devastatingly handsome and charming man... you know, so I don't know he's a psychopath...stranger. He invites me back to his place and of course, I can't say no because he says all the right things." Then in an over exaggerated execution Charlotte finished with, "Next thing you know I'm chopped up in a freezer! How good are you gonna feel about yourself when on a hot sunny day some sick freak is sitting in his lawn chair enjoying a Charlotte-Sycle?"

Unable to stand it any longer, Auggie burst into laughter, saying, "Fine."

With a shocked expression, she jumped to her feet.

"Fine as in yes?"

Finding it hard to believe himself, after her display, he couldn't say no.

"Yes but..."

Charlotte's excitement faded as she griped, "Ah... But what?"

With a heavy sigh, Auggie looked her over saying, "You owe me."

"Anything," she agreed with a smile.

Shaking his head at himself for his sudden attack of weakness, he walked to his kitchen and grabbed his beer off of the counter.

∽◦∾

Charlotte's mind reeled with excitement and gratitude towards Auggie. She never expected him to actually say yes. Wanting him to know how much she appreciated his agreeing to go with her, Charlotte glanced in his direction. Before she decided exactly what to say, to thank him, it occurred to her, he probably had nothing to wear.

Meeting him next to the refrigerator, Charlotte asked, "What size pants do you wear?"

"Excuse me?"

Pursing her lips at him, she replied, "Your pants, what size are they?"

"Why?"

"I know you have this whole rugged, manly bartender thing going for you but it isn't exactly...You're going to have a hard time getting in, even with me on your arm, if you dress like that."

"What does that have to do with what size my pants are?"

Thinking, 'Boys are so dumb', Charlotte answered, "Clearly, you can't be trusted to dress yourself. Give me your sizes and I'll pick an outfit out for you."

Appearing to be offended, Auggie fussed, "I don't wear outfits and no way in hell I'm gonna let you dress me."

Giving him an irritated expression, she replied, "Don't get all excited, Augustus. I didn't offer to dress you. I am simply going to buy you something club appropriate to wear."

Narrowing his eyes at her, he pulled his wallet out of his back pocket, pulled some money out and laid it on the counter.

Glancing down at the money, Charlotte shook her head at him.

"What exactly do you expect me to buy with that? A sock?" she fussed.

Scowling, he griped, "Your socks cost fifty dollars?"

Placing her hand across her forehead, Charlotte had to take a moment.

"Since you're doing me a favor, keep your money and consider whatever I buy you a gift."

"I can buy my own clothes."

Frustrated, she argued, "I wasn't saying that you couldn't."

Pulling five crisp one hundred dollar bills out of his wallet, Auggie slammed them against the counter saying, "Here! If it costs more, I don't want it."

"Fine," she blurted, scooping his money up in her hand.

"Goodnight, Charlotte," he snapped before walking to his room and slamming the door.

Auggie waited to hear his front door close before stepping back out of his bedroom. He wasn't ready for bed yet, but he was ready for her to leave. There seemed to be a give and take pattern with her. Give a compliment and then take it right back. She had called him rugged and manly but at the same time she seemed to insinuate that he was incapable of being either. As he thought to himself, she was a frustrating pain in the ass, he wondered what the hell he was thinking getting involved with Charlotte in the first place.

❦10❧

Chivalry

Grateful Jackson asked no questions when Auggie requested the night off as he stood in his bedroom staring at the clothes Charlotte expected him to wear. When she called the bar right at closing Friday night, he had quickly given her his sizes after she threatened breaking into his house, again if he didn't tell her. The dark blue button down wasn't too bad, he guessed but maroon slacks? Who did she think he was? She was lucky he was still going after seeing what she bought him to wear. If she hadn't shown up in those high heels and tiny black shorts, he might have changed his mind. Shaking his head at himself as he pulled his pants off of the hanger, Auggie thought 'Oh lord, this is an outfit'.

Stepping out of his bedroom Auggie noticed Charlotte sitting in his chair. The second she caught sight of him in his 'outfit' a satisfied smile spread across her face. Every muscle in his body tensed as she stood up and made her way to him. Stopping in front of him, Charlotte slid the top two buttons of his shirt open before reaching up and carefully adjusting his collar. She was too close for him to think clearly. Between the way she slowly smiled up at him and the way her sweet smell hovered around him, he felt his fingertips start to tingle. Everything about her appeared so soft, he wanted to touch her.

Clearing his throat, he said, "Thought you weren't going to dress me."

"It looks better this way and technically I think it would count as undressing you."

☙❧

Charlotte could feel her heart beat faster as the words 'undressing you' left her mouth. He was too close. He hadn't backed away or fussed at her for touching him. His tone was low as he questioned her and when she replied, he stood there gazing at her until she took a step back. Feeling a rush of warmth to her cheeks, she had no choice but to turn away.

Quickly making light of the moment, Charlotte said, "I have to get a picture."

"What?" he snapped, back to his normal self.

Pulling her cellphone out of her back pocket, she shared, "This is a momentous occasion. Years from now I want to be able to look at it and remember the day I got Augustus Caffrey to wear something stylish."

Auggie cringed, saying, "I hate you right now."

"You should be thanking me. If you dressed like this more often you probably wouldn't be coming home by yourself every night."

With an amused expression, he replied, "I'm thinkin' that has less to do with what I wear and more that nine outta ten times a crazy blonde shows up."

Pretending to be offended, Charlotte huffed, "I am not crazy. I'm lighthearted and fun."

"Lighthearted?"

"Okay, maybe not but you have to admit, you like having me around."

With a low groan Auggie griped, "Let's go before I change my mind."

☙❧

On the way to Club 76 Charlotte couldn't decide if twenty minutes was too long or not quite long enough to ride with

Auggie in his truck. The smell of his grey leather interior, mixed with his freshly showered scent, was affecting her. Charlotte always enjoyed the smell of cologne but had no idea a man could smell so good without it. Auggie's soap and deodorant aroma suited him to a tee. No frills just him. And it was all him, all man like him.

The moment Auggie parked, Charlotte didn't wait to see if he would open her door for her. She needed the fresh air to clear her head. It was an instant relief to feel the cool night air and hear the music pumping from inside the building.

Auggie made his way to the passenger side to meet her as she asked, "Can you hang onto my cell for me?" pulling it out of her back pocket.

With a confused expression, he answered, "Uh...Sure."

"Thanks, I don't like the way it looks with these shorts." As she started to hand it over, her phone vibrated in her hand.

T: Hello lovely.

Glancing at Auggie, Charlotte informed, "Just a sec," before texting back.

C: Hi!

T: Are you enjoying yourself?

C: Not yet ;) just parked.

T: What are you wearing?

C: I'm naked.

T: O_O Did you wear the skirt and blouse I suggested?

C: No

T: :(

Glaring at the disappointed frowny face Trace sent, agitated her.

C: I can't dance in that skirt unless you want everyone to see my panties.

T: Why would I mind?

Just before she could text back, Auggie snatched her phone out of her hand, fussing, "Are we doing this or what?" before shutting her cellphone off and sliding it into his pocket.

A bit startled, Charlotte nodded at him and headed towards the entrance of the club.

❧❦

Auggie tried not to look at Charlotte's phone while she was texting the douche. When he noticed her scowling, he couldn't help but look at what was upsetting her. He'd known guys that caught a beat down just for hinting at possibly thinking of a girl's panties and this creep didn't care if a room full of strangers saw hers. How could she want to be with someone like him? Reminding himself Braden said her boyfriend was 'loaded', Auggie was not only disappointed in who she really is but angry that he had let her fool him into thinking otherwise.

The closer they got to the entrance the slower Auggie walked until Charlotte turned around and stopped in front of him.

"What's your problem," she snapped.

"I didn't realize you were one of those, that's all," he shared in a gruff tone.

"One of what's?"

"A peacock," he blurted.

Taken aback by his comment, she frowned.

"You strut around all proud but under all those pretty feathers you're just another scrawny ass bird so you get with whoever can give you what you think you deserve, no matter what worthless sorry excuse for a man he is. 'Cause he's got money. 'Cause it's all fake anyway."

Narrowing her eyes at him, Charlotte tugged at the bottom of her blouse, assuring, "I am as far from fake as you're ever gonna get, Augustus. And FYI my last name is Roberts, I have my own money and it's way more than he's got. So next time you decide to get your panties all in a bunch because you've snooped on my text message, try asking me why I'm with someone like Trace instead of assuming because of what you have heard about me." Stopping to relax slightly, she added, "And by the way, my feathers aren't pretty, they are stunning and underneath them is a sexy female wearing a lovely little pair of peacock blue satin panties."

Auggie was speechless.

Making their way through the crowded club, Auggie felt Charlotte slide her arm around his and quickly jerked away. She seemed to have forgotten all about telling him off outside of the club, but he hadn't. He could admit he was wrong, never to her but to himself. However, he was still mad. Was it necessary for her to mention panties so many times? Now all he could think about was if hers really were peacock blue and satin like she said or if she was simply making a point.

As they reached the bar, Auggie noticed the bartender eyeing Charlotte with an interested expression.

"Charlotte?" the bartender exclaimed.

Stopping for a second to inspect the guy behind the bar wearing a white shirt, black vest and slicked back blonde hair, Charlotte replied, "Jeremy?"

Sucking air in through his teeth, Jeremy said, "Mmm girl, you grew up nice."

Turning away from the situation, Auggie thought 'lame', trying not to be aggravated.

"I heard you moved off to...France was it?"

"Spain," she corrected before nudging Auggie and introducing, "Augustus, this is Jeremy."

Glancing back, Auggie gave an unimpressed nod before Jeremy said, "Hey I know you," catching his full attention.

"The Dog House right? My cousin and I hit that place up a few months ago. The band was tight."

"Yea," he confirmed, reaching into his pocket to grab his wallet as he said, "Guinness."

Jeremy gave him a blank look before saying, "Sorry man, only liquor here and it's on me. Charlotte and I go way back."

Watching him raise an eyebrow and smile at Charlotte, Auggie said, "Whiskey then."

"Whiskey Sour?"

"Whiskey in a glass."

"Can't do straight liquor man."

Auggie stared in disbelief wondering what circle of hell Charlotte had brought him into.

Charlotte stepped in, saying, "I'll have the strongest drink you've got and he'll have a water."

Jeremy filled their order while flirting with Charlotte.

Charlotte's drink was empty in no time at all before she headed out to the dance floor. Sipping his water, Auggie was glad she knew better than to ask him.

"You been with Charlotte long?"

Glaring at Jeremy, Auggie hadn't realized he came for social hour.

"Hey, I wasn't tryin' to pick her up or anything I'm engaged. Great girl too."

"Mmhmm," Auggie grumbled before Jeremy continued, "Besides, and don't get me wrong, Charlotte's a good time and all. Not really a keeper though." Before Auggie could lose his temper, Jeremy pointed to the dance floor, saying, "Know what I mean?"

Scanning the crowd of people dancing, Auggie spotted Charlotte letting some stranger put his hands all over her.

Instantly heading in Charlotte's direction, Auggie knew she wasn't his but they had come together and it was damn disrespectful of her to show up with him and then dance that way with someone else.

Charlotte didn't mind some physical contact on the dance floor it was expected in places like this. She had already warned him twice and this guy was a bit too grabby for her taste.

"Baby, don't go. We're just getting started."

With a smirk, Charlotte shared, "No we're about done," as she started to walk off.

"Come on..."

As she felt something barely brush against her backside, she turned around to slap him when she saw Auggie standing there holding her offender's wrist in his hand.

"You wanna lose that hand," Auggie growled, shoving him as he let go.

"She was all over me," he lied, falling onto his back.

Auggie wrapped an arm around Charlotte warning, "Take a walk."

Surprised at Auggie's chivalry towards her, she watched her former dance partner, scramble to his feet and stomp away.

As the song changed to a down beat, Charlotte placed her hands on Auggie's shoulders. His arm that was wrapped around her fell to his side as she leaned into him. It wasn't a slow song playing but it was slow enough for her to slide her arms around his neck and sway with the rhythm comfortably close to him. With her heels on she was just an inch or two short of eye level with him. He stood perfectly still staring at her. Unable to hide what being so close to him was doing to her, she moved one of her arms to his waist and leaned her forehead onto his shoulder. Breathing in and out slowly, she waited for him to end the dance while savoring the moment while it lasted. Closing her eyes, Charlotte felt his hands on the center of her back. He wasn't pushing away or pulling her closer, he was simply holding her in place.

The song ended, forcing her to let go. When she did, he was still staring at her. Charlotte had no idea what to say. She started to slowly smile up at him when they were interrupted by a large bouncer and her touchy-feely dance partner.

Pointing at Auggie, the guy announced, "That's him. His girl was all up on me and he knocked me down."

Moving Charlotte away, as the bouncer reached to grab him, Auggie held his hands up, saying, "I didn't knock him down, he fell down."

"Sir, he says you knocked him down, now I'm gonna have to ask you to leave."

Taking a step towards the bouncer, Auggie replied, "I'll leave but just so ya' know, if I'd a knocked him down, it would looked like this," elbowing the bouncer in the chest so hard, he sat down on the floor as the wind was knocked right out of him.

Charlotte took a few steps back as Auggie swung and punched the grabby guy in the face and laid him smooth out.

Unable to hold in a laugh, when Auggie leaned over him, saying, "Tattle-tale," Charlotte noticed the bouncer getting up.

"I think we better go," Charlotte urged.

Nodding at her, Auggie took hold of her hand as they both made a mad dash to the exit door.

❧

When they made it to Auggie's house, Charlotte was still reeling from what happened at the club. It wasn't just Auggie fighting. It was putting him in his place before they walked in, slow dancing with him and then seeing him knock someone out that had Charlotte's adrenaline spiked to the point she felt she could have jogged home without getting tired.

"I still can't believe you did that," she laughed.

"You never heard the saying, 'snitches get stitches'?" he questioned with a smile.

Taking a moment before following him through the doorway, she had never seen him smile like that before. One side of his face was scrunched up into a genuine smile that made his eye squint closed in the cutest way.

The same feeling that filled her on the dance floor, coursed through her before settling in the pit of her stomach. He'd been holding out on her. Auggie's smile was the best thing she had ever seen.

Stretching out on his couch, Charlotte kicked her heels off saying, "Tell me this wasn't the best night you've ever had."

Sitting down on the coffee table in front of her, Auggie handed her a beer and said, "Not the best, but not as bad as I thought."

Propping herself up on her elbow, she gave an inviting smile as she asked, "What would make it the best?" in a whispery voice.

Suddenly his scowl was back as he griped, "A good night's sleep," before standing up and heading to his room advising, "And a word to the wise, if you don't want guys tryin' to grab your ass, consider wearing longer shorts."

Rolling onto her back with a loud huff, Charlotte stared at the ceiling.

ॐ11ॐ

Breakfast

Rolling over and burying his face in his pillow, Auggie woke up the same way he fell asleep. Thinking about Charlotte. She irritated him like no one else. No matter how hard he tried he couldn't get a handle on her. When he expressed his dislike for the way her so call boyfriend treated her, she accused him of being judgmental and read him the riot act. When he stepped in to correct some sleaze ball for disrespecting her, she was grateful. It seemed like she was all over the place. And what was with that dance? She'd appeared at ease that close to him, like it was the most natural thing in the world. Meanwhile, he could barely move. The most he could do was place his hands in a safe zone and even then, if the song hadn't ended when it did. He would have lost every ounce of control he had. He did not want her to know, but if she had any idea what she did to him, she would never have looked at him that way before he went to bed.

Groaning into his pillow as he slid his arms under it, he wrapped the sides of the pillow around his head. Auggie knew it was going to be another cold shower morning. He couldn't let her keep coming over like this. His house took too long to air out when she left and his chair had never fully recovered from her sitting in it. She was the best thing he'd ever smelled and it lingered in his furniture and his mind. So much so, he could have sworn she was in the room with him now.

Stopping to dwell on that a moment, he lifted his head from the pillow and opened his eyes finding Charlotte standing at the side of his bed.

"Morning!"

Pulling the comforter higher as he sat up, Auggie fussed, "What is wrong with you?"

"I'm hungry."

"Get out of my room," he snapped.

Ignoring his demand, Charlotte asked, "Will you get up and make me breakfast?"

'She was out of her mind', he thought, persisting, "No, get out!"

Placing her hands on her hips, she huffed, "Please?"

"Make your own breakfast."

In her tiny black shorts from the night before and a white tank top, she threw her hands out to the side as she griped, "I only know how to make scrambled eggs and you don't have any eggs."

At that moment, Auggie didn't know whether he wanted to pull her into the bed with him or choke her.

"Fine! I'll make you breakfast! Just get out of my damn room!"

Fluttering her eyelashes as she rolled her eyes at him, Charlotte left his room.

Thinking to herself 'geez, that was rude' Charlotte made her way back to his kitchen. He was probably going to take his sweet time rolling out of bed. That would be just like him. Every time she wanted something, he insisted on doing the opposite. Like him running to his room like a little girl because she simply asked what would make his night better. She wasn't even offering him anything. It was just a question. Okay, maybe she was putting herself out there a bit and it was most likely for the best that he responded the way he did, but she was normally the one doing the turning down. Opening the freezer with a heavy sigh, Charlotte thought she might as well give up. Clearly, if he was attracted to her, he wasn't going to do anything about it and it was just as well that he didn't. Convincing herself, the crush she had developed on him had more to do with the fact that he was different from every other man she knew and less genuine fondness for him, Charlotte found a box of waffles.

After checking to make sure he had syrup, Charlotte went to tell him never-mind. Walking into his room, she found Auggie wearing his Dickies and no shirt. Hunched over with his forehead pressed against the wall, he was practically panting.

"A...am I interrupting?" she blurted with a laugh.

Leaning all the way onto the wall, he let out a frustrated groan before holding his cupped hand out to her snapping, "It's tattoo goo."

Stepping closer, she inspected the jellied substance in his hand.

"What are you trying to do?"

"I can't reach the middle," Auggie griped in an almost pleading tone.

Having some compassion for him since it appeared as though he was about to have a breakdown over it, she offered, "Here, let me help."

Charlotte stepped next to him and dipped her first two fingers into the goo. Charlotte had been dying to touch the cross on his back since she first laid eyes on it.

৵৽৲

Every muscle in Auggie's body tightened the second Charlotte's fingers touched the middle of his back.

"Am I hurting you?" she asked.

Realizing his response to her was obvious, he tried to think of anything other than her touching him as he shook his head.

"Could you relax then," she said with a laugh before adding, "You're making me nervous."

Grinding his back teeth together, he leaned his head down and closed his eyes.

Charlotte's tone was as soft as her fingers on his back as she shared, "I would say your cross is beautiful but I don't want you getting all offended. I've always wanted a tattoo."

Swallowing hard, he replied, "You have?"

Sliding her fingers into his hand to retrieve more goo before branching out from the middle to his shoulder blades, she shared, "I'd like to have a mark on me that I chose to have, if that makes sense."

Understanding where she was coming from, Auggie informed, "My cousin Kieran's done all mine. I kinda sprung this one on him the night Will died. He just finished the center a few days ago," before adding, "He does the family's, old school, at his house but he has a shop on fifth street."

"If I ever decide on something, I might stop in."

Without thinking it through, he said, "Anything would look good on you."

Charlotte ran her fingers down the length of his cross before she stepped away, saying, "I found some waffles in your freezer. I'll just make those."

By the time he turned around, she was out of his room.

Popping the waffles in a toaster after she washed her hands, Charlotte leaned against the counter. Planning to suggest they work on the ledger right after breakfast, she needed to get out of there and limit her time with him to Sundays only, like their agreement. Thankfully he brought up William, reminding her why she was associating with him in the first place.

As she pulled the heated waffles out of the toaster, Auggie walked into the kitchen, saying, "Since you're already here, why don't we go over the books then you don't have to come back later?"

Whipping around, to see him with his shirt on, Charlotte thought 'I was supposed to say that' as she agreed, "That's fine."

Without another word, Auggie went behind her to make his waffles.

৵৹৵৾

They ate breakfast and worked out the weeks totals together. When they were done, Auggie remembered her cellphone in the back pocket of his slacks that were lying on his bedroom floor.

"Hang on let me grab your phone."

Charlotte nodded at him, waiting by the door.

Quickly bringing it to her, he handed it over, saying, "You almost left without it."

Another nod from Charlotte confirmed the awkwardness of the moment. Both were being polite and it was weird.

"So, I'll see you next Sunday then."

Reaching for the knob, he replied, "Yep."

He opened the door and started to move to let her through since she was on the opposite side, when he heard Penny complain, "Don't you ever answer your phone?"

Charlotte's eyes were wide just before he shoved her between the wall and the door and leaned against it.

Penny made her way into his house and set a few containers on his kitchen table before walking back to the living room.

"What are you doing?" she asked.

Trying to make it seem like his leaning against the open door was natural, Auggie kept his hand on the knob saying, "What's up Henny-Penny?"

Making a face at him, she fussed, "I hate when you call me that," before sharing, "Mom sent me over to bring you leftovers and to tell you it's your turn at Aunt Neica's."

"Can't you go?"

"Gross, no!"

"Fine, who's out there?"

"Nobody. Brennen left this morning and won't be back until Tuesday."

Staring at her as he waited for her to leave, Auggie asked, "Is that it?"

With a secretive expression, Penny replied, "Well...Guess what I heard?"

"Bye Pen."

Rolling her eyes, at him she stated, "I'm going to tell you anyway because Sophia doesn't want you ruining her shower."

With a slight laugh, he said, "You mean the one at the bar."

Stepping closer, she continued, "Anyways, Ren is making her invite Charlotte."

"So," he snapped, hoping she would drop it.

"Oh, you don't care?"

"What makes you think I give a damn about that girl?"

With a suspicious expression Penny replied, "Well, I think it's strange. All this time you hated her and now you get all butt hurt anytime someone mentions her."

"What? You're crazy," he blurted, trying to remember what he'd said each time her name was mentioned.

"Am I?" Penny questioned before walking towards the door saying, "Mom said you defended her being at the hospital with Will. We all know you let her into the bar and you cussed Sheryl up and down and told her she better stay away from Charlotte. And now you're just fine having her attend family gatherings with us."

It took Auggie a minute to think of something to say.

"Maybe if you got a job and did something with your life you would have better things to do than go around imagining things off of gossip you've heard."

Pursing her lips into a smile, Penny assured, "I don't think it's my imagination, Auggie. I wasn't asking if you cared about her; I was asking if you cared that she would be at Sophia's shower."

Ignoring her statement completely, Auggie said, "Tell mom I'll be by tomorrow afternoon."

Penny started to leave then stopped right outside his front door.

"What?" he griped, still holding the doorknob as he pulled it closer to him, ready to close it on his sister.

"Remember my friend Nina?"

"Sure..."

"She was at a club last night and said she could have sworn she saw you there."

"Yea, I don't think so."

"That's what I said too," Penny agreed with a hint of hidden agenda before she shared, "But she was pretty sure it was you that got in a fight over some blonde girl."

Closing the door a little more on his sister, Auggie stated, "Nope."

Raising an eyebrow at him, she glanced at his hand gripping the doorknob before asking, "So how did your knuckles get all red and swollen then?"

The only thing Auggie could think to do was to slam the door in her face and lock it.

ॐ‿ॐ

Hearing Penny shout 'Rude' through Auggie's front door, Charlotte watched as he pressed his back against the door. With a serious scowl he shook his head staring at the floor.

Feeling bad about putting him in a position where he had to lie to his family, Charlotte said, "I would never have asked you to take me to Club 76 if I thought someone would see us there. That was a little too close this time. Maybe we should figure out another way to work on the books together. It's only a matter of time before someone sees me here."

Appearing to ignore what she had just said, Auggie asked, "You wanna go somewhere with me?"

"Where?"

Appearing as though he was holding back a smile, Auggie replied, "My Uncle's place."

"What's there? Is that what your sister was saying 'gross' about?"

"Trust me, when we get there you'll feel right at home," he assured before informing, "I'll grab you a shirt."

"I didn't say I would go with you."

"You owe me, remember."

Knowing that she did, Charlotte shared, "Okay, but I don't do the manual labor thing."

"You can just stand there and look pretty while I do all the work."

Narrowing her eyes at him, Charlotte couldn't tell if he was being sarcastic, making fun of her or if he had really just called her pretty. When he cleared his throat and quickly walked to his room, Charlotte couldn't help but smile. He thought she was pretty.

❦12❦

Peacocks

Sitting in the passenger seat of Auggie's truck wearing one of his old plaid shirts that he said was too small for him, Charlotte couldn't quite put her finger on the way she was feeling. It was a mixture of excitement, nervousness and anticipation. Combined, it was an unfamiliar feeling that had her on edge.

❦❦

Watching Charlotte stare out of the passenger window of his truck, from the corner of his eye, Auggie fought the urge to reach over and place his hand on her knee. There was a good chance she'd be mad when she found out what they were doing but no matter what her reaction was, it would be worth it, seeing her wearing his shirt. It was the closest he was going to get to actually touching her. Knowing he shouldn't want to, there was a huge part of him that thought if fair is fair, he should be allowed to drag his fingers across her skin like she had done to him.

❦❦

After driving down a country road, they pulled up to an old wooden barn. Auggie handed her a pair of his socks before getting out of his truck. Charlotte slid his socks onto her feet before pulling them all the way up to her knees. Opening her door, she watched him return from the barn with a pair of black rubber boots. Instantly apprehensive about putting them on as she noticed him smack the soles to clean them out, Charlotte thought 'No way I'm putting my feet in those'.

Walking around the open truck door, Auggie handed her the rubber boots, saying, "Here ya go."

Charlotte turned her nose up at them, complaining, "I brought you nice things to wear and all I get from you is a pair of old nasty water boots?"

"I checked for spiders," he said, smiling at her disgusted expression.

Hesitantly, Charlotte stuck one leg out of the truck waiting for him to place one on her.

❧❧

Looking down at her leg stretched out to him, Auggie paused. She really expected him to put them on her?

Setting the rubber boots down, he laughed, "Hop on in sweetheart, we don't have all day," as he took a few steps back.

With a slight huff, Charlotte slid out of his truck and right into the rubber boots.

Stomping towards him, she snapped, "I don't feel right at home."

Even though Charlotte was clearly irritated with him, Auggie couldn't help smiling at her. The rubber boots she was wearing ended a few inches below white socks, his socks, that went all the way up to her knees. Then nothing but thigh for what seemed like miles until those tiny black shorts and his old plaid shirt that hung open, covering her tank top. Glaring at him as she tapped the toe of her boot, she was the best thing he'd ever seen. Looking her over as she placed her hands on her hips, Auggie's first impulse was to scoop her up off of her feet and toss her in the bed of his truck.

Snapping him right back to reality, Charlotte fussed, "Oh you can think this is funny all you want, but I'm starting to think your wardrobe isn't the only reason you don't have a woman."

Out of instinct to argue, Auggie griped, "So you don't like being dressed up in clothes that you normally don't wear? That is funny. Now how would you feel if I suddenly started rubbing up against you?"

Charlotte's expression instantly changed as she patronized, "Do you want me to rub up against you?"

Thinking to himself, 'like you wouldn't believe', he griped, "You wish I did."

"Please, if I wanted you to, trust me, you would be."

"Like last night?"

Auggie could tell he had struck a nerve with her as she fluttered her eyelashes, saying, "Silly boys always read more into things than are actually there."

Angered by her slight to his manhood, he growled, "Like little girls that think they are more than what they are. Stunning feathers my ass, you have no idea what real beauty is."

Auggie turned away from her and headed around the side of the barn.

Mentally questioning why he kept subjecting himself to Charlotte, he grew more and more agitated by the moment. Picking up two large rectangle baskets from the side of the barn, he could hear her dragging her feet as she walked behind him. Seriously, she strutted around in those incredibly high heels of hers and she couldn't maneuver a pair of rubber boots.

When Auggie reached the large pen with coops inside, he knew Charlotte had stopped too. Ready to see the expression on her face, he expected irritation maybe even a hint of anger toward him but definitely not the look of wonder he saw spreading across her face as he turned around.

Stopping the moment she caught sight of what was in the coops, Charlotte still didn't know what exactly they were going to do there but it didn't matter anymore.

"They're beautiful," she breathed, looking over at him.

With a confused expression on his face, Auggie replied, "Yea," before clearing his throat as he informed, "Let's get started."

Charlotte watched Auggie open the pen and allow her to step in before latching it behind them.

In awe she shared, "I've never seen a real peacock in person before."

Auggie seemed all business as he instructed, "We can let the first two pens out then once we collect the feathers, we'll let the last one out."

"Is that what we're doing here?"

"Once a year, they molt. We'll clean the feathers out of the coops and then round them back up."

As Auggie opened the first two coops, Charlotte watched the peacocks cautiously strut out to the surrounding pen, questioning, "Why did your sister say this was gross? This is amazing. And y'all take turns?"

Pulling a pair of work gloves out of his pocket, Auggie put them on, saying, "Penny doesn't like work in general." Waving her closer, as he handed her a basket he continued, "My Aunt Neica died about three and a half years ago. Brennen won't get rid of 'em because she loved them so much, but I think it's too hard for him to tend to them. So his sons handle the feed and the rest of us take turns with everything else."

"Is he too old?"

Shaking each feather gently as he placed them in the basket Charlotte was holding, Auggie scowled at her, saying, "No, he misses her."

"Oh," she replied, growing uncomfortable with how heartwarming she found the situation.

Deciding it was best to keep quiet, Charlotte followed Auggie with the basket until he had collected all the feathers from the first two coops.

꙰

After rounding the birds back into their coops, Auggie took the basket of feathers from Charlotte, placed it outside the pen and handed her the empty one.

"You might want to stand back a little, he isn't a friendly one," he warned.

Pulling the pin on the last coop, Auggie patted the door in order to urge the last peacock out.

When a solid white peacock strutted out of the coop, Charlotte gasped, "He's gorgeous."

"Mean as hell too," he cautioned before saying, "And I have the scars to prove it."

Charlotte took a few steps back just as he had instructed before dropping the basket she was holding and slowly backing away from the white peacock as he moved closer to her.

"What do I do?"

Carefully watching the old peacock as he continued to strut his way to Charlotte, Auggie replied, "Stand still."

Her eyes questioned how good of an idea that was as Auggie slowly walked behind the peacock.

Charlotte stood completely still as the old white peacock made a circle around her. Moving closer, Auggie prepared himself to grab ahold of him and tell Charlotte to go, when the strangest thing happened. Tilting his head from side to side the peacock seemed to be inspecting her before standing at her side and resting his head and neck against her.

Holding her hand out, Charlotte gently touched the peacock's head and started to pet him, saying, "I think he likes me."

Auggie stood there in shock thinking, 'You bastard' as he watched the old peacock rub up against her.

Stepping back to the coop, Auggie grabbed the empty basket, griping, "Birds of a feather I guess."

As he collected the white feathers, Charlotte teased, "Don't be jealous."

Tossing the feathers into the basket, he figured she meant not to be jealous that the bird liked her more, but that wasn't the case. Not even close. He envied the old white peacock.

Scooping a hand full of feed out of the feeder, Auggie made his way over to lure the peacock back into his coop. As soon as he was a foot from Charlotte, the peacock stepped in front of her. Scratching at the ground with his feet, the peacock ruffled his feathers seeming guarding her from Auggie.

Clearly amused by the situation, Charlotte offered, "Since he likes me better, why don't you step out and I'll walk him back."

"Fine with me," he replied, pretending the entire situation wasn't infuriating him.

Walking out of the pen, Auggie watched Charlotte walk the old white peacock back to his coop.

Inside the barn, Charlotte stood next to Auggie watching him snip the stems off of half the colored feathers and set them to the side.

"What do y'all do with them?"

Pulling a few plastic pouches out from under a shelf, Auggie answered, "There's a flower shop in town that will get them in a few weeks." As she nodded, he offered, "Do you want some?"

"Is that okay?"

"I wouldn't have offered if it wasn't," he assured.

Thinking, 'Do you always have to be a jerk?' Charlotte asked, "Can I have a white one too?"

Appearing to be too busy to answer, he opened a drawer and pulled out a gallon size ziplock bag.

Snipping one white feather off of its stem and placing it flat in the bag with several colored ones, Auggie sealed it, saying, "Here ya go."

Taking them, she replied, "Thank you."

Without a response, Auggie finished bagging the feathers.

Back at the truck, Charlotte started to open the passenger door when Auggie grabbed the handle and swung it open for her.

Turning to face him in the space between the truck and open door, his gesture compelled her to say, "Whatever your reason for taking me out there today, it means a lot that I got to do this with you."

Taking a step closer to her, Auggie questioned, "Does it?"

Noticing there was nowhere to go as she felt the door jam of his truck against her back, Charlotte answered, "I've never got to do anything like this before and..." Stopping as he leaned closer, saying, "Damn your eyes are blue."

Anticipation started to build inside her as she reached forward and placed her hand on his chest.

Sliding her hand down the buttons of his shirt, Charlotte gave it a little tug of encouragement. Shuffling his feet towards her, Auggie was as close as possible without touching her. With anyone else, she would have tapped the edge of her jawline directing them where to go but with him, she was curious to see where he went on his own.

~·~

Resting his hands on the doorframe above Charlotte's head, Auggie looked down at her. As she looked up at him with an expression that he knew was meant to be innocent, her eyes revealed she was anything but. Feeling his self-control slip, he noticed her pull her lips into her mouth and offer her cheek to him.

Remembering he couldn't let himself get caught up with her, Auggie stepped back, imparting, "You need to keep your hands to yourself."

Charlotte's eyes narrowed at him before she let go of his shirt.

"Didn't mean to make you uncomfortable," she replied in a condescendingly snotty tone.

Charlotte's tone pushed his focus back where it needed to be as he said, "Get in and hand me the boots so I can put 'em back before we go."

Hopping into his truck, she slid her legs together letting each boot fall to the ground before swinging her legs forward.

Auggie grabbed the rubber boots off of the ground and headed back to the barn. Walking faster than necessary, the second he made it inside the barn, Auggie threw the boots down. Grabbing his beanie off of his head, he ran his fingers through his hair and let out a frustrated groan. She was killing him. He was a grown man with willpower and she was reducing him to a hard up teenager that couldn't get his mind right.

⤸⤹

Sulking in the front seat of Auggie's truck, Charlotte thought for sure he would at least try to kiss her. She could see it on his face. All she was doing was letting him know how much she appreciated spending the day with him and he started it. She was going to let him kiss her but only once just to know what it felt like. What was his problem? It was almost like he was purposely... 'That's it' she thought. He was just messing with her.

As soon as Auggie climbed in the truck, Charlotte stated, "I don't appreciate being messed with."

"Yea? Neither do I," he griped, slamming the driver side door and starting the engine.

"Of course you don't. No one likes to be made fun of."

Before he put his truck in reverse, Auggie turned and snapped, "I've never made fun of you."

Feeling more offended than before, Charlotte fussed, "No? So you knew I would like coming here to see the peacocks after you accused me of being one last night?"
Without responding, he slammed his truck into reverse and peeled out of Brennen's property.

کچ٭٭

Driving back to town, Auggie wondered how she could think he was making fun of her. Teasing her a bit, maybe, but he'd never made fun of her. Charlotte, on the other hand, was constantly making fun of him. From his clothes, to saying he couldn't get a woman and even calling him a boy, all she did was pick, pick, pick and now because he wasn't all over her at the drop of a hat, he was the bad guy. She was out of her mind.

By the time Auggie pulled into his neighborhood, he decided he had enough of her.

Out of the silence he informed, "I'll handle the books on my own next week."
As he glanced at her, Charlotte appeared as though he had slapped her.

"Whatever, Augustus."
Scowling while shaking his head, he focused on the road thinking she had to be the most frustrating person on the planet. Slowing to a stop at her car, parked a few houses down from his, Auggie was happy to be rid of her for the day and possibly forever.

❧❧

Charlotte wasted no time, flinging the passenger door open and hopping out. She grabbed her purse and her feathers before slamming his door as hard as she could. If he didn't want her help anymore, that was fine. She didn't want to have anything to do with him in the first place. He was rude, infuriating and had criticized everything about her since day one. Refusing to look back at him as she noticed his truck remained idling beside her car, she slid into the driver's seat, shoved her key in and sped off before he pulled away.

The entire way back to her house, Charlotte was furious. It was obvious there was nothing more she could do to help him. If Auggie refused to see her, then she had done all she could and she was off of the hook. What had she been thinking getting involved with him in the first place? Clearly, it was this town causing her lapse in better judgment. She needed to get out of there, go back to Spain where she belonged. At least in Spain, there were no scruff bearded bartenders with ugly plaid shirts who complained that her shorts were too short. There were social events and night clubs, where she was on the arm of a handsome man who loved her revealing attire and appreciated her appeal to everyone around them.

Surprised to see Emerson's car parked in the back driveway when she arrived, Charlotte pulled the socks Auggie loaned her and his shirt off and balled them up before shoving them into her purse with her bag of feathers. Looking around the car, she realized she'd left her heels in Auggie's truck. Deeply regretting that, Charlotte got out of the car and headed inside.

Stepping into the kitchen, Charlotte was instantly greeted by a disapproving glare from Emerson and a sigh of relief from Amila.

"Oh, thank goodness you're alright honey. We were so worried when we got here and you weren't home," Amila shared, giving her a tight squeeze.

"I thought y'all were coming back tomorrow afternoon."

With a soft smile as she let go, Amila informed, "Jenna caught a stomach virus, so we came back early."

"I didn't mean to worry you," Charlotte assured before adding, "I would have been here if I had known y'all were coming back today."

"We came home last night," Emerson stated.

Fully aware that was his way of letting her know, he thought she was up to no good, Charlotte looked at Amila, saying, "Sorry if I had *you* worried."

Charlotte walked out of the kitchen and through the living room to the stairs as Silvia stood at the bottom blocking her path. Wearing jeans and a Peace Love & Cheer tee with her light brown hair pulled high on top of her head with an oversized bow and way too much mascara, Silvia's hazel eyes seemed to delight in the fact that Charlotte had upset her parents.

"Guess some things never change," she said with an 'I'm better than you' smirk across her face.

Ignoring her snotty comment, Charlotte pushed past her and headed up the stairs.

"Excuse you," Silvia snapped.

Charlotte glanced back with a smile, saying, "Appreciate it, because there's no excuse for you."

As she reached the top of the stairs, she heard Silvia shout, "Daddy!" and quickly stepped into her room before locking the door.

Desperately wanting to go back to stay with Erin, Charlotte pulled her phone out of her purse and turned it on as she sat down on her bed. Amongst the missed calls from Amila and Ren, there were seven text messages from Trace.

T: Do not be upset with me.

T: Hello...

T: Charlotte????

T: Are you ignoring me?

T: There is no need to act like a child!

T: I received a call from your father...

T: I am not upset. However, please *note* when you chose to 'enjoy yourself' discretion is always appreciated.

Thinking to herself, 'Well that's just great' Charlotte texted back.

C: I'm home... Sorry to have worried you.

Tossing her phone on her bed, Charlotte stood up before hearing it buzz.

T: It was very uncomfortable to take a call from your father while I was...in the middle of something.

A feeling of reproach grew from deep inside her as she texted back.

C: In the middle of something or 'someone'?

T: Does it matter?

C: No...but you are getting a bit free with the info.

T: Honesty is the key to any good relationship.

C: I know that but how would you feel hearing I was with someone last night?

T: Would you like to tell me about it?

He couldn't be serious.

C: Are you serious?????

T: Would that be too much to ask?

No way, he meant what she was thinking he meant.

C: I'm confused...

T: Stop being so childish for a moment

C: I'm not!

T: Then tell me.

What the hell?

C: You want me to describe being with someone else to you?

T: If you are comfortable doing so.

That is so gross.

C: Why?

T: I find the idea of you with another man sexy.

Wait, what?!

C: You won't have sex with me until we're engaged but you want to hear details of me doing it with someone?

T: And perhaps at some point in the future, watch

What?!

C: Watch?

T: I enjoy watching.

I can't do this, conversation over.

C: I have to go.

As her stomach turned, Charlotte dropped her phone onto her bed in disgust thinking 'I need to take a bath'.

13

Ransom

Sitting at the table in his mom's kitchen, Auggie looked around. As soon as he walked in, Sarah appeared to have something on her mind. He hated when she was like this. Growing up, that look on her face was usually followed by, 'How many times have I told you' or 'Son, I have just about had it'. The suspense was killing him.

"What's on your mind, Ma?"

Slowly sitting down at the table with him, Sarah answered, "Braden said you weren't at work Saturday."

"I took the night off."

"Are you feeling alright?"

Flashes of being at the club with Charlotte entered his mind as he griped, "Why wouldn't I be?"

"Don't take a tone with me, son," she snapped, pursing her lips at him.

Leaning back in his chair, Auggie laced his fingers behind his head, saying, "Sorry, Ma."

With a heavy sigh, she insisted, "I wish you would tell me what's going on with you."

"Nothing. Gah, why is everyone on my a... So interested in what I'm doing."

"Maybe because you haven't seemed the same since..."

Quickly standing up, Auggie said, "I don't wanna talk about her."

Looking up at him with a strange expression, Sarah asked, "Her?" before questioning, "There's a her?"

Gritting his teeth, Auggie couldn't believe he opened the conversation up to that.

"No."

Sarah started to smile, asking, "What's she like?"

Thinking, 'Frustrating, irritating and an all-around pain in my ass', he answered, "There's no her."

"Did something happen between y'all?"

This was the exact reason Auggie kept his life to himself. The second his mom thought there might be someone, she needed to know every detail and he never was interested in any details or anyone for more than one night.

"Nothing, because there is no one," he did his best to swear.

Standing up in front of him, Sarah patted his arm, saying, "My, it must be serious."

Throwing his hands in the air out of frustration, he griped, "I gotta go."

As he headed out of the door, she shouted, "Love you. And if she has any sense at all she'll stick around."

"Love you too, Ma," he grumbled, closing the door behind himself.

Walking out to his truck, Auggie thought 'I need a drink'.

Before he could open the door to his truck, Ren pulled up next to him. Quickly hopping out of her car, she smiled wide at him.

"Hey Auggie," she chirped.

Giving her a head nod, he opened his door.

"What's the matter with you?"

With a heavy sigh, he replied, "Just got the third degree in there."

Raising an eyebrow at him, she questioned, "What'd ya do?"

"Nothing," he snapped.

"Alright, alright, so did you hear?" Auggie shook his head at her before Ren shared, "You're going to have a niece!"

Slightly smiling, he said, "Knew Ailin couldn't make a boy."

Rolling her eyes, Ren laughed, saying, "At least he's makin' babies, which is more than you can say."

Laughing back, he assured, "Oh, I'm makin' out just fine. Grandma."

Wrinkling up her nose, Ren said, "I'm not a grandma, I'm a Nonna thank you very much."

"Whatever you say," he replied as she turned and walked toward the house.

Auggie barely got in his truck and closed the door before Ren made her way back to him. Rolling his window down, he waited to see what she wanted.

"Can you do me a favor?"

"Whatcha need?"

Hesitant at first, Ren replied, "I'm asking you because I know you won't say anything, Okay."

Confused, he questioned, "So what are you asking?"

"Have you heard anything about Charlotte seeing anyone or anything like that?"

Scowling at her, he asked, "Why?"

With a light sigh, she shared, "She stayed out all night and didn't say where she had been."

"So, isn't she grown?"

Ren tilted her head back and forth slightly before saying, "Yea, she is but it's not like she has any friends here so..."

"So wouldn't want to ruin things with that boyfriend of hers, right?"

Ren gave him an interested look as she asked, "What does it matter to you?"

129

"It doesn't," he snapped, wondering when he was going to stop having outbursts where Charlotte was concerned.

"Oh-kay..." Ren replied before saying, "Just let me know if you hear anything."

"Fine," he blurted before rolling his window up.

Pulling out of his mom's driveway, he noticed Ren look back at him before shaking her head and continuing to the house.

≈≈≈

Standing behind the bar at The Dog House, Auggie noticed a sweet little brunette eyeing him from the end of the bar. The bar was practically empty and he hadn't served a drink in around half an hour. Making his way over to her as she raised her eyebrows and flashed a smile at him, he thought this is what I need. All night long he was planning on getting drunk after closing up but bringing home the brunette would be so much better. Besides, he could still get drunk after she went home.

The closer he got the more he realized, although she was good looking, she was makeup pretty. Charlotte's light pink lips with their white scar running down them entered his mind as he looked at the brunette's hot pink mouth.

"Can I get ya somethin'?"

Her perfume wafted towards him as she replied, "Yes you can."

She smelled like she'd tried to drown herself in whatever fragrance she wore.

Thinking, maybe he'd get drunk before instead, he asked, "What'd ya have in mind?"

Leaning against the bar, the brunette's low cut top showed him exactly what she had to offer but before she could reply, he heard Jackson holler, "Auggie, come to the back a minute."

Patting the bar in front of him, Auggie said, "Gimme just a sec." and headed to the back.

Making his way through the swinging doors, Auggie stopped right inside the manager's office.

"I'm kinda workin' on something out there," he shared, hoping whatever Jackson wanted wouldn't take very long.

Smiling wide while shaking his head, Jackson replied, "I just went over the books and I needed to talk to you."

"Is something wrong?"

In a surprised tone, Jackson answered, "No. In fact the last few weeks, they've been perfect."
Auggie gave a silent nod.

"I have to say, I'm impressed. You seem to have gotten a real handle on things."
Remaining silent, Auggie couldn't take the credit. Charlotte was the reason.

With a heavy sigh, Jackson apologized, "I had my doubts, but I'm sorry. I should have had more faith that you could do it."

"Yea, thanks," Auggie choked out unable to even look at Jackson at this point.

Jackson gave him a reassuring look, saying, "You're doing a great job."

"Is that it? Can I go?"

Halfway out of the office already, he heard Jackson say, "Keep up the good work," causing Auggie to push through the swinging doors and head straight for the men's room, instead of back behind the bar.

Shaking his head at himself, Auggie pulled his beanie off and splashed cold water on his face. He yanked a hand full of paper towels out of the dispenser and dried his beard off. Running his fingers through his hair, Auggie pulled his beanie back over his head as he thought of Charlotte. It wasn't Jackson's misplaced pride in him or the fact that she was the reason he was managing the bar so well. It was her and the way one side of her mouth would curl into a smile when his totals would balance out. It was having her sit at his kitchen table reading off receipts and how her hair brushed his arm when she leaned over to look at the ledger. It was Charlotte that was making him miserable.

Leaving the restroom, Auggie decided he needed to get her out of his system completely. She was like a disease. An infectious disease that started off slowly then spread like crazy. First thing tomorrow, he would rent a steam cleaner and get the smell of her out of his house. That would be a good start.

As he headed back behind the bar, the perfumy brunette offered, "Maybe you could drive me home. I have been drinking, you know."

Auggie stared at her as she pushed her chest against the bar.

"Brooks," he shouted across the bar, causing her to give him a startled expression.

The drummer to his brothers' band jogged over, saying, "What's up man."

Introducing him to the brunette, Auggie said, "This is Brooks, he's a drummer. Brooks, this is..." She quickly shared, "Larissa," before saying, "I like music."

Taking his backwards baseball cap off to reveal his shaggy blond hair, Brooks said, "Oh yea," with a wide smile.

Auggie stepped back letting them get to know each other.

It wasn't long before Brooks took off with Larissa. After showing her his setup on stage, he gave Auggie an appreciative smile and thumbs up before walking out of the front door with her. As he thought to himself, 'It never hurts to do a friend a favor' he knew it was better to pass on an easy opportunity then to accept and not be able to follow through. There had been an instant change in the way he felt thinking of Charlotte and then looking at Larissa. One that he had a feeling wouldn't end on a good note if he took her home.

The Dog House was quiet as Auggie closed up the bar. As he shut everything down the phone behind the bar rang.

"Dog House, we're closed," he answered.

"What did you do with my heels?"

The memory of seeing them on the floorboard of his truck but being so mad at her he didn't want them in his house as he shoved them under the passenger seat entered his mind.

It took him a second before he griped, "Did you break into my house again?"

There was a pause before Charlotte replied, "It's not breaking in if I use a key."

"Damn it, woman," he fussed before he heard a little girl's voice in the background, saying, "I can't sleep."

Charlotte's voice sounded muffled as she asked, "Did you have a bad dream?"

Auggie listened intently as he heard the girl say, "Can I stay in here with you?"

Charlotte answered her, "Of course you can," in a sweet tone before snapping, "I need my heels back," directly at him.

Trying not to smile, Auggie replied, "You're not at my house."

"I never said I was. You assumed I was. Just because I've done something once doesn't mean I'll do it again."

Feeling there was a double meaning to her statement, Auggie informed, "I'm closing up. Give me your number and I'll call you. We can discuss your shoes then."

With an irritated tone, Charlotte gave him her cell number before hanging up on him.

⤳⤳

Mulling it over in his head, over and over, Auggie decided to work out a trade for her shoes. That way he could say, while you're here we can go over the books one last time. Thinking that was reasonable since she all but said she

133

wouldn't come on to him again, he could deal with her until she left and by then he'd figure out a way to handle his manager duties without her.

He'd showered and had two beers before sitting down in his chair, that still smelled like her, staring at his cellphone. Thinking he might need a third beer, for some strange reason he was nervous.

Finally biting the bullet, he dialed her number and received a sleepy, "Hello."

"So, you want your shoes back."

There was a loud huff into the phone before she replied, "Did you plan on keeping them?"

"I am holding them for ransom," he stated with a smile on his face.

"You have got to be kidding me."

"Nope."

Making an angry sound into the phone, Charlotte questioned, "Fine. What do you want?"

"My Socks."

There was a long pause before she replied, "Seriously."

"Yes. I like my socks and if you value your fancy little black heels, you will return my socks to me."

Auggie could hear her masked amusement as she asked, "When would you like to make the exchange?"

He thought for a moment before saying, "I will contact you with the time and location soon."

Trying to imagine the look she must have on her face, Auggie waited for her reply.

Choking back a laugh, she said, "Oak...Oh-kay."

There was something about making her laugh that provoked him to say, "Goodnight, Charlotte."

"Um, 'night," she replied with a confused tone in her voice.

Pressing the end button on his cellphone, he disconnected the call and sat in his chair thinking.

❧14❧

Legacy

Making her way down the stairs, Charlotte could smell breakfast cooking. The last few days had been interesting to say the least. Between going out with Auggie, visiting his uncle's farm, finding out Trace was a voyeuristic perv and having her favorite stilettos held for ransom, she needed a day to herself. Excited and honestly a bit nervous over her plans for the day, she stepped into the kitchen.

Amila placed a plate of pancakes in front of her the moment she sat down.

"Good morning honey," Amila greeted with a smile.

Drowning her pancakes in syrup, Charlotte replied, "'Morning, I am going into town after I eat, do you need anything?"

Amila gave another smile while shaking her head before asking, "Anywhere specific?"

After a short mental debate, Charlotte shared, "Actually, I'm going down to..." before Emerson walked in.

"Down to where?" Amila asked.

Shaking her head at Amila, she could feel Emerson staring at her as she answered, "Nowhere. Just into town."

Sitting across from Charlotte at the kitchen table, Emerson asked, "If you do not have any specific plans, would you like to come to the foundation with me?"

"No thank you."

Appearing disappointed, Emerson shared, "I am doing my best to make an effort with you."

Giving him a dirty look, she shook her head before focusing on her pancakes.

⊷⊶

Sitting in the parking lot of Legacy Ink on fifth street, Charlotte tapped her steering wheel. There were already cars in the parking lot, which she had not expected. She wasn't second guessing her decision, more the timing of it. With most of her back and stomach scared from her mother's drug-induced tirade, she looked forward to it. No one would truly understand how important marking herself was. She even hoped it hurt. She wanted to close her eyes, remember and forget, while finally, in her mind, settling the score. Her mother wanted to make her ugly and she was going to turn what happened that night into something beautiful. But the last thing she wanted was for everyone in town to know about it.

A little bell rang as Charlotte stepped into the shop. Looking around at photographs framed on the walls with half naked men and women covered in full body tattoos, she spotted a familiar face.

Thinking, 'Damn it', she crossed her arms and glanced away as Penny let go of the guy she was hanging on and greeted, "Hey," in a 'what are you doing here' tone.

"Hello," Charlotte replied before clearing her throat and asking, "Is Kieran available."

"Say girl," said a voice from the other side of the shop.

Making his way towards her was a tanned muscular blonde in a muscle-t with full sleeve tattoos covering his arms.

"K's out but a... I'll be happy to a... assist you," he assured, sucking air in through his teeth.

Before Charlotte could reply, Penny shared, "He'll be back in about five minutes."

Charlotte took a seat, looked at Penny and said, "Thank you."

Pulling a red chair with chrome legs from against the wall and turning it to face Charlotte, Mr. Muscles sat down.

"Want some help decidin'?"

Smiling at his attempt to flirt, Charlotte should have been all over the slick smiling, tattooed bundle of muscles, flirting back. He was ideal. A fast stress reliever and unlike the shoe ransoming jackass, this guy would welcome anything she had to offer. Unfortunately, there was something lacking and as cute as he was, she wasn't into him.

"No thanks, I know what I'm getting," she replied with a kind tone.

"How 'bout a location then?" he grinned, raising his eyebrows at her.

She couldn't help enjoying the attention as she rolled her eyes thinking, 'Gah that was lame'.

"What's your name sweet thing?"

"Charlotte."

"Jimmy. You from here?"

As she nodded, Charlotte said, "I have been in Spain for the past few years."

"You're Silvia's big sister?"

Curious, she nodded, asking, "You know my sister?"

"Yea, she goes with my brother, Shawn."

Thinking, 'interesting', she said, "Oh, that's nice."

"I guess," he blurted before informing, "I let 'em use my apartment sometimes. Not sure what he sees in her she's such a stuck up little bitch. Well, guess I do know, ya know." Charlotte gave him a dirty look as he laughed before asking, "So you wanna hook up later?"

Without responding, Charlotte faced forward wondering how Jimmy could think telling her that his brother was putting it to her younger sister and then insulting her would make her want to do anything with him.

After Jimmy gave up, mumbling 'must run in the family', he left with Penny's 'friend'. Wondering how much longer it was going to take for Kieran to get back, it had been more than five minutes by now, Penny walked up to Charlotte and placed her hand on her hip.

"I don't suppose you could keep seeing me here to yourself."

Standing up, Charlotte replied, "Can you?"

Pursing her lips up into a smile, she questioned, "From everyone, or just my brother?" without giving Charlotte a chance to speak, Penny shared, "Before you act like I'm stupid, I know you were there when I stopped by Sunday."

"I think you're mistaken."

Penny stepped back, flipping her long auburn hair over her shoulder, "But I'm not."

Charlotte stared at Penny, wondering what her angle was as she asked, "What do you want?"

With a light sigh, she answered, "Just don't tell anyone I was here and I'll return the favor."

"What about your cousin? Won't he tell?"

"Kieran? No."

Nodding, Charlotte couldn't help her curiosity.

"Why does it matter if you're here?"

Appearing disappointed, Penny replied, "Nothing I do is ever right, so... What about you?"

"No big secret here."

"Then why are you and Auggie hiding that y'all are seeing each other?"

"We're not!" Charlotte insisted as she explained, "We're just helping each other out."

"Eww!" Penny blurted making an ugly face.

Charlotte had to laugh, assuring, "Not like that."

As Penny shook her head and laughed with Charlotte, the bell at the top of the door rang.

Charlotte turned to find a tall man with short black hair and no shirt standing there. As he crossed his arms, Charlotte took in the full sleeve tattoo on one of his arms and the random ones on the other before settling her focus on the Celtic heart on the left side of his chest.

"What do we have here?"

Pursing her lips into a smile, Penny answered, "Looks to me like you have a client."

Kieran looked Charlotte over, asking Penny, "Friend of yours?"

Glancing at Charlotte, she replied, "A...Yea."

Passing by Charlotte, he walked to the back after saying, "Grab Ms. Roberts a consent form and have her fill it out." Charlotte couldn't help being irritated and it didn't help that Kieran already knew who she was.

Watching Penny do as she was told, Charlotte had to wonder if Auggie had been there bad mouthing her. Why else would he treat her this way.

When Penny handed her the form, Kieran stepped out of the back, saying, "Why don't you take lunch Pen, I'm booked up for the rest of the afternoon and it's gonna get busy."
Penny rolled her eyes and gave Charlotte a 'he's the boss' smile before grabbing her purse from under the counter and walking out.

Stopping Charlotte before she could fill out the consent form, Kieran questioned, "What are you doing here?"

Waving the pen she was holding around, she sarcastically replied, "I'm in a tattoo shop filling out a consent form. Wow, that is a mystery."

"Look, Penny's real sweet and way too trusting. She doesn't need anyone pretending to be her friend."

"I think you have me confused with someone else. I wouldn't have come if I'd known she works here."

With a suspicious expression, he asked, "Sophia didn't send you down here so she could run back to Sarah and tell her that Penny's working here?" before adding, "I know your families are close."

"Hold on there," she snapped before griping, "I'm close with Ren and Sophia just happens to be...her daughter. The only reason I know about this place is because I mentioned wanting a tattoo and your cousin said you've done all of his."

Kieran gave her a curious smile before glancing down at her legs.

His smile grew wide as he said, "Sign the form and let me see your license."

Frustrated that he obviously knew something he wasn't sharing, she did as he asked.

Once Kieran made a copy of Charlotte's driver's license and filed it with her consent form, he waved her behind the counter.

Sitting on a stool next to a small rolling table, he asked, "Any idea what you want?"

"A white peacock feather on my right shoulder blade."

"That's a simple freehand," he said before informing, "Just to let ya know white ink won't look as clean after a while if you like to tan, it'll yellow and more than likely gonna look like a scar after it heals."

Nodding, Charlotte replied, "I know."

"Is this your first tattoo?"

"Yes."

"What's your pain tolerance like?"

"Extraordinary."

"Alright, watch me and initial that you witnessed me open and place a sterile unused needle on the gun, then take your shirt off and we'll get started," he said, preparing his table.

Freezing where she sat, it never occurred to Charlotte she would have to do that.

Kieran was ready to go when he noticed Charlotte hesitating.

"Are you having second thoughts?"

Holding her head high, she snapped, "No."

Flipping a switch, he set his tattoo gun on the table, offering, "If you're not sure, maybe you should take some time to think about..." before she cut him off, stating, "I want it."

"You rethinking the location?"

Charlotte pulled her lips into her mouth and shook her head.

"If you're worried about me seeing you, I only look where I'm working and usually girls hold their shirt to cover their breasts."

Shaking her head with a loud exhale, she admitted, "I'm not worried about that. If you saw something...would you be able to keep it to yourself?"

Giving her a questioning look, he asked, "You got a third nipple or a head growing out of your back?"

With a slight laugh, she said, "No, nothing like that."

Smiling wide, Kieran shared, "Don't know if Auggs told you but I've been tattooing for my family since I was fifteen. I doubt you have anything I haven't seen before and even if ya did, I'm like a vault. Swear."

Glancing around the shop, Charlotte turned her back to Kieran, pulled her arms out of her top, so the back of her shirt fell just below the center of her back.

"Is this good?" she asked deciding to think of it like a doctor's appointment.

After a long moment of uncomfortable silence, he answered, "That'll work."

Feeling him draw a rough outline on her shoulder blade, she asked, "So you've been doing this since you were fifteen?"

"Yep," he replied before informing, "I'm gonna do a short line so you know what to expect. Ready?"

Nodding, Charlotte braced herself.

141

The vibration from the tattoo gun radiated into her shoulder blade as the needle marked her skin. Charlotte slowly exhaled thinking, 'perfect'.

"Ya good?"

"Yes," she replied soaking in the pain.

"Can I ask you somethin' personal?"

Taking slow controlled breaths, she replied, "How personal?"

"What happened to you?"

Charlotte's voice was strained as she said, "Nothing."

"Do you need to take a break?"

She gritted her teeth, saying, "No."

"You sure?"

Finding it harder than she thought to control her reaction to the pain, Charlotte focused on a small black frame surrounding a Celtic heart with light blue shading that had Liv written at the top. Recognizing it as the same one that he had tattooed on the left side of his chest, she was curious.

With a sharp inhale she all but demanded, "What's with the Celtic heart?"

"Well now, that's my favorite story to tell," he assured before sharing, "Celtic tattoos started out as warrior markings. Intimidating the enemy going into battle. Along time ago, a Celt named Fergus marked his heart for everyone to see. Fergus was a hard core warrior and womanizer. Battles, different women, that sorta thing. Legend has it, a neighboring clan was being invaded. Fergus, who was always up for a good fight, left without hesitation. The battle was won and the neighboring clan was so grateful for his assistance, he was offered... Well, pretty much whatever he wanted. The idea was brought about to join the clans through Fergus and Cinnie, the neighboring clan elder's daughter. Cinnie was of course obedient to her father but not so interested in having a man like Fergus as a husband. He was rough, rude and from years of battle not the best looking. However, Fergus was instantly attracted to her. Cinnie was young and beautiful and Fergus swore the moment he saw her, his heart beat as if he were rushing into war. Cinnie would not refuse her father and the two were joined but she had no problem refusing Fergus, in the bedroom that is. He tried everything from bringing her flowers to learning to play the harp in hopes to woo her. Years passed and not much changed, he still wooed her everyday and she still refused him just the same. Until one day Fergus didn't return home. Now it's been said, he was ambushed and captured and he fought his way out and its also told that he was in a drunken stupor caused by Cinnie not returning his affections." Stopping a moment to laugh, he shared, "I believe the latter. We are Irish ya know." Charlotte smiled as he finished by saying, "Regardless of the reason, for the first time since they had been wed, Cinnie spent the night alone. There was no one there to lay flowers on the table, attempt to play and sing made up songs of her beauty or even snore to keep her awake at night. The next morning, she woke to a quiet house. As she sat there praying for the rough, rude, often obnoxious and almost hideous man she had been forced to share a home with, Cinnie remembered all the things Fergus had done to gain her affection. When he wandered up the next afternoon, Cinnie flogged him something fierce, damn near knocking him unconscious. She then told him that he was never to leave her again because she loved him. After she gave him a homecoming that would put any honeymoon to shame, he went down and had a knotted heart marked on the left side of his chest. When the man marking him asked why, he said it was because the greatest battle he ever fought was the one for her heart."

"Is that true?"

Charlotte felt a damp cloth and then cool liquid against her tender skin as Kieran laughed, "Don't think anyone's asked that before."

"So was Fergus a Caffrey?"

"No, the man who tattooed him was. The story has been handed down from father to son along with the trade."

Shaking her head with a smile, Charlotte felt having Kieran mark her somehow made her part of a legacy in the process. When she stood up and viewed her beautiful white peacock feather tattoo in the mirror, she felt honored to have received it from him.

❧ 15 ❧

Irritation

As happy as Charlotte was with her new tattoo, it had grown itchy over the last few days. Unfortunately, an itchy tattoo was not her only irritation. She had not heard from her shoe ransom-er, which was a bit of a let-down, making her wonder if Penny kept her word or if Kieran was really a vault like he swore. However, the main source of her irritation was Trace. No matter how many times she told him she needed time to herself, he insisted on continuing to text her as if he hadn't just shared something she felt she had every right to be uncomfortable with.

Laying on her bed, Charlotte scrolled through pictures on her phone. She was feeling a bit homesick. When she reached the last picture of her camera roll, she had to smile. Remembering Auggie appearing close to miserable when she took the picture, as she stared at the picture he didn't seem so unhappy with her. He was staring back at her. With a slight scowl to his brow, it occurred to her that was the same way he looked at her at his uncle's farm, before he told her to keep her hands to herself. Saving the picture as his contact photo, Charlotte took a moment to think about what, if anything, that look meant.

Groaning as her phone vibrated in her hand, Charlotte rolled her eyes.

T: Are you getting ready for bed?

Having had her fill of politely replying to his persistence, Charlotte decided to speak her mind.

C: Did you want to WATCH???

T: Is that meant to be a joke?

C: Take it however you like.

T: What I would like is to have my Charlotte back.

Startled by the way Trace calling her his, suddenly made her uncomfortable, it took her a minute to reply.

C: I need some time to figure out what I want.

T: Are you seeing someone?

C: No.

T: Would you like to?

C: ?

T: Let's be honest with each other. You know why I escorted you down and you know what I will ask when I return for you. Why do you feel the need to make this more than what it is.

C: So what is it? I thought more was what we were moving towards...

T: I strongly dislike when you are childish.

C: K bye.

T: Do not be that way.

C: K bye.

T: Charlotte.

C: Bye.

T: You are very frustrating at the moment. I will txt you later when you are in a better mood.

Without feeling the need to respond, Charlotte didn't need to be in a better mood, she needed to put some serious thought into her future with Trace. The fact of the matter was, everything was fine between her and Trace before she came back. Yes, the voyeurism thing was new but aside from that, he was the same man as he always was. So why was she bothered by him now? Charlotte decided it could only be one of two things. After a year with him, the break gave her a chance to step back and view things differently. Or, this town was messing with her mind.

Curling up on her left side, Charlotte reached out to place her cellphone on her nightstand when it vibrated again. With a slight huff, she glanced at the screen.

A: You will receive a message at 4:30 tomorrow.

Feeling the corner of her mouth curl up into a smile, she texted back.

C: No deal.

A: No?

C: I need proof of life.

A: What?

C: How do I know what deranged things you have done to my babies?

A: Now I'm deranged?

A slight laugh escaped Charlotte as she shook her head at her phone.

C: You are holding my heels hostage for the ransom of a pair of socks... feel free to draw your own conclusion to the situation.

After a moment, there was a picture on her phone of her heels sitting neatly together on Auggie's coffee table and another text message.

A: Satisfied?

C: Yes.

A: Tomorrow you will receive the exchange location.

Charlotte continued to smile at her cellphone when the picture she took of Auggie flashed across the screen. Surprised by the way her heart skipped a beat, he was calling her.

ଚ∼ଚ

Auggie tossed his cellphone onto his chair.

As he started on his way to grab a beer from the refrigerator, he heard, "Hell-oo!" coming from his phone.

Quickly turning back to his chair, he realized he accidentally called her. After staring at it and trying to decide what to do, Auggie picked up his phone to disconnect the call.

Just before he hung up, he heard Charlotte say, "This is moving into creepy territory."

Quickly putting the phone to his ear, he griped, "I called you by accident."

"Oh, alright then."

Confused by how much he missed the sound of her voice, Auggie shared, "But I mean, you don't have to hang up."

There was a long pause before he heard her give a soft, "Okay."

Settling down in his chair, he asked, "You been keeping busy?" wondering why the last few days without her had felt like an eternity.

"Not really. There's not much to do especially with everybody back. I mostly just hang out with Lola."

"Your little sister?"

"Yea, the little one," with a light sigh she continued, "She was three when I came here and five when I left. She's not really little anymore though. I wish she still was."

"That must be a woman thing."

"What do you mean?"

"You know, wanting kids to stay babies and all. If you ask me, it's better for them to grow up so you can do stuff with 'em."

"I guess, it might be. I just feel that way about Lola because I feel like I've missed her growing up."

"You say that now but I bet you'll be just like that," Auggie laughed into the phone.

There was frustration in her tone as she assured, "No, I won't because I can't."

"Can't what? Have kids?" he blurted.

The regret of sharing was clear in her voice as Charlotte explained, "I guess I could if I adopted them like Amila."

Sounding a bit more accusatory than he intended, Auggie questioned, "Why not?"

With a loud huff into the phone, she replied, "I don't know, nature maybe... I was in the hospital for about a month when I was fifteen and they ran all kinds of tests on me and that was the result of one of them."

Trying to make her feel better for what he thought most women would be devastated by, he quickly said, "That's pretty great when you think about it."

"Is that right..."

"If you're not roped up in anything steady, it'd be awesome not to worry about that. Condoms suck."

"Umm...Having unprotected sex with strangers isn't okay."

Wondering why the hell he didn't just leave well enough alone, he tried to back peddle, saying, "I wasn't saying that. I was..." before she interrupted him, "So you use a condom every time you have sex?"

Stopping a second to think, he answered, "Other than a few times in high school, yes."

"Unhuh..."

Determined to turn the conversation in his favor, he shared, "I'm clean. I had a full physical almost seven months ago when Will went into the hospital in case he needed blood or something. Everything came back clean as a whistle."

"Unhuh..."

"I haven't been with anyone since."

"Wait, is this your way of propositioning me?"

Irritated with himself for feeling like he needed to prove anything to her and wishing he hadn't shared how long it had been, Auggie snapped, "Hell no and what Mrs. High

And Mighty, you gonna lie and say you and that douche of yours always do."

"After a year I would hardly call us strangers."

"You didn't answer which means you're lying."

"I'm not lying!"

"So you do?"

"No, okay. But I would if we had a reason to."

Stunned, he questioned, "He doesn't even f... a ... have sex with you? What the hell *does* he do?"

"That, Augustus, is none of your business," Charlotte stated right before hanging up on him.

Damn that went bad fast.

Leaning his head back, Auggie growled to himself wondering what she saw in that boyfriend of hers. He wouldn't kiss her, didn't have sex with her and had no problem with her revealing her underwear to the world. In Auggie's mind, he was about as worthless as a man could get.

৯৵৶

Gah, Auggie was nothing short of ridiculous, Charlotte thought to herself. She was just messing with him. She sort of appreciated his attempt, after the whole baby conversation, to make her feel better about something that truly never bothered her in the first place. She was giving him a hard time like he always did to her. Then he took it to the next level and got all personal.

The more Charlotte thought about it, she decided it was no wonder he was so cranky all the time. That was probably a long time for him to go without. She wasn't about to apologize for hanging up on him, he had deserved it. However, she did have great compassion for him on that particular issue, so she did the next best thing. She sent him a text.

C: 'Night, Augustus.

After a few minutes, he texted back.

A: Goodnight, Charlotte.

Satisfied, she closed her eyes, tried to pretend that her shoulder wasn't itching like crazy and waited to fall asleep.

Invitations

Charlotte received a text at 4:30 on the dot from Auggie, stating the exchange would take place at his house and to expect another message with the date at ten thirty. He was, of course, in ransom-er mode so he just wrote the address, still, she couldn't help being excited. She liked Auggie's house. There was something about it that felt homey and no matter what his mood was, she was always comfortable being there.

It was getting late and the ridiculous family movie Amila made her feel guilty for not wanting to watch with everyone in the living room, was finally over. It was one of those, everything is messed up but it all works out in the end feel good movies. She hated every minute of it. She even had to control herself while watching so she didn't blurt out things like 'Whatever' and 'Yea right'. It really was further proof that she didn't belong there with the rest of her family. Everyone else seemed to love it. Even Silvia, who cried a little at the end, enjoyed the movie.

Heading up the stairs after everyone but Amila had shuffled off to their rooms, the doorbell rang. Half way up, Charlotte waited to see who it was. Amila appeared surprised at first then moved to allow Penny inside.

Trying to make up for her rudeness the other day, Charlotte walked to the bottom of the stairs, greeting, "Hi Penny."

"Hi," Penny cheered at her with a wide smile before turning back to Amila informing, "I have y'alls invitation to Sophia's shower."

"Oh, thank you honey," Amila said, closing the door behind her.

Handing Amila the invitation, Penny offered, "Sorry it's kinda late. Sophia was gonna bring it herself but she was tired and I said I'd run it by here on my way home."

"This isn't on your way home," Amila shared with a soft smile before assuring, "You are such a sweetheart for coming out here just to deliver it for Sophia."

Not being able to stand it, Charlotte questioned, "She was tired or because I was here?"

Penny appeared as though she had no idea what to say.

Amila quickly said, "I'm sure she was just tired. Your name is on the invitation."

Charlotte replied, "Only because Ren's making her invite me."

Penny instantly raised her eyebrows and pursed her lips into a smile. The second Charlotte saw the look on Penny's face, she knew she'd messed up.

What was wrong with her? She had just out-ed herself to Penny. No way she would be able to deny being at Auggie's now. Charlotte was always careful and thought about what came out of her mouth before she said anything. Lately, speaking without thinking had become a problem for Charlotte.

While Charlotte was still reeling with regret, Amila offered, "Would you like to stay for a little bit?"

"I'd better get going. I have one more to deliver, thank you though," Penny said before asking, "Charlotte, you wanna ride with me?"

Caught off guard, Charlotte replied, "Where?"

"To deliver the last invitation," Penny answered with a secretive expression.

Since Charlotte didn't know Penny all that well she said, "Okay," just in case Penny decided to share what she knew in front of Amila.

Amila walked over to Charlotte and gave her a hug, whispering, "I'm glad you're making friends."
Forcing a smile, Charlotte met Penny at the door before they left together.

As Penny pulled away from the house, Charlotte sat in the passenger seat, debating on possible reasons Penny invited her along. She wanted to like Penny but the knowledge that her best friend was Sophia, the biggest gossip in town, was making it a little hard to.

"Where are we going?"

"The Dog House," Penny replied, glancing at her to see her reaction.

Wondering what she was up to, Charlotte griped, "Then you might as well turnaround because you know I can't go there."

"Says who?" Penny asked as if it was the first she'd heard of it.

"Your brother!"

"So, it's not even his bar. It belongs to Jackson."

Charlotte was making an effort to not be angry with Penny as she griped, "I don't know what you're trying to start here, but I'm not interested in causing trouble."

"Neither am I," Penny replied.

"Then what is the point of going?"

Appearing frustrated at first, Penny gave a short exhale, smiled and said, "I'm tired of being asked when I'm gonna settle down, why I haven't, getting advice on how I can

155

make that happen and honestly, if I hear about one more baby anything, I am going to lose it."

Charlotte started to smile, then questioned, "I thought your family hated me."

Giving Charlotte an absurd look Penny blurted, "Who said that?" before informing, "I don't think my family knows how to hate. We're more water under the bridge people."

"Augustus isn't."

"Augustus," Penny laughed, "Isn't the spokesman for our family."

Trying to steer the conversation away from him, Charlotte asked, "So do you really have an invitation to deliver?"

"Yea, I have Auggie's. I thought about bringing it by his house, but the last time I was there, he was acting all rude because he was hiding a girl behind the door."

Seeing as her idea to sway their talk in a different direction didn't work, Charlotte questioned, "How did you know I was there?"

Pursing her lips into a smile, Penny replied, "Other than the fact that Auggie was acting weird, I smelled your perfume."

"I don't wear perfume."

"I swear if you say that's just your natural smell, I'm gonna throw up on you!"

Laughing out loud, Charlotte said, "Gross!" As Penny laughed with her, Charlotte shared, "Its lotion."

"Lotion?"

Nodding with an excited smile, Charlotte replied, "Erin gave it to me for by birthday one year in a gift set. Its pure seduction from Victoria's Secret. She said the fragrance matched my appearance. I don't know about that, but it smelled so delicious the first time I wore it, I spent the whole afternoon smelling my own arm."

Penny laughed, saying, "It does smell good and yea, she was right."

Thinking about how much fun she was already having with Penny, Charlotte said, "Thanks for asking me to ride along."

With a shoulder shrug, Penny smiled pulling into a parking spot in front of the bar.

ॐॐ

Auggie was surprised The Dog House was so busy considering the fair was in town. It wasn't as packed as a normal Friday night, his brothers' band was even playing at the fair instead of at the bar. Watching the clock, he intended to send a text at exactly 10:30.

"Lou, I'm gonna step into the office for a minute."

After Old Lou gave him a nod in response, Auggie headed to the back.

Stepping into the office, Auggie closed the door behind himself and leaned his back against it. Pulling his phone out of his back pocket, he typed 'Sunday' and watched the clock as he waited to hit send. While he waited, Auggie couldn't help thinking of seeing Charlotte walk through his front door. She made him crazy in every way possible. He couldn't stop thinking about her or the feeling he got every time he thought about her.

At 10:30 Auggie hit send and stepped out of the back office. Pushing through the double doors that led into the main area of the bar, he stopped, unable to believe what he was seeing. At first he thought he might be hallucinating. Then he thought maybe Charlotte had been on his mind so much, he was fantasizing seeing her at the bar, since it was remarkably similar to a dream he had the other night. If it weren't for Penny standing next to her, he'd never have believed she was really there.

Making his way back behind the bar, Auggie's eyes trailed the length of her legs from her sandals all the way to the bottom of her tiny blue skirt. His mouth went dry and his throat felt like it was closing up on him when Charlotte glanced at him. He wanted to be alone with her.

"This is for you," Penny announced, holding a pink envelope out towards him.

Penny's distraction irritated him in the worst way.

Snatching it out of her hand, Auggie griped, "Thanks," before sliding it in his pocket.

"You're welcome," Penny sarcastically replied before turning to Charlotte saying, "I'm gonna run to the bathroom. Do you wanna grab us a table? I'll be right back."

Auggie watched Charlotte nod at Penny as she headed towards the restrooms.

"Two beers," Charlotte ordered, not making eye contact with him.

"You mean a beer and a club soda. Penny doesn't drink."

Almost glaring at him, Charlotte replied, "The beers are for me. I assumed Penny could order her own drink."

Scowling at her, he snapped, "You're starting with two?"

Charlotte narrowed her eyes, correcting, "You know, you're right. Give me two shots and two beers."

"You tryin' to get drunk?"

"Why else would I be here?"

Without fully understanding what had come over him, he was angry she wasn't there to see him.

Keeping his voice low, Auggie growled, "Damn it Charlotte, you don't need to be here."

"Don't tell me what I need."

"Fine, I won't but I don't have to serve you either."

"Are you serious?" Charlotte snapped as Penny slid onto the barstool next to her.

"Oh, we're staying at the bar?" Penny asked with a smile.

Auggie fussed, "No, y'all are leaving."

"Why?" Penny blurted before Charlotte snapped, "What is your problem?"

"I don't want you here," he growled, causing nearly everyone at the bar to take notice of their argument.

Turning to walk away, Charlotte stated, "Then I'll leave."

Penny appeared genuinely sorry as she hopped off of her barstool, saying, "Let's go," before she turned to Auggie assuring, "You're such a jerk."

Auggie quickly snapped, "Stay out of it Pen. This doesn't have anything to do with you."

Charlotte whipped around and fussed, "How about you stay out of things that have nothing to do with you."

"Excuse me?" Auggie questioned in disbelief.

"You heard me," Charlotte said before adding, "Nothing I do has anything to do with you."

Giving her a dead stare, he shrugged his shoulders and motioned towards the doors.

Auggie watched Charlotte turn, hook her arm around his sister's and walk out. Nudged from behind he turned to find Lou with a disappointed expression on his face.

"You were a little hard on Penny and her friend, don't ya think?"

Auggie griped, "She just... She makes me so damn crazy."

"Penny?"

With a heavy sigh, Auggie placed his hand over his mouth, slid it down his beard and shook his head.

❧

The second Charlotte and Penny stepped out of the bar, Charlotte let go of Penny's arm and stepped away from her. What made her think going to The Dog House would end any other way? He didn't even acknowledge her presence at the bar until she ordered drinks.

Appearing concerned Penny swore, "I'm so sorry. I promise, I didn't..."

Forcing a smile, Charlotte assured, "I know."

With an astonished expression, Penny asked, "You're not mad at me?"

"As long as the next time you ask me to ride with you, we go anywhere but here."

Heading to the car, Penny laughed a little, saying, "I sure hope you hold out on him for a while after he acted like that."

"What?"

Penny waited until they were both seated in the car before replying, "I must really look stupid." As Charlotte shook her head, Penny continued, "Look whatever y'all have goin' on is none of my business."

Leaning her head back, Charlotte started, "There is nothing..." stopping suddenly when there was a knock at Penny's window.

As Charlotte turned her head towards the window, Penny arched an eyebrow at her asking, "Nothing huh?"

Charlotte didn't say a word as Penny rolled her window halfway down.

"What do you want?"

"Get outta the car Pen," Auggie stated in a gruff tone.

"What for?"

"Because I'm asking you to."

Penny glanced at Charlotte before rolling her window up, opening the door and stepping out of the car.

Charlotte watched Penny walk in front of the car with her brother. Feeling a little betrayed by Penny at the moment, she couldn't be that mad at her for helping her brother. After a moment, Penny walked back to the bar as Auggie made his way to the driver's side of the car.

As soon as Auggie slid into the driver's seat, Charlotte blurted, "Save it," adding, "I have nothing to say to you."

Auggie shut the driver's side door, saying, "Yea well, I don't know what to say to you."

With a loud huff, she stated, "An apology would be nice."

Shifting to face her, Auggie confirmed, "I don't want you in there."

Adjusting herself in her seat, she leaned toward him, saying, "Awe, your right. That's not mean at all."

"What's mean about that?"

Charlotte stared at the baffled expression on his face. She had been so busy trying not to look at him inside, she didn't get the chance to appreciate how good he looked. Even with that stupid beanie on, he was a sight for sore eyes. Being in such a small space with Auggie caused her to let go of what had happened inside. She just wanted to sit there close to him.

"Nothing. It doesn't matter."

Auggie's eyes scanned her face, "What doesn't matter?"

"I don't care that you don't want me at the bar."

"Then why are you mad?"

"I would have at least said hello to you."

Scowling with an irritated expression, he asked, "So why didn't you?"

"I was going to."

"But you didn't," he snapped at her.

Why did he insist on arguing with her? She needed silence. Quiet while she was sitting there with him so she could figure out the feelings she was having for him.

"'Cause you didn't look happy to see me," she blurted, knowing that would shut him up.

Auggie couldn't believe what he had just heard come out of Charlotte's mouth. Facing forward, he leaned his head back against the headrest, rubbed the sides of his face with his hands and closed his eyes. He needed to get out of the car. He needed to go back into the bar. He needed to stop all this nonsense. Drawing in a deep breath, Auggie opened his eyes and shifted in the seat to face her.

Charlotte was looking at him, not staring just looking with an interested expression on her face. Whatever Auggie thought he was going to say to her quickly fell by the wayside.

"I a...I was surprised, not unhappy."

Her expression remained the same as she questioned, "Surprised in a good way?"

Clenching his teeth to keep himself from being too honest, he waited a moment before answering, "It wasn't bad."

Charlotte curled the corner of her mouth into a smile as she glanced to the side, whispering, "Good."

The air between Auggie and Charlotte grew thick as he watched her hand slowly make its way towards his. His entire body was fully aware of her touch the instant her fingers slid against his palm.

"What are y'all doing in there?" followed by a tap on the windshield caused them both to jump.

❧

As Auggie quickly opened the door and jumped out, Charlotte noticed the car windows were foggy. Shaking her head at herself, she thought 'Great'.

"Really? In mom's car?" Penny teased as Auggie griped, "Grow up."

Penny slid in the car giggling.

The moment she shut the door Charlotte swore, "We were just talking."

Penny rolled her eyes, saying, "I know. He's my brother, giving each other a hard time is what we do."

Charlotte nodded, trying to recover from the shock of Penny interrupting her and Auggie's moment.

The car ride was silent for about ten minutes before Penny started to ask questions.

"So, is it still nothing?"

Unsure herself, Charlotte admitted, "I don't know."

"Because you have a boyfriend?" Penny questioned in a serious tone.

"It's not like that."

"What's it like then?" Penny asked clearly unhappy with her.

"Look, it's... Trace and I aren't together right now. I mean, we were seeing each other but now I'm not sure if marrying him is really what I want to do."

"You're engaged?"

"He was gonna ask when he comes back to get me. I guess he still will, but we aren't together like that."

"I'm confused."

Charlotte gave a slight laugh, saying, "That makes two of us."

Penny seemed okay with Charlotte's confusion as she laughed, "Finally, someone with a more complicated love life than mine."

Interested, Charlotte decided it was her turn to ask some questions.

"What about the guy at Legacy Ink?"

Shrugging as she made a face, Penny replied, "He's alright."

"That doesn't sound so complicated."

"I'm friends with every ex I've ever had."

"Oh."

"Yea well, I'm a lot of fun to be around ya know."

Charlotte noticed the disappointment on Penny's face.

"You are a lot of fun. I think maybe you just need a better class of people to hang around."

Penny laughed, "Easier said than done. I have quite the reputation around here."

"So do I..."

"Yea but I earned mine."

The car was quiet for a minute.

"Anyway, sorry tonight was kind of a bust."

Charlotte smiled wide, saying, "I had a great time."

"You really need to get out more!"

They both laughed as Penny pulled up to Charlotte's house.

❧ 17 ❧

Tattoo

What started out as a wonderful day, one Charlotte was sure would only get better, turned into a gigantic mess, in the span of ten minutes.

Charlotte had received her last ransom text the night before. Not only was she excited to get her favorite stilettos back, the meeting was early enough that she could still have a girl's night with Lola. She even found the perfect dress to make the exchange. Originally, she thought it would be funny but once she slipped into the pink and green plaid sundress she bought, she actually liked it. It was strapless but had a high enough back that her tattoo was the only mark that showed and she hoped Auggie would like it too.

Tossing Auggie's socks in her purse, she grabbed her phone and tossed that in too. Before she could open her bedroom door, it swung open.

"It's polite to knock," Charlotte griped at Silvia standing in her doorway.

"Mom said you left this in her car," Silvia said, throwing a shopping bag on her floor.

Bending down to pick up her glue that rolled out of her bag from the craft store, Charlotte shouted, "Gah, you are such a..." when Silvia cut her off taunting, "Oh my gosh!"

To make matters worse, Emerson walked in, holding the house phone in his hand.

Silvia flashed a malicious smile at Charlotte before turning to Emerson, announcing, "Daddy! Charlotte has a tattoo!"

Emerson stood, glancing between the two for a moment before informing, "Trace wanted to speak to you," as he held the cordless phone out to Charlotte.

Snatching the phone from him, Charlotte put the phone to her ear only to hear a dial tone.

Hearing her phone vibrating in her purse, Charlotte questioned, "Why were you on the phone with him?"

"His father is interested in making a donation to our foundation," he replied, clearly confused by her reaction.

Handing the phone back to him, Charlotte snapped. "Well, he hung up."

"When did you get a tattoo?" Emerson questioned before Silvia chimed in, "So trashy."

Furious, Charlotte stormed past them. Rushing through the house, Charlotte almost ran into Amila walking into the kitchen from the back door.

"What's wrong honey?"

Hearing her phone vibrate in her purse again, Charlotte replied, "Tell Lola I'll be back for our girls night I have to go," as she hurried past her.

Pulling into a dead end street after leaving her house, Charlotte shifted her car into park. She grabbed her cellphone out of her purse as it vibrated in her hand.

T: Please tell me I misunderstood.

T: I am calling you!!!

T: It is best you do not answer. I am incredibly disappointed in you.

After reading Trace's texts, she cleared the two missed calls from him before texting back.

C: Disappointed? Why?

T: How could you do that to yourself?

C: Excuse me????

T: You did not even consult me!

C: That's because it's my body!

T: You don't have enough defects already without purposely adding another one?

C: F-YOU!

Charlotte was so angry she almost threw her phone out of her car window. She threw her cell phone in her purse instead, slammed her shifter in reverse and peeled out onto the main road.

The drive to Auggie's did nothing to calm Charlotte down. Pounding on his door with the side of her fist, she wished it was Trace's face instead. When the door slowly opened, she looked right past Auggie as she walked into his house.

"Come on in," Auggie griped as she threw her purse down on his coffee table and made her way straight to his kitchen.

Flinging his refrigerator door open, she grabbed a Guinness then started digging through his kitchen drawers for a bottle opener.

❧☙

Picking his bottle opener up off of the coffee table on his way to the kitchen, Auggie wondered what had gotten into her. She looked pissed.

Stepping next to her, he cleared his throat before asking, "Can I help you?"

Charlotte slammed a drawer closed before shoving her beer at him, blurting, "No."

Auggie couldn't take his eyes off of her as she stood there in front of him. She had a wild look about her. It was clear she was angry. Her face went flush and her hands were shaking. He was never one for overly emotional girls but on her, it was extremely attractive.

An overwhelming need to calm her, compelled him to whisper, "Baby," as he reached out to touch her.

Charlotte's eyes flew open wide as if he had called her something else that started with a B as she leaped back, shouting, "My name is Charlotte!"

Auggie's mood instantly changed with Charlotte's outburst.

"You can take all that yellin' somewhere else," he growled, adding, "Sweetheart," simply because he knew it would irritate her.

All of the sudden, she was right in front of him, shouting, "I am Charlotte! Not Sweetheart! Do not call me names! Not honey! Not Defective! Charlotte! My name is Charlotte!"

Auggie started to yell back, stopping when part of her rant didn't make sense to him.

Backing away slightly, he fussed, "I never said that about you."

Charlotte turned and walked out of his kitchen.

Not understanding what was going on, Auggie was furious with her. Confused was something he wasn't fond of being but it was something that had become fairly common since she had come back to town. Watching her grab her purse, he couldn't let her leave without knowing what was wrong with her.

"Charlotte."

Auggie watched her stop dead in her tracks.

"Charlotte," he repeated, waiting for her to turn around.

She dropped her purse at her feet.

Watching her slowly turn towards him, from the kitchen, Auggie assured, "I would never say that to you."

Charlotte appeared calm as she narrowed her eyes and asked, "Do you think it?"

"If I thought it I would say it."

Reaching down, Charlotte grabbed her purse and walked to Auggie's kitchen table. Setting her purse down, she reached into it before holding his socks out to him.

Auggie had never met anyone who switched gears that fast. She had been out of her mind seconds before she was eerily calm. Slowly making his way towards her, he reminded himself not to make any sudden movements. The truth of it was, he didn't know her history. She could be mentally unstable for all he knew. After all, she had flipped out when he tried to touch her.

With a loud huff, she reached back into her purse with her other hand, yanked out her phone as it vibrated in her hand, then slammed it face down on his table.

Appearing impatient with him, Charlotte waved his socks around, asking, "Do you still want them back?"

Taking his socks from her, he set them on the table, saying, "I think you cracked it," as he lifted her cellphone off of the table.

Charlotte opened her mouth as if to say something, then stood there staring at him. The corner of her screen was shattered with several hairline cracks spreading across it. Through her broken screen, Auggie read the texts on her phone.

As soon as he read what that creep had said to her he tossed her phone back on the table, saying, "What the hell?"

"I got a tattoo."

Those four words burned their way into Auggie's mind causing his only reaction to be, "Can I see it?"

Hesitantly, she nodded.

His mind ran wild with possibilities as he asked, "Where is it?"

Without answering him, Charlotte reached around her head with her left arm and pulled her hair away from her right shoulder.

Auggie stepped around her to see what her hair had been covering. He was pretty sure he stopped breathing for a minute when he saw a white peacock feather on her back. He could tell it was still healing, but he couldn't stop himself from touching her.

Softly running his finger against her skin next to her feather, he whispered, "Beautiful."

Auggie expected her to flinch. When she relaxed her shoulders and looked down instead, he spread his fingers across the top of her bare shoulder.

Leaning closer, he swore, "A real man would know that every mark on your body is beautiful because it's a part of you."

Charlotte turned, looking up at Auggie with surprise. As Auggie leaned closer, she pulled her lips into her mouth, and started to tilt her head to the side. Finding that unacceptable, he caught her chin, gently tilting her face back to his. Softly grazing her lips with his thumb as she released them from her mouth, he couldn't help himself.

Closing the space between them, he breathed, "Lotte," as he pressed his lips against hers.

The softness of Charlotte's lips against his, mixed with the subtle firmness of her scar was the best thing he had ever felt. How could anyone think this was a defect? It was like a blessing. No woman in the world had lips like hers. Smooth like her skin, sweet like her smell and beautiful just like her.

૱∘ஒ

Charlotte swore she could still feel Auggie's lips against hers after he pulled away. The moment felt more intimate than anything she had experienced. How was this possible? Slowly opening her eyes, she felt closer to him than she had to anyone in her entire life. Seeing one side of his face crunch up into his smile, she felt like she was sinking. Trying to remember what her first kiss felt like, a couple of years before her scar, she couldn't. There was nothing. There was no one. Just him, until she heard her phone vibrate against the table.

The noise coming from her phone seemed to break the moment for both of them. Charlotte watched Auggie's smile fade into a scowl as he took a step back.

"I have to go," Charlotte blurted, unsure of what was happening to her.

Taking another step back, Auggie nodded.

Feeling the need to explain, she shared, "I made plans with Lola."

Without saying a word, he nodded again.

Her feet didn't seem to listen to her as she repeated, "I have to go," more for herself this time.

Seemingly helping her out, Auggie stated, "Lola," as she continued to stand there waiting for him to say something else.

Charlotte glanced around the room and nodded before grabbing her phone and purse off of his kitchen table. As she made her way to his front door, she wondered why he wasn't saying anything to her. Thinking maybe she should say something, she hesitated before deciding against it and walked out of his front door.

18

Temporary

Sitting in his chair after Charlotte left, Auggie couldn't seem to get his mind right. He should have stopped her from walking out. He should have said something. He couldn't. Auggie actually thought for a moment he was having a heart attack. Frustrated with himself, he thought he shouldn't have kissed her at all. She was upset. He wanted to make her feel better. Why didn't he just say, 'Your boyfriend's a douche' and leave it at that? Then he wouldn't be sitting there alone wondering what she thought about the kiss.

Auggie's front door suddenly swung open. His body tensed in anticipation. The thrill of seeing her again was almost too much until he saw Braden instead of Charlotte walk in.

Strolling to the couch, Braden flopped down greeting, "What's up brother?"

Auggie groaned, relaxing back in his chair, "Nothing."

"Man, what did you do?"

Scowling at his brother, a hint of panic coursed through him.

"You look like the cat that ate the canary."

Thinking to himself 'It was a peacock', Auggie griped, "What do you want?"

"I need a reason to come visit my big brother?"

"Usually."

A wide smile spread across Braden's face as he admitted, "Lily and her mother in law are back. So I'm waiting for the nosy ol' bat to leave."

"Back from where?"

"County."

Shaking his head, Auggie fussed, "Let me get this straight, you're hiding out here so you can hook up with her after she's been to see her husband in jail."

"Don't make it dirty, she only went to get his mom off her back."

"Yea, that's why," Auggie sarcastically replied.

"You don't know."

"Neither do you."

"I know she's gonna ask him for a divorce when he gets out."

Shaking his head at his brother, Auggie stood up and walked to his kitchen. He'd need a beer for this conversation.

Grabbing the beer Charlotte had pulled out of the fridge from the counter Auggie's mind flashed back to her standing in his kitchen. Shaking it off, he grabbed his bottle opener and popped the cap off of his beer before making his way back to the living room.

Before Auggie made it back to his chair, Braden shared, "I'm thinkin' about making an appointment with Kieran. I still have it."

Recalling the heart Braden had their mom draw the night he was going to propose to Lily, Auggie discouraged, "She's still married."

Braden shot him a dirty look, saying, "Jackson got his while Ren was still married."

"I know you're not comparing her to Ren," Auggie snapped.

"Still have a little crush on her do ya?"

"Want me to put you through the door again do ya?"

"Don't know. You still hidin' her picture in your underwear drawer?"

Remembering the crazy crush he had on Ren during his teenage years, he had long since grown out of it. Ren was gorgeous, but it was her attitude that had been most attractive to him. He respected her. Auggie never thought he would meet a woman that compared to her, until now.

Focusing back on his brother, to keep his thoughts of Charlotte at bay, Auggie fussed, "Man you know damn good and well, Lily's gonna go back with him the minute he's out."

Standing up, Braden argued, "I already told you, she's gonna ask for a divorce."

"Why ask? Why wait for him to get out? Why not file for divorce now?"

Braden appeared hurt as he replied, "Why not be my brother and have my back?"

"I always got your back, just like the first time around."

"That's not gonna happen again."

"The girl that cheated on you is cheating with you and you think things will somehow turn out different?"

"She was mine first!"

"Is that what this is? A pride thing? You tryin' to get back at Keven for doin' her behind your back?"

"Like your hard-hearted ass would understand," Braden snapped, turning towards the front door.

"I'm your brother."

"Act like it then." Pulling his cellphone out of his back pocket, Braden replied, "Lily texted, I gotta go."

Shaking his head, Auggie said, "Be careful."

"You know I will."

Thinking to himself 'Damn fool', Auggie gave his brother a nod.

৵৵

Charlotte arrived home to find Emerson and Amila waiting in the kitchen for her. She had hoped to go straight to her room. Maybe scream into her pillow. Definitely think about the kiss. Now she was stuck in the kitchen having a conversation with her parents.

"Lola's friend invited her to spend the night," Amila shared with an apprehensive expression on her face before Emerson stated, "We would like to talk to you."

Thinking, 'What is this, an intervention', Charlotte stood next to the kitchen table where Emerson and Amila sat, saying, "I would like to go to my room."

Emerson cleared his throat before questioning, "Where have you been?"

"Out."

With a disapproving stare, he stated, "You cannot tell us where you were?"

Glancing at Amila's sweet yet concerned smile, Charlotte replied, "I can. I just choose not to."

"Because you think we will not approve?" Emerson replied.

With a loud huff, Charlotte assured, "Because I am a grown up and it's none of anyone's business what I do. And trust me, approval isn't something I need."

Amila quickly broke in, saying, "Charlotte, we know you are a grown up but you are also back under our roof and it's common courtesy to be respectful."

"I'm not trying to be disrespectful."

Emerson stood up, "It must come naturally to you then because that is exactly what you are being."

Counting backwards from ten in her head, Charlotte focused on Amila, asking, "Is this because I got a tattoo?"

Emerson answered before Amila had a chance to, "We are having this conversation because you brought a very nice and respectable man home to meet us and as soon as he left, you have been going out doing God knows what."

Amila chimed in, saying, "We just want to make sure you are okay," as she gave Emerson a 'That's enough' stare.

As Charlotte felt herself growing angrier at Emerson's statement, she looked at Amila and informed, "Since Lola's not coming home tonight, I'm going out. I will call if I stay the night somewhere, so you don't worry." Then glaring at Emerson, she stated, "As far as where I go and what I do while I'm there, that's not any of your business."

Charlotte started to walk out of the kitchen, when the phone rang.

Amila answered the phone, motioning for Charlotte to stay.

While Amila seemed to be listening to whoever was on the line, Emerson lowered his voice, saying, "Trace called after you left. He said he may have upset you and would like to apologize."

Charlotte could not believe what she was hearing.

Amila walked up and handed Charlotte the cordless, saying, "Sorry is just a word," loud enough so Trace could hear her.

Charlotte's hand started to shake as she took the phone, answering, "Hello."

"My lovely, please forgive me."

Glancing between Emerson and Amila, who clearly were not going to leave the room, Charlotte replied, "Why should I."

Trace's voice was low as he explained, "I was shocked. Much like you were when I shared something I enjoy with you and you found it unpleasant."

"I don't feel we are on the same page with that," she replied, filtering her answer in front of her parents.

"I know your environment there is trying. I understand. I am also suffering. Being so far from you has affected me in many ways. I do apologize for overreacting. My behavior was uncalled for. Please take the time you have left there to think things over. You and I have a significant amount of time invested in each other. You do not have to forgive me. All I ask is that you consider the time we have spent together and recognize whatever takes place while you are away will have no bearing on your life once you are home."

Charlotte took a moment to consider what Trace was saying.

"You are coming back?"

"Yes," she replied, reminding herself that this town and the people in it were temporary for her.

"Then please my beauty, do not decide anything until I return for you."

A bit overwhelmed by her own thoughts, she replied, "Okay," and hung up the phone.

As Charlotte set the phone down on the table, Amila asked, "Are you alright honey?"

Nodding, she walked past Emerson and Amila and headed to her room.

There was a lot of truth in what Trace said. Whether she ended up accepting his proposal or not, this was not her home and she had no intentions of staying.

∂∾∾∾

Fighting the same battle with the dreaded ledger book as he had before Charlotte intervened, Auggie got up from his kitchen table and grabbed a Guinness out of his refrigerator. He thought about calling her then quickly decided against it. He wasn't about to let her think he couldn't handle things without her. If she had been interested in the least she would have stayed.

Just as he was about to sit down at the table and get back at it, there was a knock at his door. Taking a seat, he figured it was Braden. It was unlocked so eventually he would let himself in once he got tired of knocking.

Focusing on the ledger, Auggie asked, "Change of plans?" when he heard his front door open.

"Something like that."

Auggie quickly looked up and almost fell out of his chair when he saw Charlotte step in and close the door behind herself.

"I thought you were Braden."

"Oh-kay."

"He was here earlier."

Nodding, she made her way to the table.

Confused Auggie had no idea why she was there or why she was dressed the way she was. Standing next to the table without taking a seat, Charlotte was wearing a pair of black slacks and a grey v-neck t-shirt. He would never have guessed she owned a pair of pants, but he figured it was her way of saying keep your hands to yourself.

⇜⇝

Charlotte eased herself into the seat next to him. After several occasions when Auggie made disapproving comments about her wardrobe, now that she was dressed a bit more modest he was looking at her like she was wearing a trash bag.

"Need some help?" she asked, glancing at the ledger.

Scowling at her, he griped, "Nope."

Deciding the kiss was an error in his judgment, she stood back up, saying, "I'll just take my heels and go then."

He gave her a blank stare before standing up and walking to his room. Shaking her head at herself, she felt stupid. She knew what was going on and she didn't appreciate it one bit.

Standing in the living room, Charlotte waited for her heels. Once she had her favorite stilettos back, she would tell him off and then finally be done with this particular member of the Caffrey family once and for all.

"Here ya go," Auggie said, handing them to her.

Snatching them out of his hand, Charlotte did a quick inspection to make sure nothing had happened to them in his care.

"Look a... earlier."

Hugging her heels tight to her chest, she assured, "I had a moment of uncertainty."

"Is that right?"

"Yes. So don't put yourself out. I don't need pity from someone like you."

"Someone like me? I don't do pity so don't go thinkin' I would feel sorry for you. Even for a second."

Furious he wouldn't admit what she had decided he was guilty of, Charlotte questioned, "Then what was it?"

"Uncertainty," he replied with a sarcastic expression.

Nodding, Charlotte said, "Well, that's it then."

৵৽

Standing in front of Charlotte, Auggie couldn't believe she thought he felt sorry for her or that he would kiss her out of pity. She's the one that walked out earlier. Deciding she was working some sort of angle, he was tired of having to defend himself to her.

"That's it? That's all you have to say for yourself?"

Charlotte's mood had noticeably shifted as she replied, "What would you like me to say?"

"Unbelievable," he blurted throwing his arms up in the air before correcting himself, "No, I do believe it. You have been tormenting me since the moment you got back to town..."

Cutting him off as she shoved her finger in his face, Charlotte fussed, "You are the one that has been ridiculous this whole time."

"I'm ridiculous?" he shouted at her before taunting, "Augustus, let me help you. Let me strut around your house in next to nothing. Augustus, take me to a club. Let me rub up against you every single chance I get. Augustus, I'm gonna mess with you as much as possible but wait I don't like to be picked on. Augustus..."

"If I'm so horrible then why did you kiss me?"

Having reached his breaking point, Auggie snapped, "'Cause you're sexy as hell especially when you're not tryin' and I can't get you outta my damn head."

Taking a deep breath, she spouted, "I'm leaving."
Instantly thinking, 'Good riddance', Auggie waited for her to walk out.

The longer he stood there waiting for her to leave, the harder it was for him to be happy about her walking out of his door. Why wasn't she going? She was just standing there looking like there were a million things going through his mind without saying a word.

Feeling her presence and her silence pulling him closer to her, he asked, "Why did you let me kiss you?"

Her voice was soft as she replied, "You make me feel... I'm leaving."

Scowling at her he wondered 'Feel what, good?' as he said, "You haven't left yet. Answer me."

࿊

Something clicked and Charlotte realized he was right. She hadn't left yet. Why spend the rest of her time here miserable when she could be spending it with him. There was no big decision to make there. He'd kissed her, not proposed. How was she supposed to make the right choice for the rest of her life when she's holding out on herself.

"Kiss me."
Without hesitation, Auggie's hands slid to the sides of her face as his lips pressed against hers.

A slow sideways smile spread across Auggie's face as Charlotte opened her eyes.

Feeling a smile of her own forming, Charlotte shared, "Good. You make me feel good."

181

Auggie closed his eyes and leaned his forehead against hers for a moment before reaching down and taking her heels away. After carefully setting them on his coffee table, he wrapped his arms around her waist and pulled her against him.

"I want you to stay the night."

Charlotte's entire being instantly responded to his words.

"Not tonight."

"Tomorrow?"

Sliding her hands up Auggie's chest and around to the back of his neck, Charlotte replied, "Don't ruin this."

His eyes reflected a genuine understanding of her request as he slowly nodded before pulling her into another kiss.

19

Rules

Penny was sitting on the front porch of their mom's house when Auggie walked up. Seeing her sitting on the porch swing holding the bottom of her long auburn hair in her hand as she skimmed her finger along the ends, something she only did when she was upset, he sat down next to her.

"What's wrong Henny Penny?"

Turning away from him, Penny grumbled, "Shut up Auggie."

"Come on, now," he urged nudging her a bit.

"Just go inside and leave me alone."

Shaking his head at her, Auggie stood up and headed into the house.

Wondering what Penny's problem was as he made his way to the kitchen, he could hear his mom banging pots and pans around.

"Hey Ma," he greeted as Sarah swung around and slammed a pot against the kitchen table.

"That girl needs to get her priorities straight."

Taking a deep breath, Auggie stepped towards his mom. This wasn't an unusual conversation. Every few months Sarah would get tired of Penny's lack of motivation and life goals.

Shaking her head at him, Sarah sat at the kitchen table placed her hand across her forehead, sharing, "Your sister has crossed the line this time. At least you have some sense."

"How am I in this?"

Sarah quickly stood up and turned toward the sink, saying, "The last thing she needs is to start running around with someone like Charlotte."

Deciding she was talking about the other night at the bar, he replied, "Ma, I..."

"And don't you worry, I told Sheryl I was sure you were avoiding a scene by going out to the car to speak with her. That girl sure has it in for you and I don't want the whole town to think your sneaking around with Charlotte Roberts."

Auggie shook his head and scowled as he agreed, "Yea."

With a heavy sigh, Sarah turned to him, assuring, "Don't get me wrong, I don't hold any ill will against her and neither should you. She just isn't for this family."

If Sarah only knew, 'Ill will' wasn't what he wanted to hold against Charlotte, she would probably disown him.

"Let me go talk to Penny, okay."

Nodding, Sarah hugged Auggie, "Maybe she'll listen to you."

The second Sarah let go, he headed out of the kitchen unable to look at his mom.

Once again, Sheryl was causing trouble for him and for no good reason other than, she could. As he made his way out of the front door Penny was on her way in. Shaking his head at her, Auggie shooed her back outside.

"I'm not allowed inside now?"

Frowning at her, Auggie snapped, "Calm down."

"It's not fair! She acts like y'all are saints and I can't do anything right."

With a slight laugh, he assured, "We're not."

"I know that, stupid," she blurted before griping, "I haven't even come close to doing what y'all have done. It's not fair."

"I know Pen, but you're the baby and mom's only girl," he reminded before teasing, "Except for Ailin but he's already married off."

Holding back a smile, she warned, "Don't do that, I'm mad right now."

Placing his arm around his sister, Auggie advised, "If you moved out, you wouldn't have to answer to her."
Penny shrugged his arm off of her shoulders and rolled her eyes.

As Auggie stood there staring at her, he realized she was exactly who he needed to talk to.

"So you're a girl."

Penny instantly laughed, saying, "If I'm not, I know quite a few guys that are fixing to have a real identity crisis."

Scowling, he griped, "I don't want to hear that."

Pursing her lips at him, she replied, "Fine, yes Auggie I'm a girl."

Stopping a moment to think, he said, "Say I met someone..."

"Am I supposed to pretend I don't know who we're talking about?"

"I'd appreciate it."

Rolling her eyes as she shook her head, "Go on."

"How do I not ruin it?"

"What makes you think you would?"

Scowling at her, he said, "Walk with me out to my truck."
Making their way off of the porch, Auggie mentally questioned how much he really wanted to share with his sister.

"I'm not good at this Pen," he admitted.

"In case you hadn't heard, neither am I," Penny replied as they reached his truck.

"Never mind," he mumbled, reaching for the door handle of his truck.

"Okay, wait. What does she like?"

Shrugging, he replied, "She drinks beer."

"Seriously?"

Racking his brain, he blurted, "Clothes!" before sharing, "I've never seen her wear the same thing twice."

Taking a slow deep breath, Penny said, "Oh my goodness... Auggie, as simple as you are, women are a little more complicated than that."

"What do you mean?"

"Look, since you've never had anything steady, it's probably better if you take it back to high school," as he gave her a confused stare she added, "You know how did you get a girl to go out with you then?"

"I never asked."

"How did you go on dates then?"

"I didn't. Before I started working at the bar with dad, I'd go to a party and..."

With one hand against the top of her stomach and the other stretched out facing him, Penny stopped him, "No. Just... No."

"What?"

"I can't believe you're that guy."

"That guy?"

"Yea, the drunken mistake, my boyfriend cheated on me, the guy I like doesn't like me, make myself feel better, unreliable, don't call, get dressed and go home right after, only in it for himself guy."

Never having thought about it in those terms before, he questioned, "What's wrong with that?"

Penny had a disappointed expression on her face as she scowled at him, answering, "Because if your that guy there will never be anything there to ruin."

Auggie gave her a serious look as he said, "I see."

Shrugging, "Sorry," Penny turned and headed back to her house.

Climbing into his truck, Auggie knew Penny was right but he had no idea what that meant for him and Charlotte.

Pulling into his driveway, Auggie planned on calling Charlotte to ask if she wanted to stop by and see him when he got home from the bar later. As he climbed out of his truck and made his way to the door, he found a pleasant surprise standing next to his front door.

"Tryin' to put your career of breaking and entering behind you?" he teased.

With a wicked little grin, Charlotte reached over, turned the doorknob showing him he caught her in the act.

Pushing the door open, Auggie motioned for her to step in first, saying, "After you, criminal."

"Takes one to know one, hostage taker," Charlotte laughed, making her way into his house.

As he closed the front door, Auggie pulled her against him.

Charlotte felt his kiss throughout her entire body. Sliding her hands up his chest as his arms tightened around her waist, she was fully aware of how she made him feel. With every brush of his lips, there was a slight tug in her chest.

Breaking the kiss before the moment got the better of her, Charlotte asked, "What time do you have to go?"

Leaning his forehead to hers, Auggie assured, "We have plenty of time."

Easing him back, she replied, "Don't get ahead of yourself, Augustus. We need to have a conversation."

Slowly letting go of her, he took a step back, saying, "About what?"

"We need to set some ground rules."

Charlotte watched a disapproving scowl form on Auggie's face before she turned and sat down on his couch.

While she waited for him to sit, which seemed to take longer than necessary to do, Charlotte thought about the rules she had been laying down since she was sixteen. She would have to modify them of course, for one he had already kissed her. In addition to what was previously off limits, she had no idea what to do about the way he made her feel. Everything was different with him. Charlotte never considered what it might be like to have real feelings for someone, until now. Thinking it might be nice to have something like that, she reminded herself that her time in town was limited.

When Auggie finally made his way around the coffee table to sit next to her, he kept his distance. Although Charlotte found his behavior irritating, she was grateful. His disposition made it easier to share her guidelines.

"Obviously, this isn't anything serious."

When his only response was an unhappy expression accompanied by a glare, she decided to continue.

"Sex. If it happens, it happens but I don't want to feel pressured into it or guilty for not putting out when you think I should. So, if we're messing around, don't push yourself farther than you can go without stopping. I'm very aware that there is a point of no return for men and I will be respectful of that. On the other hand, I expect you to be prepared. It isn't that I don't believe what you have told me, but I have never had unprotected sex and you're not going to be the exception."

Auggie gave a slight nod, saying, "That seems fair," then asked, "Anything else?"

"My shirt doesn't come off."

"Ever?"

"Most of the time I wear a camisole or tank top since I don't wear a bra. I don't mind getting down to those but that's as far as I'm willing to go. It can be a serious mood killer if, in the moment, I have to remind you."

"That it?"

Charlotte thought for a moment before replying, "If any of this is a deal breaker let me know now because nothing I've said is up for negotiation or debate."

Auggie sat staring at Charlotte as he pretended to mull over her rules. He was a bit disappointed about the shirt thing but from what he'd seen the first night she stayed at his house, he understood why. All in all, he was impressed with her. She knew exactly what she wanted and none of it seemed unreasonable. She wasn't going to play games.

"I have a few conditions," he shared, mainly to feel like he had some control in this.

Charlotte appeared confused as she asked, "Really?"

"Whatever we do here is between us."

Nodding, she said, "Of course."

"No more breaking into my house."

With a slight frown, she replied, "Okay."

"And I want to see you every day."

Fluttering her eyelashes as she rolled her eyes, Charlotte questioned, "That it?"

Auggie nodded, holding his hand out to her.

As Charlotte slipped her hand into his to shake on it, Auggie closed his hand around hers. Leaning closer, he kissed the top of her hand. Her skin smelled so sweet, there was no way he would be happy until he was able to kiss every inch of her. Charlotte wanted to be in control of whatever this was and he could respect that but that didn't mean he wasn't going to do everything possible to have her begging for what he couldn't stop thinking about.

A sense of satisfaction filled him as Charlotte inched closer. The look in her eyes showed him she was willing, but there was hesitation in her movements. That was one of his favorite things about her. Although she was forward, Charlotte let him be a man. Auggie knew she wanted him, but he wanted Charlotte to need him as badly as he did her. He'd never had the desire for the same girl twice, but he knew, if she let him, he would want her every day until she left.

Ready to take full advantage of having her on his couch, Auggie released her hand.

"Come here," he whispered pulling her closer.

Charlotte leaned forward, wrapping her arms around his neck. He quickly grabbed her by the waist and pulled her sideways onto his lap. Leaning her back against the arm of the couch, he glanced down at her legs stretched out, wishing they weren't covered by the cream colored pants she was wearing. There was too much he wanted to do all at once. Feeling her tug on the back of his neck, Auggie turned his focus just in time to see Charlotte pressing her lips together as she pulled them into her mouth.

He knew it was just a reflex of hers but couldn't stop himself, "Those are mine."

There was a conflicted look in her eyes as Auggie traced his finger along the edge of her lips. Slowly releasing her lips from her mouth, Charlotte closed her eyes just before he claimed them.

∞∞∞

Auggie's words echoed through Charlotte's mind as he kissed her. Her chest started to burn. The feeling was so intense, she wanted to dig her fingers into her chest to make it stop. Her hands disobeyed her as they moved to the sides for Auggie's face instead. Weaving her fingers into his beard, the burning sensation spread throughout the rest of her body until the rhythm of her heart gave away a little secret. It was beating for him.

Relaxing her hands, Charlotte let them fall from his face. Auggie slowly pulled away causing her to open her eyes. The questioning look in his eyes made Charlotte wonder if her heart had revealed its secret to him too.

"You alright?" he whispered.

The word 'No' rang in her head as she replied, "Yea."

Scowling at her, Auggie asked, "You sure?"

Charlotte opened her mouth to answer, but nothing came out.

Lifting her up and off of his lap, Auggie stood up and walked away, mumbling, "Alright then."

Counting backwards from ten in her mind, Charlotte pulled her thoughts together.

Standing up, Charlotte saw Auggie in the kitchen with his back to her. The unfamiliar feeling that was growing inside her was replaced by anger when she realized he was mad simply because she didn't answer him.

Swiftly making her way to the kitchen, she griped, "Is this what it's gonna be like?"

Turning to her, he snapped, "You tell me."

"Tell you what?"

"Feelin' guilty?"

Giving him a stupid look, Charlotte questioned, "What?"

"Aren't you getting engaged or something?"

Taken aback by his issue, Charlotte asked, "This is about Trace?"

With a disgusted expression he griped, "I have to leave to open the bar in a few."

Placing her hand on his arm, she assured, "Augustus, Trace and I are not together. I don't know what I'll do when I go back but whatever it is, it won't be with him."

His eyes searched hers before asking, "Why'd you stop?"

"Why did you?" she countered, unwilling to answer.

A sideways smile formed as Auggie said, "You can't answer a question with a question."

"I can do whatever I want."

Nodding, he pulled Charlotte into a kiss before asking, "You wanna hang around here until I come back?"

The tingling in the pit of her stomach forced her to reply, "I'll see you tomorrow."

With a loud sigh, he walked her to the door.

Each time Charlotte reached for the doorknob, Auggie gave her another goodbye kiss. After around fifteen minutes of saying goodbye, she left with a smile that radiated from deep inside her and a lot to think about.

❧ 20 ❧

Wager

When Charlotte woke, she knew what she needed. There was no better way to clear her head than to go shopping. She needed a dress for Sophia's baby shower, not that she needed a reason to shop but at least Emerson seemed happy, for a change, with her reason for leaving the house.

Trying to decide if she was willing to settle for a dress that was 'Okay' at the local clothing store or if a forty-five minute trip to an actual department store was warranted, Charlotte headed toward the shoe section. A flash of plaid caught her eye, causing an almost giddy feeling to build inside her as she watched a gray beanie making its way through the men's department.

The store was practically empty, aside from a few sales clerks and an old lady. Charlotte thought, so much for clearing her head, she was going to have a little fun.

Finding Auggie standing in the underwear isle, she quietly crept up beside him before warning, "Choose carefully."
Startled, he jumped a little as he turned toward her.

With a serious expression, Charlotte tapped her index finger against her chin, "Decisions, decisions."

She could tell he was holding back a smile as he shook his head at her.

"Now, are you a tighty whitey man or boxer kind of guy?" Stopping to glance at the front his pants as if she could see right through them, she shared, "Ah, boxer briefs."

"What are you doing here?" he quietly asked with a laugh.

"Shopping."

"For men's underwear?"

"Now I am."

With a 'You're crazy' look he blurted, "What?"

Deciding to see what he was made of, Charlotte suggested, "I'll buy yours and you can buy mine."

His crazy look was replaced by a shocked expression as he snapped, "I am not going to the panty department."

Glancing around to make sure no one was looking, she ran a finger down the buttons of his shirt, asking, "Are you scared?"

Auggie quickly blurted, "No," before lowering his voice saying, "That's stupid."

"Because you're scared?" she taunted.

Charlotte could tell she was getting under his skin as he griped, "What kinda man buys panties?"

"The kind that's not scared."

His glare was a tad on the hateful side for a moment.

Auggie's eyes softened into a seductive expression that Charlotte had never seen on him, "You want me to buy your panties?"

Holding her breath, she nodded.

"Stand still, then."

Auggie looked her up and down before stepping directly in front of her. Even if she had wanted to, Charlotte couldn't move.

Staring down at her, Auggie placed his hands around her waist. Moving them lower, he rubbed his palms up and down her hips. Charlotte sighed at the feeling. He stopped for a second, but her relief was short lived. His hands slid to her backside before taking a firm grasp on her behind. Fighting to keep her composure, Charlotte slowly exhaled.

Leaning to her ear, Auggie whispered, "Just getting a feel for your size," as he slowly released her.

Wide eyes, she watched him turn and walk away.

᪢᪡

Auggie made his way out of the store with a package of women's underwear in his bag, wondering what the hell had gotten into him. He couldn't help himself. Charlotte just didn't understand what she was asking of him. Buying her panties was going to drive him insane. Even though he picked out the most boring one's he could find, there was no way he would be able to think about anything else. It was hard enough to control himself around her and now every time he saw her, he would need to know if she were wearing the ones he bought for her. It was going to eat away at his brain. Not to mention she had the nerve to challenge him like that, like he was afraid of her little dare. When the idea came to him, he acted on it. An irresponsible impulse. He knew better than to touch her like that in public. Someone could have seen them together.

His palms were still tingling from having her in his hands as he walked up to his truck. Auggie started to open the door when he heard a voice from behind him.

"Caught ya!"

Swinging around at the sound of his brother's voice, Auggie froze.

"Damn, did you rob The Store?"

Caught between thoughts of Charlotte's panties and the realization that his brother was standing right in front of him as he held a bag with them in his hand, he snapped, "What?"

195

Braden laughed, saying, "You might wanna consider going to confession man, whatever you got goin' on, looks like it's getting to you."

"Shut up," Auggie griped before asking, "Are you here for a reason or do you spend your afternoons harassing people in parking lots?"

"Nah, that's only on Thursdays," he joked before sharing, "Lily's birthday is coming up."

Auggie started to gripe at Braden when he heard the clicking of heels against the pavement.

Without looking, Auggie knew it was Charlotte walking to her car. It was just his luck that this moment was going to be as uncomfortable as possible. Auggie tried not to look over at her but he couldn't stop himself. Charlotte's face appeared flushed and it looked like she was trying to pass by without being noticed.

"Hey, hey Charlotte," Braden called out to her.

Auggie instantly glared at his brother wanting to smack him.

Through gritted teeth, he griped, "What are you doing?"

"Dude, she's hot," Braden blurted.

Forget smacking him, Auggie was going to choke him out.

Apparently, Braden didn't know the hazards of what he was doing as he asked, "Wanna help me out with somethin'?"

Charlotte gave Braden a suspicious smile before heading in their direction.

Tightening his hold around his shopping bag, Auggie held it behind his back. Leaning against his truck, he looked away from her.

Charlotte's tone was guarded as she greeted, "Braden."

Braden's tone was friendlier than Auggie liked as he replied, "It's good to see you."

"Is that right?"

"Mmhmm... It's always good to see you."

Auggie gritted his back teeth so hard his jaw started to ache.

With a slight laugh, Charlotte questioned, "What do you want, Braden?"

He gave a laugh back, answering, "I'm lookin' to get a present for my girl Lily, any suggestions."

"Is it a special occasion?"

"Her birthday."

There was a hint of sarcasm in her voice as she suggested, "Buy her some lilies and play her a song."

Braden was oblivious as he replied, "That's a great idea," before swatting Auggie on the arm saying, "See, harassin' folks in the parking lot pays off."

సౌఐ

Even though she didn't want anyone knowing what they had going on, it dug on her that Auggie was ignoring her. It was the bar all over again.

"Hello, Augustus," she stated.

Auggie stared at her for a moment before replying, "Charlotte."

Charlotte knew she was being irrational, but that didn't change the fact that he had just groped her in the store, yet wouldn't crack a smile at her in front of his brother.

"Whatcha got there?" she asked, glancing at the bag behind his back.

Auggie looked so angry, his nostrils were flaring.

"Is it a secret?" she teased, knowing he was furious with her.

Narrowing his eyes at her, he replied, "Nope."

Curling the corner of her mouth into a smile, she shared, "What a shame, I like secrets."

Braden cut into the conversation, laughing, "Man, how can you not like her?"

Appearing as though he was about to lose it, Auggie pushed off from his truck.

Giggles erupted from behind them as a group of teenage girls slowly walked up. Whisper's followed as they were shushed by what appeared to be their leader. As soon as Charlotte saw the sparkly oversized bow step out in front of the group she thought, 'Fantastic', Silvia and her minions.

"Hi Braden," Silvia practically cooed at him.

Braden politely replied, "Hey there Silvia."

Gasps and giggles from the crowd caused Charlotte to roll her eyes.

Silvia stepped closer to Braden, saying, "I saw you play at the fair. You were amazing."

"Yea," he replied, adding, "Glad you enjoyed it."

Nodding as she bit her bottom lip, Silvia shared, "I'll be eighteen soon."

Charlotte glanced at Auggie who was staring at the display in front of him with a confused yet humored expression on his face as she thought 'Oh, you have got to be kidding me'.

Braden gave a wary smile as he said, "Well, happy birthday in advance."

Batting her eyelashes, Silvia replied, "Thank you," before asking, "Will you come?"

"Uhh..." was all Braden could say before Silvia informed, "Daddy is throwing me a huge party. It would be like a personal favor to me if you would come and play."

"Oh! Sure thing!" Braden blurted in relief.

"Fabulous. I'll be in touch," she replied, giving him a wink before heading back to her friends.

As Silvia's minion's crowded around her, oohing and aahing over Braden's 'Personal Favor' to her, she was just showing off for her friends. Apparently, simply being a Roberts just wasn't enough these days.

Charlotte started to wonder if Silvia's little display was really about impressing her friends or if the fact that she was standing there with Braden caused her to walk over and showoff.

Narrowing her eyes at Braden, she asked, "Are you friends with my sister?"

"Nah, I just know her."

Even though it seemed like Braden had a good heart, he was seeing a married woman.

"She made it seem like y'all are friends."

Braden looked at her like she was jealous as he replied, "I see her at the foundation all the time. I volunteer there, teaching a music class."

With a serious expression, Charlotte nodded.

"Silvia's a sweet kid, but she is just a kid to me," Braden assured.

Charlotte blurted, "Sweet? She's a demon."

Looking back to glare at Silvia as Braden laughed, Charlotte saw her break off from her group of friends. Thinking 'And a sneaky little one at that' she watched as Silvia hopped into an old blue mustang and rode away with some knucklehead with a neck tattoo.

Charlotte knew there was no way Silvia's 'Daddy' would approve. Shaking her head, she turned back just in time to see Auggie hop into his truck.

Guessing he was going to stay mad at her for a while, she said, "See you around Braden," and headed to her car.

Hearing Auggie's engine fire up as Braden shouted, "Thanks again," Charlotte figured she would go home and see if Lola was back from day camp.

☙❧

Thankful Charlotte's kid sister showed up when she did, he was seconds away from cussing Charlotte smooth out. What the hell was she thinking? She knew what was in the bag. He knew what she was doing though. He could see it in her eyes. She was pissed at him for not speaking to her. But how was he supposed to in front of his brother when he had just felt her up and was holding a bag of panties for her in his hand.

Stopping before he pulled out of the shopping center, Auggie decided to send Charlotte a text.

A: My house?

He stared at his phone waiting for a reply.

C: Depends...

A: On what?

C: Are you going to speak to me?

A: Yes.

C: Will there be yelling?

Shaking his head at his phone, he smiled.

A: Probably.

C: On my way ;)

When Auggie pulled up to his house, he grabbed his shopping bag and jumped out of his truck. Charlotte must have sped like a crazy person to beat him there, but he was glad that she had. It gave him a good feeling to walk up and see her standing at his door.

"Is it already unlocked?" he teased.

Giving him a serious look, Charlotte replied, "You said not to break in anymore."

Staring at her, he was at a loss for words. Pulling her in front of him, Auggie eased Charlotte into the corner of the porch and kissed her. He heard her purse fall to the ground a second before her arms slid under his. Auggie's shirt was pulled tight against his chest from the grip Charlotte had on it as she pressed him into her. Needing more, his hands pulled at her hips, so that she was firmly against him. It wasn't enough.

Frustration called him to a halt as Charlotte leaned her head back, breathing, "We're on the porch."

Loosening his grip on her, Auggie remained close, whispering, "I'm giving you fair warning."

He could see the indecision in her eyes as she moved her hands to the sides of his face.

Guiding his face to her's Charlotte placed a soft kiss against his lips before saying, "See you tomorrow."

Auggie let her slip away from him.

Lifting her purse off of his porch, Charlotte quickly stepped out of view. Auggie pulled his beanie off and ran his fingers through his hair. Unable to think straight, he stood there on the porch, mentally reliving what had just taken place.

❧ 21 ❧

Secrets

Smoothing her hand over the crisp fabric starched and ironed into a square, Charlotte smiled at the shirt Auggie gave her when they went to the peacock farm. Although the emotion was new to her, she knew what she felt every time she thought, saw, touched him was her falling for him. Lifting the shirt off of the ironing board, she pinned the four corners of it to her wall. After tacking it in a few more places, she placed a spray of peacock feathers in the pocket. Stepping back to look at the finished project, she thought that was a good day.

Continuing to admire her sentimental work of art, Charlotte heard a knock on her bedroom door before Amila walked in.

Glancing around Charlotte's room, Amila asked, "Do you have plans today?"

Reluctantly focusing on Amila instead of the shirt and feathers, she replied, "I was planning on going out in a little while."

Sitting down on Charlotte's bed, Amila questioned, "Anywhere special?"

Charlotte shook her head.

"I was hoping we could spend the day together."

She started to say, "I already..." when Amila interrupted her, "It will just be you and me until later this evening. It's sports night."

"Amila, I really can't."

With a disappointed expression, she shared, "School is starting soon and I'm afraid you'll leave and we won't have spent any time together at all."

Nodding at Amila, Charlotte gave in, saying, "I'll change my plans," before adding, "Be down in a minute."

Standing up, Amila gave Charlotte a little squeeze before stepping out of her room.

Charlotte looked at Auggie's shirt on her wall before grabbing her cellphone.

C: Can't stop by. Family thing.

A few seconds later, Auggie texted her back.

A: Do I get to break one of your rules then?

Nice try.

C: I'll be by when you get off.

A: After midnight...I won't get to see you today.

Charlotte thought for a moment before smirking at her phone as she snapped a picture of herself and sent it to him.

C: There, now you've seen me.

A: Cheater!

C: No sir! That is what's known as a loophole.

A: Playing dirty now?

C: See you later ;)

A: Later.

The knowledge that Auggie wanted to see her caused Charlotte to smile as she slid her phone in her back pocket.

Amila was sitting on the couch in the living room when Charlotte made her way down the stairs. Rounding the side of the couch, Charlotte flopped down next to her.

"What do you want to do?" Charlotte asked.

Amila smiled softly at her as she replied, "I'd like to talk."

Instantly disappointed, Charlotte said, "Oh," as she leaned back against the arm of the couch.

"Did you settle things with Trace?"

"I guess," Charlotte mumbled as she shrugged a shoulder.

Appearing hesitant, Amila said, "You seem to be enjoying your time here." As Charlotte narrowed her eyes at Amila, she added, "You've made some friends."

Charlotte cleared her throat before assuring, "I really hate when you beat around the bush."

"Okay, I guess I thought you would be home more."

Thinking, 'So did I', Charlotte questioned, "If I had been home when y'all got back from vacation would we still be having this conversation?"

"I know you always felt closer to Ren and found her easier to talk to but I was hoping that would change."

"There's nothing to talk about."

With a loud sigh, Amila asked, "Are you seeing someone?" A blank expression covered Charlotte's face as Amila clarified, "And I don't mean Trace."

Sitting perfectly still, Charlotte stared at her.

"Is it serious?"

Charlotte couldn't respond.

"I see..."

Shaking her head at Amila, Charlotte replied, "There's nothing to see or talk about. I'm just having a good time which is what everyone wanted in the first place. Right?"

Amila nodded then looked away.

Shaking her head at herself this time, Charlotte felt bad for being that way with Amila. She loved her. Knowing that Amila was simply trying to bond with her, something that she had been trying to do since they brought her home from the foundation, she decided maybe she could share a little.

"It's a secret."

Amila turned back to Charlotte with an interested expression.

Cautious, Charlotte shared, "I don't want anyone to know anything about this. Not even Ren."

"Go on," Amila urged, literally on the edge of her seat.

"He's..." Charlotte started to say as excitement swelled in her chest just thinking of Auggie. "I like him."

A wide smile spread across Amila's face as she questioned, "Well, who is he?"

Charlotte shook her head.

A disappointed scowl formed as Amila said, "I won't say anything."

"I know but we agreed not to tell anyone."

Appearing offended, Amila questioned, "Why wouldn't he want anyone to know he's seeing you?"

Smiling at Amila's protective nature, Charlotte assured, "It's not just him. I'm only here for a little while and you know how people here are. I just want to enjoy whatever it is that we have until I leave without everyone ruining it for us."

"So what's he like? Is he cute?"

Charlotte couldn't help but laugh as she wondered what Auggie would say to being called cute.

"He's a...different."

"Different?"

"Than what I'm used to. He's a little intense sometimes, but he can be sweet too. He has this way about him and he's got this smile that just, turns me inside out when..."

"Oh my gosh, you're in love!" Amila blurted.

"I don't think so."

"No? Then what's with that silly grin on your face?"

Shrugging her shoulder at Amila's question, Charlotte replied, "I like him, that's all."

Smiling as if she knew better, Amila said, "Unhuh."

Charlotte started to defend herself when the front door flew open.

Silvia pranced into the house with a tall blonde haired boy following close behind her.

"Home to change," she announced as she darted through the living room and up the stairs.

As the boy closed the front door, Amila smiled at him, offering, "Jonah, come in, have a seat."

Jonah gave a polite smile, greeting, "Hello, Mrs. Roberts."

Suspicious, Charlotte looked him over, thinking 'Huh, no neck tattoo'.

Charlotte gave a slight smile as Amila introduced, "This is Silvia's boyfriend," before asking Jonah, "Where are y'all off to?"

"I'm not sure ma'am. Wherever Silvia wants to go," he politely replied.

There was something not quite right about, Jonah. Continuing to observe him sitting there, Charlotte noticed he was nice and well-mannered but he didn't seem excited at all about their plans.

Curious, Charlotte asked, "How long have you been seeing my sister?"

"A few months."

"Do you have any brothers or sisters?"

Jonah appeared nervous as he replied, "No, I'm an only child."

"What kind of car do you drive?"

Shifting in his seat, he answered, "My mom's Volvo."

As she started to ask another question, Amila broke in, "Stop, you're making him nervous."

Narrowing her eyes at Jonah, Charlotte questioned, "Am I?"

Jonah shook his head at her as Silvia came down the stairs.

Making her way to Amila, Silvia wore a sparkly pink sundress. Charlotte glanced at Jonah to see his reaction to her. She couldn't stand Silvia herself but she was pretty and any guy with the slightest interest in her would have taken notice. Instead, he quickly stood up focusing on the front door.

"I'll be home by curfew," Silvia assured before leaning down to hug Amila.

Charlotte planned on dropping her suspicions until Silvia gave her a, 'I'm better than you' dirty look as she made her way to Jonah.

"It was nice to meet you, Jonah," Charlotte smiled before adding, "If you ever decide to trade up on your mom's Volvo, I hear old school mustangs are the way to go."

All the color seemed to drain from Jonah's face. The boy looked like he had just been convicted of murder.

Noticeably swallowing back a guilty look of her own, Silvia eyes grew wide as Charlotte suggested, "Maybe a blue one."

Amila gave Charlotte a strange look before saying, "Okay, y'all have a nice time."

Jonah seemed unable to move as Silvia swung the front door open and practically shoved him out.

'Ah, sneaky, sneaky' Charlotte thought, wondering what Silvia had on Jonah to get him to be her fake boyfriend. Silvia was brave enough to mess around with a bad boy but not quite brave enough to bring him home to meet mommy and daddy. It wasn't so different than what Charlotte did growing up, but she was bold enough not to need a stand in for appearances. Either way, there was no judging on her end. Charlotte had her own secret relationship to tend to.

༂∙❦

Everyone was asleep when Charlotte left for Auggie's house. She didn't consider it sneaking out, although that was exactly what she was doing. When she sent him a text letting him know she was on her way, he said he'd leave the door unlocked. She found that a little strange but shrugged it off in her excitement to go see him.

After letting herself in, Charlotte stood in Auggie's living room debating on whether to wait or look around for him. Setting her purse down on the coffee table, she stepped into the kitchen just as Auggie was walking in from the back door.

"There you are," she smiled.

She could tell Auggie was freshly showered. Without his beanie or shirt on, Charlotte had to concentrate on not going up and running her fingers through his damp hair.

"Dang your fast," he laughed before saying, "Have you been here long? Had to throw my clothes in the washer."

Leaning her back against the counter, Charlotte asked, "Rough night?"

"A group of girls came in, bachelorette party or somethin' and one of 'em spilled her drink all over me."

A strange feeling from deep inside caused Charlotte to narrow her eyes and snap, "Were you the main event?"

Auggie's expression was confused as he answered, "I was bringing a bottle to their table and the girl slipped. I caught her, but her long island went everywhere. I've been sticky all night."

Charlotte rolled her eyes and stepped to the refrigerator, griping, "How unpleasant."

"Yea, it was."

With a slight huff, Charlotte reached into the refrigerator and grabbed a beer, not knowing why that bothered her so much.

"You mad?"

Setting her beer on the counter, she fluffed, "Oh, please."

"You look mad," he said in a taunting tone.

How could she admit to anything when she didn't know what the feeling was.

"I'm not."

She watched his eyes carefully as they softened, "Are you jealous?"

Yes, yes she was.

"Of what? Some tipsy trick that can't walk?"

Charlotte had no idea why that came out of her mouth.

Clearly holding back his amusement, Auggie replied, "That's what I'm thinkin'."

"Well, think something else."

As Auggie scowled making his way closer, Charlotte backed up.

"So you wouldn't care if I said she asked me back to her place?"

Glancing off to the side as she felt her stomach twist into a knot, Charlotte stated, "We agreed this was nothing serious, so I guess it really doesn't matter."

He stepped closer until her back was all the way against the wall.

"You said it wasn't, we never agreed."

Charlotte wanted him to clarify what he was saying, but she couldn't get the question out of her mouth, she could barely breath.

Auggie seemed to read her mind as he shared, "I couldn't want anyone else if I tried."

An involuntary shudder shook her from the inside out as Auggie placed one hand against the wall next to her and the other around her hip.

"I'll lose my damn mind if I have to share you."

Tugging her closer, his hand slid from the wall to the back of her head.

"And I want you to stay."

Charlotte's heart raced as Auggie leaned his forehead against hers.

"I'm serious."

Feeling the exact same way, Charlotte placed her hands on his bare sides. Tilting her chin up, she brushed her lips against his before leaning the side of her head against his shoulder.

తళ

Auggie wanted her to admit she was jealous and somehow it turned into something else. She was relaxing against him and although it wasn't what he was going for, he slowly realized he wanted this. Charlotte's fingers made lazy trails down his sides and across his back as he wrapped an arm around her, gently holding her head to him with the other. He could have stood there with her like that forever.

When he felt her lips drag against the side of his neck, Auggie reached down to the back of her thighs lifting her off of her feet. Charlotte held on tight until he sat her at the edge of the kitchen table. It only took a second to readjust with those long wonderful legs of hers around his waist. Her arms were around his neck and he felt like she was wrapping him up in herself. There wasn't a better place to be on earth. Wishing they were bare, Auggie slid his hands up the sides of her pant legs before wrapping them around her hips. With a deep inhale, he kissed her, pulling her as close as possible. His scalp tingled as she slid her hands into the back of his hair. As their kiss deepened, he could feel the tingling sensation travel down his shoulders along with her fingers. It wasn't enough. He needed more, more of her. Charlotte's hands were now sliding down his chest and the friction between them was more than he could stand.

Without warning, Charlotte's palm was planted firmly against his chest, breaking him away from her.

Glaring at him, she demanded, "Let go."

Confused and lightheaded he had no idea what had gone wrong until he felt the sides of her shirt bunched up in his hands. Auggie took note of the furious expression on her face. The hand that wasn't pushing into his chest held tight to the bottom of her shirt pulling it down to the table. He couldn't help looking at her exposed ribcages.

"Let go."

Scarred unlike anything he had ever seen, he still wanted to see and touch all of her. Slowly letting go, he brushed his thumb against her side.

Jerking away from him, Charlotte shouted, "Now!"

Auggie quickly held his hands up and took a step back.

∂∽∾∾

Charlotte swung her legs to the side so she could slide off of the table without standing next to him. Frantic, she couldn't believe he did that.

Walking away from the kitchen she heard Auggie call, "Lotte."

Whipping around, she stated, "I told you," before fussing, "We had a conversation and I told you."

"I didn't realize what I was doing until you stopped me."

If his knuckle hadn't brushed against one of her scars, she wouldn't have realized either. For the first time in Charlotte's life, she lost control with someone. And it scared the hell out of her.

"That's unacceptable," she snapped, at herself as well as him.

She could see his frustration building as he griped, "Why is taking your shirt off even that big of a deal?"

Thinking if he knew, he wouldn't push the issue, she replied, "I'm ugly underneath."

Making his way closer, Auggie swore, "I don't believe you."

"I'm scarred."

The sincerity in his eyes shook Charlotte's disposition as he assured, "That doesn't matter to me."

With a loud huff, Charlotte explained, "It matters to me."

Stepping in front of her, Auggie shared, "Just so there's no misunderstanding. No part of my body is off limits to you."

"You're really hard to stay mad at," she confessed as the side of her mouth curled into a smile.

With a hopeful expression, Auggie raised his eyebrows, questioning, "Too bad I was a mood killer?"

"There's always tomorrow," she teased before saying, "Unless, of course, you have plans with the clumsy girl."

He scowled before smiling as he said, "I knew you were jealous."

Charlotte ran her finger against the tattoo across his collar bone assuring, "Well, Mr. Augustus Carrick Caffrey, I don't want to share you either."

❧ 22 ❧

Cake

Charlotte was doing her best to hurry knowing Ren was waiting for her downstairs. After a long goodbye at Auggie's just a few hours ago, she'd overslept. Since she was only going to hang out with Ren at her house for the day, Charlotte slid on a pair of gray shorts matching it with a gray camisole covered by a loose sheer black tank. Quickly pulling her hair into a banded up-do, she slipped her feet into her black strappy sandals.

Thinking ten minutes had to be some kind of record, for her 'get ready' time, she grabbed her chubby stick and smoothed it over her lips before tossing it back in her purse. As she opened her bedroom door, Silvia barged in.

Swinging the door closed behind herself, Silvia warned, "Don't even think about telling on me."

With a slight laugh Charlotte asked, "Why? Are you going to rough me up or something?"

"I'll tell daddy that you snuck out last night."

Rolling her eyes, Charlotte said, "You do that then," reaching for her doorknob.

Pushing her hand away from the knob, Silvia threatened, "I'll make something up then."

Charlotte narrowed her eyes at her sister, sharing, "I wasn't going to tell on you. What's there to tell? Your little punk ass boyfriend thinks your good enough to do on the weekends at is brother's place but not worth enough to meet your parents," stopping for a moment to see the embarrassed expression on Silvia's face, she continued, "I think I'll just let that playout on its own."

Tears welled in Silvia's eyes as she swore, "I hate you," before swinging the door open and stomped out.

Thinking to herself, 'Truth hurts, doesn't it. Brat', Charlotte went downstairs to meet Ren.

෧෨

Auggie woke twisted in his sheets, clutching his pillow tight to his chest. Stumbling out of bed, he thought, 'This is pure hell'. Bracing himself before he stepped into another cold shower, Auggie decided he had to step things up if he was going to survive Charlotte. There had to be a way to speed things along. Gritting his teeth as the icy shower stung his shoulders, he knew he was going to have to eat crow and get some advice.

෧෨

Pulling up to Jackson's house, he was only able to pull a few feet inside the gate. Ren and Jacks' property was a little over ten acres and their entire front yard was filled with pickups and Southern Trees service trucks. Hopping out of his truck, Auggie didn't get very far before he saw Jackson walking towards him.

"What's goin' on, Auggie?"

Looking around, Auggie laughed, "That's what I'm wonderin'. You plan a family reunion and didn't invite me?"

Shaking his head with a wide smile, Jackson replied, "We have some trees that need to come down," before asking, "What's up?"

"I called your office. Seth said you were home today. Didn't know you had all this goin' on. I'll come back."

"Is everything okay?"

"Yea, just needed some advice that's all."

"About what?"

Glancing at the ground, Auggie answered, "I been talkin' to this girl and a..."

Jackson had a shocked yet proud expression on his face as he blurted, "I knew you had a girl."

"Damn Jacks, keep it down," Auggie snapped.

Jackson started to say something when Oran walked up.

"Hey Bartender, come to do some real man's work?" he teased.

Reaching out, Auggie shook his cousin's hand, saying, "Ah, don't be mad I ended up with the better trade."

Oran laughed, "Better trade? Passin' out cocktails isn't a trade. You wouldn't last an hour out here, boy."

"Boy? You want me to show you how it's done," Auggie laughed back as Oran's brothers Niall and Dillen walked up.

Dillen shouted, "Place your bets! Bartender's gonna get his hands dirty!"

"You believe this boy, Jacks," Oran taunted.

Laughing and shaking his head at his family, Jackson told Auggie, "I'll let Ren know you're here," as he headed back to the house.

Auggie didn't understand why telling Ren he was there was important but was quickly distracted as Oran mocked, "You know our tools are bigger than a bottle opener."

"I can out swing you any day," Auggie swore.

"Ah, ah, ah, no swingin' or sawin' unless you're a regular member of the crew," Niall corrected.

"Only haulin'," Dillen added.

Oran shrugged, saying, "Sorry, crew rules."

Auggie shook his head at his cousins, "Crew rules, huh."

"Laid down by the old man himself," Niall assured.

Pulling his shirt off, Auggie tossed it in the bed of his truck, recalling all the summer's he worked for his Uncle Brennen.

Heading to the back of Jackson's property with his cousins, Auggie thought some good hard physical labor might relieve the frustration Charlotte was causing him.

As they walked, Dillen blurted, "Nice!" before asking, "Kieran do that?"

Nodding, Auggie shared, "Yea, when Will passed."

They were all quiet for a moment before Oran griped, "Damn Kieran."

Niall agreed, "He outta have to come out here and supervise the idiot."

"What?" Auggie asked.

"Kieran heard Frank broke his leg and asked if we could hook his buddy's brother Shawn up with a job," Oran replied.

"Stupid ass Jimmy from the shop's kid brother?" Auggie questioned.

Dillen nodded, saying, "Yep."

"Ah, man," Auggie laughed before Oran shared, "Don't laugh too hard, you're babysittin'."

Auggie was about to complain when Shawn strolled up to them.

Wearing tennis shoes instead of work boots with jeans that were baggy enough to be a hazard out there working, Shawn stopped in front of Auggie.

"Sup," Shawn greeted with a slight head nod.

Auggie gave his cousins an 'I hate you all' glare as they laughed and headed back to work.

Tightening the bandanna around his head, Shawn asked, "Auggs, right?"

Unhappy with Shawn's use of what Kieran always called him, Auggie corrected, "Not if you wanna make it through today. It's Auggie."

"That's cool man. Hey, you know that fine ass woman that's here?"

"You wanna die?" Auggie blurted before saying, "That's my cousin's wife."

Shawn got a strange look on his face before a smirk appeared as he said, "Nah man, she's smokin' hot too though. I was talkin' about the blonde."

A mixture of excitement and irritation filled Auggie as he realized it had to be Charlotte. She was there.

"No," he stated, hoping for the boy's own safety, he would leave it at that.

"Dang man, you gotta see her. She got legs that you can just imagine...
Auggie's arms flexed as he tried to keep from snatching the boy up by his undershirt.

"No," he repeated, cutting Shawn off.

"Oh yea," Shawn assured before informing, "I'm definitely gonna try and hit that."
Grinding his back teeth together a flash of Shawn laying on the ground, disfigured and bloody entered Auggie's mind.

Utilizing the last thread of control he was hanging on to, Auggie growled, "Shut your mouth and let's get to work."

As he turned to get started hauling, Shawn mumbled, "Shut my mouth, you shut yours," oblivious to how near death he actually was.
Auggie shook his comment off as he lifted the end of a large branch dragging it towards the burn pile.

∾∾

Sitting in the kitchen, Charlotte was enjoying the smell of strawberry from the cake Ren was baking. It smelled so good she almost wanted to stay for dinner, but that would mean not going to see Auggie and she liked him even better than her favorite strawberry cake. Watching Ren pour herself another cup of coffee, she had been acting strange since Jackson came up behind her and whispered something in her ear. Something was up but Charlotte couldn't quite put her finger on what it was. She seemed apprehensive, which was unusual for Ren.

"So your broke up with Trace, how'd Emerson take it?" Ren asked.

With a slight laugh, Charlotte replied, "Just fine. He doesn't know."

"Are you going to tell him?"

Charlotte thought for a moment before saying, "I hadn't planned on it."

"Don't you think he's going to wonder why he's not there to pick you up?"

"He's still coming."

Ren raised an eyebrow at Charlotte before questioning, "Does Trace know y'all broke up?"

Rolling her eyes, she answered, "Yes Ren, he said for me to do whatever I wanted while I was here and I could give him my final answer when he comes down."

"That's...odd," Ren said with a confused tone.

"Why is it odd?"

Ren set her coffee cup down, sharing, "I think it's strange that he doesn't care if you see other people."

Thinking 'Oh you have no idea how strange he is', Charlotte asked, "Who says that's what I'm doing?"

With a loud sigh, Ren replied, "I didn't say you were. It was implied by him saying you could do whatever you wanted here, that he didn't care if you did."

"Oh," Charlotte said before Ren asked, "Are you?"

"Am I what?" she replied, not wanting to lie to Ren but trying to think of a way around answering.
Ren's golden retriever, walked into the kitchen providing a temporary distraction.

Honey barked at them before running over to the back door, pacing back and forth in front of it.

"I think she needs to go out," Charlotte shared.

Ren smiled at Honey, saying, "You need to go outside girl?" Honey barked again before Ren asked, "Can you go tell Jacks, she needs to go out?"

"I'll take her," she offered.

There was that apprehension again, as Ren said, "They're still cutting down trees and it's just a big mess out there.

"That's okay, I'll take her," she insisted, standing up and grabbing the leash by the door.

"Wait," Ren blurted as Charlotte clipped Honey's leash onto her collar.

Giving Ren an irritated expression, Charlotte questioned, "Is Jackson's family going to throw rocks at me or something if I go out there?"

"Auggie's out there," Ren replied, appearing as though she wanted to keep it a secret.

Charlotte froze as the excitement of knowing he was there caused her heart to beat a little faster.

Honey barked, snapping her back to the conversation as she fluffed, "I'm not worried about him."

Ren shook her head as Charlotte gave a sarcastic smile and walked out of the back door with Honey.

Purposely walking Honey around the side of the house where she could get a good view of the workers, it was like a sea of red hair and beards to match. She didn't want to stare but the thought of catching a glimpse of Auggie working compelled her to glare at each and every man out there. Then she saw it, a large Celtic cross moving with every step its owner made. Mesmerized, Charlotte watched as Auggie's cross stretched with his arms as he lifted and flexed with the muscles on his back. After briefly considering pulling up a lawn chair and setting up camp there to watch him all day, she looked down at Honey who was tugging the leash to go back inside. Frowning at Honey, she thought 'Well you're no fun' before walking back towards the house.

She only made it a few steps before a, "Say girl," caused her to stop.

Blinking a few times at the boy who stepped around in front of her, she asked, "Can I help you?"

Puffing out his chest he introduced himself, "I'm Shawn. Big Shawn."

Remembering her conversation with the guy at Legacy Ink, Charlotte stared at the tattoo on the side of his neck, saying, "Shawn, huh. I'm Charlotte, just Charlotte."
The fact that Silvia was seeing someone that referred to himself as Big Shawn was slightly amusing to her and she smiled.

Assuming she was smiling at him, Shawn took a step closer, saying, "You got plans later."

"Excuse me?"

"You got plans," he repeated.

Offended he was hitting on her while dating her sister, Charlotte replied, "Is that a statement or were you asking me a question?"

Shawn gave her a confused look before saying, "I get it, you're funny girl. Yea, you got plans with me."

With a sarcastic smile, she assured, "Not gonna happen."

"Don't be shy now girl, I saw you starin'," he shared before a masculine voice came from behind them growling, "It sure as hell wasn't at you."
Charlotte whipped around as Honey instantly pulled her in Auggie's direction, darting towards him.

Taking a knee in order to pet Honey, who apparently was overjoyed to see him, Auggie looked up at Charlotte. Pulling her lips into her mouth, she winked at him.

Clearing his throat, Auggie stood up and glared at Shawn, ordering, "Get back to work."
Charlotte turned to look at Shawn as he gave Auggie a dirty look but did exactly as he was told.

After waiting a moment for Shawn to be far enough away, Charlotte said, "Awfully territorial these days, aren't you Augustus."

"You were starin'?"

"I was."

Holding back a smile, he complimented, "You look pretty."

Itching to touch him, Charlotte placed her free hand behind her back, saying, "You look sweaty."

Auggie's expression changed from pleased to a scowl as he shared, "I'll only have enough time to run home and take a quick shower before I go to the bar."

With a mischievous expression, Charlotte asked, "Are you implying if you had time for a long shower, I would be invited?"

His scowl intensified as he griped, "Knock it off."

"Why? Are you picturing me in the shower?" she questioned, thinking it was only fair for him to suffer a little after what seeing him hauling branches with his shirt off did to her.

"Go inside," he fussed.

"And take a shower?" Charlotte taunted.

Raising his voice at her, Auggie snapped, "Damn it, you're..." before Ren's voice came out of nowhere asking, "Is there a problem?"

Charlotte cringed as Auggie looked past her at Ren stating, "Nope," and walked off.

Knowing it more than likely looked like they were fighting, Charlotte turned and led Honey back inside without saying a word. Ren was close behind her with a frustrated look on her face.

"What is wrong with the two of you? It's like y'all seek each other out just to be mad! And you're just as stubborn as he is," Ren complained as Charlotte unhooked Honey's leash from her collar.

Nodding as she hung the leash up and walked to the table, Charlotte said, "Sorry."

Ren turned and gave her an 'I'm not really mad' expression before saying, "Just stay inside. I'll be right back."

Watching Ren walk out of the kitchen, Charlotte felt her cellphone vibrate in her back pocket.

Pulling her cell out, there was a text from Auggie.

A: You're making me crazy woman!

Charlotte thought for a moment before replying.

C: Me? Whatever, Mr. Sweaty Muscles.

A: Yes! Miss Sexy Legs.

Trying not to smile wide at Auggie's reply, she texted back.

C: That was hard for me ;)

A: You wanna talk hard? I'm dyin' over here.

C: Bahahahahah!

A: My pain is funny to you?

C: That's what you get for telling me to go inside :p

A: Did you just stick your tongue out at me?

C: Yep

A: You make me smile! See you later?

Charlotte much preferred his words to a smiley face.

C: Sure thing ♥

Sticking her phone in her back pocket, Charlotte wondered if attaching the heart was too much. In her next thought, she shrugged off her concern. A smile formed as she realized she could now stay for dinner and have some delicious strawberry cake. Seeing Auggie today was sort of delicious also. Laughing to herself, Charlotte thought, 'I get to have my cake and eat it too'.

Worth

When Auggie made it to The Dog House, he was surprised to find Jackson was already there. Sitting behind the desk in the office, he stood up when Auggie walked in.

"Still need some advice?" Jackson asked.

Nodding, Auggie leaned against the wall, saying, "I can't get a handle on her, man."

"Hold on. You have to do me a favor first," Jackson shared.

Laughing, Auggie asked, "Your advice comes with a price?"

Shaking his head with a smile, Jackson answered, "No but I promised Ren I'd talk to you about Charlotte."

"What about her?" Auggie asked, trying to appear serious when it was such a coincidence, he wanted to smile.

"Just lay off of her okay."

Covering his mouth with his hand before running it down the front of his beard to compose himself, Auggie was having a hard time keeping a straight face.

"You don't have to be on her ass every time you see her," Jackson said, clearly getting frustrated with him.

Unable to hold it in any longer, Auggie let out a laugh.

"If you knew what she had been through, you might take this more seriously," Jackson snapped.

Suddenly Auggie was serious as he asked, "Do you know?"

"Some of it."

"What happened to her?"

Sitting back down behind the desk, Jackson assured, "That's none of your business. But both of you will be at Sophia's baby shower so be civil with her. And if you can't be polite to her, keep your distance."

Wanting to argue, Auggie was irritated, it was his business and he wanted to know what happened and who it was that hurt her. Not only that, he knew how to treat her and no way he would be keeping his distance.

After stewing for a moment, Auggie knew he needed to keep his cool around Jackson where Charlotte was concerned. He was smart and if he figured it out, Ren would find out and she'd have a damn conniption fit.

Walking to a chair facing the desk, Auggie sat down, saying, "I'll be nice."

A wide smile appeared on Jackson's face as he said, "Thank you. Now tell me about this girl of yours."

Shaking his head, Auggie shared, "She's incredible."

"So what's the problem?"

"I don't know what the hell I'm doin'," Auggie admitted.

Jackson laughed, saying, "That's not unusual. The good ones always keep you confused."

Leaning back in his chair, Auggie rubbed his palms across his forehead.

"Is it serious?" Jackson asked.

Auggie shrugged, "Sorta, I like her."

Resting an elbow on the desk, Jackson scratched the side of his head, saying, "So you're in a sorta serious relationship with an incredible woman you like. I'd say whether you know what you're doing or not, you're doing pretty good."

Scowling, Auggie complained, "I was really hoping for more."

"From her?"

"From you man. Damn Jacks, I'm losing my mind over here and you're telling me that's a good thing."

Placing his other elbow on the desk, Jackson leaned forward, imparting, "When I first met Ren, your dad told me, I needed to ask myself what she was worth to me."

"Like on a scale from one to ten?"

With a heavy sigh, Jackson replied, "No, like your time, patience, forgiveness, loyalty, friendship, love, understanding, compassion, trust. If she's not and you still care about her then, she's worth more than you have to offer and you should let her go."

"How did you figure it out?"

"I got to know her. Slowly but surely over time the questions answered themselves. She was worth everything I had to give."

Auggie looked down at the floor, asking, "What if I already know it's a temporary thing."

"Well then, enjoy what you have while you have it."
Nodding, Auggie stood up and started to walk out.

"You alright, Auggie?"

Stretching his elbows out to the side, Auggie lied, poking fun at himself saying, "Yea, sore from today. Those branches were bigger than a bottle opener."

Jackson laughed before sharing, "See you next Sunday and don't forget to wear a suit."

"I won't. Thanks Jacks. Later."
Feeling heavy, Auggie walked out of the office into the main area of the bar.

&~&

When the night that seemed to drag on forever finally ended, Auggie closed up the bar and headed home. He was still frustrated but confused as hell now too. Did that mean she was a good one? Jackson's advice was probably good but it made him feel bad and he had no idea why.

227

Remembering all the sayings and advice his dad used to give, he started to miss him even more. Gus passed away almost six years ago of a heart attack before Ailin and Sophia's wedding. Maybe that's what was making him feel bad. Hearing his dads words come from Jackson. He tried to imagine hearing his dad's voice saying what Jacks had but it didn't help.

Seeing Charlotte at his door, when he arrived home, instantly put him in a better mood. She was like a beautiful breath of sweet smelling fresh air, refreshing him from the inside out as he reached his doorstep. The value Jackson advised he put on her was insignificant. She was his until she left and that was enough.

"Have you been here long?" he asked, allowing her to walk in first.

"Yes but I couldn't stand being at the house anymore."

Auggie kicked the door closed before pulling her to him. Making up for not being able to touch her at Jackson's, he made sure to kiss her long and slow.

Pulling back, he asked, "Wait, what did you mean?"

Charlotte stared at him with a dazed expression before answering, "Too much crying for me."

"Crying?"

"Silvia's boyfriend broke up with her and apparently now her life is over."

"That bad, huh," he said with a laugh.

"She was practically howling. It was ridiculous."

"Were they together for a long time?" he asked slowly letting go of her.

Making a disgusted face Charlotte walked to the couch and replied, "All I know is, it was an undercover thing. She even had a pretend boyfriend for show. She was putting out and evidently, that's all he wanted from her. I mean, he didn't have enough respect for her to come meet Emerson and Amila. Really, he did her a favor she is just too stupid to realize it."

The heavy feeling returned as Auggie asked, "You think so?"

Charlotte sat down on the couch, sharing, "Oh, I know so. Obviously he was playing with her because otherwise he would have been man enough to be upfront with everyone about what they had going on instead of doing her whenever she could sneak away."

Auggie scowled at her before turning towards the kitchen to grab a beer.

Charlotte didn't seem to be talking about him but he felt convicted all the same. Wondering if that was how she felt about him and what they were doing, he made his way back to the couch carrying a six pack of Guinness. He noticed Charlotte's remorseful expression as he set the bottles down on the coffee table in front of her.

Looking up at him with a light smile, she shared, "I don't think there's a similarity there. Silvia's a kid. We are consenting adults who made an agreement."

"I didn't take what you were saying personal," he lied.

"Then what's wrong?" she questioned, staring right into his eyes.

Stretching, so he could look away without it appearing intentional, Auggie lied again, "Just sore from today."

With a suspicious expression, Charlotte questioned, "So lying is what we're doing now?"

"No," he snapped giving her an offended look.

"Augustus, I'm a fairly upfront person. If whatever's bothering you is none of my business then say so and I'll respect that but don't lie."

Nodding, he flexed his arms, saying, "I am kinda sore."

The side of Charlotte's mouth curled into a smile as she offered, "Come, sit down."

Auggie walked around the coffee table and sat down next to her.

Shifting to face him, Charlotte gave a light smile. Reaching over she unbuttoned his shirt. Auggie leaned in to kiss her and was confused seeing her shake her head at him.

"Where are you sore?"

Auggie narrowed his eyes at her before replying, "Everywhere."

With a little laugh, she said, "Nice try," as she slid his shirt off of his shoulders. "Turn around and I'll rub your back."

"You will?" he asked wanting her to but caught off guard by her offer.

"Well, I did just call you a liar so consider it my way of apologizing."

Swallowing hard, he admitted, "I was lying but I'd rather listen to you talk."

With a knowing smile, Charlotte repeated, "Turn around." As Auggie moved to comply, she asked, "What would you like me to talk about?"

"Yourself," he breathed as Charlotte placed her hands on his shoulder blades.

Auggie instantly relaxed. Just her touch seemed to sooth him.

"What do you want to know?" she questioned pressing her palms into his back as she slid them to the tops of his shoulders.

"What happened to you?"

৵৵

Charlotte continued to massage his back, allowing the question he asked to sink in. She knew what he was asking. It didn't bother her. As she debated on how to answer, her concern grew wondering if it would bother him.

"That is an incredibly broad question," she replied in a light tone.

"It's not."

Pressing into his spine as she slid her hands down the center of his back, Charlotte assured, "It is, and we can play this game all night if you like or you can be more specific."

She could feel the muscles in his back tense as he replied, "No need to play games. If you don't want to tell me, I understand."

"I'm not sure that you do," she shared before explaining, "I think it's natural for you to be curious. I'm sure it comes off as mysterious and interesting. The truth is, it's not much of a story."

"Everyone should tell their story at least once," Auggie urged.

"It's not my story, just something that happened."

"Then tell me," he pressed

"If you want to feel sorry for me then there's no need for me to share. You can use your imagination for your own pity purposes. I am who I am. I carry nothing with me from the past with the exception of scars. And they only affect my choice in apparel, nothing else."

There was a long pause before Auggie replied, "They affect me."

"How's that?"

"You've had the honor of seeing me with my shirt off. In all fairness, if you can't return the favor, you could at least explain to me the reasons for such an injustice."
Charlotte couldn't help but smile.

As she decided where to start and what information to share, Charlotte knew Auggie was a rare breed of man and felt comfortable telling him. Gazing at the cross on his back, she smoothed her hands over it before sharing the event for only the second time in her life.

"I didn't have a whole lot of parenting before the Roberts'. I can't remember ever having a curfew or rules.

The only time I got in trouble was when my mom felt like I was disobeying her. There was never a rhyme or reason to her. She did a lot of drugs. Things would seem fine and then in the next second, they weren't. She had quite a few boyfriends. One in particular was a regular, Jack. He would bring presents when he showed up and he was always nice to me." Feeling Auggie's back straighten, she started to massage him again, assuring, "Not pervy nice, he really was a sweet guy." As he started to relax again, she continued, "I actually think he was her dealer. Anyway, Jack came over one evening and saw what she did to my mouth. He blew up at her and told her he was cutting her off and left."

Charlotte paused, recalling the pain of the moment before saying, "I was changing my clothes to go out when she came in my room. She hit me on the back of the head, not sure with what, but I fell down. I was dizzy but I remember thinking that I really needed to get dressed. When I got up, I reached for a shirt and I think she thought I was going to hit her. She grabbed my metal flowers. They were daisies, thirteen of them with the stems welded together, so they stood up by themselves without a vase. Jack gave them to me when I turned thirteen. I stumbled toward her to grab my shirt off of my bed and she started swinging them at me. I don't remember seeing the flowers hit me but I could feel them. I covered my stomach with my hands and laid face down on the floor trying to inch under my bed to get away from her. She just kept swinging. She was screaming and telling me how ugly I was. I can remember wanting to move, but she was hitting me in the back with them so hard I couldn't."

"Did that guy come back?" he asked.

Thinking that was a strange question, she answered, "No. I stayed there for a while staring at my flowers lying on the floor next to me. They were twisted and broken with petals missing. I know it sounds gruesome but with silver shining though the red they were coated in, they were kinda pretty that way."

"Did you call the police?"

With a slight laugh, Charlotte replied, "No, I didn't."

"How did you end up with the Roberts' then?"

"I did the best I could to clean myself up. Some of the petals were pretty deep and I couldn't get them out. I knew it was getting worse because I started to feel sick but my mom acted like nothing happened so I did too. A couple of weeks later a girl who sat behind me in class told the teacher I was bleeding. I was sent to the nurse's office. When I got in there, she tried to pull my shirt up and I shoved her. She called the police and it took four officers to hold me down and when they saw me, they called an ambulance. I don't remember a lot from the hospital. As soon as they examined me, I was rushed into surgery. The infection from not being treated properly could have killed me they said. I was sedated most of the time because whenever they would come in to check me I had to be restrained. A Social Worker showed up at the hospital and said they arrested my mom because she was high when officers questioned her and there were drugs in the house," Charlotte paused thinking 'Almost done' before continuing to say, "They sent me to the juvenile detention center because I wouldn't say what happened. The hospital said I was hostile and under the circumstances I was a detriment to myself. I didn't mind it there. I was in the infirmary the whole time. They ended up sending me to the foundation because they didn't know what else to do with me and that's when the Roberts' adopted me."

࿇

Auggie sat still trying to absorb what he had heard. He wanted to react and felt like he should, but he had no idea how. It was the most horrific thing he had ever heard. Through her entire story, Charlotte rubbed his back and the only inflection in her voice was humor. Understanding now why she questioned his reasons for wanting to know. Auggie would never be able to look at her the same again. She was damn near righteous in his eyes.

Charlotte clearly didn't want sympathy. She didn't need it. He wanted to assure her that although he'd never hit a woman before, if he ever ran into her mom, he'd gladly beat that bitch to death but it seemed like the wrong thing to say. Then it hit him, what Jackson said at the bar. He knew something she was worthy of.

"I respect you."

Sliding her arms around his waist, Charlotte pressed her lips against the center of Auggie's back before saying, "That's a nice thing to hear."

Auggie shifted in her arms to face her.

"I really like you," he swore placing a soft kiss on her lips.

Scooting closer, she tightened her arms around him, saying, "I like you a lot too."

Smiling at her, Auggie let go of his urgency to have her. He still wanted her with a need that he knew would end up eating him alive, but he was no longer in a hurry. Whatever pain she caused him simply by being herself was worth it if he got to share little moments like this with her. She was now worth his patience too.

When Charlotte started to yawn, Auggie realized how late it was getting. He'd agreed to help his cousins finish up in the morning with the trees at Jackson's place and being too tired to work hard would give them a good year's worth of lazy bartender jokes. As much as he hated to, Auggie needed to call it a night.

"I have to get some sleep, you wanna stay?" he asked, knowing she was going to say no but still feeling the need to make the offer.

Appearing to give it serious consideration, Charlotte replied, "Everyone was still up dealing with Silvia when I left so I better not."

Nodding, Auggie stood up before holding his hand out to her.

Auggie held Charlotte's hand as he walked with her out of his front door and onto the porch. Standing on his doorstep with her, kissing her goodbye, Auggie thought about her standing there waiting on him to arrive home.

"I wanna give you something."

With that mischievous little smile of hers, Charlotte questioned, "Out here on the porch?"

An instant mental image made Auggie want to push her back into the house.

"Anywhere you want. Just say the word."

"And what word is that?" she asked, pushing to see how far he was willing to take this.

Knowing she was taunting him, Auggie drew in a deep breath before leaning closer.

Stopping before their lips touched he breathed, "Want. Tell me you want me."

A look of pure lust coated Charlotte's expression as she stared at him.

Thinking, 'This is going to hurt me more than it does her' Auggie gave her a quick kiss before stepping away saying, "I guess since your speechless, I'll just give you something else."

Narrowing her eyes at him for a moment, she said, "That wasn't nice."

Auggie reached down behind a potted plant and grabbed his spare key before turning back to her saying, "It wasn't meant to be."

"You are very lucky I like you Augustus Caffrey," she assured with a smile.

Closing his fist around the key, he replied, "That sounded a little threatening."

"Watch yourself, if you make this into a game, I will show up at the bar in my little turquoise shorts that you pretended to hate so much."

Auggie was desperate to come out on top for once as he swore, "If you do, I'll take you right over the bar."

"Promises, promises," she laughed not taking him seriously.

Shaking his head at her, Auggie admitted defeat saying, "I'll never be able to get to sleep if we keep going."

A satisfied expression appeared on Charlotte's face as she wrapped her arms around his neck.

"Kiss me goodnight then."

Auggie did as she asked before holding his spare key between them, offering, "This is for you. I don't want you to have to wait outside on the porch for me."

Charlotte seemed genuinely appreciative as she said, "Thank you."

Feeling good about it, he added, "You can use it anytime you want."

Charlotte wore a soft smile as she nodded, taking the key from him.

❧ 24 ❧

Falling

An early morning wake up call from Penny, that originally irritated an exhausted Charlotte, turned out to be a fun day of shopping with a friend. They shopped and laughed until both found perfect dresses for Sophia's shower. It was a great day and after stopping for lunch, Charlotte and Penny headed back to town.

Charlotte sat in the passenger seat while Penny drove them at what Charlotte considered a snail's pace. At this rate, a forty-minute drive was going to take them two hours.

"You know you drive like an old grandma," she laughed.

Penny pursed her lips into a smile, firmly holding the steering wheel at the ten and two position, saying, "There is nothing wrong with being a cautious driver."

"You know they give tickets for going too slow."

Laughing, Penny swore, "Excuse me, I go the speed limit."

"I'm just saying you're allowed to go with the flow of traffic."

Penny smiled, asking, "Got somewhere special to be?"

Auggie instantly entered Charlotte's mind as she replied, "Next time I'm driving."

"Ah, you're going to see your secret boyfriend," Penny teased.

Rolling her eyes with a smile, Charlotte replied, "Oh please, he's not my boyfriend. We are just seeing each other."

"I get that. So are y'all seeing other people too?"

"No," Charlotte answered, disliking the question but pleased at what she and Auggie had decided.

"Just so you know, that's what *we* call, having a boyfriend."

Charlotte sighed with a laugh, saying, "Well, *we* doesn't know everything and should not make more out of this than what it is."

Penny started to pout before blurting, "Oh, I almost forgot to tell you!" Charlotte jumped a little at her outburst as Penny shared, "Sophia is naming the baby Keely but spelling it K-e-y-l-e-e."

"Any particular reason?"

Shrugging a shoulder at Charlotte, Penny explained, "She doesn't want people to call her Kelly by mistake."

"Oh-kay."

Penny gave her a scolding expression saying, "Look, I know you don't like Sophia but she is my best friend and you're my friend, I don't want that to be a problem."

Charlotte mentally counted back from ten before she replied, "Well, you won't have a problem from me. I don't have an opinion of her at all. She's Ren's daughter, that's it."

With a curious smile, Penny asked, "Are you still going to feel that way if things work out with you and Auggie?"

"Things are working out with us."

Penny laughed, shaking her head, "Long term."

Suddenly uncomfortable with the conversation, Charlotte replied, "There is no long term. I'm leaving in a month and a half."

Appearing sad at first, Penny nodded before asking, "Just out of curiosity, what would you do if he asked you to stay?"

"He won't."

"You sure about that? When the Caffrey men fall, they go down hard," Penny imparted.

Penny's words filtered down into Charlotte's heart causing her to wonder if he was really falling hard for her and if he would ask her to stay.

Charlotte knew they agreed to keep their relationship a secret but recognized the fact that she really needed to talk to someone about it. Since Auggie knew that Penny knew and if no real details were shared, maybe it would be okay.

"How would I know?" Charlotte questioned before adding, "If he was falling for me."

Rolling her eyes with a laugh, Penny replied, "Oh you mean the fact that my brother has never spent more than a few hours with a woman even once in his life and wants to spend all his free time with you isn't convincing enough."

Hesitant, Charlotte said, "William said he loved me but once I was gone he moved on."

With a light sigh Penny shared, "Look, I hope I don't hurt your feelings but I'm gonna be honest with you. Will moved on because he was never in love with you." Charlotte gave Penny a confused look as she continued, "There's no doubt in my mind he loved you until the day he died but... Okay, none of the girls around here would give 'Weezy Will' the time of day until you, which is a shame because as far as brothers go, I think he was the cutest one. Then here you came all blonde and long legs wanting to get with him. Do you see what I'm sayin'."

"So he really was okay after I left?"

Penny gave her a 'Don't be silly' look as she replied, "He was sad that it didn't work out but yea, he was fine. And... I happen to know having you go to the hospital to say goodbye was for you, not him."

Nodding, Charlotte offered, "I thought I really screwed him up."

"You're not Lily," Penny cheered with a smile.

Letting go of something she didn't realize she was still carrying around, Charlotte exhaled, leaning back in her seat.

The car was silent for a few moments before Penny decided to share some background information on the Braden and Lily situation.

"By the way you know how I said we're forgiving people, that doesn't apply to her."

Charlotte found that somewhat interesting. She honestly couldn't see Penny disliking anyone.

"Lily?"

Nodding, Penny had an irritated expression as she shared, "She didn't just break my brother's heart, she crushed him."

"Braden doesn't come off as wounded," Charlotte replied.

With a heavy sigh, Penny informed, "That is because he's the dumbass brother." Charlotte started to laugh before Penny continued, "I'll admit we all loved her at first, even mom. She cheated on him a few times in high school. She complained he was too busy playing every weekend, wasn't paying attention to her, but that was between them and he forgave her, so it was whatever. High school stuff."

Listening to Penny, Charlotte tried to remember what she had overheard between Auggie and Braden when she was hiding in his bedroom.

"Lily always made a big deal about marriage. She said it was just a piece of paper and she didn't agree with labels or institutions. So they got a house together. About three years ago Braden and the rest of the band had the opportunity to be the opening band for six months on a tour. Everyone was so excited for them, except Lily. He wanted her to go with them, Sophia was going too. She said no and told him they were done if he went."

"He went anyway?"

Shaking her head, Penny answered, "Nope. He didn't want to lose her. Ailin and Brooks didn't want to go without him so they turned down the offer. They were bummed but we're a pretty understanding bunch, Lily was his girl and he had to do what he felt was right."

A thought quickly occurred to Charlotte as she blurted, "Wait, isn't she married now?"

Making a 'Mmhmm' face, Penny said, "Hold on, I'm getting to that," before continuing, "About two months after that, Braden bought her a ring. He thought even though she didn't want to get married he could still make it official, ya know. Mom drew out his heart and he left work early to go surprise her. He walked in and caught her cheating with Keven. He went back the next day and found all his stuff packed and on the curb. A week later Lily and Keven got married."

"So Lily's house, down Auggie's street..."

"Was the house Braden bought and he just gave it to her. He moved in with Brooks but it was horrible. For six months he didn't leave the house, play or anything. Finally, we had an intervention. It was mostly Auggie cursing at him and shaking him until he got mad enough to take a swing. They got in a fight and then we had our Braden back."

"And now?"

"Keven's in jail. There are rumors but I don't know what really happened. She told Braden that Keven beat her up. He probably did, he had steroids and some other stuff on him when he was arrested. At least that's what I heard."

Charlotte sat straight up, suggesting, "We should go kick her ass."

With a laugh Penny replied, "Gah, if my brother doesn't fall for you I will," before taking a more serious tone saying, "We've all tried to talk him out of her. He just won't listen. Still carries the heart mom drew around in his wallet. You know how they say love is blind? Well, I know Braden can see so apparently love's a dumbass and so is my brother."

Feeling sad for Braden, didn't stop the laughter that poured out of Charlotte as they pulled up to her house.

Penny dropped Charlotte off at home with a cheerful goodbye and an invitation to hang out anytime. Finding it hard to believe that she actually did William a favor as Penny had implied, by hurting him, she was relieved she hadn't ruined his life. Feeling like a little less of a bad person, Charlotte planned on hanging out at the house for a while. However, when she walked into the house, Silvia burst into tears. More howling and violent crying ensued before Charlotte decided she had to get out of there.

The disappointment Charlotte felt in not getting to use the key Auggie gave her was quickly replaced by excitement. His truck was in the driveway. When she turned the knob and found his front door locked, she was excited all over again. After using her key to open his door, Charlotte stepped inside. Closing the door behind herself, she glanced at Auggie asleep in his chair and smiled.

Late nights and early mornings had Charlotte worn out also and she hadn't spent the last two days doing manual labor. Imagining how tired he must be, she decided not to wake him. Looking him over while thinking she might take a nap, she noticed not only was he wearing plaid pajama bottoms, of course, his hair was still wet. She couldn't help herself as she set her purse down and stepped closer.

Running her fingers through Auggie's damp hair, Charlotte leaned closer. Just as she was about place a light kiss against his temple, Auggie pulled her over the arm of the chair sideways onto his lap.

"I was trying not to wake you," Charlotte shared with a smile.

Resting his forehead against the side of her head, Auggie whispered, "Stay here with me."

Closing her eyes, Charlotte drew in a slow breath before asking, "For how long?"

"I set an alarm on my phone."

Feeling both relief and disappointment as she thought to herself 'Damn Penny putting that in my head' Charlotte curled into him, resting her head against his shoulder.

∽∾

Slowly opening his eyes, it took Auggie a minute to figure out what was going on. Charlotte was on top of him in his chair. The recollection of waking up to her fingers running through his hair had nothing on the feeling of her soundly sleeping against him. Wrapping his arms around her, Auggie kissed her forehead.

Her eyes fluttered open as she whispered, "Don't get up."

"I gotta open the bar."

Charlotte pulled away with the most beautiful still half asleep expression on her face.

"You suck, I was sleeping good."

Auggie wanted to laugh but instead blurted, "Wait," as she stood up.

Stretching her arms high above her head, she yawned, "I need to go."

Slowly getting up, Auggie asked, "Are you coming back?"

"We'll see. Depends on how Silvia's melt down is going."

Auggie looked at her and nodded before a sudden realization struck him.

Pulling her to him, he slid his arms around her and leaned to her ear, quietly informing, "We just slept together."

Charlotte's voice was soft and low as she shared, "That makes you my first."

An unbelievably territorial instinct caused him to tighten his arms around her. Wondering if he should admit to the same for him, he'd never even passed out next to a woman much less snuggled to sleep with one.

Surprised that a word like 'Snuggle' entered his mind, Auggie cleared his throat and let go of her saying, "You got a key now so come by whenever."

Charlotte narrowed her eyes at him for a moment. As she flashed a sarcastic smile and reached down to grab her purse, Auggie knew he was a jerk for responding that way. Instead of making it right or even telling her goodbye, he turned and walked to his room to get ready for work.

❧ 25 ❧

Retribution

Day three of Silvia and Neck Tattoo's breakup saga continued on to reach new levels of ridiculousness. Charlotte had her own things to think about. She needed to quit being silly about things and just have sex with Auggie already. Knowing she was holding out because she liked being around him and in the back of her mind, she couldn't shake the feeling that all the craziness with him would be over as soon as she did. She didn't want that and talking to Penny didn't help at all. She had let Penny's take on what she and Auggie had going on cloud her thoughts.

Charlotte heard the 'My life is over because I'm not with you' song restarted for the millionth from Silvia's room and snapped. Marching out of her room and up to her sister's door, she flung it open.

"Gah, would you just get over it already!" Charlotte shouted.

Silvia's face was red and swollen as she screamed, "I can't!"

Snatching Silvia's iPhone out of its speaker dock, Charlotte threw it at her, griping, "At least change the damn song then."

"You're glad this happened! I hate you! You wanted us to break up!"

Charlotte had started to walk out when she whipped around, asking, "Excuse me?"

Wiping fresh tears from her eyes with her comforter, Silvia cried, "He hooked up with Lee-Lee."

"What is a Lee-Lee?"

"He swore there was only me and to trust him. You made me not trust him and he had sex with her. I hate you! You made me question him and he...he... I hate you! You made him have sex with her," Silvia spit out in a new anger induced crying spree.

After briefly considering the 'shake and curse' approach Auggie took with Braden when his heart was crushed, Charlotte decided on a more compassionate route.

"Think about what you're saying. Do you really think someone like him wasn't already screwing around?"

And then came the howling.

Shaking her head, Charlotte realized that wasn't the best thing for her to say as she asked, "Did you really love him?"

Silvia nodded wiping her comforter down her face again.

With a slight huff, Charlotte sat down on the side of Silvia's bed, "This is going to sound mean but before you start bawling again, think about what I'm saying, okay." Silvia nodded before Charlotte offered, "It's pretty clear he doesn't feel the same." She could tell another outburst was coming as she held up her finger, "Don't. No crying. Only thinking."

Silvia nodded again, frowning as she blinked her tears back.

"Now, I know it must hurt but since he doesn't love you and y'all are not going to live happily ever after, what would make you feel better?"

After a few minutes of sniffling, Silvia replied, "I want this to hurt him too."

Charlotte thought for a moment before informing, "Sit tight. I think I can help with that."

Silvia gave an interested look as Charlotte hopped off of her bed and ran out of the room.

Grabbing her cellphone off of her dresser, Charlotte looked at the time and called Auggie.

"Hey," he answered.

"I need a favor," she asked.

"What's up?"

Huffing into the phone, Charlotte answered, "You know that guy that thought I was checking him out at Ren's."

Auggie's tone was angry as he replied, "Yea."

"That's the kid that broke up with Silvia."

"You serious?"

"Yep, so I was thinking you could scare him a little or something. You know, let him know it's not okay to hurt my sister."

There was a hint of humor in his voice as he replied, "Sure. Let me call Oran to give him a heads up and see where they're at."

"I'm going back to Silvia's room to see if she has any special requests. I'll text you."

Laughing, Auggie said, "Okay."

Pleased with herself, Charlotte headed back across the hall.

Silvia was sitting up, waiting for Charlotte when she walked back into the room.

Smiling, Charlotte sat down next to Silvia on her bed, "How hurt do you want him?"

"What do you mean?" Silvia asked with eyes wide.

Charlotte rolled her eyes, saying, "We're going to teach him a lesson."

Glancing at the phone in Charlotte's hand Silvia shouted, "Oh my gosh! Who are you going to call?"

"It doesn't matter," Charlotte snapped before saying, "Do you want him hurting or not?"

Silvia sucked her bottom lip into her mouth before nodding.

"How hurt?"

Looking down, Silvia replied, "It would be nice if he cried."

"Make him cry, it is," Charlotte confirmed before sending a text to Auggie.

C: Make him cry. You can rough him up too if you want ;)

Auggie texted back.

A: You got it.

C: Thanks!

A: I'll call you in a few.

Charlotte nodded at her cellphone feeling like a good big sister.

৯৩

Auggie was cleared to be on the property and once Oran confirmed that the property owners were gone, he let the crew know what was going on. Auggie hopped out of his truck, making a beeline straight for Shawn.

Charging up behind him, Auggie grabbed him by the back of his shirt, swinging him around as he warned, "We got a problem."

The crew gathered around them at a distance as Shawn tripped and fell backwards.

Quickly scrambling back to his feet, Shawn shouted, "What's your problem?"

"You're my problem," he snapped, giving him a little shove.

Trying to act hard, Shawn took a step back, "Man, I ain't even trying to fight you."

"And you're not gonna. You're gonna cry like the little girl you are when I kick your ass for doin' Silvia dirty."

Shawn looked around at the crew before smarting off, "That prissy trick. She's lucky I was puttin' it to her anyways."

Auggie stepped forward as Shawn took another step back.

"You talk big, why ya backin' up?" Auggie questioned, knowing he was scared.

The crew laughing apparently gave Shawn a burst of confidence as he announced, "The only one backin' up was your girl last night on my..."

Before Shawn could finish the most hazardous statement of his life, Auggie grabbed the front of his shirt, lifting him off of the ground as he growled, "What about my girl?"

Practically screeching, Shawn apologized, "No! I'm sorry! Please! No! Please! I'm sorry!"

Releasing Shawn as he hunched over, Auggie instantly shoved him backwards as hard as he could.

"Ah, what the f..."

ॐॐ

Sitting on Silvia's bed with her, waiting for Auggie's call, Charlotte looked at her sister's matted hair and kind of missed seeing those tacky bows on her head.

"You should take a shower and get dressed. He's not worth you looking like crap. You were too pretty for him anyway."

With a surprised expression, Silvia asked, "You think I'm pretty?"

Charlotte teased, "Well at the moment, no. But usually, yes, I do."

Silvia frowned, saying, "I'm sorry for hating you."

"Okay..."

"I was really excited when I found out I was getting an older sister."

Shocked, Charlotte questioned, "You were?"

Nodding Silvia sat up a little straighter and shared, "I told all my friends. I couldn't wait. When you got here you just ignored me. You were so hateful all the time," stopping to shrug her shoulder she added, "Then you were all mom and dad talked about. What's wrong with Charlotte? Where's Charlotte? We need to help Charlotte. I guess I just hated you because I didn't get what I wanted or any attention once you were here."

Charlotte felt a lump in her throat as she replied, "I'm really sorry."

Silvia made a 'Whatever' face, saying, "I guess it could have been worse. Shannon's sister steals her jeans all the time and once she squeezes her fat butt into them they are ruined forever."

And just like that snotty, shallow Silvia was back, and Charlotte couldn't help but laugh.

Seeing Silvia stare at her like stretched out jeans were a serious matter and there was no reason to find it funny, Charlotte laughed even harder. Until, the screen of her cellphone lit up with a picture of Auggie.

"Is that..." Silvia started to question before Charlotte glared at her.

She quickly answered his call, "Hey."

Auggie's voice was full of irritation as he griped, "You owe me."

"Did he cry?" she asked confused as to why he was mad.

Auggie snapped, "No. He peed his pants then threw up on my boots."

Charlotte really didn't know how to respond so she turned to Silvia, sharing, "He peed is pants."

A satisfied smile formed across Silvia's face as she leaned back against her headboard.

Knowing her sister was listening even though she pretended not to, Charlotte told Auggie, "I appreciate your help."

"Yea, you better," he griped before asking, "Are you coming over?"

"It doesn't look that way," Charlotte answered.

Auggie sighed into the phone, "Alright."

"Umm... Thank you."

His voice was softer now as he assured, "I get it. Family thing."

"I owe you one."

Back to his cranky voice, Auggie said, "No, you owe me two. One for each boot," before he hung up.

Thinking of something nice to do for him, Charlotte noticed Silvia get out of bed.

Walking to her bathroom, Silvia glanced back at Charlotte, saying, "I won't tell."

Giving her sister a 'Thanks' smile, Charlotte looked down at her phone and resisted the urge to text Auggie.

Walking back to her room, Charlotte knew she needed to regain control of herself. She had been acting on impulse since the moment Auggie kissed her. Everything she said and did were things that came from deep inside her instead of her normal calculated self. Always before, there was a purpose to what she said and did. Now, she was letting her feelings take over and guide her. But for every feel good moment there was one that made her question herself. That needed to be corrected.

❧ 26 ❧

Unsettled

One long night at The Dog House, of suffering through an old pair of boots from the back of his closet, led to Auggie to waking up early Sunday. He still couldn't believe that punk threw up on him.

In all the fights he'd been in, that was a first. All he planned on doing was slapping him around a little until he cried but when he snapped off implying he was with Charlotte, Auggie lost it. Shawn didn't have to say her name. The second he said 'your girl', Charlotte flashed in his mind. She wasn't though. It was a right now thing. He knew it. She knew it. Auggie was letting things get out of hand by letting her get to him.

The remarkable moments that kept taking place between the two of them was causing Auggie to think about more than just sex with her. No wonder she didn't come see him yesterday. He was probably scaring her off by giving her a key and a taking a nap with her. Auggie was starting to feel miserable, and although it was a little comforting to feel misery instead of confusion, he knew if his dad was here, Gus would know the right thing to say to him.

Walking into his house, Auggie stopped right inside. Charlotte was standing there, leaned up against the bar that divided his kitchen and living room, wearing the black heels he'd held for ransom, tiny black shorts and a plaid shirt that could have easily been one of his if it wasn't a few sizes smaller.

"Good afternoon, Augustus," Charlotte greeted.

"Afternoon," he replied.

Unable to move, he needed to set his bag down and walk all the way into the house.

A sly smile formed across Charlotte's face as she said, "It's good to see you too," making her way towards him.

Auggie started to feel like he couldn't catch his breath as Charlotte brushed up against him before shutting the door behind him. She took the bag from him and set it down.

The tension in his body made Auggie want to go down on his knees as he asked, "What's going on?"

"I owe you, remember," she replied, walking back to his kitchen.

With her back turned, Auggie squeezed his eyes closed while uttering a curse word under his breath before finding the will to move.

Following her into his kitchen, Auggie gave himself a mental 'Be a man' pep talk.

Charlotte stopped at the counter and turned to him, confirming, "I owe you two, right. One for each boot."

Getting his breathing under control, he scowled at her, "That's what I said."

Reaching behind her back, she revealed a bottle of whisky.

Charlotte handed it to him, saying, "One."

Auggie had a pretty good idea what two was by the way she was acting. The whole thing was incredibly sexy but there was something off about it. She was being hot as hell but at the same time, there was a coldness to her.

Holding the bottle up, Auggie offered, "Let's have a drink then."

Stepping to him, Charlotte assured, "Two, isn't a set of glasses."

In his mind, Auggie busted the bottle open, took a long swig and bent her over the counter.

In reality, he shared, "I have glasses."

He could hear Charlotte let out a loud huff and smiled to himself imagining the face she was making at him behind his back.

As he set two glasses down on the counter, Charlotte asked, "You don't want me to settle my debt?"

Opening the bottle of whisky, Auggie filling the bottom of both glasses. He turned with one of the glasses in hand to offer her a drink and found her right in front of him. Resting her hands on his sides, she leaned into him.

"I'm good with the whisky," Auggie replied before turning his head away from her as he took a sip.

Her eyes narrowed in a hateful glare at him as she repeated, "You're good with the whisky."

Taking another sip, he said, "Yea, it's good whisky."

A disgusted expression appeared on Charlotte's face as she snapped, "You'd rather drink?"

Finishing off what was left in the glass before setting it down, Auggie griped, "This Charlotte bull-crap doesn't do it for me."

Shoving away from him, she questioned, "Oh, now I don't do it for you? And did you just call me crap?"

Frustrated and tired of her little charade, Auggie pulled her to him, swung around and pressed her against the wall.

Grabbing her hips he jerked her closer, "Yea sweetheart, you do it for me. Go ahead in there and take your pants off. I'm gonna need another drink first."

As Auggie stepped away to pour another drink, Charlotte stood there against the wall staring at him.

He refilled his glass, tipped it in her direction and winked at her before drinking his whisky down. Charlotte looked at him like she hated him. Thinking 'How does that feel' he wanted her to know exactly how she had made him feel. Hoping she was just as confused and frustrated as he was, that would serve her right; he almost dropped his glass on the floor. She was unbuttoning her shorts.

Sliding his glass across the counter, Auggie practically lunged at her. Pulling her hands away from her shorts and holding them up to her chest, he wrapped his arm tight around her.

Pressing his forehead against the side of her head, he pleaded in her ear, "Stop this."

Her voice was shaky as she offered, "If I do it for you, we should stop making this more than it is and have sex."

Unable to be anything but honest with her, Auggie swore, "Charlotte does do it for me and has since the moment, I saw you being manhandled outside the bar that night. But Lotte, with her sexy peacock tattoo and soft beautiful lips, she does everything to me."

Charlotte relaxed in his arms, mumbling, "This is crazy."

Auggie pulled her around to face him, agreeing "It is."

"You're turning me inside out."

Sincere in expression, he replied, "I know the feeling."

There was sadness in her eyes as she reminded, "I'm still leaving."

Nodding, he assured, "I'm still going to want to see you every day until you do."

Looking off to the side, she scowled before giving him a dirty look as she blurted, "Damn it! Now I still owe you one."

Allowing her to slip out of his arms, Auggie thought for a moment.

"Sex isn't an option anymore?" he questioned with a smile.

The corner of Charlotte's mouth curled into a smile as she informed, "That was Charlotte's offer. Lotte wants to hold out on you for a while."

"Does she?" he laughed.

Nodding, she raised her eyebrows, stating, "Yep, that's the kind of person she is."

"Well, I guess the only thing we can do now is get drunk."

Smiling at him, Charlotte replied, "Then pour me a glass, bartender."

Happy to have his girl back to normal, Auggie handed her the other glass of whisky.

❧❧

Auggie and Charlotte laid across his living room floor somewhere between drunk and sober. After texting Amila to tell her she had too much to drink and would be home in the morning, she showed Auggie pictures of her room and places she visited in Spain on her cell. She then assured him that he was her favorite sight to see in town and took what felt like five hundred pictures of them cheek to cheek as she swore all he had to do was smile and they'd be done. When he finally smiled, the way she wanted him to, she rewarded him with a long slow kiss.

Charlotte's eyes fluttered closed before she blinked them back open while her head rested against his chest. Holding her hand, it amazed him how something so simple could make him feel so good. Even drunk, it felt good to be next to her. It was more than likely the alcohol causing him to feel the way he was; Auggie wanted people to know she was his. Not necessarily his family but strangers. How would other men know she was off limits if they didn't know she was taken?

"Gotta be a way," Auggie mumbled, not realizing it was out loud until Charlotte asked, "To what?"

"You can't be like this."

"Drunk?" she laughed.

Flexing his hand around hers, Auggie replied, "That either."

Charlotte lifted her head, rolled onto her back.

Propping himself up on his elbow, he leaned over her saying, "Kieran can mark you for me."

"You sir, have had too much to drink," she laughed, running her hand under his beanie and into his hair.

Shaking his head against her hand, he whispered, "With a little A, so everyone knows."

"Knows what?" she breathed.

Auggie softly kissed her after replying, "I'm the only one that gets to touch you here." He ran his finger down her arm to her wrist, adding, "Here." Continuing on, he brushed his fingertips under the waistband of her shorts grazing the skin on her hip saying, "And here."

Charlotte let out a permissive sigh, allowing Auggie to gently touch every spot he wanted to mark as his own.

❦ 27 ❦

Stay

A repeated tapping from the kitchen woke Charlotte. Stretching out her arms and legs on Auggie's couch, she wasn't entirely sure how she had ended up there. Remembering his living room floor being where she passed out, she looked up to see Auggie sitting down on the coffee table in front of her.

Crossing her arms over her face, she questioned, "How did I get here?"

"I woke up on the floor and put you there before I went to bed."

Humor coated her tone as she replied, "Guess it's good you didn't take advantage of me."

"I still may have," he replied in a slightly concerned tone. Sliding her arms down, Charlotte rubbed her eyes.

Smiling at him, she assured, "Actually, you passed out just as I was about to take advantage of you."

With a disappointed expression, Auggie replied, "That's depressing."

Charlotte let out a laugh before saying, "I thought so too."

Auggie flashed a quick smile at her before offering, "I made you some toast."

Slowly sitting up, she nodded, "I need to brush my teeth." Hopping up, Auggie quickly made his way to the kitchen.

An awful throbbing headache let charlotte know exactly how much she had drunk as she stood up. Looking around, she saw her purse on the kitchen table and headed in that direction.

Auggie popped in front of her just before she reached the table, informing, "There's stuff for you in the hall bathroom."

Charlotte's head hurt too bad to question him as she changed direction, making her way to the bathroom. Stepping in, she closed the bathroom door before seeing a small bag sitting on the counter next to the sink. Peeking inside, she found a toothbrush, toothpaste, a little cup and a washcloth inside. Closing her eyes, she let out a happy sigh before using the items in the bag.

Back at the kitchen table, Charlotte saw Auggie sitting in one of the chairs. A plate of dry toast, a cup of tea and two aspirin set in front of the empty chair next to him.

Taking her seat, she asked, "Did you leave while I was asleep?"

Nodding, Auggie answered, "After my mom's, I stopped at the store."

Charlotte nodded back, questioning, "What time is it?"

"A little after three."

Thinking, 'Great' as she lifted a piece of toast to take a bite, she remembered texting Amila she would be home in the morning.

"You okay?"

"Yea, I just know I'm going to get griped out when I get back."

"Stay here then."

Dropping her toast onto her plate, Charlotte turned her head and stared at him in surprise.

"I got you some other stuff too. In case you wanted to stay."

"Umm... stay?"

The expression on Auggie's face showed he realized how what he said sounded as he clarified, "The night."

Charlotte quickly blurted, "Oh."

"Yea," he confirmed with a confused expression before sharing, "I'll be right back."

As he walked out of the kitchen Charlotte took her aspirin, mentally scolding, 'Get a handle on yourself'. When Auggie stepped back to the table, he set a large shopping bag down on the chair he had sat in.

Charlotte immediately apologized, saying, "I didn't mean to make that weird. My head is killing me and..."

Stopping her, he laughed, "Finish your toast so I can see if you approve of what I got."

With a loud sigh, Charlotte cautioned, "I'm done unless you'd like me to throw up on you too."

"Let me take that then," he said, grabbing her plate.

Charlotte waited for him to come back before looking to see what he had bought her.

Auggie pulled a few solid colored t-shirts and pairs of cotton shorts out of the bag before showing her his personal favorite. It was a faded black tee that had Auggie written on a dog house on the front and Caffrey across the back.

"Penny had 'em made for us awhile back, I wore it a few times," he shared.

Charlotte tried to control her smile from getting too wide as she replied, "I like that one a lot."

A proud smile followed as Auggie offered, "If you wanna take a shower, there's underwear in there too."

Stopping him as he started to place her clothes back into the bag she asked, "You bought me panties?"

Giving her a stupid look, he replied, "You know I did."

She had completely forgotten about daring him to buy them as she blurted, "Show me."

Scowling, he asked, "Where are mine?"

"I didn't get you any," she laughed before informing, "I just wanted to see if you would."

Narrowing his eyes, Auggie fussed, "Are you serious?"

She nodded, admitting, "I was messing with you."

"You're wrong for that."

Continuing to laugh, Charlotte said, "Awe... don't be mad."

Raising an eyebrow, he assured, "I'm not but I will get even."

Giving him an eye roll, she urged, "Show me."

Auggie reached down into the bag before tossing a package of plain white panties in front of her.

Charlotte made a disgusted face, questioning, "What are those?"

"Panties," he replied.

Taking a deep breath, she looked up at him, asking, "Exactly what is it about me that screams granny panties?"

"They're not," he argued, grabbing the package and looking it over.

"It's not gonna say that on the package," she laughed before saying, "I'm going to take a shower, so I don't go home smelling like I was drinking all night."

As she stood, Auggie pulled her to him, asking, "Can I come?"

"No," she answered giving him an absurd look.

"Please," he tried with a wide smile.

Shaking her head at him, Charlotte grabbed her purse and bag of clothes before heading back to the bathroom.

Sitting in his chair, Auggie couldn't shake the anxious feeling that had come over him. The knowledge that Charlotte was naked in his hallway bathroom was going to give him a panic attack. The longer he waited for her to come out, the worse it got. He started imagining all kinds of things. What if she slipped and fell? She could have gotten sick and needed him. Did she see the towels? She could be standing there shivering with no way to dry off. Finally, unable to stand it any longer he decided to make sure she was okay.

Auggie was about to knock on the bathroom door when it slowly opened. The most glorious scent flowed with her as Charlotte stepped out. Wearing the grey cotton shorts and black v-neck that he bought her, her hair was still wet. He'd never seen her hair wet before.

Glancing at him as she made her way to the living room, she teased, "Hey there creeper."

Following behind her, he defended himself, saying, "It seemed like you were taking a long time, I was worried."

"How dangerous is your bathroom?"

Ignoring her smartass question, Auggie asked, "How's your head? Did everything fit okay?"

Turning to face him, she replied, "Better and yea, except for those awful underwear you got. They're dang near as big as the shorts I'm wearing."

Messing with her, he used her own words to taunt, "Awe...don't be mad."

"I'm not," she said with a smile before sharing, "I'm not wearing them."

Auggie's entire body begged to know the answer as he questioned, "Them or any?"

"Interesting question."

"Are you going to answer it?"

With an all too confident sigh she replied, "I think I'll just let you wonder."

On impulse, he blurted, "Stay."

Charlotte gave him a serious look before taking a step back.

She stared at him for a long moment before pulling the side of her shorts down, revealing she was, in fact, not only wearing panties, she was wearing the ones he bought her.

Shaking his head, he smiled, saying, "You just showed me your panties."

A soft smile appeared as she questioned, "Why do you keep asking me to stay?"

"That's a dumb question."

Back to an old familiar tendency, Charlotte gave the bottom of her shirt a tug before griping, "I know it is but I asked it so I would appreciate you giving me an answer," as she sat down in his chair.

Auggie watched her cross her legs and glare at him.

"Alright. Instead of doing this woman thing you do, where you try to coax something out of me, why don't you just say what's on your mind."

With a frustrated sigh, Charlotte snapped, "I'm not trying to coax anything from you. And if I was, it would be because getting a little clarity from you is nearly impossible."

Irritation coated every word as he replied, "You are leaving. I know this because you feel the need to keep reminding me. Every damn time I have to hear you're leaving. It's like your little way of diggin' at me."

Hopping to her feet, she fussed, "Why do you keep asking if you don't want the answer?"

"When I say stay I'm not asking you. It's not a question."

Shaking her head at him she quickly tried to make her way past him.

Stopping her, he caught her by the arm, explaining, "I know you're not going to, but I can't help it. I don't want you to lie to me, but that doesn't mean I want the truth either. I need to say it because I have no idea what I'm gonna do when you go."

Charlotte's eyes reflected the feeling behind his words as she stared at him. He wanted to kiss her but instead Auggie pulled her against him as tight as he could, wishing he wouldn't have to let her go.

❧

Parked under the carport, Charlotte tried to gather her thoughts before walking into the house. It wasn't the disappointed look she would get from Emerson or the questions Amila would ask that was bothering her, although it would be great if she didn't have to deal with them right now. All she was supposed to do was help Auggie get out more. That day at the hospital, William told her how worried he was that his brother would never see past the end of his own nose, as he put it. Anyone in their right mind would agree he was an ass, but William was right, he had a good heart and there was so much more to him than the rude bartender she thought she knew. She promised William she would show Auggie that not everything in life is cut and dry, that stepping outside your comfort zone doesn't just make you uncomfortable, it makes you want more out of life.

Dwelling on her last conversation with William, she already fulfilled her promise. She had fooled herself into thinking Auggie would be a fun way to pass the time until she left. Killing time wasn't what she was doing with him. It was more like savoring time. All of the sudden, something Penny said shook her insides causing her to roll her window down in case she threw up. That day at the hospital wasn't for William, it was for her. She was the cut and dry ass refusing to step outside her comfort zone. The metaphorical more that Trace had always spouted wasn't more at all. It was a progression of the same thing. That's why she was so content with him. Auggie made her uncomfortable from the beginning, and it was because he was the more life had to offer. Charlotte's revelation pushed every feeling she had buried deep down inside to the surface as she acknowledged that the Caffrey men weren't the only ones that went down hard when they fell.

28

Family

Waking up to a note laying over her cellphone on her dresser from Amila that said, 'Come to the dining room when you wake up', Charlotte knew when she got home the day before and they let her go to her room without saying a word was just too easy. Brushing the note onto the floor, she picked up her cellphone and saw a text from Auggie.

A: Good Morning!

She smiled, texting back.

C: It's afternoon now ;) but Hello anyway.

Charlotte started to get up when her phone vibrated in her hand.

A: I sent that 2hrs ago.

C: Just woke up.

A: Geez lazy. Come see me.

C: Can't, got a meeting with the parents :/

A: ????

C: I'm sure they're mad about yesterday and the day before. Sorry.

A: Tonight?

C: I'll let you know.

A: If you can't can I call you? I hate text messages.

C: Yes :) I'll let you know in a little bit.

A: Okay. I'm going back to sleep then. Bye.

C: Bye.

Tossing her phone on her bed, she walked to her bathroom.

Charlotte took her time brushing her teeth and getting dressed as she delayed the inevitable, 'You're a grown up but we're still going to tell you what to do' talk. Stepping out of her room into the hallway, she headed for the stairs when Silvia popped out of her room.

"Dad is really mad at you," she warned.

Rolling her eyes, Charlotte mumbled, "Yea, what else is new," continuing on her way.

Down the stairs and through the kitchen, she stepped into the dining room to find Amila and Emerson waiting on her.

Looking at their faces, Emerson's disappointed and Amila's concerned, the usual, Charlotte wondered how long they had been sitting there waiting.

Sliding into a chair at the opposite end of the table from them, she asked, "What's up?"

"Where were you?" Emerson questioned in a harsh tone.

Charlotte tried to keep a straight face as she replied, "Upstairs in my room."

Amila looked down, fighting a smile of her own as Emerson stated, "There are rules in this house and we expect you to follow them."

Narrowing her eyes at Emerson, she questioned, "What rules did I break?"

"You stayed out all night."

"I texted Amila and let her know I wasn't coming home."

"You were out drinking."

"I'm over twenty-one."

"You are being irresponsible."

Charlotte gave him a stupid look, saying, "That's your opinion."

Emerson appeared flustered as he stressed, "Staying out all night, getting drunk and tattooed is not responsible. It is also disrespectful to us."

Standing up, she replied, "I'm sorry you don't agree with my choices but to be clear, I got *a* tattoo and I was sober when I did. Yes, I had too much to drink and didn't come home. That was the responsible thing to do. I wasn't going to drive after I had been drinking. And I also happen to think not coming home drunk, where my underage brothers and sisters live, was pretty damn respectful."

Emerson stood up too, barking, "Do not curse at this table."

Frustrated, he wasn't even listening to her, Charlotte yelled, "Why am I always wrong? It doesn't matter what I do you're going to find something wrong with it."

He shouted back, "What am I supposed to think?"

"More of me than you do," Charlotte snapped as she started to walk out.

"Both of you sit back down, "Amila ordered in an 'I'm tired of this' tone.

Doing as he was told, Emerson turned to her, saying, "We agreed that..." before she cut him off, correcting, "I agreed to sit in here while you talked to her. That's not what you're doing."
Looking like a scolded child, Emerson placed his hands in his lap frowning at her.

Amila focused on Charlotte, staring at her until she sat back down. With a loud huff, she crossed her arms, taking a seat.

"Now Charlotte, you have to look at this from Emerson's perspective. He's worried because he loves you. You can't just turn off feeling parental once a kid hits eighteen."
Charlotte started to say something when Amila held her finger up in a 'keep your mouth closed' fashion.

"And Emerson, how is she supposed to feel. You rarely talk to her and when you do it's to tell her how disappointed you are in her."

The dining room was silent for several minutes before Amila stood up.

"I expect the two of you to talk to each other. Not yell or be defensive. Talk," Amila informed before stepping out of the room.

Charlotte and Emerson watched Amila close the doors to the dining room before he shared, "I do not like it when she does that."

Nodding, Charlotte agreed, "When she puts you in your place."

"Yes."

With a slight smile, she added, "And you can't even argue because of the way she says things makes you feel bad for being wrong in the first place."

"Exactly," Emerson replied before saying, "We probably should do what she says."

Charlotte took a breath, saying, "I don't have anything to say."

Emerson nodded at her before resting his hands on top of the table.

Tapping his fingers against the table, Emerson glanced around the room. Charlotte watched his eyes soften as he smiled.

"Roberts is not the most upstanding last name around."

Confused, Charlotte replied, "Could have fooled me."

Smiling wider while shaking his head, Emerson informed, "It's powerful and infamous, not upstanding."

"Is that so?" Charlotte said, finding that somewhat humorous.

With a slight nod, he shared, "It is. My father was a powerful man. He was highly respected. That does not mean he was respectable."

"Like you?" she sarcastically asked.

"I try to be. I like to think I am a better father than he was, but I imagine you feel differently."

"Hmm..." Charlotte pondered before questioning, "What was he like?"

Emerson chuckled, replying, "Always disappointed in me."

Raising her eyebrows, Charlotte said, "Well..."

A heavy sigh preceded a laugh as Emerson admitted, "No need to rub it in, I know what it feels like to be on your end of things."

Charlotte nodded before asking, "Why did you name the foundation after him if there were hard feelings between y'all."

"He was an orphan that never got adopted."

Surprised at that fact, she replied, "Oh, so he didn't have any family."

Emerson appeared uncomfortable as he shared, "He had an older brother that was adopted."

"They lost touch? You don't keep in contact with him?"

With a serious expression, he replied, "No. They stayed in contact with each other. I was not aware he had a brother until a few months after my father died. His brother is also deceased."

"I'm sorry," Charlotte said, never before thinking Emerson's life was less than perfect.

Sitting up tall, he assured, "Don't be. I'm not."

"What happened?"

Relaxing as he spoke, Emerson appeared satisfied, saying, "He was shot in the face."

Confused by the way he answered, Charlotte asked, "By who?"

Clearing his throat, he replied, "Someone who is also now deceased," before a warm smile covered his face as he bargained, "What do you say, for Amila's sake, we reach a compromise."

"Okay..."

"I'll be less of an uptight authoritarian and you can at least pretend to be happy you are a part of this family."

Charlotte thought for a moment before agreeing, "Well now that I know we really aren't an upstanding family, I don't need to pretend."

Emerson laughed as he stood, asking, "Would you like a hug?"

Shrugging a shoulder at him, she replied, "No thanks but thanks. Okay?"

Another warm smile appeared on his face as he nodded before walking out of the dining room.

Oddly pleased with the way her conversation with Emerson went, Charlotte wondered if it was an indication that she should stay. She always had Amila and Lola, now Silvia seemed to be coming around. Jenna was quiet with her nose always stuck in a book. Max and Luke had no time for her but were still nice. Trent was away doing good deeds however his return wouldn't change anything. She started to feel like she was really part of the family. Not to mention, she had friends. Always Ren, and Penny now too. When she thought about Auggie, it occurred to her there were more reasons for her to stay than to go.

As much as she wanted to see Auggie, her new found feeling of belonging prompted her to text him.

C: Hey, family time tonight. See you tomorrow :)

When he didn't text back right away, she figured he was still asleep. Rounding up her sisters, Charlotte had them follow her back downstairs.

All four of them gave a unanimous, "Ewww!" when they stumbled upon Emerson and Amila practically mauling each other in the kitchen.

Figuring Amila was rewarding Emerson for doing what she asked, it was understandable but still pretty gross.

Shaking off the disturbing image while Emerson and Amila smiled as if there was nothing wrong with that horrendous display they witnessed, Charlotte informed, "Amila, if you can tear yourself away from Emerson, we are having a girl's night."

Pushing away from her make out partner, Amila cheered, "All of you? Together!"

"All of us," Charlotte replied, making a circle with her finger that included Amila before fake frowning at Emerson as she said, "Sorry, no boys allowed."

Emerson gave a laugh, saying, "I'll get the boys and find something for us to get into. I hope you ladies have fun." Squeals and giggles of excitement erupted from Amila and Charlotte's sisters as she smiled wide at the happiness her idea created.

29

C&A

Rushing home from The Dog House, Auggie couldn't wait to see Charlotte. He had to laugh at himself for being so excited. He hadn't seen or talked to her in a whole day.

He was going to call her the previous night but when he saw her text that said see you tomorrow, he figured she was busy with her family. It was fine at the time because he had spent the morning looking for something special for her and only caught around two hours of sleep before work. By the time he got off, he was so tired he laid down on the couch and passed out.

Tonight, just as he started to close up, Charlotte texted him saying she was at his house along with the pictures she took of them drunk and laying on his floor. One picture in particular stood out from the rest. He was smiling while she kissed his cheek. Between that picture and knowing she was at his house waiting for him, he couldn't get there fast enough.

Sprinting to his front door, he knew she had missed him too when he reached the porch and the door swung open. Standing there, waiting for him to get home, wearing his Dog House t-shirt and little red shorts was his girl.

Lifting her off of the ground as he hugged her tight and kissed her he managed to say, "Gah, I missed you," in between kisses.

"I like that," she assured as he put her down.

"That I missed you?"

Nodding with a smile, Charlotte pulled away before blurting, "Oh, I got you something."

"Lotte," he said, wishing she hadn't.

Picking up a box off of the coffee table, she replied, "I know you don't like the idea of me buying you things but I still owed you one and when I saw this I had to get it for you." As he scowled taking the package from her, Charlotte swore, "It wasn't even expensive."

Shaking his head at her, Auggie opened the box and pulled out a gray beanie.

"Turn it over," she instructed as he gave her a confused expression.

It looked exactly like the one he had on until he turned it over. In little white letters, C&A was embroidered on it. Instantly he knew, Charlotte and Auggie.

As he stared at it, Charlotte said, "You don't have to wear it. I was shopping with Silvia, saw it and thought you'd get a kick out of it."

Pulling the one he was wearing off, he tossed it at her, sharing, "Are you kidding? This is my new favorite."

Auggie ran his fingers through his hair before pulling the new beanie on.

Charlotte seemed pleased that he liked it which made Auggie like it even more.

She eyed him, saying, "Looks good," before sliding his old one over her head, asking, "What about me?"

Auggie wasn't sure what it was exactly but seeing her wearing his beanie caused all the air to leave his lungs.

Scowling at him, Charlotte held out her hand and stated, "Augustus Caffrey."

"You're too pretty to be me," he replied with a smile.

Shaking her head, she pretend griped, "You wanna fight? Girls are pretty. I'm a man."

Rolling his eyes, Auggie played back, "Okay big talker, let's go."

Holding her fists up, she continued to make fun of him, saying, "Come on, I'll put you on your ass."

Auggie picked her up and tossed her on the couch before pinning her down. They both laughed as he playfully kissed her face and neck. Stopping to catch his breath Auggie was suddenly aware of their position. She was lying underneath him with her legs wrapped around his waist. As his breathing slowed his heart rate picked up. Staring up at him, Charlotte's smile faded into a look of urgency.

"Kiss me," she breathed.

There was no thought, he simply acted.

Moving under him as she unbuttoned his shirt, Charlotte's sighs of anticipation made it hard for him to concentrate. Auggie kept trying to remember not to touch her shirt. The last thing he wanted was for her to stop him but at the same time he wanted to feel her everywhere.

Breaking their kiss for a moment, he whispered, "I know under is off limits. What about over?" sliding his hand across the front of her shirt.

Nodding, she breathed out, "Over's fine...over's good," before pulling him back to her lips.

Pleased with her answer, at least it was something and since he didn't plan on their first time being there only time, he could talk her out of her shirt another day. For the moment, those little red shorts were his goal.

Bracing himself with one hand on the arm of the couch, he hovered over her smoothing his other hand down her side to her hip, urging, "I wanna hear you say it, Lotte."

Running her fingers into his hair while sliding his new beanie off, she swore, "Want... I want you," as she pulled him back to her.

With tunnel vision and only one thing on his mind, Auggie knew he needed to slow things down for a minute. The last thing he wanted was to shoot first and have her disappointed later. Pulling away from Charlotte, he went back on his knees.

"You're prepared, right?" she questioned as he took his shirt the rest of the way off.

Her face was flush and she was all kinds of beautiful as he looked down at her.

"They're in my room," he informed, letting her know he was, just as she'd asked him to be.

A sly smile formed on her face as she reached behind herself under the couch cushion and pulled out a little square wrapper.

"I gotcha covered," Charlotte shared, waving it in front of him between her first two fingers.

He almost questioned how it got there or why she asked if she had one, then quickly decided it wasn't important as he grabbed the bottoms of her shorts and pulled them off and her legs against his chest in one fluid movement. Charlotte slid her legs down his sides before wrapping them around his waist. Tucking the wrapper against her palm, she grabbed the front of his pants. Popping the button from its hole as she unfastened his pants, Auggie couldn't believe the feeling it created. It felt like a pulse or even maybe a spasm.

It wasn't until Charlotte gave him a strange look, asking, "Are you vibrating?" that he realized his phone was still in his pocket.

She gave a slight laugh as he pulled his cellphone out and tossed it on the coffee table.

Auggie's cellphone continued to vibrate loud against the coffee table with each incoming text message. Reaching over, he picked it up and tossed it on the floor next to the couch where the only sound was a light hum.

"Do you need to get that?" she asked, sounding disappointed.

Laying over her, he kissed her before saying, "It's just Kieran."

"What if something's wrong? It's really late. There could be an emergency."

"It can't be that serious if he's sending a text."

Charlotte nodded before running her lips from the side of his neck to the top of his shoulder. She glided her hands down his back until her fingers met the waistband of his boxers. Sliding her hands under, she stopped when his phone started to ring. 'Somebody's gonna die' Auggie thought as he reached for his phone on the floor.

"What?" he growled into the phone as Charlotte slid her arms to the center of his back.

Kieran's voice was stressed as he demanded, "You need to get out here."

"I'm with my girl," Auggie snapped into the phone as Charlotte gave him a soft smile.

A bit more hostile now Kieran shared, "Braden's here with a damn heart."

Auggie scowled, glancing at Charlotte before scooting back and sitting up.

"Tell him no!" Auggie griped into the phone.

Charlotte sat up next to him as Kieran reminded, "You know I can't. It's not up to me to decide who gets what."

Frustrated and torn, Auggie looked at Charlotte as she whispered, "You need to go."

Auggie placed his hand over his mouth before running it down the front of his beard saying, "I'm on my way."

Ending the call, Auggie leaned to Charlotte and softly kissed her.

"It's okay, take care of your family," she assured.

Pulling her closer he shook his head onto her shoulder, "Braden's..." before she stopped him, saying, "I heard Kieran. You need to stop him."

The drastic change, from we're doing this to my dumbass brother is ruining his life, made Auggie feel slightly woozy and if he was honest, sad.

"Don't go until I get back," he requested before giving her another soft kiss.

Charlotte reached down and grabbed the beanie she had bought him.

Pulling it over his head, she gave him a kiss before replying, "I should go."

Reaching down, Auggie picked her shorts up off of the floor, saying "I'll walk you to your car," as he handed them to her.

Taking her shorts from him, Charlotte shared, "I'm punching Braden right in the eye the next time I see him."

With a heavy sigh Auggie stood up, buttoned his pants and pulled his shirt back on thinking, 'I'm kickin' everyone's ass when I get out there."

❧◦❧

It took around twenty minutes for Auggie to make it out to Kieran's place. When he arrived Kieran's wife, Liv, was standing on their porch waiting for him. He'd known Liv for around seven years. In fact, Auggie was there when Kieran first met her. She wasn't really Auggie's style of woman although he always thought she was pretty. Liv had long black hair, blue eyes and both her arms were completely covered with brightly colored tattoos. Kieran was smitten the moment he saw her. All in all, she was fun to be around because she always felt like the girl version of Kieran to Auggie.

Stepping onto the raised porch, all he had to do was look at the expression on Liv's face to know he was too late.

"What's goin' on Auggs?" she greeted with an irritated tone.

Shaking his head at her, Auggie griped, "Where are they?"

"You know where they are," she snapped back at him.

Auggie started to walk past her when she jumped in front of him, warning, "You can't go in there."

"The hell I can't," he argued.

Pushing him back a little, Liv fussed, "What are you gonna do? He already started."

Narrowing his eyes at her, he answered, "I'm gonna knock him out and have Kieran cover what he's already done with a pink unicorn or maybe a princess."

"Ha!" Liv blurted before sharing, "That'd be funny but you know you can't."

Taking a step back, Auggie snapped, "He should of told him no."

Nodding, she agreed, "I told him the same thing but you know he takes this serious. His legacy and all."

Auggie paced back and forth for a few minutes before saying, "Kieran should have called me as soon as he showed up."

"He did, the second Braden handed him the heart, he walked out of the house and called you."

"Y'all couldn't have stalled him 'til I got here?"

Giving Auggie a dirty look, Liv fussed, "You think we didn't try? We don't want him to do this anymore than you do. Braden made Kieran feel bad, like he wasn't following behind his dad right."

"It's just a damn tattoo!"

Pointing her finger at him, Liv snapped, "You and I both know that's not true. If it were, you wouldn't be here right now."

Stepping away so her finger was no longer in his face, Auggie shook his head.

Auggie was at a loss. Furious and disappointed in his brother all he could think about was Charlotte lying under him. He could have been wrapped up in Charlotte, all of her, instead of standing outside his cousin's house arguing with Liv if Braden wasn't such a dumbass.

"I'm gonna go."

Liv appeared confused, asking, "You don't want to wait for him to come out?"

"I don't want to see him at all right now," he replied, stepping off of the porch.

Walking back to his truck, he turned to see Liv wave at him before stepping back into her house.

Hopping into his truck, Auggie noticed his phone flashing from the dashboard. Swiping the lock screen picture of Charlotte kissing his cheek, he smiled at the picture, then the text message from her that said 'Nite' with a little heart beside it. Instead of texting her back, he called.

"Hi there," Charlotte answered in a hushed tone.

"Did you make it home okay?" he asked, adoring the sound of her voice, low and sleepy.

"Yea, did you stop him?"

With a heavy sigh, he replied, "Kieran had already started it by the time I got there."

There was a long pause before she consoled, "Sorry."

"Yea," he muttered before saying, "I'm on my way home now."

"Okay. Oh, I almost forgot, I made plans with Penny tomorrow so I'll see you Friday."

Disappointed, he said, "Alright, see you Friday."

He could hear the smile in her voice as she whispered, "Goodnight Augustus."

"Goodnight Charlotte."

Setting his cellphone in the dash compartment, Auggie drove home, wishing she would have stayed. There wasn't a whole lot of things he could think of that were better than knowing she was there waiting for him.

30

Plans

Charlotte's bed shook, startling her awake. Rolling over she saw Silvia lying next to her. Even though they had sort of buried the hatchet, Charlotte didn't find her intrusion pleasant in anyway.

"Do you not understand the concept of knocking," Charlotte griped.

Silvia rolled her eyes in a 'whatever' fashion as she asked, "What are we doing today?"

"No idea what you're doing, I have plans with Penny," she replied, dragging herself out of bed.

Making her way to the bathroom, Charlotte stopped dead in her tracks when she heard Silvia taunt, "And where did you sneak off to last night, Mrs. Caffrey."
Looking over, Charlotte caught a glimpse of herself in the mirror. She was still wearing Auggie's dog house shirt.

After mumbling a curse word under her breath, Charlotte reminded, "Guess it's good we're friends now, right."
Silvia started to say something when Lola pranced in the room with Jenna right behind her.

Thinking 'When did my room become so popular', Charlotte hurried into the bathroom. Sitting down on the edge of the bathtub, she had to laugh at the situation. In what world is a grown woman afraid of children tattling on

283

her. She had been dead set against anyone knowing she had anything to do with Auggie even when it was nothing more than fulfilling a promise. Although she still liked the idea of having him as her little secret, she was never big on sharing her personal life. The fact that she was thinking about staying, made her wonder if it would always be this way or if there was a chance of them going out together in public without all hell breaking loose.

As Charlotte started to brush her teeth, the bathroom door swung open and Silvia popped her head in.

"Seriously?" Charlotte tried to blurt with a mouth full of toothpaste.

Silvia gave her a stupid look, handing her a t-shirt.

"By the way, we're not friends. We're sisters. I kinda think that's better."

Charlotte nodded at her sister and gave her an appreciative glance as Silvia left the bathroom.

As the door closed, she heard Silvia shout, "You're welcome."

After brushing her teeth, Charlotte leaned against the counter staring at herself in the mirror. She wasn't just Charlotte anymore. She was Emerson and Amila's daughter, a sister, a friend and Auggie's girl.

☙❧

Laughing so hard, Charlotte didn't know whether she was going to pee her pants or spit her drink all over the table she and Penny were sitting at. The stories of her growing up were hysterical.

Like the time Auggie and Braden wouldn't stop arguing so Sarah decided she would force them to get along by duct taping their hands together. After only an hour, Auggie had two broken fingers and Braden's shoulder was dislocated. Sarah gave up and cut them apart.

Then there was the time they glued Ailin's hand to the side of his head. Sarah shaved his head but couldn't get all the hair off his hand and he spent two days walking around with a hairy palm. And of course, the first and only boy Penny ever brought home, Auggie and Braden took him out back and showed him a few crosses in the backyard, where various childhood pets were buried. They told him that's what happened to the other boys that took their sister out. He was so terrified he sat a seat apart from her at the movies and brought her home two hours early.

When the waiter brought their food, he gave them both a polite smile before winking at Penny. Pursing her lips into a smile, Penny gave him a little wave as he turned and walked away. Charlotte turned and looked back at him, noticing how he kept looking back at Penny.

"I think he likes you," Charlotte shared.

Penny let out a deep sigh, informing, "I liked him too, a year ago, when he took me out. That was before he asked me to call him Ramone and spank him." Charlotte's eyes were wide and she didn't know if she should laugh of feel bad for Penny as she continued, "Which I guess would have been fine to try if it wasn't our first date or if his is name wasn't Danny."

"How do you do that?" she asked.

"What?"

Smiling, Charlotte replied, "You make everything sound good. Even when it's not."

"I like to be happy. Things happen or they don't and there's no good reason not to look for the best in every situation. I get upset like everybody else, but I never dwell on anything negative because I'm alive and I have a family that loves me."

"I'm glad we're friends," Charlotte assured.

Penny gave a laugh, saying, "Told ya, I'm a lot of fun to be around."

Charlotte swore, "You are but you're also a really good friend."

Giving her a suspicious look, Penny questioned, "Are you buttering me up for something."

Charlotte frowned, assuring, "No, I really mean it," then smiled, "Well, there is something."

Giggling at being semi right, Penny said, "Let's hear it."

"I was thinking about staying," Charlotte shared in a quiet voice.

Penny's eyes and flew open wide as she clapped her hands and bounced in her seat.

"I knew it! Y'all are in love and y'all are going to get married and have lots of babies and..."

"Whoa!" Charlotte blurted at her before fussing, "First of all, shush. None of that is going on."

With a pouty expression, Penny complained, "Awe, you got me all excited for nothing."

Charlotte couldn't help laughing a little at Penny's reaction.

"Second, I'm still not completely sure, so don't say anything to anyone. But I thought if I did... Would you want to get an apartment with me?"

Penny looked like she was about to cry as she replied, "Really?"

"Yea," Charlotte stressed, not fully understanding why Penny was so emotional.

A happy sigh, preceded Penny saying, "That sounds great."

It was strange to Charlotte how making other people happy could bring her so much joy. First with Amila and her sisters and now with Penny.

She was almost one hundred percent sure about staying. The only question left was how would Auggie feel about it. He kept telling her to stay but would that change if she wasn't going to leave. It's easy to say you want something when there's no real commitment involved.

ൟ

After finishing the day off by having dinner with the family and family movie night, Charlotte sat on her bed. Working on Sophia's baby shower present, she decided she just wanted to sit and think. Her visit home had gone nothing like she thought it would. In fact it was turning out not to be a visit at all.

Deciding she should get some sleep, Charlotte slid under her covers. Grabbing her phone off of her dresser, she was about to send Auggie a goodnight text when his picture flashed across the screen.

"Hey," she answered with a smile on her face.

"Did I wake you up?"

"No, I was just about to text you goodnight."

There was a hint of amusement in his voice as he asked, "Yea, are you already in bed?"

"Yes."

"So, any chance you sleep naked?"

Laughing, Charlotte answered, "No, I don't."

"Whatcha wearin'?"

"My awesome dog house t-shirt and panties but not the grandma kind you like."

Auggie laughed before saying, "I like that."

"That I'm not wearing granny panties?"

"Yea, that too," he replied, laughing again.

Charlotte liked the fact that he liked her sleeping in his shirt.

"Just so you know, I am naked underneath."

His tone lowered as he said, "Is that right."

Curling up in her sheets, Charlotte offered, "Would you like to come over here and check?"

There was a long pause before he questioned, "If I did would you let me?"

Realizing, she suggested he would get under the shirt privileges, she corrected herself, saying, "Hmmm... No but you can touch me here."

"Where is here?"

"Right there."

"Where is right there?"

"If you were here, I could show you," she teased in a soft tone.

"Woman, you're lucky I know your messin' with me. Otherwise I'd be under the sheets with you right now."

Charlotte gave a slight laugh as she said, "Sweet dreams Augustus."

"Yea, like I'm gonna be able to sleep now," he griped with a hint of humor in his tone.

"Goodnight Charlotte."

Ending the call, Charlotte tucked her phone under the covers with her.

❧ 31 ☙

Marked

Somewhere between sleep and reality, Auggie felt at ease. The last two nights he'd dreamed about Charlotte but not the usual, he had his way with her kind. Twice she'd disappeared while he was holding her and once his door actually ate her. They weren't nightmares, more like bad dreams that made him feel uncomfortable when he woke. Keeping his eyes closed, he took a deep breath, swearing he could smell her. It was relaxing and soothing until he heard the alarm on his phone go off.

Slowly opening his eyes, Auggie reached to grab his phone. Not fully awake yet, he looked at his empty night stand. His phone wasn't there but when he looked up, Charlotte was.

"Nice background," she said, waving his phone at him.
Without a second thought, he reached out and grabbed her, pulling her onto the bed with him. She let out a squeal as he rolled them both over keeping his arms and legs firmly around her.

"Good morning," Charlotte whispered, most likely because he was squishing her against the bed.

Burying his face in the side of her neck, he breathed her in, saying, "Morning."

Charlotte's arms slid around him, pulling herself even closer as she rested her head against his.

It felt so amazing to have her curled up with him in his bed. He didn't want to ruin the moment, but the possibility of making it better was driving him crazy.

Sliding his hands down to her hips, Auggie pushed her down into the mattress, whispering, "Stay right here."

As he started to let go, Charlotte softly asked, "Where are you going?"

"I wanna kiss you."

Charlotte appeared confused, then smiled as she let go. He hated to tear himself away from her, but there was no way he was going to do anything else without kissing her. Kissing Charlotte was better than anything in this world, only because he hadn't had sex with her yet. That would be the best feeling and kissing her would become a close second. Still, the two weren't separate for him. He needed to kiss her. Before her, he'd always viewed kissing as a means to an end, not that he disliked it, it was never his goal. Until Charlotte. Gah, he could kiss those perfectly imperfect lips of hers for hours.

Leaping into the bathroom from the bed, he swung the door closed. He wasn't nervous, but he was so excited he dropped his toothbrush in the sink a few times and had trouble squeezing the toothpaste on. After taking care of a few other morning necessities, Auggie swung the door open ready to climb back in bed with her and show her the kind of man he was. The kind of man he wanted to be and would only be with her.

Instantly deflated when all that was waiting for him was an empty bed, he didn't understand what was going on. Had he imagined the whole thing? Was he hallucinating? Walking out of his room, Auggie stepped in the living room and found her on the couch. It was hard for him not to be irritated with her. He told her to stay in bed. It couldn't have taken him more than five minutes to come out and she bailed on him.

As the unpleasant feeling of 'It's not going to happen, again' set in, Auggie noticed a look of regret on Charlotte's face. Her eyes were saying she was sorry but since her ass was still on the couch instead of in his bed, he continued to be frustrated with her.

"What the hell?" he griped at her.

Patting the spot next to her on the couch, she replied, "I'm not trying to mess with you. I actually came over to talk to you."

With a heavy scowl, Auggie made his way to the couch and sat down, informing, "You're gonna end up giving me a damn stroke. I hope you know that."

"Well, I didn't know you were going to tackle me into your bed when I got here," she argued.

"What did you think I was gonna do with you in my room?"

Giving a slight huff, Charlotte rolled her eyes, answering, "I went in there to wake you up. When your alarm went off, I saw the picture on your phone and got distracted."

"Distracted?"

There was a sweet smile on her face as she shared, "You have a picture of us on your phone."

Auggie was still upset with her but between the look on her face and knowing he was responsible for it, he slowly got over his feeling of being hung out to dry.

Shaking his head at her, he couldn't help but smile back. He leaned in to kiss her, stopping half way when he remembered he had something for her.

"Sit tight," he blurted, patting her on the leg as he hopped up.

Swiftly making his way back to his room, Auggie opened his dresser drawer. He pulled out a small black box and headed back into the living room.

Handing her the box as he sat down, he said, "I got this for you."

"What is it?" she asked, holding the box in her hand.

"It's a present," he replied, confused by the way she was acting.

Nodding at him, Auggie could tell she was holding her breath as she opened the box.

A slow smile spread across her face as she looked over at him. That expression on her face and the anticipation she built by holding her breath as she opened her gift made him want to go out and buy her something to open every single day.

"Will you put it on me?" holding her hand out to him.

Auggie took the thin silver bangle that had a silver peacock feather and a tiny letter A hanging from it, out of the box and slid it over her hand onto her wrist.

One moment she was sitting there admiring her gift and then in the next, Charlotte was straddling his lap kissing him like she was going to eat him alive. Still in his pajama bottoms, there wasn't a whole lot between them causing him to feel every movement, no matter how slight, she made.

Pressing his hands into the small of her back, Auggie breathed out, "You're welcome," as her kiss made its way down his neck to his shoulder.

Pulling up, Charlotte placed her hands on the sides of his face, asking, "Is this your way of marking me?"

Knowing she was referring to the little A that hung next to the peacock feather on her bracelet, he replied, "Yes."

Closing her eyes, she leaned her forehead against his, whispering, "Then I'll never take it off."

She acknowledged what he was doing and was happy about it. A sense of peace settled over him, knowing whenever she left no matter where she went, she would still be his.

Auggie's insight was quickly replaced by urgency. He had a

distinct need to christen the moment and physically claim her as his own.

Auggie wrapped his arms around her tight and kissed her while standing up. Her legs were wrapped around his waist as he hurtled the coffee table, heading straight for his room. His heart was pounding and his mind was racing as everything he planned to do to her flashed in his mind. A sudden jolt stopped him as he noticed her grab hold of the doorframe before they could enter his room. Pulling back out of the doorway, he continued to kiss her as he turned around and pushed her up against the wall.

Breaking their kiss, Charlotte breathed, "Wait."

Pressing into her, Auggie leaned his forehead against the wall, pleading with her, "Lotte, please."

It was at that moment, as he heard himself beg for her, he knew she had him. It was an irrational and unreasonable thing that he had made fun of all his life. When someone has you so strung out all you can do is want them. There's nothing rational about it and it makes no sense whatsoever but right then and there he knew, she could have him on his hands and knees begging if that's what she wanted. She had him.

༄✦

Guilt among other things settled in Charlotte's chest as she unwrapped her legs from him, letting her feet fall to the floor. Earlier, he was just being Auggie in bed but this was all on her. She couldn't help it. Staring at the bracelet, he gave her and knowing the meaning behind it, twisted her insides to the point to where she felt like she would explode if she continued just to sit there. He was going to start hating her if she kept this up. Hell, she was starting to hate herself for stringing things along.

Taking a few moments to catch her breath and try to relax, Auggie hadn't let up.

"Hey," she soothed as he continued to breath heavy, shaking his head against the wall.

Slowly loosening his grip on her, he breathed, "Stay."

Charlotte's hands started to shake as she slid them to the sides of his face, saying, "I know this is going to sound a little crazy coming from me, but I want it to be special."

Scowling, he blinked a few times before asking, "You want me to take you out? On a real date or somethin'?"

"No. Well, I wouldn't say no but that's not what I meant." Auggie was still so close to her it was hard for her to concentrate.

"I was thinking, Sunday."

"Sunday?"

"Yea, this Sunday. After the baby shower."

Appearing confused, he questioned, "Any particular reason?"

Taking a deep breath she gave him a soft kiss before sharing, "We'll be all dressed up and you won't have to go to work."

A light smile played on his lips as he confirmed, "Special."

Nodding, she gave him another soft kiss.

After walking Charlotte out to her car, Auggie sat in his chair thinking. Sunday. She said Sunday. Although today would have been better, he was glad to know it would finally happen. He honestly didn't know how many more times she could bring him to the edge of sanity and then body slam him to the ground before it killed him.

Charlotte wanted special; he could do special. Getting up out of his chair, he walked to the bathroom. Looking at himself, he decided it wouldn't hurt to trim his beard a little neater and maybe while he was out getting the suit he forgot to buy, and get a haircut.

32

Drunk

Stepping into her silver heels, Charlotte turned and looked in the mirror. The floor length sundress that she found while out shopping with Penny was a perfect peacock blue, matching some of the feathers from Brennen's peacock farm, she attached to the band of her white sun hat. She still thought having a baby shower tea at a bar was a crazy idea but it turned out to be a great set up for what was to come that evening.

Checking her eye makeup in the mirror one last time, she smoothed her chubby stick across her lips as she smiled at the A hanging from her bracelet. Laughing to herself at how she had to pinch Silvia to remind her to keep her mouth shut when she saw it, maybe it wouldn't always be a secret. Hopefully, when she told him tonight that she was staying, they could ease everyone into the idea of them being together.

❧

Standing behind the bar in his dark grey Glen plaid suit and tie, Auggie watched the door like a hawk, waiting for his first glimpse of Charlotte for the day.

"You gotta date comin' or somethin?" Braden asked, startling Auggie away from his thoughts.

Giving his brother an unhappy glare, he answered, "Quit being stupid."

"You still pissed at me?"

Glancing back at the door before turning to Braden, Auggie replied, "Yea, but it's your life do whatever you want with it."

Braden looked shocked as he blurted, "Since when?"

"What do you mean?"

"You get a new suit, cut your hair and trim your beard and suddenly you're a new man?"

Checking the door again, Auggie informed, "I'm never gonna like her but she's your girl and I can respect that. What's going on between the two of you is your business. So yea, it's your life."

"Who the hell are you?" Braden laughed.

Shaking his head at his brother, Auggie made a 'Shut up' face at him before focusing back on the door.

Auggie's keeping a watchful eye on the door paid off, the second he saw Charlotte walk in with her family. No way he was going to make it through the shower pretending to ignore her. She had a flow to her walk and with that dress, she was a classy kind of gorgeous.

"Hey, Charlotte!" Braden shouted out to her, causing Auggie to growl at him under his breath.

Charlotte turned to her parents for a moment before heading towards the bar. For a second, Auggie wondered if she was going to punch Braden in the eye like she said. The thought made it hard for him to keep a straight face and he decided if she did, he just might grab her and kiss her in front of everyone for being such a bad ass.

Keeping a reasonable distance, Charlotte replied, "Hi, Braden."

Auggie stood up tall, stating, "Charlotte," with a nod.

Lifting her hand, to adjust her large white sunhat with peacock feathers that he was sure came from their day at the farm together, she wiggled her wrist making the bracelet he gave her move against her arm as she replied, "Augustus."

Out of nowhere there was a clapping sound as his sister suddenly appeared in front of them, cheering, "Charlotte!"

Charlotte instantly held her arms in the air, "Penny!"
Auggie watched in a daze as Penny and Charlotte laughed, walking away from the bar together.

Once again, Braden's voice interrupted his thoughts, asking, "You alright?"

Auggie scowled at him, snapping, "Did you want somethin'?"

Braden smiled wide, "Nah brother, not a thing," as he stepped away.
Rolling his eyes at his brother, Auggie stepped from behind the bar to find a spot where he could keep an eye on Charlotte without being obvious about it.

Quickly finding a spot next to Kieran and Liv against the wall, it was crazy how fast the bar was filling up for a baby shower.

"What's up sexy," Kieran laughed, reaching out to shake Auggie's hand.

Laughing back, Auggie said, "Damn, you clean up nice."

"Y'all need a minute to go make out with each other?" Liv teased them as she bumped Auggie with her shoulder before saying, "Wow, who is that?"
Auggie scanned the room wondering who she was talking about.

Kieran asked, "Who?"

"Peacock girl over there sitting with Penny."

Kieran and Auggie glanced at each other before Kieran answered, "Charlotte Roberts."

"No way," Liv blurted before sharing, "I'm going to go introduce myself."

Kieran laughed, shaking his head saying, "Serious man, I can't take her anywhere."

With a loud exhale, Auggie thought 'It's gonna be a long day'.

⊱⊰

Once all the greeting formalities were over, Charlotte sat at a table with Penny off to the side. Everyone, including her family, were taking turns oohing and aahing over Sophia. It was her shower, so that was expected. When Sarah walked by she looked so much like an older version of Penny, it made Charlotte want to smile at her. She settled on a polite 'Mrs. Caffrey' instead. Sarah turned and although there was sort of a smile on her face it was more 'Why are you speaking to me' than anything else. Also to be expected. What Charlotte didn't expect was company at their table

A woman with long black hair, colorful full sleeve tattoos wearing a blue and white striped tank dress, aviator sunglasses and a navy blue sunhat pulled out a chair and sat down across from them.

"Hey beautiful," she greeted Penny with a wink before asking, "So is this the outcast table?"

Penny laughed, answering, "Men are men and boys will be boys but us girls are the black sheep of this family."

Nodding in agreement, she asked, "So, are there drinks at this thing?"

"It's a baby shower," Penny reminded, pointing to Sophia.

"Ah, that's right. You know this having it in a bar just throws the whole thing off."

Charlotte started to laugh thinking the exact same thing as Penny introduced them, "This is Liv by the way. Kieran's wife."

Remembering the framed heart on the wall at Legacy Ink, Charlotte replied, "It's nice to meet you."

Liv made a clicking sound with her mouth and winked before asking, "So, Charlotte Roberts, what brings you to our festive family gathering?"

"Ren made Sophia invite me," Charlotte replied.

"Don't you just love her! She's so badass!" Liv practically shouted, receiving a few glares in the process.

Penny placed her hand across her face and shook her head, warning, "Mom's gonna kick you out if you don't behave."

"Oh yea?" Liv asked before looking at Charlotte saying, "Watch this." Holding her hand high in the air, Liv shouted, "Hi, Sarah!" waving at her.

Sarah looked like it actually hurt her so reply as she stated, "Liv."

Turning back to them, Liv shared, "She secretly loves me," with a nod.

Charlotte tried not to laugh but couldn't help it as she thought, Liv might be the most awesome person she'd ever met.

As Liv chattered away, poking fun at various family members, they heard a whinny voice call out to Penny.

Sophia had a helpless look about her as she said, "We ran out of cups. Do you know if there are more in the back?"

Penny gave her a sweet smile as she started to stand up.

"Where are you going?" Charlotte asked.

"Oh, you don't know. That was code for 'Penny to get her highness more cups'," Liv shared.

Charlotte thought 'You have got to be kidding me' as she offered, "I'll go look."

"Are you sure?" Penny questioned.

"Yep, I'll be right back," she assured, not because she was just dying to go get cups but because she disliked the way Sophia was sending Penny instead of Braden, who was standing right next to her.

ॐॐ

Breaking off his conversation with Kieran the second he saw Charlotte walk through the swinging doors to the back, Auggie tried to be covert in making his way in the same direction. Taking a look around before pushing through the doors, it didn't appear anyone was paying him any attention. Being as quiet as possible, he crept down the hall and up to the storage room.

Charlotte was staring at the wire shelving against the wall with her back to him. He watched her for a moment, place her hands on her hips and look up at the top shelf.

Leaning against the doorframe, Auggie complimented, "You are lookin' mighty fine today, Miss Lotte."

Slowly turning around, she peeked up at him from the brim of her hat, saying, "Why Mr. Caffrey, are you flirting with me?"

Auggie could feel the side of his face scrunch up into a smile as he took a few steps closer, sharing, "You look beautiful."

A mischievous grin formed as she replied, "Do you know how hard it was for me not to pull you over the bar by your tie and give you a proper greeting?"

Closing the distance between them, he dared, "So what's stopping you now?"

"I came in here to grab some more cups, not fool around with you," she said with a laugh.

Charlotte reached up to grab a sleeve of cups off of the shelf when Auggie caught her by her forearm. He smiled at the little A on her bracelet before pressing his lips against her wrist.

"You may have come back here for cups. I came back here for you," he shared in a low tone before lowering her arm, whispering, "And I do intend on greeting you properly."

Her opposition faded into a welcoming expression as she looked into his eyes.

"Hey, did you find the cups," Braden chimed from the doorway, causing Auggie to turn his head and scowl at his brother.

Charlotte jerked her arm away from Auggie and grabbed the sleeve of cups, confirming, "Yep, got 'em," and turned to walk out.

Auggie watched her leave the storage room when Braden stopped her, saying, "Sophia wanted me to make sure y'all were behaving yourselves."

She gave him a crazy look as she snapped, "Excuse me?"

"She doesn't want y'all causing a scene at her shower. We all know how you feel about each other," Braden shared with a wide smile.

Charlotte flashed a sarcastic smile as she stated, "I'm bringing the princess her cups, now."

Auggie wanted to smile but the fact that his brother interrupted them kept an unhappy expression on his face.

Shaking his head at Braden, Auggie started to walk out of the storage room.

"Seriously, you've got to like her at least a little."

Glaring at his brother, Auggie snapped, "You need to shut up."

"Come on man, she's gorgeous and she always smells nice. Not only that, she seems like she'd be a lot of fun to be with."

Charlotte was all the things Braden was saying and so much more. He started wondering why he was still pretending to hate her when it was just Braden.

Auggie started to confess when his brother added, "I mean Will thought so. Gah, can you believe our Will got with her in the first place."

Suddenly, Auggie felt his mouth start to water like he was going to be sick.

Grabbing Braden by the front of his suit jacket, he growled, "I said, shut your mouth," then let go with a little shove.

As he walked out of the room, Auggie heard his brother gripe, "Damn, lighten up."

All the things that brought Charlotte into his life seemed to assault him as he made his way back through the swinging doors.

How could he have forgotten? Another wave of nausea hit him as he changed his course and headed straight for the men's room. Loosening his tie as he stepped in, his guilt was suffocating him. Charlotte wasn't his girl; she couldn't be. She was Will's first. Trying to catch his breath, he clinched his fists remembering all he was supposed to do was look out for her. What kinda of a man was he? He was a sorry excuse for a brother, a disloyal son of a bitch that was dishonoring Will with every move he made. And he was in desperate need of a drink.

Pulling himself together, as best he could, Auggie headed behind the bar. He pulled a bottle of whisky from the top shelf before heading into the kitchen. He opened the cooler and grabbed a box of Guinness. Heading to the office in the back, where he planned to drink himself into oblivion, he caught sight of Charlotte. She was watching him with a concerned expression on her face. Everything he felt for her was still there, except now, his head was telling him what a low down dirty excuse for a brother he was for feeling that way. Auggie slammed the office door and locked it behind him, pulled his suit jacket off, rolled up his sleeves and took a long swig out of the whisky bottle.

ॐ•ॐ

Sitting still as Liv and Penny continued on with their conversation, Charlotte didn't understand what had happened. Auggie appeared upset and when he came through with his arms full of alcohol, he glared at her like he couldn't stand the sight of her.

"Hey, I think something's wrong," she whispered, leaning closer to Penny.

Penny gave her a confused look, asking, "What?"

"Your brother just walked through with a bunch of beer and a bottle of whisky."

Liv put her two cents in, sharing, "I don't know that I've ever been to a gathering when Auggs didn't get mad or drunk or mad and drunk."

Nodding at Liv, Penny said, "He probably got into it with Braden or something."

With a heavy sigh, Charlotte glanced off to the side thinking there had to be more to it.

Charlotte sat disappointed through the rest of the shower. Even when everyone, including Sarah, complimented the name plaque she made for Keylee's nursery wall, she couldn't bring herself to smile or even gloat at their surprise that it was a nice gift. She just sat there hoping Auggie would come out of the back. Wondering what was wrong and trying to convince herself that their special night was still going to happen.

ॐ∘ॐ

Charlotte sat down on her bed after riding back home with her family. Giving up on any ideas for the evening, she had just changed out of her dress when she received a text from Penny.

P: I'm at the bar. Can you come over here? Auggie's DRUNK.

C: Who's there?

P: Just me. I dropped mom off and came back because I forgot my hat.

C: Okay.

Shaking her head as she stood up, Charlotte thought 'If there's not something seriously wrong with him, there's gonna be'.

Penny was waiting right inside of the back door when Charlotte arrived. She appeared frustrated as she waved Charlotte over to the locked office door.

"I can't get him to come out. I don't even know what happened. Did y'all get in an argument?"

Trying to think what could have happened, Charlotte replied, "No, everything was fine when I left the storage room."

Penny shrugged, asking, "Do you think you can get him to come out?"

"Yea, why don't you go. I'll text you and let you know how he is."

Giving her a halfhearted smile, Penny said, "Thanks."
Charlotte smiled back, waiting for Penny to walk out before knocking on the office door.

She could hear mumbling coming from inside and decided to knock harder.

"Augustus," she shouted at the door.
A shuffling and then banging sound preceded the sound of the office door unlock. Turning the knob, she opened the door and saw him sitting on the floor.

Frowning at him, she informed, "I guess you really would rather drink."

Auggie's chest was heaving as he slurred, "I rather...wanted...you," with and incredibly sad expression on his face.

Closing her eyes a moment, she took a breath before offering, "Come on, let's get you home."
She reached down to help him, but he pushed her hand away using the chair against the wall to pull himself up.

As soon as he was on his feet, Auggie practically hugged the doorframe next to her to remain upright.

"You smell like the bad end of a bottle."

"You smell sweet," he forced, reaching out for her.

Rolling her eyes at him, Charlotte asked, "Do you think you can make it to my car?"

Frantically shaking his head, he mumbled, "No...you're not...won't stay."

Grabbing his face with her hand so she could look him in the eye, Charlotte stated, "Look at me."

Auggie's eyes appeared sorrowful and anguished causing her to feel nothing but compassion for him.

"If you make it to my car, I'll stay with you."

Allowing him to go first, she watched as he stumbled to the back door, bracing himself against the wall the whole way. Charlotte looked back at all the beer bottles on the floor and the empty whisky bottle on the desk and wondered how he wasn't already in a coma.

By some miracle of luck, Auggie made it into his house and then onto his bed all by himself. She helped him take his shoes off and since he couldn't seem to manage the buttons on his shirt, she did that too.

Leaning over him, as he sat on the bed, Charlotte fussed, "Stop doing that and let me help you," when he kept trying to kiss her.

"You...no...want...to?"

Growing more frustrated with him, she griped, "No I don't."

"Why no kiss...ess."

Finally getting his shirt off of him, Charlotte snapped, "Because your drunk and I don't like sloppy."

Shaking his head back and forth at her, Auggie leaned his head against her stomach slurring, "Not...that's why. I know...why."

Rolling her eyes, she pushed him back on the bed, griping, "Glad you know."

She moved to the head of the bed, to pull his sheets back while he mumbled, "Special. Not...this." As Charlotte thought, 'You're telling me', he continued babbling, "I'mma ya out...Nice an out. I shouldn't a...this isn't...nice."

Scowling at him, she asked, "You want to take me out?" Nodding, he rolled over and found his pillow.

Charlotte still had a feeling something else was wrong but she started to wonder if the whole making this special had put too much pressure on him.

≈33≈

Almost

Everything hurt as Auggie rolled over in bed. He wouldn't have thought it was possible, but he was in more pain than when he had a concussion. He felt like he'd been run over. Even his hair hurt. The last thing he remembered was drinking in the back office of the bar. Auggie was wondering how he got in bed. Then what took place before that slowly filtered into his mind, making him feel worse.

Letting out a loud groan as he tried to get up, he froze hearing Charlotte say, "Hung over?"
Whipping his head around to see her made his brain throb. As he laid his head back on his pillow to keep it from spinning, he tried to figure out why she was under the covers in his bed.

She seemed to read his mind as she informed, "I promised you I would stay if you left the bar."

Scowling at her, he asked, "You slept in here?"

Charlotte made a stupid face at him before fussing, "I don't know why you're looking at me like that. I wasn't the one that got drunk and was talking crazy before passing out."

"What was I saying?"

Letting out a sigh, she looked up, saying, "Oh, something about you trying on your mom's dresses when no one was home?"

"What?" he blurted, sitting straight up causing a sharp pain to radiate through his head.

The corner of her mouth curled into as smile as she admitted, "Okay, I made that up but that's what you get for ruining last night."

With a heavy sigh, he shook his head asking, "So no crazy talk?"

Shrugging she answered, "More like slurry mumbles and I think you tried to ask me out on a date."

"I did?"

"You kept saying this wasn't nice and something about out. I asked you if you were asking me out and you nodded then passed out."

Auggie placed his hands over his eyes thinking.

That could work. Maybe if he took her out, in public, it would ease his conscience. He could then prove to himself that there was nothing wrong with wanting her. Maybe then it wouldn't feel like he was keeping a dirty little secret. The truth was, even with the most hellacious hangover he'd ever had and feeling like low life scum for dishonoring his brother, he still wanted her. Charlotte could have easily left him at the bar; he deserved that. He ruined her special night and she still took him home and stayed with him. It was worth a try to keep her around just a little bit longer. Until she left.

Trying to focus and not sound like the jackass that he was, Auggie turned to Charlotte.

"I want to take you out."

Looking at him like he was out of his mind, she snapped, "Are you still drunk?"

"I know I screwed up yesterday. I can make it up to you, tonight," he swore, hoping that was the truth.

With a suspicious expression, Charlotte said, "You have work."

"Monday's are never busy. Old Lou can handle it, and Braden can help out if he gets in a bind."

She sat there staring at him as if she was waiting for something.

Realizing what she was waiting for, Auggie asked, "Will you go on a date with me?"

With a soft smile, she replied, "Yes."

"I'll pick you up at six."

Shaking her head, she corrected, "I'll meet you here at six," before assuring, "That's really sweet that you want to pick me up. Maybe next time you can."

Trying to think of a nice way to get her to leave, Auggie said, "Let me get up and try to get rid of this hangover. See you tonight."

Charlotte gave him a well-deserved 'You're acting strange' look before saying, "Oh-kay."
When she leaned towards his cheek to kiss him, he quickly slid away from her and out of bed.

Closing the bathroom door behind himself, he heard her shout 'Bye' right before he turned the shower on. Auggie's head was pounding and his conscience was stinging as he stepped in, trying to wash both feelings away with a cool shower. When it was clear neither were subsiding, he stepped out of the shower, wrapped a towel around his waist, set an alarm on his phone and went back to bed.

৵৽

Looking through the clothes in her closet, Charlotte forgot to ask where they were going. She was still in shock that he asked her on a date. Maybe that was his problem. Reminding herself how much he'd had to drink the day before, she decided she was over thinking things.

৵৽

When Auggie's alarm went off, he drug himself out of bed. After taking more aspirin and another shower, he started to feel a little better. He wanted to take her someplace nice, she deserved nice after the way he acted yesterday. Standing in his kitchen, waiting for his bread to finish toasting, he decided to try pushing everything except tonight out of his mind and dwell on the way he felt about her. He needed to start completely over with her. Starting with the night he saw her standing in front of The Dog House. She was worth his effort.

Forcing his last bite of toast down, it wasn't easy but he knew an empty stomach after drinking was always bad. Back to thinking of where to take her, Auggie called Jackson.

"Were your ears burnin'?" Jackson answered his call laughing.

Ignoring his question, Auggie knew Ren would be mad at him for bailing on Sophia's shower.

"Do you still have the hook up at Mansurs?"

"Do you need a reservation?"

"If you can swing it, tonight at seven thirty."

"Shouldn't be a problem, you know its tie and jacket, right?"

Auggie replied, "Never mind then," knowing he couldn't wear his funeral suit and there was no time to get the one he wore yesterday cleaned before tonight.

"You know what, I think I have one that would fit you," Jackson offered.

"You sure?"

"Yea, I'll run it over in a few."

"Thanks."

"No problem," Jackson said before hanging up.

Auggie walked to his living room and sat down in his chair. He sent Charlotte a text to let her know where they were having dinner, figuring she would want to know and waited for Jackson. So far, so good.

Jackson arrived around forty-five minutes later. Auggie had taken another nap in the meantime and was close to a full recovery. After letting Jackson in, Auggie took the dark grey suit, white shirt and tie he brought and hung it up in his room.

Walking back into the living room, Auggie noticed the serious expression on Jackson's face.

"Thanks. Appreciate the loan," Auggie said.

"Anytime, keep it. Ren's been on me to get rid of the one's I don't wear anymore."

Nodding, Auggie walked to his kitchen.

Jackson rested his arms on top of Auggie's bar while leaning against it as he shared, "Ren is furious with you," before asking, "Didn't you and I have a talk about Charlotte? Didn't you say you'd be nice for the shower?"

Scowling, Auggie griped, "I didn't do anything to her."

That wasn't technically true but Auggie knew Jackson thought they had gotten into it at some point.

"We all saw you go to the back after her. Then you got drunk and she was noticeably upset."

Half-truthing his way through defending himself, Auggie griped, "I didn't do anything to her. Just like at y'alls house that day. We were just talking."

Jackson stared at him for a moment before a wide smile spread across his face.

The 'Happy I figured it out' look he had was quickly replaced by a 'What the hell are you thinking' one as he shared, "You sure like to make things hard on yourself."

Shaking his head, Auggie replied, "You have no idea."

Concern spread across Jackson's face as he asked, "Do you know what's going to happen when you take her out, here?"

Auggie gave a heavy sigh as he answered, "It's gonna eat me alive and I'll lose her if I don't." As Jackson shook his head, not understanding, Auggie explained, "Everything was fine. Well, not fine but I liked what we had going on.

311

Yesterday, Braden was...being Braden. He said something about Will getting with her."

"And you think parading her on your arm through town is going to make it better?"

Shrugging, Auggie said, "I gotta do something. All I keep thinking about is her being with Will."

Jackson nodded, advising, "Then you should talk to her about it."

Giving Jackson a stupid look, Auggie fussed, "I can't tell her that the idea of being with her makes me sick because she was with Will."

"If you talk to her, she can tell you what was between them and what happened."

Horrified at the thought of hearing Charlotte describe being with his brother, Auggie snapped, "I don't want to hear that come out of her mouth."

Appearing frustrated, Jackson said, "You don't know what she's going to say."

"You give terrible advice."

Pushing off from the bar, Jackson assured, "It's only terrible because you won't take it. You need to quit being such a stubborn ass and talk to her," as he headed toward the door.

"Hey, don't tell Ren, okay."

When Jackson reached the front door, he turned back, saying, "Are you kidding? My house is already an emotional war zone and that is 'shoot the messenger' news. I accidentally called her grandma the other day and she didn't talk to me for two hours. No way I'm going to admit I have any part in this situation."

As Jackson walked out of his house, Auggie sat down at his kitchen table. Stretching his arms out across the table, he rested his forehead against the cool surface. That could have gone better. It also could have gone a whole lot worse. Jackson didn't say he was wrong or call him a vile betrayer, even though he still felt like one. There was a tiny bit of relief in admitting they were together. This could actually work.

࿎࿎

Charlotte pulled into Auggie's driveway about five minutes to six. When he said that he was taking her to Mansurs, she was genuinely surprised. She wasn't sure where she thought they would go, but Mansurs was definitely never a thought. Stepping out of her car, she looked down before giving herself a once over in her reflection on the side of the car. It took a bit to figure it out, but she was happy with the strapless black dress she picked out. Especially because it worked perfect with the lace straps from the lingerie she wore underneath. No one would know they were two separate pieces and the lacy straps on her shoulders made the dress appear fancier than it was. Charlotte nodded at her reflection and headed to his door.

Smiling to herself as it occurred to her she was picking him up for their date as she knocked. The door opened, slowly revealing Auggie wearing a charcoal grey suit with white shirt and black tie.

"Well hello," Charlotte blurted.

Auggie looked her up and down, assuring, "You look gorgeous."

With a slight laugh she smiled, saying, "I feel like I should have brought you flowers, since I came to pick you up."

Smiling back, he offered, "You wanna make it a thing and drive too."

"Are you serious?"

"Why not? But we're taking my truck," he replied.

Charlotte was thrilled, not only to be the one driving she was also getting to drive his truck.

Although it took her a ways down the road to get used to driving such a large vehicle, he never cringed or corrected her. Auggie sat in the passenger seat appearing relaxed and looking incredibly sexy as she drove them.

When Charlotte put the blinker on to make a turn, Auggie instructed, "Don't turn there. Go up to the next light."

Confused she replied, "But that will make a big loop and I'll have to make a u-turn to get there."

"Our reservation is at seven thirty. I thought we could stop by the bar for a drink first."

Flipping the blinker off, Charlotte headed in that direction, asking, "You want to take me for a drink at the bar?"

Auggie flashed her a quick smile, answering, "I'll just have a ginger ale after yesterday."

"That's not why I was asking."

Giving her a serious look, he shared, "I have more than last night to make up for."

An amazing feeling overwhelmed her as she realized this would be a night she was never going to forget.

Auggie gave her a 'don't you dare' expression as she started to open the door. Placing her hands in her lap, Charlotte waited for him to get out, walk around and open hers. When Auggie opened her door, he didn't just help her out, he grabbed her waist and lifted her out. After closing the driver's side door, he held his hand out for hers. Charlotte's heart was racing as she thought, we are going to walk into The Dog House holding hands. So much for easing everyone into the idea of us being together.

Right outside the doors, Auggie stopped. Charlotte thought he might be having second thoughts.

Tightening his hold on her hand, he looked at her offering, "Would you like to go inside?"

When Charlotte nodded, Auggie opened the door for her.

They stepped into The Dog House never letting go of the others hand. Auggie's grip was firm and almost protective as the made their way to the bar.

Leaning to her ear, Auggie asked, "Table or bar?"

"Table," she whispered, loving the feel of him close in public.

When they reached the bar, a salt and pepper gray haired man was standing behind it, staring at them in complete and total disbelief.

Auggie let go of her hand and placed it on the small of her back as he told the bartender, "Ginger ale and a..." then looked at Charlotte as she replied, "Two please."

Lou laughed, "I almost didn't recognize you. This your girl?"

"Yea, this is Charlotte," Auggie introduced before Charlotte replied, "Hi."

Giving a nod as he set their drinks on the bar, Lou said, "Don't know what you're doin' to this guy. Boy you sure lucked out."

Auggie shook his head with a laugh before they picked up their drinks and walked to a table by the corner.

As Auggie pulled out her chair, Charlotte stopped, looking at the wall full of pictures.

"Oh my gosh, is that Ren. Geez, she looks so young."

Stepping beside her, he shared, "Yea, she was. Jackson worked here his senior year and from what I understand she was always up here."

Charlotte inspected the picture then looked at him, assuring, "That has to be your dad. You look just like him."

Nodding, he replied, "There's the original Augustus," pointing to a hard looking man in a black and white photo.

"You look like him when you're mad."

Auggie laughed, "Alright, let's sit down."

Charlotte sat, pleased to see Auggie pull his chair around right next to hers before sitting down.

Glancing around, Charlotte noticed although they were getting plenty of looks, no one looked like they were going to say anything. Even Braden stayed on stage after giving her a big smile.

Auggie lifted his ginger ale in his brother's direction and tipped the glass at him before turning to Charlotte saying, "I should have done this sooner."

Charlotte started to reply but before she could get a word out, Auggie pressed his lips against hers.

As he pulled back, she noticed a look of relief in his eyes as he whispered, "I'm gonna be honest. I was half expecting torches and pitchforks."

Closing her eyes, she leaned her forehead to his, saying, "You did say it was a slow night."

Laughing together, they sat close until it was time to leave.

Dinner at Mansurs was wonderful. Charlotte and Auggie laughed and talked about things they had never gotten around to discussing. What music they liked, favorite movies, mostly first date stuff. As their meal ended, the anticipation of what was to come was getting the better of Charlotte. When the waiter offered dessert, she declined and Auggie followed suit. Their date had been close to perfect and the only thing Charlotte could think about was sealing their relationship before the night was over.

প্র০

The night had gone so much better than Auggie expected. He felt relaxed and pleasantly surprised at how comfortable he felt out in public with Charlotte. It was strange to him how effortless the whole thing was. He'd always viewed taking a girl out as more trouble than it was worth because there were always the ones that were ready no matter what. Charlotte was worth whatever hoops he had to jump through but it never once felt like he was working for it. Everything about their date felt right, from the suit he was wearing, to letting her drive, all the way down to kissing her at the bar.

Auggie's fingers were tingling as he itched to get his hands on her. She was making him wait outside of his bedroom door, he really had no idea why. Waiting for her to welcome him in, he pulled out his cellphone, that he had on silent, out of the inside pocket of his suit jacket to see what time it was. After viewing a slew of missed calls from random numbers, he saw a text message from Sheryl of all people. He almost didn't check it but since he was waiting and a little curious, he did. Scanning the rather lengthy text message, the majority of it was asking if he was blocking her calls, telling him he had missed out on her and that he must think he was better than everyone else. Laughing to himself, he assumed she was drunk texting and found it pretty funny until he read the last part.

S: Do you know what a slap in the face bringing HER to The Dog House was to everyone. I hope you enjoy your brother's leftovers you piece of sh*t.

Standing there staring at the last sentence, Auggie tried to be rational. He turned his cellphone off and threw it. Watching it skim across his coffee table before bouncing off the edge of the couch onto the floor, he gritted his teeth trying to somehow unread the message.

Running his hand down his face, he turned away from his bedroom door as the same sickening feeling from the day before started to overtake him. When he did, William's door was right there, staring at him. Taunting him with the knowledge that Charlotte had been behind that door with his brother.

He turned back to his door, hearing Charlotte announce, "You can come in now."

Standing at the foot of his bed, Charlotte was wearing a red and black plaid corset that covered only the parts he knew he wasn't allowed to touch. As his eyes appreciated the length of her, he noticed the only other things she had on were a pair of little black panties and her black heels. Auggie tried to take a breath but couldn't. She was absolutely glorious.

Every single fiber of his being wanted her with the exception of the little nagging part of his brain that was trying to convince him this was wrong. Slowly walking towards her, he didn't see how being with her could be anything but right. She was beauty, lust, sweetness, sex and passion. When he reached her, she stepped out of her heels before reaching up and running her hands through his beard. Guiding his lips to hers, her kiss was soft and slow. She slid her hands up his chest and under the shoulders of his suit jacket. Once his jacket hit the floor, she made short work of his tie before starting on the buttons of his shirt. Half way down, he couldn't stand it anymore. Pulling her down on the bed with him, he kissed her, kicking his shoes off before scooting them both farther onto the bed.

Auggie pulled her as close as possible before rolling them over. Charlotte's legs found their way around his waist. Pushing up on his hands, he leaned his head down, brushing his lips across her collar bone. The most exquisite breathy moan escaped her lips, and it was the best thing he'd ever heard until that nagging voice started messing with his head.

All of the sudden, he wondered if that was the how she sounded with William. Knowing what thoughts like that would do to him, he moved to her side and pulled her to him. Frantically kissing her while inhaling deeply every chance he could, Auggie thought smelling her and feeling her might drown everything but her out of his mind. The harder he tried, the worse it got. His brother was fixated in his mind.

Pulling away from her, Auggie tried to sit up.

Charlotte caught the side of his face, saying, "I trust you."

He had no idea what to say to her.

The look in her eyes damn near killed him as she declared, "I don't want anything between us."

"I can't go where my brother's been," he choked out.

Charlotte narrowed her eyes at him. She laid there completely still, staring at him for several minutes.

Her voice was hurt an angry as she questioned, "What kind of a man does this?"

Auggie opened his mouth to answer, but nothing came out. He didn't know.

Charlotte jumped out of bed, yelling, "Congratulations. You are the best damn brother in the entire world."

Shaking his head, he swore, "That's not what this is."

Pulling her dress back on, she snapped, "No?"

"I didn't want for this to happen."

Offended, Charlotte questioned, "So you didn't want me to believe that you wanted me? That this was real? And then make me feel like I'm not worth anything to you?" Taking a step closer to the bed, she shouted, "Because that's what just happened."

Jackson was right. He should have talked to her before something like this happened. Jackson was right about everything. Sliding to the edge of the bed, he stood up in front of her.

Auggie looked into her eyes, trying to make her understand, "The right thing to do is to let you go."

Instantly slapping the side of his face, she informed, "It's not right. It's not alright to break my heart."

The spot where she hit him stung but the hurt he felt in his heart was excruciating as he noticing the tears in her eyes. He'd made her cry.

Hearing his front door slam shut, Auggie clinched his fists. Hurt and anger brewed deep inside him until he exploded.

Rushing to William's door, he kicked it open shouting, "Why? Why would you do this to me?"
Grabbing the picture of he and his brother from the dresser, Auggie threw it against the wall.

"You did this! You left me! Why? You left me with her!" Going down on his knees, he leaned his forehead against William's bed.

"Why would you do this to me? You're gone! I can't have her!"
Auggie rubbed his eyes as they started to burn. Sitting back on his heels, he looked down at his fingers. The reality that he was blaming his dead brother for losing Charlotte, hit him as he saw tears on his knuckles. He couldn't remember ever crying before now. Not when William passed or when he lost his dad, not even as a kid.

Looking around the room, he admitted, "I love her." Moving off of the floor to sit on his brother's bed, Auggie said, "I miss you."

Curled up in Amila's arms the tears wouldn't stop. Charlotte now understood all of Silvia's howling sobs when her heart was broken.

Nothing had ever hurt this bad. There was no physical pain that could match the crushing feeling she felt on the inside. She wanted to tell her how badly it hurt, but she couldn't stop crying long enough to make a sound come out of her mouth.

34

Timing

Curled up in bed, Charlotte was on her fourth box of tissues when Amila left the room, to make breakfast for everyone. She held her cellphone in one hand swiping through pictures of her and Auggie with the other. Charlotte was glad Amila had stayed the night in her room, loving on her as she cried. Especially since she had no idea what was wrong. Every time Amila asked, Charlotte tried to answer but couldn't. Now, that she was alone all she wanted to do was look at pictures of him and remember what it felt like to be in his arms.

Pulling her cellphone to her chest, Charlotte squeezed her eyes closed, hugging her phone. When it vibrated, the thought that it might be him sent chills down her arms. She was new to this feeling and her heart felt so raw and broken, it didn't matter what he had to say, she just wanted him to talk to her.

Lifting her phone, she blinked a few times surprised at who the message was from.

T: Hello my beauty.

Shaking her head, Trace always had impeccable timing.

T: All meetings have come to an end. Would you like me to fly down and bring you back early or are you enjoying your stay?

Pausing for a moment, Charlotte swallowed hard.

C: No, come now. I want to go home.

T: I am pleased to hear that. I look forward to seeing you and resolving your concerns considering our future.

There was no future with Trace, at least not for her, but she wanted to get as far away from her heartache as soon as possible.

C: We can have a conversation.

T: Your father will expect a proposal when I arrive.

C: He'll get over it.

There was a few minutes delay before his reply.

T: I may not...

She didn't have the patience to deal with his ego.

C: Are you coming or not?

T: Will you at least wear the dress I sent?"

Charlotte rolled her eyes.

C: Sure.

T: Thank you my lovely. I will arrive Friday morning. We will depart at seven that evening.

C: Perfect!

Turning her cellphone off before placing it on her nightstand, Charlotte's heart hurt at the thought of everything she would be leaving behind. There was no way she was going to allow herself to stay in this stupid town feeling heartbroken and lovesick for someone who didn't give a damn about her.

Loading a box into the back of his truck, Auggie had stayed up all night talking aloud to Will as he packed up his brother's room. He talked to him about how much it sucked to manage the bar, how crazy Charlotte made him before he realized how wonderful she was and even told him he was sorry for not being a better brother to him when he was alive. Will's mattress and dresser went into the garage while he packed bags for Goodwill to pick up. Aside from a few things he decided to keep, he was bringing the rest to his mom.

It was actually a relief to have the door to his brother's room open. As he pulled up to his mom's house, he had a feeling he needed to stop closing doors and leave a lot more open. Something about getting everything off his chest the night before made him realize he had always closed himself off. He was still a stubborn judgmental ass but now he knew what it was like to fall and hit the ground, onto rusty spikes that twisted into you as you were being hosed down with lemon juice just to remind you with the added sting, no matter how much pain you're in, it was your own damn fault.

Carrying the box for his mom into the house, he set it on the coffee table when he saw Sarah standing there.

"Hey, Ma."

She appeared angry, snapping, "What's this?"

With a shrug, he replied, "I finally cleaned out Will's room. There's some stuff in there I thought you might want."

Nodding, she questioned, "So one night and you're ready to just throw your brother out."

Confused, Auggie said, "You've been on me for over a month to do this?"

Ignoring his reply, Sarah fussed, "How dare you disrespect your brother, not to mention our entire family by bringing her to the bar."

He honestly couldn't believe what his mom was saying to him as he blurted, "Ma?"

"You're willing to trade your brother's memory for someone like her?"

Having already lost this battle with himself, Auggie answered, "I'm not going to see her again."

Penny walked in, giving her brother a dirty look, asking, "You're not?"

Sarah seemed relieved, "At least one of y'all has some sense, that girl doesn't belong with our family."

Penny blurted, "Mom!"

"Well, it's the truth. She's a disposable mistake. That's why the Roberts shipped her off. The whole town knows it too. Not everything that looks good on the outside is good on the inside and I guess I can just be thankful it didn't take you as long as it did your brother to realize it."

Auggie couldn't sit back and let her talk about Charlotte like that, "You want some truth? I've been seeing her. Since Will's funeral. And it's no wonder she moved to another country. This whole town can go straight to hell because she is better than damn near everyone in it."

Sarah stared at Penny, asking, "Did you know about this?" Before Penny could open her mouth, Auggie replied, "No, Ma. No one knew until last night."

"Get out," Sarah stated before shouting, "Get out of my house!"

Clenching his teeth, Auggie gave a heavy sigh, nodding as he turned and walked out of his mom's house.

Walking back to his truck, Auggie mentally questioned 'Anything else?' wondering what was next. His mom's words were like a double blade that twisted inside his heart. Not only did it hurt like hell to hear what she said about Charlotte, he knew he was just as bad as everyone else because that was exactly the way he felt about her before he knew her.

"Auggie!" Penny called out, running up to his truck.

Stopping before he opened the door, he waited for her to meet him before saying, "Now's not a good time, Pen."

"Maybe she just got scared, hang in there, I know..." she started before he stopped her, saying, "It was me."

Scowling, she questioned, "Why?"

"I had to let her go," he replied.

Giving him a hard shove, Penny griped, "What is wrong with you?"

"It was going to end anyway."

Furious with him, she informed, "She was gonna stay."

A new level of regret burned inside him as he clenched his teeth.

Penny had tears in her eyes as she berated, "You're such a selfish hard hearted bastard."

Looking down at the ground, Auggie nodded, confirming, "I know, Pen."

As Penny stormed back to their mom's house, Auggie opened the door and climbed into his truck.

❧⸾❧

Amila walked into Charlotte's room with a plate of eggs, bacon and toast. Setting Charlotte's breakfast on her nightstand, Amila sat down on the side of her bed and patted her arm.

"Do you feel like talking, honey?" Amila asked with a sweet smile.

Shrugging, Charlotte replied, "What's there to say? It's over."

Giving her another smile, Amila shared, "Honestly, I'm still trying to wrap my mind around your secret guy being Auggie. Not to mention, this is the first time I've ever seen a relationship outed and over, all in the same night."

"I don't know what made me think it would work out," Charlotte thought aloud.

With a concerned expression, Amila said, "It sure seems like he went through a lot of trouble to break it off with you. I doubt anyone is going to let this go for a while."

"Do you think it's possible to love someone because of how they are and at the same time wish they weren't the way they are?"

Amila made a face, asking, "Pardon?"

Charlotte stared at her for a moment before deciding to catch Amila up to speed on.

After Amila swore whatever was said stayed between them, Charlotte shared what William had asked of her, how absolutely ridiculous Auggie was the first few times she went to his house, the day at the peacock farm and how everything changed the night he kissed her.

Amila gave a heavy sigh as she admitted, "You're right, Auggie is different...then I thought he was."

Nodding, Charlotte replied, "He said he had to let me go because of William."

Amila gave her a strange look, asking, "Because of his dead brother?"

"Because I was with him."

"Why didn't you tell him what happened?"

Shrugging, she replied, "At first, I thought about telling him... Then, I guess I wanted it not to matter. He said that wasn't what he wanted to happen, but he was doing what was right."

"Do you think he feels like he's being a bad brother?"

"Yea, I do. The worst thing about it is, I could see how hard it was for him to say those things. But he did it anyway."

Appearing to be in deep thought, Amila scooted farther onto the bed.

Charlotte noticed the apprehensive look on her face as she hesitantly opened her mouth.

"I was married before Emerson." Interested, Charlotte sat up and waited for her to continue, "I cheated on him with Emerson. It was only once and I felt terrible. Romero wasn't perfect, but he was my husband and I betrayed him. To this day, I'm sorry for that."

Shocked, to say the least, Charlotte questioned, "So y'all got divorced and you married Emerson?"

Shaking her head, Amila replied, "No, we worked through it."

"Wait, I'm confused," Charlotte replied.

As if she was trying to keep a terrible memory at bay, Amila blinked a few tears away, replying, "He died."

Charlotte thought, 'Dang, do Emerson and Amila have any stories where people survived' as she continued to listen.

"Several months later, The Society held a birthday party for Ren. She left early and a few of the ladies were being a bit tacky, so I decided to go outside to get some air. Emerson walked up, apologized for what happened and gave me a ride home."

"And y'all lived happily ever after."

Amila smiled as she shared the moral to her little story, "A lot of things, serious things were happening but in the process, I fell in love with him. He was all the things I really wanted and never bothered to look for in a man. But Emerson didn't see it that way. He felt because he had made some poor decisions he wasn't worthy of me. See, it didn't have anything to do with me. It was how he felt about himself."

"I understand what you're saying."

Nodding, Amila said, "Good. Because although it took a little time, you see he got over himself and here we are."

Charlotte nodded back before saying, "I'm so happy it worked out with you and Emerson but I'm leaving for Spain Friday, so if Augustus ever gets over himself, I won't be here waiting to find out."

"You're leaving Friday?" Amila blurted.

Wishing she was a better person, Charlotte replied, "I'm sorry. I can't stay."

Amila appeared sad but understanding as she reached her arms around Charlotte, hugging her tight.

❦ 35 ❦

Brothers

Wednesday was a blur of hurt feelings and mixed emotions for Charlotte. Lola refused to believe Charlotte leaving wasn't meant to personally hurt her, Jenna wouldn't look at her and Silvia was extra snotty. On the upside, her sisters seemed to be forging a tight bond over their opinion of her. Emerson didn't say much to her, but she was pretty sure he was more disappointed in finding out about her and Auggie than the fact that she was leaving. Even though Amila had tears in her eyes every time she looked at her, she never said anything to make her feel bad for leaving.

As happy as she could be, considering every single thing she did made her heart hurt, Thursday meant she was one day closer to leaving this town, including Auggie, behind her. Penny was sitting on her bed as she folded clothes and placed them in her suitcases. Charlotte was really going to miss her.

"Maybe you can come visit me?" Charlotte offered.

"Maybe you could stay and then I won't have to leave the country to see you," Penny retorted.

Rolling her eyes, Charlotte replied, "Please stop, I feel bad enough."

Laying Auggie's plaid shirt from her wall in her suitcase, Charlotte blinked back tears.

"Does he know I'm leaving?" she asked.

Penny's voice sounded gloomy as she answered, "Yea, I told him."

Charlotte tried to make light of things as she forced a laugh, asking, "Did he say good riddance."

"Do you really wanna know?"

Charlotte was close to breaking down again at the thought that he really might have as she nodded at Penny, needing to know.

With a distressed expression Penny informed, "He told me to get out of his house."

"Is he going to be okay?"

With a heavy sigh, Penny replied, "No, but I'll be here to look after him."

Shaking her head, Charlotte griped, "Why should I feel bad? He's the one that did this."

"Same reason you're still wearing the bracelet he gave you. You're in love with him."

"This is so ridiculous. I should be mad. I should hate him. I shouldn't care at all," Charlotte spouted before sitting down on the bed next to Penny, admitting, "All I can think about is how much I already miss him."

Placing her arm around Charlotte, Penny said, "I know he misses you too. He's just a stubborn ass and when he gets something in his head... Let's just say I've yet to meet anyone able to knock some sense into him."

Charlotte rested her head on Penny's shoulder. It did make her feel better to know he was hurting too.

A steady Thursday night crowd poured into the bar, giving Auggie plenty of distraction from his thoughts. Some of the fuss of his bringing Charlotte had died down, but that didn't change the fact that it hurt to be there. Braden and Penny had done a pretty good job of keeping everyone away from him over the week. When Ren and Jackson came in, Ren just shook her head at him, which was worse than if she had told him off. It didn't matter though because no matter if he was home or at the bar, Charlotte was all he thought about.

And now she was leaving early, he'd never forgive himself for hurting her.

There was a slight lull in orders allowing Auggie to step back and regroup for a moment when Penny made her way behind the bar.

"I need to talk to you," Penny stressed with a serious expression on her face.

"Not now, Pen," he replied, already knowing what the subject would be.

Placing her hand on her hip, she asked, "When then?"

"Never."

Appearing fed up with him, she lowered her voice saying, "She's packing."

Auggie forced a shrug as he said, "Makes sense if she's leaving."

"She was crying too."

Penny's words struck him and he was pretty sure that's what being struck by lightening felt like. There was a sudden jolt to his heart, his muscles tensed and he couldn't move away from the pain.

"Why would you tell me that?"

"Because..." Penny started to say before stopping at the same time the music in the bar abruptly stopped.

Auggie noticed Braden just standing on stage looking down at the crowd. Ailin and Brooks were looking at each other as if they weren't really sure what was happening.

As Penny gave Auggie a questioning look, he suggested, "You should go see what the problem is."

Nodding, Penny headed in that direction.

It was hard for Auggie to see what was happening at the front of the stage with the crowd that was gathered around it, so he watched Braden. His brother appeared confused and was noticeably breathing hard. Auggie thought maybe he needed a little break until his cellphone vibrated with a text from Penny.

P: Lily's here with Keven.

Watching his brother carefully, he texted her back.

A: Stay right there, I'm going to call Jacks."

Braden slowly walked up to the microphone continuing to stare down. The entire bar was silent. Auggie moved from behind the bar, to call Jackson.

"Hello?" Jackson answered.

"You need to get up here."

Auggie kept his focus on his brother as he lifted his guitar and started to play, hearing Jackson ask, "What's wrong?"

"Lily brought Keven up here and..."

"Where is he?"

"Braden's playing, I think they're right at the front."

"Try to keep things calm, I'm on my way."

Auggie hollered for Lou to take over the bar as he moved closer to keep an eye on things.

Braden looked like he was fixing to lose it as he started to sing, 'I Don't Love You' by My Chemical Romance. Brooks and Ailin slowly started to keep time with him, both still appearing confused and a little worried now too. Auggie couldn't see Lily and Keven but had a pretty good idea from Braden's direct glare, where they were. It was clear the song was for Lily. Keven was dangerous and Auggie doubted he was there to enjoy the show, but as long as Braden was on stage he could keep an eye on him and wait for Jackson.

It was hard for Auggie to stand by and watch his brother unravel on stage. Listening to the lyrics as Braden sang them in anguish to Lily. A guitar solo that sounded like it came from every part of Braden's soul rang out through the bar before he took the strap from around his shoulder, dropped his guitar and held onto the microphone with both hands whispering. It damn near tore Auggie's heart out when all the music stopped and he saw his brother break on stage, shouting the end of the song at her. The bar was silent as everyone stared at his brother.

All of the sudden, Braden was yanked off of the stage.

Pushing his way through the crowd that was tightly gathering to get a better look at what was happening, Auggie heard Penny shout, "Get off my brother!"

Shoving people out of the way to get to Braden, Auggie caught sight of Penny sliding across the floor before making it close enough to see her leap onto Keven's back and wrap her arms tight around his neck as he punched Braden in the face over and over.

"Move Pen!" Auggie shouted, rushing up behind them and pulling her off, so she didn't get hit by accident.

As Auggie swung and hit Keven in the side of the head, he heard Penny yelling, "If he kills my brother you're next!" Without letting go of Braden, Keven reached around and nailed Auggie right in the eye. Dazed for a moment, he glanced around and saw Lily holding her mouth with blood pouring through her fingers as Penny shoved her down and grabbed hold of Keven's arm. Auggie grabbed his other arm thinking between the two of them Braden would have a chance to get away.

Brooks appeared out of nowhere right in between Keven and Braden and punched Keven in the face. Keven let go of Braden, shook Penny off, elbowed Brooks right above his eye and punched Auggie hard enough to send him flying back. Auggie pulled himself up and grabbed Braden's guitar off of the stage. Brooks leaped over and pulled Penny back as she attempted to stop Keven from hitting Braden again.

Auggie looked up at Ailin frozen on stage and tried to shake off the ringing in his ears. Brooks wrapped Penny in his arms, moving her further out of the way as Auggie turned and swung Braden's guitar, hitting Keven in the back with it as hard as he could. 'Well hell' Auggie thought as Keven let go of Braden, stood up straight and turned to him.

A stern voice shouted, "Hey!" causing Keven to focus in that direction.

By the time Auggie realized Jackson had finally made it, Keven was lying on his back with blood rushing out of his nose and Jackson had his foot firmly planted in his chest.

They all stared as Jackson stated, "You don't wanna do that," when Keven tried to lift his head.

Keven let out a loud groan before he was out cold.

Breathing heavy, Auggie slid to the ground trying to let his adrenaline level out. Glancing around as he surveyed the damage. Ren had cleared everyone back before tending to Braden. He was pretty beat up but coherent and seemed like he was going to be okay. Lily was sitting in a chair crying and still holding her mouth as Auggie thought 'That's what your ass gets'. Brooks had a nice size knot forming across his eyebrow and would be fine unless he didn't get his hands off of his sister, soon. Penny looked a mess but he couldn't see any visible marks on her. And of course Ailin was alright, he'd never left the stage.

The police arrived shortly after the fight had ended. They questioned everyone and arrested Keven. When the bar closed for the night, Penny, Braden and Auggie retold everything that took place during the fight and gave Jackson the respect he rightly deserved by ending it.

Luckily Jackson didn't give a lecture, he just said he was glad they were alright and told them to clean up the bar. Once he and Ren left, Ailin wasn't far behind. Auggie assured Penny and Brooks they could go ahead and take off, that he and Braden could handle the rest of the cleanup. They left, at the same time, in separate cars.

Auggie swept up the last bit of broken glass while Braden sat holding a cold beer against the side of his face. Turning around to see who was at the front doors when they heard a knock, Auggie shook his head at his brother as he watched him get up and unlock the door for Lily. Unable to watch his brother make the same mistake, again, Auggie turned his back to them, dumping the glass from the dust pan in the trash.

Auggie heard Braden lock the doors before informing, "She said Keven hasn't seen the judge but the officer's assured her, with his record and being on probation, he's going away for around ten years."

Nodding, Auggie replied, "Good."

Braden sat back down, saying, "Can you believe she asked me to come over."

"Do you need to go?"

With a loud sigh, Braden shook his head, replying, "I may be slow but I do learn."

Propping the broom up against the table, Auggie pulled a chair up and sat down.

"You alright?"

Braden shrugged, saying, "Everything hurts."

Nodding at him, Auggie scowled, asking, "You're not gonna cry now are ya?"

Shoving his brother a little, Braden laughed, "And get my ass beat twice in one night? No thanks."

Shaking his head with a laugh, Auggie questioned, "Seriously, you alright?"

"Yea, how about you?"

Shrugging, Auggie answered, "No better, no worse."

"So now that you've had a steady girl, you going back to your old ways or you gonna do the girlfriend thing?"

"Neither," he replied before sharing, "She was it for me."

Braden nodded, swearing, "You know, I'm starting to think we're frickin' cursed. You, me and Penny."

"Ah, I think we're all just dumbasses," Auggie replied before teasing, "You for sure."

They laughed together for a little bit before Braden gave his brother a serious expression.

"Thanks for having my back tonight."

Crossing his arms, Auggie said, "We're brothers."

Nodding, Braden informed, "And thanks for being a good big brother. You're always looking out for us. I know we give you hell for it but this whole family would fall apart without you."

Clearing his throat, Auggie, griped, "Come on man."

"It's true. Mom was always too upset to deal and Dad was always here at the bar, you're the one we've always looked to." Auggie stared at him as Braden continued, "Every time Will got real sick, when Penny needed help with homework, you took Ailin's side when mom found out he was dating Sophia and hell, I can't remember a time when you weren't there for me."

Auggie gave a heavy sigh, assuring, "Well brother, it's 'cause I love y'all."

Braden smiled wide at Auggie as he stood up and patted him on the back.

It felt good to be appreciated but it also made him feel bad in a way. If he had looked to them more, instead of thinking he knew everything, maybe he could have made things work with Charlotte.

❧ 36 ❧

Goodbye

Getting the bar set up for Friday night, Auggie laughed with Penny as they joked, wondering how the night before could ever be topped. Braden had said he wasn't feeling playing lead, so he and Ailin were switching places and were busy changing the lineup. In the back of his mind, Auggie knew Charlotte was leaving today, but having his brothers and sister at the bar with him helped alleviate the burden it was putting on his heart.

It didn't take Auggie long to notice Penny looking over at Brooks as he sat behind his drum kit. When Brooks smiled at her, Penny blushed and let out a little giggle.

"Seriously?" Auggie griped at her.

Rolling her eyes at her brother, Penny said, "What? He's cute."

Giving her a stern look, he snapped, "Pen."

Resting her elbow on top of the bar, she sunk her cheek down onto her hand, pouting, "Fine."

Shaking his head with a slight laugh, he asked, "What are you doing here anyway? Besides trying to break up the band."

Penny stuck her tongue out at him before saying, "I figured stopping here was better than going home."

Auggie started to ask where she'd been, and then realized he already knew.

"How is she?"

Penny shrugged, replying, "All packed up and ready to go."

Scowling, he questioned, "So she's okay?"

"Her flight leaves at seven and she's ready to go."

Suspicious, he asked, "Why aren't you answering me?" Shrugging at him, Penny looked off to the side.

Auggie felt offended, "She doesn't want me to know how she is?"

Penny frowned at him, saying, "If you want to know ask her yourself. Even Braden called her and told her goodbye."

Shaking his head, he admitted, "I can't."

Pushing off from the bar, Penny fussed, "You at least owe her a goodbye text if you're going to be too much of a coward to say it."

Watching Penny storm off towards the stage, he knew she was right.

Pulling his cellphone out of his back pocket, Auggie pressed the center button and stopped. Staring at his lock screen that he couldn't bare to change from the picture of Charlotte kissing his cheek, he couldn't do it. He could accept being called a coward if that's what it was. He was letting her go, but there was no way in hell he was telling her goodbye. Suddenly he didn't really know what to do with himself. Somewhere between hyperventilating and on his way into full on panic mode, Auggie swiftly made his way from behind the bar heading straight for the back office.

Passing the stage, he was about to head through the swinging doors.

"You alright?" Braden called out.

Ignoring his brother, he continued through the doors into the hallway until he heard Ailin spout, "He's not man enough to stop himself from letting her go."

Stopping dead in his tracks, he turned and pushed back through, glaring at his brother.

"Come again? I don't think I heard you."

Hopping down from the stage, Ailin assured, "Oh I think you heard me just fine."

Auggie looked to Penny and Braden to make sure he hadn't just lost his mind. Braden held his hands up and took a huge step back while Penny stared at Ailin as if he'd just sprouted a big toe out of his forehead. Yep, his mind was intact but clearly Ailin's wasn't.

"Have you lost your little punk ass mind?" Auggie fussed before shouting, "You're going to say I'm not man enough? Hell, last night Penny was more of a man than you are."

Ailin stepped closer to Auggie, shouting, "I'm fixing to be a father. None of y'all know what that's like. You think I didn't want to jump in? I have more to think about than just myself. I have a pregnant wife at home. Putting her before myself makes me a man," stopping to take a breath, he continued, "So yea, I'm saying you're not being a man."

Auggie shoved him back, growling, "You think you're more of a man than me? Come on."

Without hesitation, Ailin swung as hard as he could, hitting Auggie right in the mouth and knocking him on his ass.

Stunned that Ailin not only hit him but put him on his ass, Auggie rubbed the corner of his mouth and saw blood on his thumb. Before he could say anything, Ailin was standing over him, red faced and shouting.

"I'm sick of this. I'm not a real man? Why? Because I have someone that loves me? Sophia loves me exactly the same way I love her. And I'll gladly kiss her ass every day for the rest of my life because showing someone you love how important they are to you isn't being a girl. I'm man enough to admit, I'm not a man at all without her."

Auggie nodded in respect to Ailin. Not only for knocking him on his ass but because he knew what he was saying was the truth.

Ailin held his hand out to Auggie, saying, "You had that too. Why would you let her go?"

Taking his brother's hand, Auggie pulled himself up, answering, "She was Will's first."

Giving him a ridiculous look, Ailin fussed, "Are you kidding me? All this because for about two weeks five years ago she was talking to Will? They never even slept together."

Auggie's heart stopped as he blurted, "What?"
Trying to make sense of what Ailin was saying, Auggie looked at Penny.

"Emerson and Ren got there before they did anything," she shared.

Braden chimed in, questioning, "You didn't know that?"

Auggie glanced around the room, trying to think as Ailin imparted, "You know, if you had talked to any of us or even her about it, you might have known that."
In two heartbeats, Auggie was out of the door and in his truck, headed to the Roberts' house.

Auggie rang the doorbell five times and knocked four, wondering what was taking them so long to answer. An immediate pang of 'What if they already left' struck him.

Breathing a sigh of relief when Emerson opened the door, Auggie blurted, "Charlotte. I need to see Charlotte."

Emerson gave him a concerned look, asking, "Are you aware that you are bleeding?"

Auggie rubbed the side of his mouth with his hand before saying, "I really need to talk to her."

"Now is not a good time."

Growing frustrated, Auggie snapped, "Damn it Emerson, I need to see her."

Emerson glared down at him, assuring, "You are not welcome here."

Taking a step back, Auggie pulled his beanie off of his head.

With hat in hand he begged, "Please, Mr. Roberts."

Amila's voice startled them both, saying, "For goodness sakes, Emerson, let him in."

Rolling her eyes, she pulled the door away from Emerson to open it wide.

"Thank you," Auggie appreciated, stepping into the house.

"Oh honey, do you know you're bleeding?" Amila blurted.

Pulling his collar up to wipe the corner of his mouth, he gave Amila a questioning look.

Pointing to the other room, Amila informed, "Through the kitchen and out the back door."

Nodding at her, he dashed through the house. Pulling his beanie back on, he took a deep breath and opened the back door.

৵৽৾

Hearing the back door open, Charlotte mentally counted back from ten.

"Don't rush me, we'll leave in a little bit," she snapped.

"I'm not in any hurry for you to go," Auggie replied, causing Charlotte to whip around in surprise.

As her heart started beating faster, she wondered why he appeared confused while staring at her. Narrowing her eyes at the sight of him, she noticed he had a dark purple black eye, his cheek was bruised and his lip was bleeding.

"What happened to you?"

"There was a fight at the bar last night. It's a long story but..."

Giving him a stupid look, Charlotte cut him off, saying, "No, you're bleeding."

"Damn, still?" he griped before pulling the front of his shirt up to wipe his mouth saying, "Ailin's got a mean right hook."

Shaking her head at him, she asked, "Why are you here?"

"I owe you an apology."

"Ya think?" she snapped.

Flinching a little as he smiled at her, Auggie shared, "I was wrong."

"That's it? You came all the way over here to tell me something I already know?"

Shaking his head as he took a step closer, Auggie replied, "No, I came here to tell you that I'm sorry for the way I acted. I'm sorry that I assumed something about you without asking you myself." Reaching down, he took her hand, saying, "I'm sorry I hurt you."

Looking at the C&A on his beanie, Charlotte replied, "I'm sorry that you did too."

"I won't say goodbye," he said, before looking down at the bracelet he gave her on her wrist.

Feeling as though her heart was tearing into tiny pieces, Charlotte let go of his hand, saying, "I didn't want anything between us. But that's impossible. This time it was William next time it could be anything. There's too much history here for it to be any other way."

"Lotte, I swear to you..."

Auggie stopped midsentence as they heard the back door open.

Trace had a smug expression on his face as he coolly made his way towards them.

"Bartender, right?" he questioned, holding his hand out.

Auggie glared at his hand before focusing on Charlotte, "I guess you've got your clean slate right there."

"If it looks like it, that must be what it is," she spit out at him, wondering how in the hell he could keep hurting her like this.

Nodding at her, Auggie stated, "Goodbye Charlotte," before turning and walking back into the house.

Charlotte's mind snapped 'Unbelievable' as she stared at the ground.

Realizing how it looked and what the original plan concerning Trace was, Charlotte was still baffled that Auggie did the exact same thing he had just apologized for. As she stood there trying to think, she could hear Trace tapping his foot.

"Can I help you?" she snapped at him.

With an unpleasant expression, "We are already fifteen minutes late."

"The plane's not going to leave without us," she griped, wishing he would shut up and go inside so she could think.

"It's time to go," he stated.

Looking at Trace and thinking about Auggie, Charlotte remembered Amila saying 'He was all the things I really wanted and never bothered to look for in a man'.

"I'm not ready."

Trace gave a loud sigh before stating, "You are behaving like such a child. All of this over a mick bartender? Someone who could be so easily forgotten? I might understand if he was in a position of any importance."

Charlotte gave him a light smile as she replied, "His name is Augustus Caffrey and you're not even good enough for him to shake your hand."

"That is it," he snarled at her before informing, "Don't you think for one second you can end this without there being serious repercussions. You will not make me look bad in front of everyone. Do you actually think I would go this far without looking into your past? I know all about your crack-head mother, I have seen the pictures of what she did to you. In fact, I can name every person you ever had sex with. I was willing to overlook your history, how grotesque you are under those fancy clothes of yours. All of it. But since I'm not as good as your bartender, rest assured, I will make it my personal mission in life to share what I know about you, everywhere I go to everyone I meet."

Seeing Trace for who he really was made Charlotte's skin crawl.

She had never met anyone, including her mother, so vile in all her life. Aside from that, his threat had no effect on her at all.

Accepting the fact that this was on her, she never cared what was below his handsome surface any more than he cared what was under her thick lipstick and designer clothes. She was going to own it. So be it if the whole world knew. The people who really mattered already did and they loved her anyway.

Trace flashed his all too perfect toothy grin at her. Charlotte gave a slight huff, motioning for him to go ahead and go.

"You're going to regret this," he stated with a smug expression on his face.

As he turned to leave, Emerson stepped out and assured, "No she won't", before backhand bitch slapping Trace to the ground.

With eyes wide and her mouth hanging open, Charlotte watched as Emerson crouched down eye level with Trace on the ground.

Flipping his tie over his shoulder, Emerson rested his arms on his knees, swearing, "How dare you disrespect my daughter. Who the hell do you think you are? You think you're someone because your father owns a company? Boy you have no idea how far my reach goes. You will not utter one word against Charlotte because rest assured if you do, they will never find you." Standing up tall, Emerson demanded, "Get the hell off of my property, out of my town and you will not use my plane to do so."

Trace was shaking and white as a sheet as he scrambled to his feet and sprinted away.

Amazed at what had just taken place in front of her, Charlotte stared at Emerson.

With a soft smile and warm caring eyes, he asked, "Are you alright?"

Shaking her head, she walked up to him and wrapped her arms around him. As Emerson hugged her back, he was softer than she would have thought and warm.

Keeping her in his protective arms, Emerson shared, "There are some people who are able to love blind. However, most people need to be reassured they're not making a horrible mistake. Not everyone is able to believe someone's side of things without all the information."

Charlotte held onto him tighter, nodding into his chest before looking up at him.

With a smirk on her face, she questioned, "They will never find you?"

Emerson let go of her as he laughed, "I believe I already shared that Roberts is not the most upstanding last name around."

Raising her eyebrows at him, she remarked, "Powerful and infamous."

"Well, it certainly put Mr. Delgado in his place."

Charlotte laughed out loud before it occurred to her there was something she needed to say.

With a sincere expression, Charlotte said, "Emerson, thank you for adopting me."

Emerson's eyes filled with tears as he scooped Charlotte up in another warm and loving hug.

❧37❧

Declaration

It was seriously the night from hell. After leaving the Roberts', as if that wasn't a nightmare in and of itself, he was finally man enough but it turned out Charlotte wasn't the woman he thought she was. Or maybe it was that he really wasn't sure about anything anymore. All he knew was, he still missed her. The fact that she was just ready to pick up where she left off before they were together didn't change that. Seeing her wearing that thick lacquer lipstick because her douchebag never saw how beautiful she really was, made it worse.

Once he got back to The Dog House to open up, a pipe in the kitchen burst causing water to rush everywhere. When they got that under control, one of the draft spigots broke off in his hand and shot beer all over him. Then, the wire shelf in the storage room broke off of the wall and knocked him down, covering him in an avalanche of bar supplies.

When Jackson showed up, he told Auggie to take the rest of the night off. The only plus side of the evening was that his lip finally stopped bleeding.

Stepping out of the shower, he was glad to be home a few hours early. He was going to drink a beer, relax in his chair

347

for a while and try to put this horrible day behind him. He dried off, pulled his boxer's on, looked in his bottom drawer for pajama bottoms and realized he forgot to wash clothes this week. With a slight laugh, Auggie shook his head at himself. What difference did it make, he was by himself anyway.

Making his way into the kitchen, Auggie grabbed a beer, popped the cap off and headed to the living room to relax. He had the feeling of being struck by lightening again, but it was for a different reason this time.

Once the shock of seeing Charlotte sitting in his chair wore off, he set his beer down and griped, "What the hell?"

"Why did you apologize to me?" she snapped at him.

Thinking she had some nerve, he sarcastically replied, "Because I'm a grown up and I felt it was necessary."

As she stood up out of his chair wearing tiny hot pink shorts, a thin white t-shirt and the peacock bracelet he gave her, Auggie wished he was wearing more than a pair of boxers.

Giving the bottom of her shirt a little tug, she questioned, "Why would you go to all the trouble of saying you're sorry, if you were just going to turn around and do the same damn thing?"

Irritated, he barked, "Look here woman, I'm not the one that just picked up where I left off before you."

"Neither am I," she griped at him.

Thinking to himself 'Unbelievable', Auggie shook his head, saying, "If it looks like it, that must be what it is. Right?"

Charlotte glared at him before asking, "Is that a question?"

Running his hand over his face in frustration, Auggie wondered what kind of crazy ass game this was that she was trying to play with his head.

Deciding to play along, he replied, "Alright, I'm game. Was it what it looked like?"

Holding her head high, she stated, "No."

Standing there baffled, he asked, "What was he doing there?"

Rolling her eyes at him, Charlotte replied, "He came to escort me back."

"You're not going to marry him?"

Shaking her head while giving him a stupid look, she informed, "Why would I marry him when I'm in love with you?"

Auggie's whole world came crashing down on him in an instant.

Every single thought, feeling and moment he had with Charlotte surged through him as he walked up to her. Placing his hands on the sides of her face, he kissed her like he never had before. The way he should have been kissing her all along. Without restraint. Like she was truly his because she was and he sure as hell belonged to her.

Without hesitation, Charlotte wrapped her arms around his neck as she kissed him back.

Picking up where he left off before his ignorant mistake earlier, Auggie said, "Lotte, I swear to you, I will never let anything come between us again."

"I love you," she whispered in response.

Between his promise and her words, they were declaring themselves to each other and Auggie was determined to make it official. After breathing her in as he kissed her, he hoisted her high in the air and threw her over his shoulder.

Setting her back on her feet next to his bed, there was so much he wanted to say and do, he wasn't sure where to start. Her face was flush, his breath heavy as he stood in front of her.

"I want all of you," he whispered, running his hands down her sides.

As she nodded, he wrapped the hem of her shirt around his fingers.

Seeing the resistance in her eyes, he reminded, "I gave you my word."

"That's not..." she started to argue before he softly kissed her, swearing, "Nothing between us."

With a firm hold on the bottom of her shirt, he leaned his forehead against hers.

"There's no more you or me. Only us from this moment on," Auggie whispered before placing another soft kiss against her lips.

Charlotte slowly nodded as she looked into his eyes.

Carefully removing her shirt, he glanced down at her and smiled. She was insanely beautiful, scars and all. Pulling her all the way against him, he slid his hands from her hips up her bare back. Running his fingers back down to her hips gave him the same feeling as the first time he kissed her. There was not a woman in the world like her and all her scars said about her were that she was one of a kind. Auggie felt Charlotte tense in his arms as he realized there was something he forgot to say.

"I love you," he swore before pulling her down onto the bed with him.

It wasn't about showing her the kind of man he was anymore because without her he didn't feel like a man at all. She made him the man he was.

෨෧

Falling asleep, completely naked in Auggie's arms, Charlotte felt complete in every way. The man that she was in love with was now asleep beside her. He had been greedy with her in such an insatiable way he allowed her to be fulfilled over and over. Her man, Augustus Caffrey was in love with her, all of her. Even the parts that she, herself had trouble accepting. Smiling to herself as she drifted off, she felt at home in the arms of her scruffy bartender.

❧ 38 ❧

Attached

Rolling over in bed, Charlotte started to smile then frowned, realizing she was by herself. Peeking over the side of the bed, she saw her clothes from last night. She slid out of bed and grabbed her panties off of the floor, pulling them on before picking her shirt and shorts up off of the floor.

"What are you doing?" Auggie questioned from the doorway.

Turning to see him holding a plate of waffles in one hand and a glass of juice in the other, she answered, "Getting dressed."

Auggie looked at her like she just ruined his day.

"Why?"

Shaking her head at him, she laughed, "Did you expect me to stay naked all day?"

Nodding his head vigorously, he blurted, "Yea."

Charlotte rolled her eyes, saying, "You can't be serious."

Placing the waffles and juice on top of his dresser, he made his way over to her.

"Oh, I'm serious," he assured, running his hands across her breasts.

The side of her mouth curled into a smile as she replied, "Well, Mr. Serious, I'm going to go brush my teeth and get dressed."

After giving her a quick kiss on the lips, he flopped down on his bed.

There was no way Charlotte would have believed she could be this happy. Almost giddy, she hurried to the hallway bathroom, quickly pulled her shirt and shorts on, brushed her teeth and washed her face before heading back to Auggie's bedroom.

Picking the plate of waffles up off of his dresser on the way to his bed, she confirmed, "These are for me?"

Nodding, Auggie placed his hands behind his head as he laid back, asking, "You're staying, right?"

"I was thinking about it," she replied, winking at him as she took a bite of her waffles.

"You wanna stay here?" he questioned.

Placing her waffles on his night stand, Charlotte answered, "I never liked the idea of living with someone unless we're married."

"You wanna get married?"

"Umm, I don't know how to answer that," she replied with an uncomfortable smile.

Auggie gave her a confused look before shaking his head correcting, "Oh, I wasn't proposing."

Raising her eyebrows, Charlotte nodded as she glanced off to the side.

"Well, I just made this awkward as hell," he shared.

Leaning over him, Charlotte kissed his lips.

"We can have this conversation another day."

Nodding, he pulled her on top of him, asking, "So, what do you wanna do?"

Giving him another kiss, she replied, "Take a shower."

Charlotte raised up to climb off of him when he pulled her back down. Holding her tight against him, he stood up with her in his arms, kissing her all the way to the shower.

ক৽৽ঌ

Standing in his driveway, Auggie watched Charlotte drive away. He didn't want her to leave. In fact, he had planned on trying to keep her there, naked, all day. When Penny called to tell him Sophia went into labor, Charlotte thought it was best to go home and assured him she would see him at the hospital later. Shaking his head as he climbed in his truck, he laughed to himself, thinking 'Leave it to my family to ruin naked sex day with Charlotte'.

The hospital waiting room was pretty intense. While everyone was waiting for Sophia to have her baby, Sarah was ignoring Auggie and Ren was giving Sarah dirty looks for ignoring Auggie because of Charlotte.

Braden who at this point looked like a red headed plum after the fight at the bar, was also getting the silent treatment from Sarah and Penny was 'in trouble' too, simply for being a part of what her brothers had done. No one said a word for two hours until Ailin walked in, announcing that Keylee Marie Caffrey had arrived.

Auggie decided to hang back in the waiting room after Ren basically shoved Ailin out of the way to beat Sarah to see the first grandkid on both sides.

Jackson watched Ren and Sarah practically race down the hall as he laughed, "I'll just wait here then."

"Women and babies," Auggie remarked, shaking his head as Braden and Penny laughed.

Ailin appeared startled as he said, "Maybe I should have mentioned they took Keylee to clean her up and moved Sophia to a different room."

The waiting room erupted in laughter.

They all took turns visiting the new edition to the Caffrey family. When Auggie took his turn to meet his niece, Penny was smiling at them from the chair next to Sophia's bed. He carefully held Keylee in his arms, rocking her as she slept.

"She looks like Ailin with brown hair," Auggie shared before glancing at his brother saying, "You did good man but I think she's too pretty to be one of us."

Sophia smiled as Penny blurted, "Excuse you," with a laugh.

"You hear that little girly, your Aunt Penny's already jealous of you."

Rolling her eyes at him, Penny hopped up from her chair. saying, "Okay, it's my turn again," holding her arms out to hold Keylee.

Auggie carefully handed her over to Penny, asking, "Where did Jacks go?"

Sophia looked at Ailin before answering, "I think he's trying to keep mama away from your mom." As Auggie gave her a questioning look, she shared, "Charlotte's here with her family."

෴

Standing outside the waiting room, Charlotte congratulated Ren and Jackson after Amila and Emerson headed to see the baby.

Swatting Charlotte on the arm, Ren fussed, "I can't believe you didn't tell me."

"About?" she questioned, pretending not to know.

Raising an eyebrow at her, Ren said, "I don't know. Let's ask him," pointing past Charlotte.

As Charlotte turned, Auggie made his way beside her. Sliding his hand around hers, he leaned to her cheek and kissed her.

Smiling at Ren, she replied, "Oh, that."

Auggie appeared confused, asking, "What?"

Ren and Charlotte laughed as Jackson just shook his head with a wide smile.

"Can I steal her away for a minute," Auggie asked.

Both Ren and Jackson smiled while nodding as they walked into the waiting room to sit with the other Roberts' kids.

Leading Charlotte around the corner by her hand, Auggie pointed to the door marked 'stairwell'. Opening the door, he let her step in first before double checking to make sure no one saw them go in.

Pulling her against him, Auggie whispered, "Wanna sneak out of here?"

"I sure do but things are tense enough without us bailing on Sophia's baby day."

"And?"

Giving him a stupid look, she replied, "And? When your mom saw me, she held onto her cross pendant and said 'God be with me' like I'm the devil or something and Ren looked like she was fixing to throw down before Jackson's parents walked in."

Laughing, Auggie shared, "Welcome to another Caffrey family gathering."

"This is normal?"

"No, it's usually much worse," he assured.

Charlotte let out a laugh before pulling Auggie into a kiss.

Auggie's hands instinctively moved to her hips as he guaranteed, "After dinner, you're staying with me."

"We're going to dinner?" she asked with a smile.

Shaking his head, Auggie replied, "Emerson said I was having dinner with y'all tonight."

"He invited you to dinner?" she questioned, excited by Emerson's invitation.

With a slight laugh, he said, "No, he told me I was."

Rolling her eyes, she wondered how well dinner was going to go before a mischievous expression formed.

"How brave are you?"

Tugging her closer, he asked, "What did you have in mind?"

"Depends, you scared?"

The door to the stairwell swung open causing them both to jump.

Ren shook her head at them as she peered into the stairwell, fussing, "You two come out and behave yourselves."

With a heavy sigh, Charlotte took Auggie's hand leading him out of the stairwell.

Continuing to shake her head at them, Ren walked up to Jackson and whispered something to him that made him laugh out loud.

Turning to Charlotte, Ren informed, "Sophia wants you to come see Keylee."

Giving Ren a crazy look, she replied, "Umm, okay."

Auggie gave Charlotte a quick kiss before letting go of her hand.

As Ren led the way to Sophia's room, Charlotte heard Auggie say, "Can I talk to you a minute, Jacks."

Glancing back, she watched Auggie and Jackson head in the opposite direction.

Hesitant, Charlotte followed Ren to Sophia's hospital room.

Sophia appeared exhausted as she looked up at Charlotte, asking, "Do you want to hold her?"

"Oh, no thanks," Charlotte replied with an uncomfortable smile.

"Mama, can you give us a minute?"

Ren kissed Sophia's forehead before gently brushing her fingers across Keylee's arm as she nodded.

As soon as the door closed behind Ren, Sophia looked at Charlotte, saying, "I'm a mom."

Wanting to laugh, Charlotte cleared her throat, agreeing, "Yep."

Nodding, Sophia shared, "I keep looking at her thinking... I just love her so much. I hope I'm a good mom."

"Well, I think if you love her that's a great start," Charlotte replied not sure what she was really looking for in this conversation.

With a loving sigh, Sophia gazed at Keylee as she said, "I don't know what to say except I'm sorry."

Trying not to appear as shocked as she truly was, Charlotte replied, "Umm, Thank you."

"I don't want to be friends with you but I don't see why we can't get along."

Charlotte smiled, saying, "The feeling is mutual," with a slight laugh.

"You know, Sarah was furious when she found out Ailin and I were seeing each other."

"Seriously?" Charlotte blurted.

Nodding, Sophia said, "Good luck. Will you send my mom back in?"

Making her way to the door, Charlotte turned to Sophia, saying, "Congratulations, Keylee is beautiful," before turning back and walking out of the hospital room.

When Charlotte stepped out of the room, Ren hugged her before going back in with Sophia. Jackson flashed a smile, motioning for Charlotte to follow him. Thinking that was strange, she had never really spoken to Jackson before other than a polite hello.

They reached an empty waiting room when Jackson offered, "Have a seat."

Charlotte accepted, asking, "Yes?"

Pulling a chair in front of her, Jackson sat, informing, "I just had an interesting conversation with Auggie." Confused, she listened as he continued, "It seems he's had some help keeping up with the books."

Taking a breath, Charlotte asked, "You're not mad are you?"

Smiling wide, he assured, "No, I'm not mad."

Nodding, she said, "Okay. So?"

"So, I would like to offer you the job."

"The job?"

Jackson nodded at her clarifying, "The Dog House needs a manager. I'm not sure what your plans are but from what Auggie says they include staying here. So, if you wouldn't mind taking a business course or two and you think you could put up with him every night, I'm offering you the job."

Charlotte didn't know what to say exactly but it was for sure a, "Yes," that came out of her mouth.

Another smile and a happy nod proceeded Jackson saying, "I'll meet you there Monday around noon and we can go over the details."

"Okay, thank you," Charlotte appreciated.

As Jackson stood up, he imparted, "Welcome to the family Charlotte."

Nodding back at him with a smile of her own, she watched him walk out.

As Charlotte sat by herself, thinking, she had spent so much of her life unattached to anything or anyone. It is amazing what happens when you open your heart a little. It makes it nearly impossible to stop letting people in at that point. After years of thinking she was content with no sense of family, she now had two.

☙❧

Sitting at the dining room table with Emerson, Auggie thought dinner with Charlotte's family was going well, until it was over and it was just the two of them behind a closed door.

Emerson had a stern expression on his face as he cleared his throat, "What are your intentions with my daughter?"

This was a situational first for Auggie. Not only being questioned by someone's father but this was Emerson. He'd grown up hearing the stories of Emerson, Jacks, Ren and Hert as teenagers and he'd known friendly, easygoing Emerson for years. Although Auggie knew this was important, it was a little hard to take him seriously, now that Emerson was 'Mr. Roberts' standing in front of him, questioning his intentions.

Sitting up straight in his chair, Auggie replied, "I intend to love her for the rest of my life."

Almost mocking him, Emerson stated, "As heartfelt as that is, life is not always that simple."

Slightly agitated, Auggie adjusted himself in his chair, replying, "I happen to think it is that simple."

Emerson glared at him, reminding, "Your mother seems to have a problem with her."

"Have you ever known a person my mom didn't have a problem with?"

"You do not see that as a challenge for your relationship?"

"Nope."

Growing agitated himself, Emerson, questioned, "I was under the impression family is important to you. Was I wrong?"

"No. My family is very important to me."

"Then how do you expect to please everyone when your family is not welcoming to her?" Emerson asked with an 'I've got you cornered expression'.

"I'm not a people pleaser."

"Who do you aim to please?"

"Charlotte."

With a short exhale, Emerson stated, "You have an answer for everything don't you."

"No disrespect, Mr. Roberts but you know me. And I think you already know how I'm going to answer every question you have. For some reason you feel you have to ask anyway. The long and short of it is, I love Charlotte. She loves me back. I want you and your family to be happy for us and I want my family to be too. If that happens, great. If not, oh well. Because I gave her my word that nothing would ever come between us and whether it's a party of two or a whole congregation, I'll be keeping that promise."

"Very well then, allow me to rephrase the question. What are your plans?"

"My family has a tradition that I intend to uphold."

Emerson cracked a smile, "Then is there something you would like to ask me?"

Auggie nodded as he replied, "Yes sir, there is."

 The End

Epilogue

Sitting behind the desk in the office at the back of The Dog House, Charlotte was going over the weeks receipts when her cellphone vibrated against the desk.

A: Happy Anniversary-its 12:01

Smiling at the text message, Auggie sent, she texted back.

C: Your so sweet ♥ Happy Anniversary.

A: I love you.

C: Love you ;) almost done.

A: I got you something.

C: Like a present?

A: Sort of.

C: What is it?

A: Can you please just come out here? I hate texting.

Rolling her eyes at her phone, she set it back down and walked to the main area of the bar.

Finding him standing next to a table in the corner, she gave a happy sigh making her way over to him.

Glancing at the bouquet of peacock feathers on the table, where they sat on their first date, Charlotte leaned in to kiss him, saying, "I love you."

Auggie gave her his squinty eyed smile as he reached out, holding onto her arms to keep her from coming too close as he said, "You know in the six months you've forced me to date you," before she cut him off.

Giving him a crazy look, Charlotte snapped, "Oh, now I've *forced* you to date me?"

"Yep. And I'm still pretty insulted you'd rather live with my sister," he fussed back at her.

With a slight huff, she griped, "Well, what do you expect from someone who *forces* you to date them."

"Gah damn woman, just... Do you want your present?" Smiling with the satisfaction of frustrating him, Charlotte nodded.

"Okay, but you have to find it," he informed, taking another step back.

Eyeing the front of his pants, she questioned, "Is it on your person?"

"It's not there," he blurted with a laugh.

"But that's the gift that keeps on giving," she said with a mischievous smile.

"Damn it Lotte, I'm trying to have a serious moment with you," he fussed at her with an uncontrollable smile.

Giving him a wink, Charlotte said, "Hmm, let's see." Stepping directly in front of him, she placed her hands on Auggie's shoulders.

Sliding her hands down his chest, she felt something under his shirt. Nervous and excited she quickly unbuttoned his shirt to find a white bandage taped over the left side of his chest.

"It's not the prettiest wrapping but what's underneath belongs to you," Auggie shared as she stood there staring at it.

He flinched a little as she slowly pulled the tape away. In awe of his permanent declaration to her, Charlotte felt like she was falling in love with him all over again. Auggie had marked his heart with a black peacock feather and keeping with tradition, there was a Celtic heart where the eye of the feather would be. The stem was her name and on the left side of the heart from the top all the way down there was a thin strip missing from it, signifying the scar on her lips.

Wishing it wasn't brand new so she could touch it, Charlotte placed her hand on the center of his chest, holding his shirt away from his tattoo with the other.

"There's no way for me to top that."

Auggie gently kissed her before running the tip of his finger across her ring finger as he suggested, "You can always get an A right here."

With a laugh she assured, "Yea, I don't think so," before kissing him.

Reaching into his back pocket, Auggie informed, "I guess I'll give you this instead," handing her a small black box.

Holding her breath Charlotte slowly opened the box. Inside was a princess cut peacock blue diamond engagement ring. A slow smile spread across her face as Auggie went down on one knee in front of her. Taking the box out of her hand, he pulled out the ring.

"Charlotte Persephone Roberts, you are worth more than I will ever have to offer but if you marry me, I swear I'll do everything possible to be worthy of you."

Nodding as Auggie slid the engagement ring onto her finger, she breathed, "Kiss me."

Auggie was on his feet with Charlotte in his arms in an instant. Kissing the woman he loved, just like he was going to for the rest of their life together.

Acknowledgments

As always, thank you to my family for continuing to put up with my craziness on a daily basis.

Thank you to my readers! Without y'all my characters would never see the light of day.

All the INDIE blogger/reviewer/supporters out there, I appreciate everything that you do to keep writers writing.

Thank you to my editor Margaret Civella, who keeps me from getting all verb-y and has the best editorial comments.

And very special 'thank you' to my beta readers Susanne Lancello, Nicole Griffin, Kasey Fitzgerald, Lucii Grubb, Katelynn Luna, Addison Kline and Charity Sembera for taking *Charlotte* with me one step at a time. I am honored to have each of you in my corner, loving my characters.

Playlist

Music has a way of inspiring the smallest ideas. It allows me to create an entire scene or chapter from just the right song. For me, music is one of the most important creative tools there is. These are the songs that brought C&A to life.

Hey Brother-Avicii
Oh Love-Green Day
Wake Me Up-Avicii
Come With me Know-Kongos
I Don't Love You-My Chemical Romance
Bartender Song-Rehab
Stay-Rihanna
Let Her Go-Passenger

Special Playlist additions

Lucii Grubb~This is War-30 Seconds to Mars
Katelynn Luna~Human-Christina Perri
Margaret Civella~Glitter in the Air-Pink
Kasey Fitzgerald~I Chose You-Sarah Bareilles
Addison Kline~Poison & Wine-The Civil Wars
Nicole Griffin~You and Me-Lifehouse

About the Author

M. Sembera was born in Baton Rouge, Louisiana and now lives in Brazoria, Texas with her husband, three kids, three dogs and two cats. After writing her first short story when she was in high school, M. instantly fell in love with writing. However, life sometimes gets in the way of aspirations and it wasn't until years later, when her life calmed down, M. was able to start writing again.

'For me, each new book I write or character I create feels like the first time and I find myself falling in love with writing all over again'

Past works include Enduring Everything, 'The Rennillia Series', 'Life with Him: Novelette' & 'Louisiana Spice, Italian Intrigue, and Texas Bull: A Memoir'.

www.BrokenBirdMedia.com

Work in Progress

www.ingramcontent.com/pod-product-compliance
Lightning Source LLC
Chambersburg PA
CBHW070733180626
46818CB00007B/2828